Critical Acclaim for
The *Weetzie Bat* Books

"Magic is everywhere in Block's lyrical and resonant fables, which always point back to the primacy of family, friends, love, location, food, and music. At once modern and mythic, her series deserves as much space as it can command of daydream nation's shrinking bookshelves."

—*The Village Voice*

"A poetic series of books celebrating love, art, and the imagination, all in hyper-lyrical language." —*Spin*

"Ms. Block's far-ranging free association has been controlled and shaped into a story with sensual characters. The language is inventive Californian hip, but the patterns are compactly folkloristic and the theme is transcendent."

—*The New York Times Book Review*

"[Block's] extravagantly imaginative setting and finely honed perspectives remind the reader that there is magic everywhere." —*Publishers Weekly*

Weetzie Bat . . .

"[WEETZIE BAT is] one of the most original books of the last ten years." —*The Los Angeles Times*

"WEETZIE BAT burst on the scene like a rainbow bubble showering clouds of roses, feathers, tiny shells, and a rubber chicken. Hardened critics were astonished by the freshness of Francesca Lia Block's voice." —*The New York Times*

"Francesca Lia Block's writing style is a dream—minimalist yet poetic." —*Sassy*

Witch Baby . . .

"This sequel to the extraordinary WEETZIE BAT revisits L.A.'s frenetic pop world, again using exquisitely crafted language to tell a story whose glitzy surface veils thoughtful consideration of profound contemporary themes." —*Kirkus Reviews*

"Wonderful." —*The Los Angeles Times*

"Sparkling writing." —*Publishers Weekly*

Cherokee Bat and the Goat Guys . . .

"Ms. Block writes about the real Los Angeles better than anybody since Raymond Chandler." —*The New York Times*

"Not to be missed." —*Kirkus Reviews*

Missing Angel Juan . . .

"An engagingly eccentric mix of fantasy and reality, enhanced by mystery and suspense. . . . Magical, moving, mischievous, and—literally—marvelous." —*School Library Journal*

"This moving novel shares the super-hip aesthetic of its predecessors." —*Publishers Weekly*

"Uniquely fascinating and provocative." —*Kirkus Reviews*

And Baby Be-Bop

"The writing is as fevered as life in Los Angeles." —*The Horn Book*

"BABY BE-BOP can be read for the straightforward story and then re-read to enjoy the sumptuous layers upon layers of meaning, which cover each other like fine gauze." —*Sassy*

DANGEROUS ANGELS

ALSO BY FRANCESCA LIA BLOCK:

Weetzie Bat

Missing Angel Juan

Girl Goddess #9: Nine Stories

The Hanged Man

Dangerous Angels: The Weetzie Bat Books

I Was a Teenage Fairy

Violet and Claire

The Rose and the Beast

Echo

Guarding the Moon

Wasteland

Goat Girls: Two Weetzie Bat Books

Beautiful Boys: Two Weetzie Bat Books

Necklace of Kisses

Psyche in a Dress

Blood Roses

How to (Un)cage a Girl

The Waters & the Wild

Pretty Dead

House of Dolls

With Carmon Staton:

Ruby

The *Weetzie Bat* Books

DANGEROUS ANGELS

FRANCESCA LIA BLOCK

HARPER TEEN
An Imprint of HarperCollinsPublishers

Special thanks to Gilda Block, Lydia Wills,
and all the people who contributed to this edition.

"Song of Encouragement" (Papago), from *Singing for Power: The Song Magic of the Papago Indians
of Southern Arizona* by Ruth Underhill. Copyright © 1938, 1966 by Ruth Murray Underhill.
Reprinted by permission of the University of California Press

"Wind Song" (Pima), "Song of Fallen Deer" (Pima), "Omen" (Aztec), and "Dream Song"
(Wintu) are excerpts from *In the Trail of the Wind* edited by John Bierhorst. Copyright © 1971
by John Bierhorst. Reprinted by permission of Farrar, Straus and Giroux, Inc.

Library of Congress Cataloging-in-Publication Data
Block, Francesca Lia.
Dangerous angels : the Weetzie Bat books / Francesca Lia Block.
p.   cm.
Contents: Weetzie Bat — Witch Baby — Cherokee Bat and the Goat Guys — Missing Angel
Juan — Baby Be-Bop.
ISBN 978-0-06-200740-7
[1. Los Angeles (Calif.)—Fiction.] I. Title.
PZ7.B61945Dan 1998   97-40933
[Fic]—dc21   CIP
                                                                          AC

Typography by Steve Scott
❖
16 17 18 19   CG/RRDH   10 9 8
Revised paperback edition, 2010

For Charlotte Zolotow and Joanna Cotler

DANGEROUS ANGELS

BOOK ONE

Weetzie Bat

Weetzie and Dirk

The reason Weetzie Bat hated high school was because no one understood. They didn't even realize where they were living. They didn't care that Marilyn's prints were practically in their backyard at Graumann's; that you could buy tomahawks and plastic palm tree wallets at Farmer's Market, and the wildest, cheapest cheese and bean and hot dog and pastrami burritos at Oki Dogs; that the waitresses wore skates at the Jetson-style Tiny Naylor's; that there was a fountain that turned tropical soda-pop colors, and a canyon where Jim Morrison and Houdini used to live, and all-night potato knishes at Canter's, and not too far away was Venice, with columns, and canals, even, like the real Venice but maybe cooler because of the surfers. There was no one who cared. Until Dirk.

Dirk was the best-looking guy at school. He wore his hair in a shoe-polish-black Mohawk and he drove a red '55 Pontiac. All the girls were infatuated with Dirk; he wouldn't pay any attention to them. But on the first day of the semester, Dirk saw Weetzie in his art class. She was a skinny

3

girl with a bleach-blonde flat-top. Under the pink Harlequin sunglasses, strawberry lipstick, earrings dangling charms, and sugar-frosted eye shadow she was really almost beautiful. Sometimes she wore Levi's with white-suede fringe sewn down the legs and a feathered Indian headdress, sometimes old fifties' taffeta dresses covered with poetry written in glitter, or dresses made of kids' sheets printed with pink piglets or Disney characters.

"That's a great outfit," Dirk said. Weetzie was wearing her feathered headdress and her moccasins and a pink fringed mini dress.

"Thanks. I made it," she said, snapping her strawberry bubble gum. "I'm into Indians," she said. "They were here first and we treated them like shit."

"Yeah," Dirk said, touching his Mohawk. He smiled. "You want to go to a movie tonight? There's a Jayne Mansfield film festival. *The Girl Can't Help It.*"

"Oh, I love that movie!" Weetzie said in her scratchiest voice.

Weetzie and Dirk saw *The Girl Can't Help It*, and Weetzie practiced walking like Jayne Mansfield and making siren noises all the way to the car.

"This really is the most slinkster-cool car I have ever seen!" she said.

"His name's Jerry," Dirk said, beaming. "Because he reminds me of Jerry Lewis. I think Jerry likes you. Let's go out in him again."

Weetzie and Dirk went to shows at the Starwood, the

Whiskey, the Vex, and Cathay de Grande. They drank beers or bright-colored canned Club drinks in Jerry and told each other how cool they were. Then they went into the clubs dressed to kill in sunglasses and leather, jewels and skeletons, rosaries and fur and silver. They held on like waltzers and plunged in slamming around the pit below the stage. Weetzie spat on any skinhead who was too rough, but she always got away with it by batting her eyelashes and blowing a bubble with her gum. Sometimes Dirk dove offstage into the crowd. Weetzie hated that, but of course everyone always caught him because, with his black leather and Mohawk and armloads of chain and his dark-smudged eyes, Dirk was the coolest. After the shows, sweaty and shaky, they went to Oki Dogs for a burrito.

In the daytime, they went to matinees on Hollywood Boulevard, had strawberry sundaes with marshmallow topping at Schwab's, or went to the beach. Dirk taught Weetzie to surf. It was her lifelong dream to surf—along with playing the drums in front of a stadium of adoring fans while wearing gorgeous pajamas. Dirk and Weetzie got tan and ate cheese-and-avocado sandwiches on whole-wheat bread and slept on the beach. Sometimes they skated on the boardwalk. Slinkster Dog went with them wherever they went.

When they were tired or needed comforting, Dirk and Weetzie and Slinkster Dog went to Dirk's Grandma Fifi's cottage, where Dirk had lived since his parents died.

Grandma Fifi was a sweet, powdery old lady who baked tiny, white, sugar-coated pastries for them, played them tunes on a music box with a little dancing monkey on top, had two canaries she sang to, and had hair Weetzie envied—perfect white hair that sometimes had lovely blue or pink tints. Grandma Fifi had Dirk and Weetzie bring her groceries, show her their new clothes, and answer the same questions over and over again. They felt very safe and close in Fifi's cottage.

"You're my best friend in the whole world," Dirk said to Weetzie one night. They were sitting in Jerry drinking Club coladas with Slinkster Dog curled up between them.

"You're my best friend in the whole world," Weetzie said to Dirk.

Slinkster Dog's stomach gurgled with pleasure. He was very happy, because Weetzie was so happy now and her new friend Dirk let him ride in Jerry as long as he didn't pee, and they gave him pizza pie for dinner instead of that weird meat that Weetzie's mom, Brandy-Lynn, tried to dish out when he was left at home.

One night, Weetzie and Dirk and Slinkster Dog were driving down Sunset in Jerry on their way to the Odyssey. Weetzie was leaning out the window holding Rubber Chicken by his long, red toe. The breeze was filling Rubber Chicken so that he blew up like a fat, pocked balloon.

At the stoplight, a long, black limo pulled up next to Jerry. The driver leaned out and looked at Rubber Chicken.

"That is one bald-looking chicken!"

The driver threw something into the car and it landed on Weetzie's lap. She screamed.

"What is it?" Dirk exclaimed.

A hairy, black thing was perched on Weetzie's knees.

"It's a hairpiece for that bald eagle you've got there. Belonged to Burt Reynolds," the driver said, and he drove off.

Weetzie put the toupee on Rubber Chicken. Really, it looked quite nice. It made Rubber Chicken look just like the lead singer of a heavy-metal band. Dirk and Weetzie wondered how they could have let him go bald for so long.

"Weetzie, I have something to tell you," Dirk said.

"What?"

"I have to wait till we get to the Odyssey."

At the Odyssey, Weetzie and Dirk bought a pack of cigarettes and two Cokes. Dirk poured rum from the little bottle he kept in his jacket pocket into the Cokes. They sat next to the d.j. booth watching the Lanka girls in spandy-wear dancing around.

"What were you going to tell me?" Weetzie asked.

"I'm gay," Dirk said.

"Who, what, when, where, how—well, not *how*," Weetzie said. "It doesn't matter one bit, honey-honey," she said, giving him a hug.

Dirk took a swig of his drink. "But you know I'll always love you the best and think you are a beautiful, sexy girl," he said.

"Now we can Duck hunt together," Weetzie said, taking his hand.

7

Duck Hunting

There were many kinds of Ducks—Buff Ducks, Skinny Ducks, Surf Ducks, Punk-Rock Ducks, Wild Ducks, Shy Ducks, Fierce Ducks, Cuddly Ducks, Sleek, Chic G.Q. Ducks, Rockabilly Ducks with creepers and ducktails, Rasta Ducks with dreads, Dancing Ducks, and Skate-Date Ducks, Ducks in Duckmobiles racing around the city.

Weetzie and Dirk went to find the Ducks of their respective dreams.

At a gig at Cathay de Grande, Weetzie stood in front of the stage feeling Buzz's sweat flinging off him as he sang. He was bald, with tattoos all over his arms. Weetzie stared up into the lights.

"That is no Duck," Dirk said. "That is one wild vulture bird."

"But he is gorgeous, isn't he?" Weetzie said, watching Buzz's nostrils flare.

She was pretty drunk by the end of the gig. Buzz came out from backstage and grabbed her wrists.

"How was I?" he asked.

"You were okay." Weetzie swallowed.

"Okay? I was hot."

"You think you are pretty sexy, don't you?"

"Yes. So are you. Come and get a beer with me."

He turned and backed Weetzie up against the wall. She smelled leather and beer.

"Put your arms around my neck."

She did it, pretending to choke him, and he pulled her up onto his glossy, white back.

"Put me down!"

She tried to kick him with her engineer boots but he carried her toward the bar.

After he had let her down, he felt the pockets of his Levi's for change.

"Shit." He turned to Weetzie. "Let's go to my place. I got some beers."

He looked about twelve suddenly, even with the shaved head, the eyeliner, and the skull earring.

Weetzie started to walk away.

"Come on," he said softly.

Weetzie clung to Buzz's body as they rode his motorcycle through the night. Wind blew on their faces, a summer wind thick with the smell of all-night taco stands.

Buzz lived in the basement of an old house. The walls were covered with graffiti for his band, Head of Skin, and there was a mattress in one corner. Weetzie glimpsed the handcuffs for a second before Buzz had her down on the mattress. She kept her eyes on the bare bulb until it blinded her.

In the morning, Weetzie tried to wake Buzz but he grunted when she touched him and pulled the sheets over his head. She got out of bed, wincing, still drunk, and called Dirk. He came and picked her up outside.

"Are you okay?" she asked him. His eyes were red. He had met someone in a video booth at a local sex store and they had groped around there for a while, then gone to the guy's apartment. Dirk had awakened, looked at the unfamiliar face, and gone home fast.

"About the same as you, I think."

They went to Canter's for bagels, which comforted Weetzie because she had teethed on Canter's bagels when she was a baby. While they ate, a cart of pickles wheeled by, the green rubbery pickles bobbing.

"Oh, God, that's all I need to see after last night," Dirk said.

"There are no Ducks, it feels like," Weetzie said.

"What is that?" Dirk asked the next day, noticing a tattoo-like bruise on Weetzie's arm.

"Nothing," she said.

"You aren't seeing that Buzz vulture anymore," Dirk said.

Weetzie kept falling for the wrong Ducks.

She met a Gloom-Doom Duck Poet who said, "My

10

heart is a canker sore. I cringed at the syringe."

She met a toothy blonde Surf Duck, who, she learned later, was sleeping with everyone.

She met an Alcoholic Art Duck with a ponytail, who talked constantly about his girlfriend who had died. Dirk saw him at an all-boy party kissing all the boys.

Dirk didn't do much better at the parties or bars.

"I just want My Secret Agent Lover Man," Weetzie said to Dirk.

"Love is a dangerous angel," Dirk said.

Weetzie and Her Dad
at the Tick Tock Tea Room

Weetzie's dad, Charlie Bat, took her to the Tick Tock Tea Room.

"We're the only people here without white hair . . . well, naturally white," Weetzie's dad said. Weetzie's hair was bleached white.

Weetzie's dad ordered two turkey platters with mashed potatoes, gravy, and cranberry sauce. The white-haired waitress served them canned fruit cocktail, sugar-glazed rolls, and pink sherbet before the turkey came. They had apple pie afterward.

"Does your mother feed you?" Weetzie's dad asked between the fruit and the rolls. "You're wasting away."

"Dad!" Weetzie said. "Of course she does."

"And how is your mother?"

"She's okay. Why don't you come in and see her later?"

"No, thanks, Weetzie. Not a good idea. But say hello from me," he said wistfully. "Any boyfriends? You, I mean."

"No, Dad."

"What about that Dirk? Still seeing him?"

"Yeah, but we're just friends."

Weetzie smiled at her dad. He was so handsome, but he didn't look well. He reminded her of a cigarette.

"I wish you'd come in and say hi to Mom," Weetzie said when Charlie dropped her off. But she knew that Charlie and Brandy-Lynn still weren't speaking.

Charlie came to L.A. from Brooklyn in the late fifties. He wrote to his older sister, Goldy, "Here I am in the L.A. wasteland. I hate the palm trees. They look like stupid birds. Everyone lies around in the sun like dead fishes. I go back to my little hotel room and my sad bed and feel sorry for myself. Saving all my pennies. Still no work. But I keep hoping."

Charlie got a job as a special-effects man at the studios. Making cities and then making them crumble, creating monsters and wounds and rains and planets in space. But what he really wanted to do was to write screenplays. He finished *Planet of the Mummy Men* and showed it to a producer, Irv Finegold.

"I like it, I like it," Irv said. They were having martinis at the Formosa. "And I'd like to make it."

Brandy-Lynn was a starlet who got a role in *Mummy Men*. She was on the set, having a fight with the director because she thought the mummy rags were unflattering, when Charlie saw her.

"Love at first sight, I swear," he would say later. "The most beautiful woman I'd ever seen."

13

She was bleach-blonde and sparkling with fake jewels, although she was wrapped in bandages. He wrote a new part into the movie for her so she didn't have to dress like a mummy.

"He made me feel like crying the first time I saw him," Brandy-Lynn told Weetzie with a sigh. "How right I was!" she added cynically.

They made love in the heat in Brandy-Lynn's bungalow, the filmy white drapes blowing with an occasional desert breeze. They drank tequila sunrises and bathed in gin. "That was your father's idea." They drove to the beach and made love in a tent under a pink-flamingo sky. They drove down the strip in Charlie's pale-yellow T-bird, Brandy-Lynn kicking her feet—in their gold mules with the fake fruit over the toes—right out the window.

When Weetzie was born Charlie said, "Best accident I ever had." (He had crashed the T-bird twice, because Brandy-Lynn was distracting him with kisses.)

"Where did you get a name like Weetzie Bat?" Dirk had asked when they met.

"Weetzie, Weetzie, Weetzie," she had shrilled. "How do I know? Crazy parents, I guess."

"I'll say."

She wished that the romance between Charlie and Brandy-Lynn had lasted.

But Brandy-Lynn turned bitter, that's what Weetzie's dad said. "Bitter as . . . what's the bitterest thing, Weetz?"

And Brandy-Lynn said, "That man was incorrigible.

14

Chasing women. A real lush. And who knows what other substances he was abusing." She downed her cocktail and patted the corners of her mouth with a cherry-printed napkin held in tanned and polished fingers. "I need a Valium."

They had screamed and thrown glasses at each other in the heat. One night, Weetzie saw them by the luminous blue condo pool; Brandy-Lynn threw a drink in Charlie's face. "That's it," he said.

Charlie moved back to New York to write plays. "Real quality stuff. This Hollywood trash is bullshit."

He sent Weetzie postcards with pictures of the Empire State Building or reproductions of paintings from the Metropolitan Museum, Statue of Liberty key chains, and plastic heart jewelry. He wanted Weetzie to move back east but Brandy-Lynn wouldn't hear of it. And although Weetzie adored her father, who reminded her of a cigarette, of Valentino, of a prince with palm trees on his shoulders, she couldn't leave where it was hot and cool, glam and slam, rich and trashy, devils and angels, Los Angeles.

"Okay, baby, so you can come visit me, at least."

When she visited him, he took her to the Metropolitan and to the Museum of Modern Art, took her to Bloomingdale's and bought her perfume and shoes, rode with her on the Staten Island ferry, took her to the delis for pastrami sandwiches and Cel-Ray tonic, bought her hot pretzels on the street.

One night when they got back, the power had gone out

in Charlie's apartment building and they had to walk up nine flights in the dark carrying the lox and bagels and cream cheese and bon-bons. He sang to her the whole way. "Rag Mop. R a g-g M-o-p-p Rag Mop doodley-doo."

When Weetzie left, she cried into his tobacco jacket. But really she couldn't live in New York, where the subways made her nerves feel like a charm bracelet of plastic skeletons jangling on a chain. She wished that Charlie would move back to L.A.

Instead, he came to visit and took her to the Tick Tock Tea Room. And he asked about Brandy-Lynn. But he never came into the house.

Fifi's Genie

One day, Weetzie and Dirk brought Grandma Fifi tomatoes from the Fairfax market and prune pastries from Canter's. As they were leaving, Fifi called them back.

"You look sad," she said.

"We want Ducks," Dirk said.

Fifi looked them up and down. Then she pointed to her canaries in their cage.

"They are in love. But even before they were in love they knew they were going to be happy and in love someday. They trusted. They have always loved themselves. They would never hurt themselves," Fifi said.

Dirk looked at Weetzie. Weetzie looked at Dirk.

"I have a present for you, Miss Weetzie Bat," Grandma Fifi said.

She went to the closet and brought out the most beautiful thing. It was a golden thing, and she put it into Weetzie's hands. Then she kissed Weetzie's cheek.

As Weetzie and Dirk left Fifi's cottage, Weetzie looked back and saw Fifi standing on the porch waving to them.

She looked paler and smaller and more beautiful than Weetzie had ever seen her.

When she got home, Weetzie set the thing on her table and looked at it. Despite the layers of dust she could see the exotic curve of its belly and the underlying gleam.

"I'll just polish you up," Weetzie said.

So Weetzie took out a rag and began to polish the thing.

But before she knew it, steam or smoke started seeping out from under the lid. A wisp of white vapor that smelled like musty cupboards and incense poured out and began to take shape there in the room.

Slinkster Dog whined and Weetzie gasped as they saw a form emerging. Yes, it was more and more solid. Weetzie could see him—it was a man, a little man in a turban, with a jewel in his nose, harem pants, and curly-toed slippers.

"Lanky lizards!" Weetzie exclaimed.

"Greetings," said the man in an odd voice, a rich, dark purr.

"Oh, shit!" Weetzie said.

"I beg your pardon? Is that your wish?"

"No! Sorry, you just freaked me out."

"I am the genie of the lamp, and I am here to grant you three wishes," the man said.

Weetzie began to laugh, maybe a little hysterically.

"Really, I don't see what is so amusing," the genie sniffed.

"Never mind. Okay. I wish for world peace," Weetzie said.

"I'm sorry," the genie said. "I can't grant that wish. It's out of my league. Besides, one of your world leaders would screw it up immediately."

"Okay," Weetzie said. "Then I wish for an infinite number of wishes!" As a kid she had vowed to wish for wishes if she ever encountered a genie or a fairy or one of those things. Those people in fairy tales never thought of that.

"People in fairy tales wish for that all the time," the genie said. "They aren't stupid. It just isn't in the records because I can't grant that type of wish."

"Well," Weetzie said, a little perturbed, "if this is my trip I think at least you could *say* I could have one of these wishes come true!"

"You get three wishes," the genie said.

"I wish for a Duck for Dirk, and My Secret Agent Lover Man for me, and a beautiful little house for us to live in happily ever after."

"Your wishes are granted. Mostly," said the genie. "And now I must be off."

"Don't you want to go back into your lamp?" Weetzie asked.

"Certainly not!" the genie said. "I've done my duty. I owed Fifi one more set of wishes, and she used them up on you. I'm not going back into that dark, smelly, cramped lamp. Farewell."

The genie was gone in a puff of smelly smoke.

"What a trip!" Weetzie said. "I'd better call Dirk. I wonder if someone put something in my drink last night."

Before Weetzie could call Dirk, the phone rang.

"I have good news and bad news," Dirk said. "Which first?"

"Bad," Weetzie said.

"My Grandma Fifi died," Dirk said.

"Oh, Dirk." Weetzie felt her heart stealing all the blood in her body.

"We knew she wasn't going to live very long," Dirk said.

"I know, but I never really thought she was going to die! That's a whole different thing," Weetzie said. The only death she had known was a dog named Hildegard that had belonged to Charlie Bat. The dog was the same tobacco color as Charlie and followed him everywhere, walking with the same loping stride. When Hildegard died, Weetzie saw Charlie cry for the first time.

"But, Weetz, there is good news. I feel a little guilty about good news but I know Fifi would be really happy."

"What?"

"She left us her house!" Dirk said.

"Oh, my God!" Weetzie said.

"What's wrong?"

Fifi's house was a Hollywood cottage with one of those fairy-tale roofs that look like someone has spilled silly sand. There were roses and lemon trees in the garden and two bedrooms inside the house—one painted rose and the other aqua. The house was filled with plaster Jesus statues, glass butterfly ashtrays, paintings of clowns, and many kinds of coasters. Weetzie and Dirk had always loved the house.

Weetzie felt terrible about her wish, but Dirk said, "You didn't wish for that house or to get it that way. And she was sick anyway. And she wanted us to have the house. She even wanted you to have her dresses. She told me that a million times."

"I don't know," Weetzie said, chewing her fingernails with their Egyptian decals.

"Now, look at these dresses," Dirk said, opening the closet.

Weetzie had never seen such great dresses—a black dress with huge silk roses sewn on it, a cream chiffon dress embroidered with gold sequins, a gold lamé and lace coat, a white fox fur, a tight red taffeta dress.

"Lanky lizards." Weetzie sighed. "They are so beautiful."

"She's lucky she had you, because I know she wouldn't want them to go to a stranger. And I know she secretly wished that I was a girl, but you serve the same purpose."

"Oh, Grandma Fifi, thank you," Weetzie said.

Duck

"I met the best one!" Dirk said. "The perfect Duck. But what is so weird is that this Duck calls himself Duck. Now that is hell of weird!"

"Lanky lizards!" Weetzie said.

"What now?"

Weetzie could not believe how wild it was.

Duck was a small, blonde surfer. He had freckles on his nose and wore his hair in a flat-top. Duck had a light-blue VW bug and he drove it to the beach every day. Sometimes he slept on picnic tables at the beach so he could be up at dawn for the most radical waves.

Dirk met Duck at Rage. Duck was standing alone at the bar when Dirk came up and offered to buy him a beer. Duck looked up at Dirk's chiseled features, blue eyes, and grand Mohawk. Dirk looked down at Duck's freckled nose and blonde flat-top. The flat-top was so perfect you could serve drinks on it. It was love at first sight. They danced the way some boys dance together—a little awkward and shy at first but with a sturdy ease, a rhythm between them.

Dirk's heart was pounding. He didn't even feel like finishing his drink.

He imagined the feel of Duck's skin—still warm and salty from the afternoon sun. Duck grinned and looked down at his feet in their white Vans. His teeth and his Vans glowed in the dark. His long eyelashes looked so soft on his tan cheek, Dirk thought.

"I haven't asked anyone home in a long time," Dirk said. "And we don't have to do anything. I don't know. . . ."

"I'd love to," Duck said solemnly, looking straight at Dirk.

Weetzie was happy that they had their house. She was happy that Dirk had a Duck. Duck moved in with Dirk— into the blue bedroom. Weetzie had the pink one. They were a threesome. A foursome if you counted Slinkster Dog. They went surfing together, dancing together. They all sat together on Jerry's front seat. They had barbecues and ate hamburgers and watermelon. They were a threesome all day (a foursome with Slinkster Dog included).

At night, Dirk and Duck kissed Weetzie on the cheek and went to bed. Weetzie got into her bed with Slinkster Dog. Sometimes she heard muffled giggles and love noise through the walls. Sometimes she heard music drowning out any sounds.

Weetzie couldn't help wondering why the third wish hadn't come true.

Jah-Love

Weetzie was working as a waitress at Duke's. One day a tall Rastafarian man, a tiny Chinese woman with black hair tipped in orange and red like a bouquet of bird of paradise, and a baby with skin the dusty brown of powdered Hershey's hot-chocolate mix came in for breakfast. The family came in often, and pretty soon Weetzie became friends with them. The man's name was Valentine Jah-Love and the woman's name was Ping Chong. They had met in Jamaica while Ping was looking for new ideas for her spring fashion line. She had gone to Valentine's house in the rain forest to see the fabrics he silkscreened, when suddenly the sky cracked and rain poured down.

"Jah!" cried Valentine, lifting his stormy face up in the greenish electric light. "You'll have to stay here. It will rain for seven days and seven nights."

It rained and rained. The house smelled moist and muddy. Valentine carved huge Rasta-man heads, animals, and pregnant women out of wood. The second night, Ping got out of the bed she had been sleeping in and got into

24

the cot beside Valentine. They slept together every night after that until the rain stopped on the seventh night. In the morning, Ping took an armload of fabrics silkscreened with snakes and birds, suns and shells, and went out into the steamy hot hibiscus air of Jamaica. After she had flown back to L.A., Ping found that she was pregnant. She wrote to Valentine and said, "I am having your child. If you ever want to see us you can find us here."

Valentine came to L.A. with an old leather bag full of fabrics and carvings. He arrived at the door of Ping's Hollywood bungalow looking like an ebony lion. He said he had come to live with her.

The child they had was a boy named Raphael Chong Jah-Love. They all lived together and wore red and ate plantain and black beans, or wonton soup and fortune cookies, and made silkscreened clothing they sold on the boardwalk at Venice beach. Weetzie loved Valentine and Ping and Raphael. They took her to the Kingston 12 to hear reggae music and drink Red Stripe Jamaican beer and they gave her sarong mini skirts and turbans they made and told her about Jamaica.

"In Jamaica there is night life like nowhere else—your body feels radiant, like orange lights, like Bob Marley's voice, when you dance in the clubs there. In Jamaica we climb the falls holding hands and the water rushes down bluer than your eyes. In Jamaica. In Jamaica it is hot and wet, and the people are hot and wet, and the shells look like flowers, and the flowers look like shells, and when you drive down some roads men come out of the bushes wearing parrots on their shoulders and flowering bird cages on top of their heads."

Weetzie said, "Maybe in Jamaica I could find My Secret Agent Lover Man. I can't seem to find him here." At night she dreamed of purple flowers and babies growing on bushes.

One day she was driving Valentine and Ping and Raphael to the L.A. airport to fly to Jamaica for a few weeks. Driving south on La Cienega, past the chic restaurants and galleries, down by the industrial oil-field train-track area, was a wall with graffiti that said, "Jah Love."

"Jah Love," Valentine said. "See that. Jah Love. That is a sign."

"Jah Love," Weetzie said wistfully.

"You need a man," Ping said. "But just you wait. I know you'll find your Jah-Love man."

"Coffee, black," he said.

It was a Sunday morning at Duke's.

"Anything else?" Weetzie asked.

"I'd like to put you in my film. My Secret Agent Lover Man." He put out his hand to shake.

"What?" Weetzie's eyes widened. She had been mistaken for a boy before and was a little sensitive about it. All she needed now was some gay man trying to pick up on her!

"My Secret Agent Lover Man's my name."

Weetzie was relieved that he hadn't been calling her *his* Secret Agent Lover Man, and that My Secret Agent Lover Man was . . .

"Your name!" she shrieked.

"Yeah. I know it's a little weird."

"Dirk put you up to this."

"Who's Dirk?"

"Lanky lizards!" Weetzie said, sitting down at the booth, knees buckling. "No way! I mean this is the wildest!"

"I know my name's weird but that's no reason not to give me a chance," he said.

A man at the next table was grumbling.

"I've got to go," Weetzie said.

My Secret Agent Lover Man came every day to see Weetzie. He was her height and wore a slouchy hat and a trench coat. He was unshaven and had the greenest eyes Weetzie had ever seen.

"I really want you to be in my film," My Secret Agent Lover Man said. "It's about a girl who comes to L.A. to be a filmmaker, and she's always taking home movies of everything, and by accident she gets some footage of a guy, and she goes around searching for him because he's the man of her dreams. She has to search in all these places like the Hollywood Wax Museum and Graumann's Chinese and Farmer's Market and Al's Bar. It's all black and white and dim and eerie and beautiful. And then at the end you realize a guy who is obsessed with the

27

girl has been filming *her* all along."

My Secret Agent Lover Man took out his home-movie camera and started to shoot Weetzie in her waitress apron while she stood waiting for his order. She put her hand over the lens. She had always wanted to be a star, and, yes, he looked like her Secret Agent Lover Man, but she was afraid to believe this was real. She couldn't handle another disappointing Duck.

"Sorry, mister," Weetzie said.

"Then at least let me take you out for a drink after work."

"Some drink after work!" Weetzie said.

My Secret Agent Lover Man had driven her to the beach on the back of his motorcycle and pulled a bottle of pink champagne out of his trench coat. They were sitting on the sand by the sea. My Secret Agent Lover Man uncorked the champagne and handed the bottle to Weetzie. He got out his camera and filmed her taking a swig.

"I said no film!" Weetzie said, scowling into the camera.

"That's beautiful!" he said.

Weetzie splashed champagne at the camera lens, but My Secret Agent Lover Man kept filming.

Suddenly, the tide came in. It came up over them, spilling over Weetzie's skinny legs, spilling over My Secret Agent Lover Man's legs in the slouchy trousers.

"Lanky lizards!" Weetzie shrieked.

My Secret Agent Lover Man laughed and laughed and kept filming her.

"Stop it!" Weetzie shouted, trying to grab the camera away.

My Secret Agent Lover Man took her wrists in his hands. Weetzie and My Secret Agent Lover Man sat there covered with salt water staring at each other. Weetzie had never noticed how pretty My Secret Agent Lover Man's lips were.

He kissed her.

A kiss about apple pie à la mode with the vanilla creaminess melting in the pie heat. A kiss about chocolate, when you haven't eaten chocolate in a year. A kiss about palm trees speeding by, trailing pink clouds when you drive down the Strip sizzling with champagne. A kiss about spotlights fanning the sky and the swollen sea spilling like tears all over your legs.

And there were a lot more of those kisses after that. On the motorcycle, in the restrooms of nightclubs, in the bathtub, in the pink bedroom. In between kisses My Secret Agent Lover Man made films of Weetzie putting her hands and feet into the movie-star prints at Graumann's, serving French toast at Duke's, dressing up in Fifi's gowns, rollerskating down the Venice boardwalk with Slinkster Dog pulling her along, Weetzie having a pow-wow and taking bubblebaths. Sometimes he filmed her surfing with Dirk and Duck, or doing a reggae dance with Ping while

Valentine and Raphael played drums.

"My Secret Agent Lover Man is very cute and cool," Dirk told Weetzie.

"*Your* Secret Agent Lover Man?"

"No, I mean *your* Secret Agent Lover Man. Where did he get such a weird name?"

Weetzie just smiled beneath her feathered headdress.

And so Weetzie and My Secret Agent Lover Man and Dirk and Duck and Slinkster Dog and Fifi's canaries lived happily ever after in their silly-sand-topped house in the land of skating hamburgers and flying toupees and Jah-Love blonde Indians.

Weetzie Wants a Baby

"What does 'happily ever after' mean anyway, Dirk?" Weetzie said. She was thinking about buildings. The Jetson-style Tiny Naylor's with the roller-skating waitresses had been torn down. In its place was a record-video store, a pizza place, a cookie place, a Wendy's, and a Penguin's Yogurt. Across the street, the old Poseur, where Weetzie and Dirk had bought kilts, was a beauty salon. They had written their names on the columns of the porch but all the graffiti had been painted over. Even Elvis Land was gone. Elvis Land had been in the front yard of an old house on Melrose. There had been a beat-up pink Cadillac, a picture of Elvis, and a giant love letter to Elvis on the lawn.

Then there were the really old places. Like the Tiki restaurant in the Valley, which had gone out of business years ago and had become overgrown with reeds so that the Tiki totems peered out of the watery-sounding darkness. Now it was gone—turned into one of the restaurants that lined Ventura Boulevard with valets in red jackets sitting out in the heat all day waiting for BMW's. And Kiddie

Land, the amusement park where Weetzie's dad, Charlie, had taken her (Weetzie's pony had just dawdled, and sometimes turned around and gone back to the start, because Weetzie wouldn't use the whip, and once Weetzie was traumatized by a plastic cow that swung onto the track); Kiddie Land was now the big, brown Beverly Center that Weetzie would have painted almost any other color—at least, if they *had* to go ahead and put it up in place of Kiddie Land.

"What does happily ever after mean anyway?" Weetzie said.

She was still living in Fifi's cottage with Dirk and Duck and My Secret Agent Lover Man. They had finished their third film, called *Coyote*, with Weetzie as a rancher's daughter who falls in love with a young Indian named Coyote and ends up helping him defend his land against her father and the rest of the town. They had filmed *Coyote* on an Indian reservation in New Mexico. Weetzie grew her hair out, and she wore Levi's and snaky cowboy boots and turquoise. Dirk and Duck played her angry brothers; Valentine did the music, and Ping was wardrobe. My Secret Agent Lover Man was the director. His friend Coyote played Coyote.

The film was quite a success, and it brought Weetzie and My Secret Agent Lover Man and Dirk and Duck and their friends money for the first time. They bought a mint 1965 T-bird, and Weetzie went to Gräu and bought a jacket made out of peach and rose and gold silk antique

kimonos. They had enough to go to Noshi for sushi whenever they wanted (which was a lot because Weetzie was
addicted to the hamachi, which only cost $1.50 an order).
They also ate guacamole tostadas at El Coyote (which had,
they agreed, some of the best decorations in Hollywood,
especially the painting with the real little lights right in
it), putting the toppings of guacamole, canned vegetables,
Thousand Island dressing, and cheese into the corn tortillas that were served between two plates to keep them
warm. Weetzie also bought beads and feathers and white
Christmas lights and roses that she saved and dried. She
decorated everything in sight with these things until
the whole house was a collage of glitter and petals.

"I feel like Cinderella," Weetzie said, driving around in
the T-bird, wearing her kimono jacket, while My Secret
Agent Lover Man covered her with kisses, and Dirk and
Duck and Slinkster Dog crooned along with the radio.

Everything was fine except that Weetzie wanted a baby.

"How could you want one?" My Secret Agent Lover
Man said. "There are way too many babies. And diseases.
And nuclear accidents. And crazy psychos. We can't have a
baby," he said.

They had hiked to the Hollywood sign and were eating
canned smoked oysters and drinking red wine from real
glasses that My Secret Agent Lover Man had packed in
newspaper in his backpack.

"But we could have such a cool, beautiful baby,"
Weetzie said, sticking her toothpick into an oyster. "And it

would be so happy and we would love it so much."

"I don't want one, Weetz," he said. "Just forget about babies—you have enough already anyway: me and Dirk and Duck and Slinkster Dog. And you're just one yourself."

Weetzie stood up, shoved her hands into the back pockets of her Levi's, and looked out over the top of the Hollywood sign. My Secret Agent Lover Man and Weetzie had spray-painted their initials on the back of the "D" when they first met. Beneath the sign the city was only lights, safe and sparkling, like the Hollywood in "Hollywood in Miniature" on Hollywood Boulevard. It didn't look like any of the things that My Secret Agent Lover Man was talking about.

The next day, My Secret Agent Lover Man came home carrying a cardboard box that made scratching, yipping sounds. "I brought you a baby," he said to Weetzie. "This is Go-Go Girl. She is a girlfriend for Slinkster Dog. When she grows up, she and Slink can have some more babies for you. We can have as many puppy babies as you want."

Slinkster Dog wriggled with joy, and Weetzie kissed My Secret Agent Lover Man and held Go-Go Girl against her chest. The puppy's fur had a pinkish cast from her skin and she wore a rhinestone collar. She would make a perfect girlfriend for Slinkster Dog, Weetzie thought. But she was not a *real* baby.

"We'll have a baby with you," Dirk said.

He and Duck had come home to find Weetzie alone on

the living room couch among the collage pillows, which were always leaving a dust of glitter and dried petals. She was crying and blowing her nose with pink Kleenex, and there were wadded up Kleenex roses all over the floor.

"Yeah," Duck said. "I saw it on that talk show once. These two gay guys and their best friend all slept together so no one would know for sure whose baby it was. And then they had this really cool little girl and they all raised her, and it was so cool, and when someone in the audience said, 'What sexual preference do you hope she has?' they all go together, they go 'Happiness.' Isn't that cool?"

"But what about My Secret Agent Lover Man?" Weetzie said.

"Nothing has to change," Dirk said. "We'll just have a baby."

"But he doesn't want one."

"It might not be his baby," Dirk said. "But I'll bet he likes it when he sees it, and we'll all go to a doctor to make sure we can make the perfect healthy baby."

Weetzie looked at Dirk's chiseled features and Duck's glossy, tan, surfer-dude face and she smiled. It would be a beautiful slinkster girl baby, or a hipster baby boy, and they would all love it more than any of their parents had ever loved them—more than any baby had ever been loved, Weetzie thought.

When My Secret Agent Lover Man came home that night he looked weary. His eyes looked like glasses of gin. Weetzie ran to kiss him, and when she put her arms around him, he felt tense and somehow smaller.

"What's wrong, honey-honey?"

"I wish I could stop listening to the news," he said.

Weetzie kissed him and ran her hands through his hair.

"Let's take a bath," she said.

They lit candles and incense, and made Kahlua and milks, and got into the bathtub in the pink-and-aqua-tiled bathroom. Weetzie felt as if she were turning into steam and milk and honey. She massaged My Secret Agent Lover Man's pale, clenched back with aloe vera oil and pikake lotion.

"If I was ever going to have a baby, it would be with you, Miss Weetzie," he said after they had made love. "You would make a great mom."

Weetzie just kissed his fingers and his throat, but she didn't say anything about the plan.

One night, while My Secret Agent Lover Man was away fishing with his friend Coyote, Weetzie and Dirk and Duck went out to celebrate. They had received their test results, and now they could have a baby. At Noshi, they ordered hamachi, anago, maguro, ebi, tako, kappa maki, and Kirin beer. They were buzzing from the beer and from the burning neon-green wasabe and the pink ginger and from the massive protein dose of sushi. ("Like, sushi is the heavy protein buzz," Duck said.)

"Here's to our baby," Dirk said. "I always wanted one, and I thought I could never get one, and now we are going to. And it will be all of ours—My (your) Secret Agent Lover Man's, too."

They drank a toast and then they all got into Dirk's car, Jerry, and drove home.

Weetzie changed into her lace negligée from Trashy Lingerie and went into Dirk and Duck's room and climbed into bed between Dirk and Duck. They all just sat there, bolt upright, listening to "I Wanna Hold Your Hand."

"I feel weird," Weetzie said.

"Me too," Dirk said.

Duck scratched his head.

"But we want a baby and we love each other," Weetzie said.

"I love you, Weetz. I love you, Dirk," Duck said.

"'I Wanna Hold Your Hand,'" the Beatles said.

And that was how Weetzie and Dirk and Duck made the baby—well, at least that was how it began, and no one could be sure if that was really the night, but that comes later on.

When My Secret Agent Lover Man came back from fishing with Coyote he looked healthier and rested. "I haven't seen the paper in three weeks," he said, sitting down at the kitchen table with the *Times*.

Weetzie took the paper away. "Honey, I have something to tell you," she said.

Weetzie was pregnant. She felt like a Christmas package. Like a cat full of kittens. Like an Easter basket of pastel chocolate-malt eggs and solid-milk-chocolate bunnies, and yellow daffodils and dollhouse-sized jelly-bean eggs.

But My Secret Agent Lover Man stared at her in shock and anger. "You did what?

"The world's a mess," My Secret Agent Lover Man said. "And there is no way I feel okay about bringing a kid into it. And for you to go and sleep with Dirk and Duck without even telling me is the worst thing you have ever done."

Weetzie could not even cry and make Kleenex roses. She remembered the day her father, Charlie, had driven away in the smashed yellow T-bird, leaving her mother Brandy-Lynn clutching her flowered robe with one hand and an empty glass in the other, and leaving Weetzie holding her arms crossed over her chest that was taking its time to develop into anything. But My Secret Agent Lover Man was not going to send Weetzie postcards of the Empire State Building, or come visit every so often to buy her turkey platters at the Tick Tock Tea Room like Charlie did. Weetzie knew by his eyes that he was going away forever. His eyes that had always been like lakes full of fishes, or waves of love, or bathtub steam and candle smoke, or at least like glasses of gin when he was sad, were now like two heavy green marbles, like the eyes of the mechanical fortune-teller on the Santa Monica pier. She hardly recognized him because she knew he didn't recognize her, not at all. Once, on a bus in New York, she had seen the man of her dreams. She was twelve and he was carrying a guitar case and roses wrapped in green paper, and there were raindrops on the roses and on his hair, and he hadn't looked at her once. He was sitting directly across from her and staring ahead and he didn't see anyone, anything there. He didn't see Weetzie even though she had known then that someday they must have babies and bring each other roses and write songs together and be rock stars. Her heart had felt as meager as her twelve-year-old chest, as if it had shriveled up because this man didn't recognize her. That was nothing compared to how her heart felt when she saw My Secret Agent Lover Man's dead marble fortune-teller eyes.

Nine months is not very long when you consider that a whole person with fingers and toes and everything is being made. But for Weetzie nine months felt like a long time to wait. It felt especially long because she was not only waiting for the baby with its fingers and toes and features that would reveal who its dad was, but she was also waiting for My Secret Agent Lover Man, even though she knew he was not going to come.

Dirk and Duck were wonderful fathers-in-waiting. Dirk read his favorite books and comic books out loud to Weetzie's stomach, and Duck made sure she ate only health food. ("None of those gnarly grease-burgers and NO OKI DOGS!" Duck said.) They cuddled with her and gave her backrubs, and tickled her when she was sad, to make sure she got enough physical affection. ("Because I heard that rats shrivel up and die if they aren't, like, able to hang out with other rats," Duck said.) Whenever Weetzie thought of My Secret Agent Lover Man and started to cry, Dirk and Duck waited patiently, hugged her, and took her to a movie on Hollywood Boulevard or for a Macro-Erotic at I Love Jucy. Valentine and Ping and Raphael came over with fortune cookies, and pictures and poems that Raphael had made. Brandy-Lynn called and said, "I don't approve . . . but what can I get for you? I'm sure it's a girl. She'll need the right clothes. None of those feathered outfits."

Weetzie was comforted by Dirk and Duck, Valentine, Ping, Raphael, and even Brandy-Lynn, and by the baby she felt rippling inside of her like a mermaid. But the movie camera and the slouchy hat and baggy trousers and the crackly voice and the hands that soothed the jangling of her charm-bracelet nerves—all that was gone. My Secret Agent Lover Man was gone.

Weetzie had the baby at the Kaiser on Sunset Boulevard, where she had been born.

"Am I glad that's over!" Duck said, coming into Weetzie's hospital room with a pale face. "Dirk has been having labor pains out there in the waiting room."

"What about you?" Dirk said to Duck. "Duck has been moaning and sweating out there in the waiting room."

Weetzie laughed weakly. "Look what we got," she said.

It was a really little baby—almost too little.

"You can't tell who it looks like yet," Duck said. "It's too little and pink."

"No matter who it looks like, it's all of ours," Dirk said.

He put his arms around Weetzie and Duck, and they sat looking at their baby girl.

"What are we going to name it?" Duck said.

They had thought about Sweet and Fifi and Duckling and Hamachi and Teddi and Lambie, but they decided to name her Cherokee.

When they left the hospital the next day, Weetzie looked down Sunset Boulevard to where Norm's coffee shop used to be. Weetzie's dad, Charlie, had waited all night in that Norm's, drinking coffee black and smoking packs until Weetzie was born. Weetzie had always thought that when she had a baby its father would wait in Norm's for her, looking like her secret agent lover. But Norm's was torn down and My Secret Agent Lover Man was gone.

Weetzie and Dirk and Duck brought Cherokee home and the house felt different, lighter and more musical now, because someone was always opening a window to let in the sun or putting on a record. The sun streamed in, making the walls glow like the inside of a rose. But even in the rosy house, Weetzie felt bittersweet; bittersweetness was like a liqueur burning in her throat and dripping down slowly into her heart.

Then one morning, Weetzie woke up feeling different, not bittersweet, but expectant the way she used to feel on the morning of her birthday. She opened her eyes and saw the flowers—there were flowers heaped on top of the quilt. Big, ruffly peonies, full-blown roses, pink-spotted lilies,

41

pollen-dusty poppies. Weetzie blinked in the sunlight and saw My Secret Agent Lover Man standing over her and Cherokee. He looked very pale and hunched in his trench coat, and his eyes were moist.

Weetzie put out her arms, and he came and sat on the bed and held her very tight. Then he looked at Cherokee.

"Whose is she?" he asked. "She is so completely perfect."

"She looks like Dirk," Weetzie said. "Because of her cheekbones."

My Secret Agent Lover Man's mouth twitched a little.

"And she looks like Duck," Weetzie said. "Because she is blonde . . . And her nose."

My Secret Agent Lover Man wrinkled his brow.

"And she looks like me, of course, because she is so itsy-witsy and silly-looking," Weetzie said, laughing.

"But really, she absolutely has no one else's eyes but yours, and your pretty lips. I think she's all of ours," Weetzie said. "I hope that is okay with you."

Dirk and Duck came into the room.

"We missed you," Dirk said. "And we hope you stay around and help raise our kid."

My Secret Agent Lover Man smiled. Weetzie held Cherokee against her breast. Cherokee looked like a three-dad baby, like a peach, like a tiny moccasin, like a girl love-warrior who would grow up to wear feathers and run swift and silent through the L.A. canyons.

Witch Baby

One day, there was a knock on the door of the silly-sand-topped house. Weetzie opened the door, and there stood a beautiful woman with long black hair, purple, tilty eyes, and a long body. She was the type of woman Weetzie and Dirk used to call a "Lanka."

"Is Max here?" asked the Lanka in a low voice.

"Who?" Weetzie said. It came out like a screech, especially compared to the Lanka murmur, and she said again, "Who?"

"Max," the woman repeated. "I know he lives here. I've tracked him down."

"There is no one by that name here," Weetzie said. "I'm sorry I can't help you."

"I insist on seeing Max," the woman said, pressing on Weetzie's chest with five taloned fingertips.

Weetzie pushed the Lanka away and shut the door.

"Curses on both of you!" the Lanka said.

Weetzie looked out the peephole and saw her slink away down the front path in her long, black Lanka dress.

At dinner that night, Weetzie said, "A crazy woman was here today. She kept asking for some man. She was a real Lanka—a mean Lanka, too. It was a little scary."

"There are a lot of freaks around," Dirk said.

"Yeah," Duck said. "Next time something like that happens, call us."

"I can handle it," Weetzie said.

My Secret Agent Lover Man was unusually silent.

The next night, My Secret Agent Lover Man came home early from the set where he had been working on his new horror movie about a coven of witches who pose under the guise of a Jayne Mansfield fan club. His skin was burning and he looked as if there was a heavy weight pressing on his forehead and his shoulders. Weetzie put him in bed and took his temperature, which was very high. She gave him aspirin and megadoses of vitamin C and sponged him off with cool towels.

"You have been working too hard," she said.

My Secret Agent Lover Man gasped for air all through the night. Weetzie lay awake, watching him so hot and vulnerable, shivering with fever, and she wanted to hold on to him and never let go. It was as if he had no defenses, none of his usual guards up, as if they could merge together so easily.

"I love you, Weetzie," he said in the middle of the night. Then he twisted as if from a sharp pain.

"I love you, I love you, My Secret Agent Lover Man, my wish list come true," she said.

44

In the morning, he was still sick. Weetzie brought him more aspirin and vitamin C, and made him drink grapefruit juice and herb tea, and she put on cartoons for him to watch.

"I have to tell you something, Weetzie," he said.

"Not now; try to rest. I'm taking you to the doctor later."

But, in the afternoon, there was a knock on the door.

Weetzie answered it without thinking, and there stood the Lanka.

"Tell Max he had better see me or he will get worse," she said.

Before Weetzie could shut the door, she heard My Secret Agent Lover Man say, "Wait."

He had gotten out of bed and was stumbling toward them wearing his trench coat over his pajamas.

"Max," said the woman, "I must talk to you. Tell this girl to let me in. Or I will make her sick, too. I have a Barbie doll that will look a lot like her when I chop off all its hair, and I have plenty of pins to stick into it."

"Weetzie," My Secret Agent Lover Man said, "can I please speak to her? I will tell you everything after."

Weetzie looked at him and at the Lanka and then back at him. He was really sick.

"Whatever you need to do," she said, going into the kitchen.

A little while later, My Secret Agent Lover Man came into the kitchen, too. He looked better, as if the fever had broken. "She's gone. Now I have something to tell you," he said, sitting down beside her.

"When I went away I was very confused," he began. "I knew I was afraid of having a baby, and I hated myself for being afraid. And I was so jealous of you with Dirk and Duck that I couldn't even think. I just had to leave.

"So while I was away, all I thought of was you. And one day I saw a sign that said 'Jayne Mansfield Fan Club.' The picture of Jayne Mansfield reminded me of how you make that siren noise out of *The Girl Can't Help It*, and I went to the place it said. It was a house in a run-down part of town, real spooky and dark, and there were all these people wearing white wigs and doing drugs and watching weird old Jayne film clips and talking about the sick way she died. How her head got cut off in her pink T-bird or something. I was such a wreck from being without you, and from not eating, and from sleeping in my car, and from drinking too much that I just stayed and watched and listened. And then this one woman, Vixanne Wigg, the one today, she asked me if I needed a place to stay, and I did, so she let me stay in the attic of this house where she lived. But soon I realized that these people were pretty sick. They were witches. They had séances and shit, and some pretty bad things happened."

"Like you saw maggots in the sink, and then they were gone, and someone hanged himself in the backyard, and you started to leave but Vixen or Vixanne or whatever seduced you and you slept together just like in your movie, right, *Max*?" Weetzie said.

My Secret Agent Lover Man looked down at his blue suede creepers, and then he looked into Weetzie's eyes. "That's right," he said. "I was very sick then, Weetzie, and now there is more. I left the next day. We only slept together once. It was a terrible thing. But now she says she is pregnant and she needs money for the abortion, so I gave her money, and now she'll leave us alone. But I had to speak to her because she is very powerful and she could have made you sick, too."

"She could not have made me sick," Weetzie said. "You got sick because you felt guilty and afraid."

She got up and walked out of the room.

When she told Dirk and Duck that night they said, "Miss Weetzie Girl, I bet she did make him sick. But don't be mad. Don't hang on to it. He loves you."

And Weetzie remembered him sweating and shaking and gasping in the night and twisting with pain as if he were a Ken doll stuck with pins, and she knew she couldn't be mad for long, and when he came to her that night and stood there so vulnerable and naked and with painful memories tattooed on his body, she forgot everything except that he was back.

Months passed, and the Jayne Mansfield witches were only a movie, and everything was happy in Fifi's cottage.

Until the witch baby appeared on the front step.

Duck came into the house one day, carrying a basket. "Look what I found on the front step," he said.

Inside the basket was a newborn baby with purple, tilty eyes and pouty lips. There were a Ken doll and a Barbie doll with chopped-off hair in the basket, too, and Weetzie took one look at the baby and knew who it was.

"It is the witch baby," she said.

"What?" Dirk and Duck said.

"It is My Secret Agent Lover Man and Vixanne's witch baby," Weetzie said.

My Secret Agent Lover Man sat silently for a moment and then he said, "She lied. I'll find her and give it back. I'm sorry, Weetzie."

The witch baby began to cry.

"She is beautiful," Weetzie said. "Even if her mother is a Lanka witch."

Weetzie took the witch baby out of the basket and held her close until she stopped crying. Cherokee eyed her suspiciously.

Duck said, "What are those?" noticing the Ken and Barbie.

"Those are Vixanne's voodoo dolls," Weetzie said. "I think Vixanne gave them to us as a peace offering."

"Vixanne is evil," My Secret Agent Lover Man said. "I've got to give this baby back."

"If she is evil, we can't do that," Weetzie said. "We have to take care of this baby."

"Yeah, we can call her Witch Baby," Duck said. "How totally cool!"

"No, we can call her Lily," Weetzie said. "And she can be Cherokee's sister. Okay, Cherokee Love?"

Cherokee didn't look pleased. My Secret Agent Lover Man picked her up and put her on his knee and gave her the Ken doll to play with. This made her smile.

"If you can accept Cherokee as yours without being sure, then I can accept Lily, even though I know she's not mine; I can accept her because you are her daddy-o," Weetzie said. "Besides, she is cool and she likes me. What do you guys think about keeping her?"

"I hope she is not a voodoo queen already," Dirk said.

"She is only a baby," Weetzie said.

"I hope she is not going to hex me if I don't give her her favorite kind of Gerber's," Duck said.

"She is only a baby," Weetzie said.

"She is a witch baby," said My Secret Agent Lover Man.

"Look at her," Weetzie said. "She is *your* baby."

My Secret Agent Lover Man looked at Lily's pointy little face.

"What does Cherokee think?"

Cherokee smiled and clapped her hands.

"It is cool with me," said Duck. "It will be like *Bewitched.*"

"Me too," said Dirk.

They all looked at My Secret Agent Lover Man.

"Okay," he said. "Witch Baby, I mean, Lily, welcome to the family."

Weetzie put Lily onto his other knee.

It was not easy at first. Witch Baby was a wild witch baby. The name Lily never stuck. As soon as she could walk, she would run all over the house like a mad cat, playing torpedo games. As soon as she could talk, she would go around chanting, "Beasts, beasts, beasts," over and over again.

"Who taught her that?" Weetzie asked Duck suspiciously.

"I swear, she just knew it," Duck said. "Pretty creepy, huh?"

Once, Witch Baby pulled Cherokee's hair and ran away laughing shrilly. The next night, Cherokee cut off Witch Baby's shaggy black hair with a pair of toenail scissors while the witch baby slept. Witch Baby ate and ate but she stayed as skinny as bones and she became more and more beautiful.

"What are we going to do with her?" My Secret Agent Lover Man said.

"She just needs time and love," Weetzie said. "It must be hard for her, knowing she's a witch baby. Besides, I was a terror when I was little, too."

And so, Witch Baby stayed on in the house, and took turns terrorizing Cherokee and being terrorized by Cherokee, and eating up all of Duck's Fig Newtons, and using Dirk's Aqua Net, and insisting on being in My Secret Agent Lover Man's movies, and dressing up in Weetzie's clothes, and pulling heads off Barbie dolls and sticking them on the TV antenna and ruining the reception.

But that's how witch babies are.

Shangri-L.A.

Weetzie and My Secret Agent Lover Man and Dirk and Duck and Cherokee and Witch Baby and Slinkster Dog and Go-Go Girl and the puppies Pee Wee, Wee Wee, Teenie Wee, Tiki Tee, and Tee Pee were driving down Hollywood Boulevard on their way to the Tick Tock Tea Room for turkey platters.

"They are already putting up Christmas lights," Duck said.

"It's only the beginning of October," My Secret Agent Lover Man said.

"They're making a movie," Dirk said.

Cherokee clapped her hands for the feathery golden bridges of lights that were being strung from Frederick's of Hollywood to Love's.

"We live in Shangri-la," Weetzie said. "Shangri Los Angeles. It's always Christmas."

"That's it!" My Secret Agent Lover Man said.

"What?" they all asked.

"The name of our new movie."

❧

Shangri-L.A. was a remake of *Lost Horizon*, except that in the movie the horizon was a magical Hollywood where everyone looked like Marilyn, Elvis, James Dean, Charlie Chaplin, Harpo, Bogart, or Garbo, everything was magic castles and star-paved streets and Christmas lights, and no one grew old. Weetzie played a girl on her way to the real Hollywood to become a star. The bus on which she is traveling crashes, and when she regains consciousness she and the other passengers who have survived find themselves in the magic land. Weetzie falls in love with the Charlie Chaplin character from Shangri-L.A., and he tells her she can stay there with him and never grow old. She doesn't believe him and insists that they leave together. They fix the bus and drive away, but he immediately ages and dies, leaving her caught in the real Hollywood.

"Hell-A," My Secret Agent Lover Man said.

Making the movie was like dreaming twenty-four hours a day. Weetzie styled her blonde hair in Marilyn waves, and wore strapless satin dresses and rhinestones. She made fringed baby clothes and feathered headdresses for Cherokee and tutus and gauze wings for Witch Baby. Dirk had grown out his Mohawk into a ducktail, and he wore sparkling suits and bolo ties. Duck, in leather, squinted his face up, pretending to be Jimmy Dean. And My Secret Agent Lover Man, in a baggy suit, walked toes out, his eyes like charcoal stars. They drove around in the T-bird eating ice cream and filming. In the movie, they got to be a rock band. Dirk and Duck played guitar, My Secret Agent Lover Man bass, Valentine and Raphael drums. Weetzie and Cherokee and Witch Baby and Ping sang. They performed "Ragg Mopp," "Louie-Louie," "Wild Thing," and their own songs like "Lanky Lizard," "Rubber-Chicken Strut," "Irie-Irie," "Witchy Baby," and "Love Warrior."

The movie was going very well except they weren't sure about the ending.

"We should ask your dad," My Secret Agent Lover Man said. "He is great at those things."

"Maybe I'll go visit him," Weetzie said. "He hasn't seen Cherokee in a long time, and besides, I'm worried about him."

So Weetzie and Cherokee went to New York to see Charlie Bat.

Charlie was unshaven and he looked even taller because he was so skinny now. He stood in the doorway of the dark apartment shaking his head.

"My babies," he said.

Being with Charlie was always a romantic date. The first day, he took them to the Metropolitan Museum, where they looked at Greek marbles and French Impressionist paintings and costumes until their eyes were blurry and their feet were sore. Weetzie loved the Egyptian rooms the most.

"They spent their whole lives covering these walls with pictures," Charlie said, showing them gods, goddesses, stars, eyes, rabbits, birds, on the tomb walls. "And they filled the tombs with everything you could want. Now that's the way to die."

After the museum, they went to Chinatown and ate squid and broccoli and hot-and-sour soup. Then they wandered through the angled streets that smelled meaty and peppery. The Chinatown museum looked like a movie set and inside was a dancing chicken—a real, live chicken that turned on its own tunes with its beak and did a slidy dance for seventy-five cents. Charlie Bat made the chicken dance and he played air hockey with Weetzie. Then, on the way home, he bought cannolis in Little Italy for all of them.

The next day, Charlie took them to the top of the Empire State Building, and there was his city spread out in front of them. It reminded Weetzie of the time she and My Secret Agent Lover Man had hiked to the top of the Hollywood sign, and she had dreamed of Cherokee and he had been afraid. She wished that the world could be the way it looked from up here—that Charlie could live in a city of perfect buildings and cars and people if he was going to live so far away. The Chrysler Building looked like an art-deco rocket that had caught fans of stars on its way up, and the Statue of Liberty looked like a creature risen green and magical from the sea, and everything looked at peace in the blue, clear day. Charlie bought Cherokee a bottle filled with tiny buildings and blue glitter and water, and she shook it and laughed, watching the glitter come down, and Weetzie wished she could shake blue glitter around all of them—keeping them sparkling and safe.

By the time they came down in the elevator, they all had blue glitter on their eyelids and cheeks from the little bottle.

Charlie took them out for Italian food and French food and Jewish deli and lobster. He bought them strawberries and whipped cream at the Palm Court in the Plaza Hotel, where musicians played to them among the peachy marble columns, mirrors, and floral tapestry chairs. He took them to galleries and shops in SoHo and the East Village and bought them gifts: flowers, Peter Fox shoes for Weetzie, and a Pink Panther doll from F.A.O. Schwarz for Cherokee. Charlie smiled, but he looked lost.

"Are you okay, Daddy?" Weetzie asked.

They had come to Harlem for breakfast. On the street, a man in a black hat had touched Charlie's shoulder and muttered something about "Doctor Man," and Charlie went pale and started to cough as he walked away. Now they were in Sylvia's, eating eggs and grits and biscuits and sweet-potato pie.

"I'm okay," Charlie said. He was on his third cup of coffee and hadn't touched his breakfast. "How's Brandy-Lynn?"

"She is okay," Weetzie said. "She doesn't like the idea of Cherokee having three dads."

"Well, it is a little hard to get used to," Charlie said.

"I think she really misses you," Weetzie said. "You should come and visit."

"And how is that boyfriend of yours?" Charlie asked, trying to change the subject. "The one with the funny name."

"You mean My Secret Agent Lover Man."

"That sure is a funny name," Charlie said.

Weetzie laughed because Charlie had named her Weetzie and his last name was Bat.

"What is Cherokee's last name?" Charlie asked. "Is it My Secret or Secret Agent or Lover or what?"

"Bat, like ours," Weetzie said. "Cherokee Bat."

"She is a wonder," Charlie said dreamily, looking at his granddaughter in her pink fringed coat. "Cherokee Bat . . ."

Before she left, Weetzie asked Charlie how to end *Shangri-L.A.*

"Maybe this girl tries to get back by taking drugs," he said. "And she dies."

"That is such a sad ending, Dad," Weetzie said with dismay. She knew something was wrong. The paint on Charlie's apartment walls had cracked and chipped and his eyes were as dark and hollow as the corners of the room.

Charlie sighed.

"Move back," Weetzie said. "It is no good for you here. You could work on the movie. We need you. In L.A. we have a fairy-tale house. We have pancakes at Duke's, and dinners at the Tick Tock Tea Room. We have the sky set; remember, you used to take me to see it, and Marilyn's star. And we have Cherokee."

Charlie said: "Weetzie, I love you and Cherokee and . . . Well, I love you more than everything. But I can't be in that city. Everything's an illusion; that's the whole thing about it—illusion, imitation, a mirage. Pagodas and palaces and skies, blondes and stars. It makes me too sad. It's like having a good dream. You know you are going to wake up."

"Daddy," Weetzie said. "Please come home."

"I love you more than everything," Charlie said. "You and Cherokee and Brandy-Lynn still, too. But I can't come back. It would hurt you."

So Weetzie and Cherokee had to leave New York. They left Charlie Bat standing at the airport in his trench coat. He was smiling, but his eyes were like dark corners.

"Mom," Weetzie said. "I am worried about Charlie."

Brandy-Lynn looked up from polishing her nails. "What is it? What's he doing to himself?"

"I think you should call him," Weetzie said.

"It makes me too sad," said Brandy-Lynn.

Charlie was dreaming of a city where everyone was always young and lit up like a movie, palm trees turned into tropical birds, Marilyn-blonde angels flew through the spotlight rays, the cars were the color of candied mints and filled with lovers making love as they drove down the streets paved with stars that had fallen from the sky. Charlie was dreaming of a giant poppy like a bed. He had taken some pills, and this time he didn't wake up from his dream.

Weetzie and My Secret Agent Lover Man and Dirk and Duck and Cherokee and Witch Baby huddled on the pink bed and cried. Grief is not something you know if you grow up wearing feathers with a Charlie Chaplin boyfriend, a love-child papoose, a witch baby, a Dirk and a Duck, a Slinkster Dog, and a movie to dance in. You can feel sad and worse when your dad moves to another city, when an old lady dies, or when your boyfriend goes away. But grief is different. Weetzie's heart cringed in her like a dying animal. It was as if someone had stuck a needle full of poison into her heart. She moved like a sleepwalker. She was the girl in the fairy tale sleeping in a prison of thorns and roses.

"Wake up," My Secret Agent Lover Man said, kissing her. But she was suffocated by roses that no one else saw— only their shadows showed on her lips and around her eyes.

"Weetzie," he said, kissing her mouth. "You are my Marilyn. You are my lake full of fishes. You are my sky set, my 'Hollywood in Miniature,' my pink Cadillac, my highway, my martini, the stage for my heart to rock and roll on, the screen where my movies light up," he said.

Weetzie curled up in a little ball in the bed.

"Weetzie," he said, "your dad's dead. But you aren't, baby."

She put her arms around him and cried. Their clothes

fell away like clothes in a dream—like a dream peels away when you wake up. Their bodies clung together like warriors fighting out the pain in each other.

My Secret Agent Lover Man finally relaxed, his body becoming heavy with sleep. Weetzie held on to him.

"Don't sleep," she said. "Don't sleep. How can we sleep? Suddenly I felt what it is like to know I am not always going to be able to see you and touch you."

My Secret Agent Lover Man wrapped her in his pale warrior arms. The veins pulsed with blue peace like rivers that lead to a mountain lake. Weetzie shut her eyes finally, and the roses did not grow over her in the night. She dreamed that she and My Secret Agent Lover Man were holding hands and climbing a waterfall.

Weetzie went to see Brandy-Lynn the next day.

Brandy-Lynn was drinking vodka and lying on a chaise lounge by the pool. She wore curlers and she was getting very tan.

"When I was a kid my mother brought me to Hollywood," Brandy-Lynn said. "We lived at the Garden of Allah. She left me alone all day and I went around the pool with my cute little autograph book. It said 'Autographs' on the cover in gold. Clark Gable even signed it! Everyone was so gorgeous. I used to walk to Schwab's and have a hamburger and a milkshake for dinner, and I'd swivel around and around on the barstool reading Wonder Woman comics and planning how it would be when I became a star. But what I really wanted was a Charlie Bat. I always loved that man. What happened, Weetzie?"

Weetzie hugged Brandy-Lynn. She felt greasy from the suntan oil and her shoulders felt very small.

"He loved you too, Brandy-Lynn," Weetzie said. "Now that's enough." She took away the bottle of vodka. "Let's go out for some health food."

"Did he really?" Brandy-Lynn said. A blurry lipstick smile showed through her blue-mascara-tinted tears. "I haven't been a very good mother, have I?"

"You are a wonderful mother."

"He was the man of my dreams. . . ."

At the end of *Shangri-L.A.*, Weetzie played a scene in which the starlet shoots up so she can get back to the dream city. After she dies of an overdose in her apartment, she is transported back. In the final scene, she is reunited with the Charlie Chaplin bass player, and the band performs "Love Warrior" in a *Casablanca* nightclub filled with fans, fronds, and fireflies. Then darkness.

"This film is dedicated to the memory of Charlie Bat," it said on the screen.

Love Is a Dangerous Angel

One day, Duck came home crying. Weetzie and My Secret Agent Lover Man and even Dirk had never seen Duck cry before, except when Charlie Bat died. They all sat very still and looked at him. Then Dirk got up from the couch and tried to hug him, but Duck pulled away, ran to the blue bedroom, and shut the door.

"Ducky. Duckling. Rubber Duck," Weetzie called.

Dirk got very quiet and kept knocking on the door.

Cherokee and Witch Baby began to cry and My Secret Agent Lover Man took them in his arms.

Duck would not come out. They said they were going to Mr. Pizza and then rent *Casablanca* on VHS, but he would not come out. They said they were going surfing in the morning, but he would not come out. Finally, after midnight, Dirk tried the door and found it was unlocked. He got into bed next to Duck and looked at the sweatshirt with the picture of Howdy Doody (Duck wore it backward because, otherwise, he said, it kept him awake), and at the blonde hair and the boxer shorts with ducks on them that he had bought for Duck for Valentine's Day, but he didn't touch Duck. It was as if they were far away from each other and he didn't know why. Dirk watched Howdy Doody rise and fall with each sleep breath until Dirk fell asleep, too.

In the morning, Duck wasn't there. Dirk jumped out of bed, his pounding heart making him dizzy. He ran outside in his boxers and saw that Duck's bug was not there. He ran back inside and saw a note on the table:

*Dear Weetzie, My Secret Agent Lover Man, Cherokee,
Witch Baby and my dearest, most darling Dirk,*

    *I found out yesterday that my friend Bam-Bam is sick.
He is really sick. The world is too scary right now. Even
though we're okay, how can anyone love anyone when you
could kill them just by loving them? I love you all too much.
I'm going away for a while. I will never forget you. And
Dirk, I will always love you more than anyone.*

                                  Duck

Dirk grabbed his clothes and keys and ran outside and jumped in Jerry. He drove all over the city that day and Weetzie and My Secret Agent Lover Man called all their friends and the restaurants, bars, and stores where Duck hung out. Valentine and Ping made flyers and had them posted all over the city. But there was no trace of Duck.

Dirk came home the next morning unshaven and with

dark circles around his eyes. He had been driving around all night.

"I went to the picnic tables on Zuma Beach where we used to sleep, and I went to Rage and Revolver and Guitar Center and El Coyote and Val Surf, and I called everyone. I went to the hospital where Bam-Bam is. No one knew anything. No one's seen him," Dirk said in a monotone. He collapsed on the couch.

Weetzie made tea and rubbed his back, and My Secret Agent Lover Man told him Duck would come back soon, that Duck was just facing this for the first time and it would be okay. But Dirk hardly felt Weetzie's hands on his back or heard My Secret Agent Lover Man's words. His muscles felt like water, his eyes were blurry; he felt as if someone had cut him and he was losing blood. He thought of his lover and his best friend and his date—his Major #1 Date-Mate Duck Partner.

You are my blood, he thought.

"I'm going to search for him," Dirk said the next day. "Jerry and I are going to find him."

"But how will you know where to go?" Weetzie asked. "Maybe we should hire someone to help us." But she knew that Dirk had to go. She kissed him and packed bags and picnic baskets and thermoses and Spiderman lunch pails full of bagels, string cheese, chocolate-chip cookies, milk, apples, and carrot sticks. My Secret Agent Lover Man slipped some cash and a Dionne Warwick tape into Dirk's pockets. They all hugged and kissed, and Cherokee and

Witch Baby cried.

"I'll let you know," Dirk said, before driving away in Jerry.

You are my blood, Dirk thought over and over to himself as he drove north on Highway 5 in the startling mirage of heat. Everything was the same for miles—dry and yellow—the earth, the sky. He passed a herd of cattle waiting to be slaughtered. The smell made his stomach grip like a fist. He stopped at McDonald's but kept thinking of the cows and ordered a Filet o' Fish and a milkshake. The tourists stared at his black-dyed hair, his torn Levi's, round sunglasses. Some of the sunburned, blinking faces reminded him of raw meat.

Dirk got back into Jerry and drove some more. He felt as if the road were pulling him along and he followed it— he felt like blood in the road vein. He thought of Duck— seeing the blue eyes full of summer, the tan, freckled shoulders, the surfer legs gilded with blonde hair.

Dirk arrived in San Francisco at night. The lights shone and he smelled the cold, bread baking, gasoline. He drove around the Haight where people all wore leather and ate burritos. In a bar where everything looked blue, he felt like a fish in an aquarium as he watched Billy Idol videos next to a man in a muscle T-shirt. On Polk Street there were fewer men than he remembered from the last time he had been there with Duck—fewer men dressed in chains, less swaggering in the strides of the men. It was quieter on Polk

Street. The ice-cream store was crowded.

Where are you, my Duck? Dirk thought, looking at the faces of the men eating ice cream as if it would ease some pain.

Dirk drove to Chinatown and walked around the streets that were already emptying as the restaurants closed and the shop owners brought in the porcelain vases, the parasols, kites, screens, jade, and rose quartz and locked their doors. Flyers for Chinese films flapped in the wind. There were carcasses of birds strung up in the windows. Dirk zipped up his leather jacket and walked with his head down but his eyes kept sight of everything around him, of every person he passed. He moved like a piece of blown paper through the windy, hilly Chinatown streets.

It was very late when Dirk went to Hamburger Mary's. Everyone looked drunk under the old Coca-Cola signs in the rooms that smelled of meat, onions, and sawdust. Dirk remembered when he had come here with Duck and how they had held hands the whole time they ate their hamburgers, not even worrying, for once, about what people would think. He put money in the jukebox and pressed "Where Did Our Love Go" by the Supremes, but he left Hamburger Mary's before it played.

Dirk crossed the street to the bar called the Stud. The place was packed and steaming; Dirk could hardly breathe. He went and stood close to the bar while everyone pressed in around him—the leathered, studded, mustached men in boots, the little surf boys with LaCoste shirts, Levi's, and Vans, the long-haired European-styled model types in black. Dirk stood there looking around and then his heart began to beat very quickly and then he felt like crying.

Who was that beautiful blonde swaying drunkenly on the edge of the dance floor and smoking a cigarette. Who was that beautiful blonde boy?

Love is a dangerous angel, Dirk thought. Especially nowadays.

It was Duck.

Out of all the bars and all the nights and all the people and all the moments, Dirk had found Duck.

Dirk went up to him and looked into his eyes. Duck dropped his cigarette and his eyes filled with tears. Then he fell against Dirk's shoulders while the lights fanned across the dark dance floor like a neon peacock spreading its tail.

"How did you find me?" Duck asked as Dirk led him out of the Stud.

"I don't know," Dirk said. "But you are in my blood. I can't help it. We can't be anywhere except together."

"I love you so much," Duck said. "I've been so afraid. I've been to all the bars just watching and getting wasted. And I know people are dying everywhere. How can anyone love anyone?"

Dirk put Duck into Jerry and he drove them to the hotel where they had stayed another time they had visited San Francisco. Dirk ran the bath and undressed Duck and helped him into the hot water. He soaped Duck's back and made Duck's hair into Mohawks and Kewpie-doll curlicues with shampoo before he rinsed him off. Then they got under the pressed hotel sheets and held on to each other.

"It's so sick," Duck said. "I nicked myself shaving that last night at home, and I saw my own blood and I thought, How could I live in a world where this exists—where love can become death? Even if the doctor says we're okay, how could we go on watching people die?"

Duck buried his face against Dirk's shoulder and the streetlamp light shone in through the window, lighting up Duck's hair.

Dirk stroked Duck's head. "I don't know. But we've got to be together," he said.

In the morning, Dirk drove Duck home down Highway 5. They sang along with Dionne Warwick. They stopped for all-you-can-eat pea soup at Anderson's Pea Soup. Dirk made plans for when they got home—they would start working on My Secret Agent Lover Man's new movie (called *Baby Jah-Love* and starring Cherokee and Raphael as a brother and sister whose parents have been separated because of racial prejudice but who are reunited by their children in the end); they would take a trip to Mexico and drink tequila and lie in the sun and play with Cherokee and Witch Baby in the water. They would start having jam sessions and write new songs, start training to run the next L.A. Marathon; they'd become more politically active, Dirk said.

Dirk talked and talked, the way Duck usually talked, and Duck was quiet, but he laughed sometimes, sang along to Dionne, and took off his shirt and opened Jerry's windows to get a tan.

When they got home, it was a purple, smoggy L.A. twilight. Weetzie and My Secret Agent Lover Man and Cherokee and Witch Baby and Slinkster Dog and Go-Go Girl and the puppies Pee Wee, Wee Wee, Teenie Wee, Tiki Tee, and Tee Pee were waiting on the front porch drinking lemonade and listening to Iggy Pop's "Lust for Life" as the sky darkened and the barbecue summer smells filled the air.

Weetzie ran up to them first and flung her arms around Duck and then Dirk. Then all six of them held on to one another in a football huddle and the dogs slunk around their feet.

That night, they all ate linguini and clam sauce that My Secret Agent Lover Man made, and they drank wine and lit the candles.

Weetzie looked around at everyone—she saw Dirk, tired, unshaven, his hair a mess; he hardly ever looked like this. But his eyes shone wet with love. Duck looked older, there were lines in his face she hadn't remembered seeing before, but he leaned against Dirk like a little boy. Weetzie looked at My Secret Agent Lover Man finishing his linguini, sucking it up with his pouty lips. Cherokee was pulling on his sleeve and he leaned over and kissed her and then put her onto his lap to help him finish the last bite of pasta. Witch Baby sat alone, mysterious and beautiful.

Weetzie's heart felt so full with love, so full, as if it

could hardly fit in her chest. She knew they were all afraid. But love and disease are both like electricity, Weetzie thought. They are always there—you can't see or smell or hear, touch, or taste them, but you know they are there like a current in the air. We can choose, Weetzie thought, we can choose to plug into the love current instead. And she looked around the table at Dirk and Duck and My Secret Agent Lover Man and Cherokee and Witch Baby—all of them lit up and golden like a wreath of lights.

I don't know about happily ever after . . . but I know about happily, Weetzie Bat thought.

BOOK TWO

Witch Baby

Upon Time

Once upon a time. What is that supposed to mean?

In the room full of musical instruments, watercolor paints, candles, sparkles, beads, books, basketballs, roses, incense, surfboards, china pixie heads, lanky toy lizards and a rubber chicken, Witch Baby was curling her toes, tapping her drumsticks and pulling on the snarl balls in her hair. Above her hung the clock, luminous, like a moon.

Witch Baby had taken photographs of everyone in her almost-family—Weetzie Bat and My Secret Agent Lover Man, Cherokee Bat, Dirk McDonald and Duck Drake, Valentine, Ping Chong and Raphael Chong Jah-Love, Brandy-Lynn Bat and Coyote Dream Song. Then she had scrambled up the fireplace and pasted the pictures on the numbers of the clock. Because she had taken all the pictures herself, there was no witch child with dark tangled hair and tilted purple eyes.

What time are we upon and where do I belong? Witch Baby wondered as she went into the garden.

The peach trees, rosebushes and purple-flowering

jacaranda were sparkling with strings of white lights. Witch Baby watched from behind the garden shed as her almost-family danced on the lawn, celebrating the completion of *Dangerous Angels*, a movie they had made about their lives. In *Angels*, Weetzie Bat met her best friend Dirk and wished on a genie lamp for "a Duck for Dirk and My Secret Agent Lover Man for me and a beautiful little house for us to live in happily ever after." The movie was about what happened when the wishes came true.

Witch Baby's almost-mother-and-father, Weetzie Bat and My Secret Agent Lover Man, were doing a cha-cha on the lawn. In a short pink evening gown, pink Harlequin sunglasses and a white feathered headdress, Weetzie looked like a strawberry sundae melting into My Secret Agent Lover Man's arms. Dirk McDonald was dancing with Duck Drake and pretending to balance his champagne glass on Duck's perfect blonde flat-top. Weetzie's mother, Brandy-Lynn Bat, was dancing with My Secret Agent Lover Man's best friend, Coyote. Valentine Jah-Love and his wife, Ping Chong, swayed together, while their Hershey's-powdered-chocolate-mix-colored son, Raphael Chong Jah-Love, danced with Weetzie's real daughter, Cherokee Bat. Even Slinkster Dog and Go-Go Girl were dancing, raised up circus style on their hind legs, wriggling their rears and surrounded by their puppies, Pee Wee, Wee Wee, Teenie Wee, Tiki Tee and Tee Pee, who were not really puppies anymore but had never gotten any bigger than when they were six months old.

Under the twinkling trees was a table covered with Guatemalan fabric, roses in juice jars, wax rose candles from Tijuana and plates of food—Weetzie's Vegetable Love-Rice, My Secret Agent Lover Man's guacamole, Dirk's homemade pizza, Duck's fig and berry salad and Surfer Surprise Protein Punch, Brandy-Lynn's pink macaroni, Coyote's cornmeal cakes, Ping's mushu plum crepes and Valentine's Jamaican plantain pie.

Witch Baby's stomach growled but she didn't leave her hiding place. Instead, she listened to the reggae, surf, soul and salsa, tugged at the snarl balls in her hair and snapped pictures of all the couples. She wanted to dance but there was no one to dance with. There was only Rubber Chicken lying around somewhere inside the cottage. He always seemed to end up being her only partner.

After a while, Weetzie and My Secret Agent Lover Man sat down near the shed. Witch Baby watched them. Sometimes she thought she looked a little like My Secret Agent Lover Man; but she knew he and Weetzie had found her on their doorstep one day. Witch Baby didn't look like Weetzie Bat at all.

"What's wrong, my slinkster-love-man?" Witch Baby heard Weetzie ask as she handed My Secret Agent Lover Man a paper plate sagging with food. "Aren't you happy that we finished *Angels*?"

He lit a cigarette and stared past the party into the darkness. Shadows of roses moved across his angular face.

"The movie wasn't enough," he said. "We have more

75

money now than we know what to do with. Sometimes this city feels like an expensive tomb. I want to do something that matters."

"But you speak with your movies," Weetzie said. "You are an important influence on people. You open eyes."

"It hasn't been enough. I need to think of something strong. When I was a kid I had a lamp shaped like a globe. I had newspaper articles all over my walls, too, like Witch Baby has—disasters and things. I always wished I could make the world as peaceful and bright as my lamp."

"Give yourself time," said Weetzie, and she took off his slouchy fedora, pushed back his dark hair and kissed his temples.

Witch Baby wished that she could go and sit on Weetzie's lap and whisper an idea for a movie into My Secret Agent Lover Man's ear. An idea to make him breathe deeply and sleep peacefully so the dark circles would fade from beneath his eyes. She wanted Weetzie and My Secret Agent Lover Man to stroke her hair and take her picture as if they were her real parents. But she did not go to them.

She turned to see Weetzie's mother, Brandy-Lynn, waltzing alone.

Weetzie had told Witch Baby that Brandy-Lynn had once been a beautiful starlet, and in the soft shadows of night roses, Witch Baby could see it now. Starlet. Starlit, like Weetzie and Cherokee, Witch Baby thought. Brandy-Lynn collapsed in a lawn chair to drink her martini and finger the silver heart locket she always wore around her neck. Inside the locket was a photograph of Weetzie's father, Charlie Bat, who had died years before. The white lights shone on the heart, the martini and the tears that slid down Brandy-Lynn's cheeks. Witch Baby wanted to pat the tears with her fingertip and taste the salt. Even after all this time, Brandy-Lynn cried often about Charlie Bat, but Witch Baby never cried about anything. Sometimes tears gathered, thick and seething salt in her chest, but she kept them there.

As Witch Baby imagined the way Brandy-Lynn's tears would feel on her own face, she saw Cherokee Bat dancing over to Brandy-Lynn and holding a piece of plantain pie.

"Eat some pie and come dance with me and Raphael, Grandma Brandy," Cherokee said. "You can show us how you danced when you were a movie star."

Brandy-Lynn wiped away her mascara-tinted tears and shakily held out her arms. Then she and Cherokee waltzed away across the lawn.

No one noticed Witch Baby as she went back inside the cottage, into the room she and Cherokee shared.

Cherokee's side of the room was filled with feathers, crystals, butterfly wings, rocks, shells and dried flowers. There was a small tepee that Coyote had helped Cherokee make. The walls on Witch Baby's side of the room were covered with newspaper clippings—nuclear accidents, violence, poverty and disease. Every night, before she went to bed, Witch Baby cut out three articles or pictures with a pair of toenail scissors and taped them to the wall. They made Cherokee cry.

"Why do you want to have those up there?" Weetzie asked. "You'll both have nightmares."

If Witch Baby didn't cut out three articles, she knew she would lie awake, watching the darkness break up into grainy dots around her head like an enlarged newspaper photo.

Tonight, when she came to the third article, Witch Baby held her breath. Some Indians in South America had found a glowing blue ball. They stroked it, peeled off layers to decorate their walls and doorways, faces and bodies. Then one day they began to die. All of them. The blue globe was the radioactive part of an old x-ray machine.

Witch Baby burrowed under her blankets as Brandy-Lynn, Weetzie and Cherokee entered the room with plates of food. In their feathers, flowers and fringe, with their starlit hair, they looked more like three sisters than grandmother, mother and daughter.

"There you are!" Weetzie said. "Have some Love-Rice and come dance with us, my baby witch."

Witch Baby peeked out at the three blondes and snarled at them.

"Are you looking for those articles again? Why do you need those awful things?" Brandy-Lynn asked.

"What time are we upon and where do I belong?" Witch Baby mumbled.

"You belong here. In this city. In this house. With all of us," said Weetzie.

Witch Baby scowled at the clippings on her wall. The pictures stared back—missing children smiling, not knowing what was going to happen to them later; serial killers looking blind also, in another way.

"Why is this place called Los Angeles?" Witch Baby asked. "There aren't any angels."

"Maybe there are. Sometimes I see angels in the people I love," said Weetzie.

"What do angels look like?"

"They have wings and carry lilies," Cherokee said. "And they have blonde hair," she added, tossing her braids.

"Clutch pig!" said Witch Baby under her breath. She tugged at her own dark tangles.

"No, Cherokee," said Weetzie. "That's just in some old paintings. Angels can look like anyone. They can look like mysterious, beautiful, purple-eyed girls. Now eat your rice, Witch Baby, and come outside with us."

But Witch Baby curled up like a snail.

"Please, Witch. Come out and dance."

Witch Baby snailed up tighter.

"All right, then, sleep well, honey-honey. Dream of your own angels," said Weetzie, kissing the top of her almost-daughter's head. "But remember, this is where you belong."

She took Cherokee's hand, linked arms with Brandy-Lynn and left the room.

❧

Witch Baby, who is not one of them, dreams of her own angel again. He is huddling on the curb of a dark, rainy street. Behind him is a building filled with golden lights, people and laughter, but he never goes inside. He stays out in the rain, the hollows of his eyes and cheeks full of shadows. When he sees Witch Baby, he opens his hands and holds them out to her. She never touches him in the dream, but she knows just how he would feel.

Witch Baby got out of bed. She put the article about the radioactive ball into her pocket. She put her black cowboy-boot roller skates on her feet.

As she skated away from the cottage, Witch Baby thought of the blue people, dying and beautiful.

Devil City, she said to herself. Los Diablos.

Globe Lamp

Witch Baby passed the Charlie Chaplin Theater that had been shut down a long time ago and was covered with graffiti now. The theater still had pictures of Charlie Chaplin on the walls, and they reminded Witch Baby of My Secret Agent Lover Man.

Someday me and My Secret will reopen this theater, she thought. And we'll make our own movies together, movies that change things.

Witch Baby passed Canter's, the all-night coffee shop, where a man with dirt-blackened feet and a cloak of rags sat on the sidewalk sniffing pancakes in the air. She only had fifty cents in her pocket, but she placed it carefully in his palm, then skated on past the rows of markets that sold fruits and vegetables, almonds and raisins, olive oil and honey. The markets were all closed for the night. So was the shop where Weetzie always bought vanilla and Vienna coffee beans. But next to the coffee bean shop was a window filled with strange things. There were cupids, monster heads, mermaids, Egyptian cats, jaguars with clocks in their bellies, animal skulls; and lighting up all the rest was a lamp shaped like a globe of the world.

Witch Baby stood in front of the dust-streaked window, wondering why she had never noticed this place before. She stared at the globe, thinking of My Secret Agent Lover Man and the lamp he had told Weetzie about.

Then she opened the door and skated into a room cluttered with merry-go-round horses, broken china, bolts of glittery fabric, Persian carpets and many lamps. The lamps weren't lit and the room was so dark that Witch Baby could hardly see. But she did notice a gold turban rising just above a low counter at the back of the store. A humming voice came from beneath the turban.

"Greetings. What have you come for?" The voice was like an insect buzzing toward Witch Baby and she saw a pair of slanted firefly eyes watching her. A tiny man stepped from behind the counter. He smelled of almonds and smoke.

"I want the globe lamp," Witch Baby said.

The man shuffled closer. "My, my, I haven't seen one of my own kind in ages. You're certainly small enough and you have the eyes. But I wouldn't have recognized you in those rolling boots. Is that what we're wearing these days?" He looked down at his embroidered, pointed-toed slippers. "What have you come for?"

"The globe lamp," Witch Baby repeated.

"I wouldn't recommend the globe lamp. It's not a traditional enough abode. On the other hand, you may not want to be bothered with all those people rubbing the lid and whispering their wishes all the time. It gets tiresome, doesn't it, this lamp business? They don't understand that the really good wishes like world peace are just out of our league and those love wishes are such a risk. So the globe's a fine disguise, I suppose. No one bothering you for happily ever after. I understand, believe me; that's why I quit. The lamp business I'm in now is much less complicated."

"What time are we upon and where do I belong?" Witch Baby asked.

"This is the time we're upon." He blinked three times, shuffled over to the window, drew back a black curtain and reached to touch the globe lamp. Suddenly it changed. Where there had been a painted sea, Witch Baby saw real water rippling. Where there had been painted continents, there were now forests, deserts and tiny, flickering cities. Witch Baby thought she heard a whisper of tears and moans, of gunshots and music.

The man unplugged the lamp, and it became dark and still. He carried it over to Witch Baby and placed it in her arms. Because she was so small, the lamp hid everything except for two hands with bitten fingernails and two skinny legs in black cowboy-boot roller skates.

"Where do I belong?"

"At home," said the man. "At home in the globe."

When Witch Baby peeked around the globe lamp to thank him, she found herself standing on the sidewalk in front of a deserted building. There was only dust and shadow in the window, but somehow Witch Baby thought she saw the image of a tiny man reflected there. Skating home, she remembered the lights and whispers of the world.

It was late when Witch Baby returned to the cottage and tiptoed into the pink room that Weetzie and My Secret Agent Lover Man shared. They lay in their bed asleep, surrounded by bass guitars, tiki heads, balloons, two surfboards, a unicycle, a home-movie camera and Rubber Chicken. My Secret Agent Lover Man was tossing and turning and grinding his teeth. Weetzie lay beside him with her blonde mop of hair and aqua feather nightie. She was trying to stroke the lines out of his face.

Witch Baby watched them for a while. Then she plugged in the globe lamp, took the article about the glowing blue ball out of her pocket, put it on My Secret Agent Lover Man's chest and stepped back into the darkness.

Suddenly My Secret Agent Lover Man sat straight up in bed. He shone with sweat, blue in the globe-lamp light.

"What's wrong, honey-honey?" Weetzie asked, sitting up beside him and taking him in her arms.

"I dreamed about them again."

"The bodies . . . ?"

"Exploding. The men with masks."

"You'll feel better when you start your next movie," Weetzie said, rubbing his neck and shoulders and running her fingers through his hair. "You and our Witch Baby are just the same."

My Secret Agent Lover Man turned and saw the globe lamp shining in a corner of the room.

"Weetz!" he said. "Where did you find it? What a slinkster-cool gift! It's just like one I had when I was a kid."

"What are you talking about?" Weetzie asked. Then she turned, too, and saw the lamp. "Lanky Lizards!" she said. "I don't know where it came from!"

Witch Baby wanted to jump onto the bed, throw back her arms and say, "I know!" But instead she just watched. My Secret Agent Lover Man, who didn't look at all like Witch Baby now, stared as if he were hypnotized. Then he noticed the article, which had slipped into his lap.

"Two glowing blue globes," he said, gazing from the piece of paper to the lamp. "I'm going to make a new movie, Weetz. One that really says something. Thank you for your inspiration, my magic slink!"

Before she could speak he took her in his arms and pressed his lips to hers.

Witch Baby turned away. Although her walls were papered with other pieces of pain, although her eyes were globes, he had not recognized her gift. She did not belong here.

Drum Love

In the garden shed, behind a cobweb curtain, Witch Baby was playing her drums.

It was the drumming of flashing dinosaur rock gods and goddesses who sweat starlight, the drumming of tall, muscly witch doctors who can make animals dance, wounds heal, rain fall and flowers open. But it began in Witch Baby's head and heart and came out through her small body and hands. Her only audience was a row of pictures she had taken of Raphael Chong Jah-Love.

Witch Baby had been in love with Raphael for as long as she could remember. His parents, Ping and Valentine, had known Weetzie even before she had met My Secret Agent Lover Man, and Raphael had played with Witch Baby and Cherokee since they were babies. Not only did Raphael look like powdered chocolate, but he smelled like it, too, and his eyes reminded Witch Baby of Hershey's Kisses. His mother, Ping, dressed him in bright red, green and yellow and twisted his hair into dreadlocks. ("Cables to heaven," said his father, Valentine, who had dreads too.)

Raphael, the Chinese-Rasta parrot boy, loved to paint, and he covered the walls of his room with waterfalls, stars, rainbows, suns, moons, birds, flowers and fish. As soon as Witch Baby had learned to walk, she had chased after him, spying and dreaming that someday they would roll in the mud, dance with paint on their feet and play music together while Cherokee Bat took photographs of them.

But Raphael never paid much attention to Witch Baby. Until the day he came into the garden shed and stood staring at her with his slanted chocolate-Kiss eyes.

Witch Baby stopped drumming with her hands, but her heart began to pound. She didn't want Raphael to see the pictures of himself. "Go away!" she said.

He looked far into her pupils, then turned and left the shed. Witch Baby beat hard on the drums to keep her tears from coming.

Witch babies never cry, she told herself.

The next day Raphael came back to the shed. Witch Baby stopped drumming and snarled at him.

"How did you get so good?" he asked her.

"I taught myself."

"You taught yourself! How?"

"I just hear it in my head and feel it in my hands."

"But what got you started? What made you want to play?"

Witch Baby remembered the day My Secret Agent Lover Man had brought her the drum set. She had pretended she wasn't interested because she was afraid that Cherokee would try to use the drums too. Then she had hidden them in the garden shed, soundproofed the walls with foam and shag carpeting, put on her favorite records and taught herself to play. No one had ever heard her except for the flowerpots, the cobwebs, the pictures of Raphael and, now, Raphael himself.

"When I play drums I don't need to bite or kick or break, steal Duck's Fig Newtons or tear the hair off Cherokee's Kachina Barbies," Witch Baby whispered.

"Teach me," Raphael said.

Witch Baby gnawed on the end of the drumstick.

"Teach me to play drums."

She narrowed her eyes.

"There is a girl I know," Raphael said, looking at Witch Baby. "And she would be very happy if I learned."

Witch Baby couldn't remember how to breathe. She wasn't sure if you take air in through your nose and let it out through your mouth or the other way around. There was only one girl, she thought, who would be very happy if Raphael learned to play drums, so happy that her toes would uncurl and her heart would play music like a magic bongo drum.

Witch Baby looked down at the floor of the shed so her long eyelashes, that had a purple tint from the reflection of her eyes, fanned out across the top of her cheeks. She held the drumsticks out to Raphael.

From then on, Raphael came over all the time for his lessons. He wasn't a very good drummer, but he looked good, biting his lip, raising his eyebrows and moving his neck back and forth so his dreadlocks danced. For Witch Baby, the best part of the lessons was when she got to play for him. He recorded her on tape and never took his eyes off her. It was as if she were being seen by someone for the first time. She imagined that the music turned into stars and birds and fish, like the ones Raphael painted, and spun, floated, swam in the air around them.

One day Raphael asked Witch Baby if he could play a tape he had made of her drumming and follow along silently, gesturing as if he were really playing.

"That way I'll feel like I'm as good as you, and I'll be more brave when I play," he said.

Witch Baby put on the tape and Raphael drummed along silently in the air.

Then the door of the shed opened, and Cherokee came in, brushing cobwebs out of her way. She was wearing her white suede fringed minidress and her moccasins, and she had feathers and turquoise beads in her long pale hair. Standing in the dim shed, Cherokee glowed. Raphael looked up while he was drumming and his chocolate-Kiss eyes seemed to melt. Witch Baby glared at Cherokee through a snarl of hair and chewed her nails.

Cherokee Brat Bath Mat Bat, she thought. Clutch pig! Go away and leave us alone. You do not belong here.

But Cherokee was lost in the music and began to dance, stamping and whirling like a small blonde Indian. She left trails of light in the air, and Raphael watched as if he were trying to paint pictures of her in his mind.

When the song was over, Cherokee went to Raphael and kissed him on the cheek.

"You are a slink-chunk, slam-dunk drummer, Raphael. I didn't really care about you learning to play drums. I just wanted to see what you'd do for me—how hard you'd try to be my best friend. But you've turned into a love-drum, drum-love!"

"Cherokee," he said softly.

She took his hand and they left the shed.

Witch Baby's heart felt like a giant bee sting, like a bee had stung her inside where her heart was supposed to be. Every time she heard her own drumbeats echoing in her head, the sting swelled with poison. She threw herself against the drums, kicking and clawing until she was bruised and some of the drumskins were torn. Then she curled up on the floor of the shed, among the cobwebs that Cherokee had ruined, reminding herself that witch babies do not cry.

After that day Raphael Chong Jah-Love and Cherokee Bat became inseparable. They hiked up canyon trails, collected pebbles, looked for deer, built fires, had powwows, made papooses out of puppies and lay warming their bellies on rocks and chanting to the animals, trees, and earth, "You are all my relations," the way My Secret Agent Lover Man's friend Coyote had showed them. They painted on every surface they could find, including each other. They spent hours gazing at each other until their eyes were all pupil and Cherokee's looked as dark as Raphael's. No one could get their attention.

Weetzie, My Secret Agent Lover Man, and Valentine and Ping Chong Jah-Love watched them.

"They are just babies still," My Secret Agent Lover Man said. "How could they be so in love? They remind me of us."

"If I had met you when I was little, I would have acted the same way," Weetzie said.

"But it's funny," said Ping. "I always thought *Witch Baby* was secretly in love with Raphael."

While Raphael and Cherokee fell in love, they forgot all about drums. Witch Baby stopped playing drums too. She pulled apart Cherokee's Kachina Barbie dolls, scattering their limbs throughout the cottage and even sticking some parts in Brandy-Lynn's Jell-O mold. She stole Duck's Fig Newtons, made dresses out of Dirk's best shirts and bit Weetzie's fingers when Weetzie tried to serve her vegetables.

"Witch Baby! Stop that! Weetzie's fingers are not carrots!" My Secret Agent Lover Man exclaimed, kissing Weetzie's nibbled fingertips.

Witch Baby went around the cottage taking candid pictures of everyone looking their worst—My Secret Agent Lover Man with a hangover, Weetzie covered with paint and glue, Dirk and Duck arguing, Brandy-Lynn weeping into a martini, Cherokee and Raphael gobbling up the vegetarian lasagna Weetzie was saving for dinner.

Witch Baby was wild, snarled, tangled and angry. Everyone got more and more frustrated with her. When they tried to grab her, even for a hug, she would wriggle away, her body quick-slippery as a fish. She never cried, but she always wanted to cry. Finally, while she was watching Cherokee and Raphael running around the cottage in circles, whooping and flapping their feather-decorated arms, Witch Baby remembered something Cherokee had done to her when they were very young. Late at night she got out of her bed, took the toenail scissors she had hidden under her pillow, crept over to Cherokee's tepee and snipped at Cherokee's hair. She did not cut straight across, but chopped unevenly, and the ragged strands of hair fell like moonlight.

The next morning Witch Baby hid in the shed and waited. Then she heard a scream coming from the cottage. She felt as if someone had crammed a bean-cheese-hot-dog-pastrami burrito down her throat.

Witch Baby hid in the shed all day. When everyone was asleep she crept back into the cottage, went into the violet-and-aqua-tiled bathroom and stared at herself in the mirror. She saw a messy nest of hair, a pale, skinny body, knobby, skinned knees and feet with curling toes.

No wonder Raphael doesn't love me, Witch Baby thought. I am a baby witch.

She took the toenail scissors and began to chop at her own hair. Then she plugged in My Secret Agent Lover Man's razor, turned it on and listened to it buzz at her like a hungry metal animal.

When her scalp was completely bald, Witch Baby, with her deep-set, luminous, jacaranda-blossom-colored eyes, looked as if she had drifted down from some other planet.

But Witch Baby did not see her eerie, fairy, genie, moon-witch beauty, the beauty of twilight and rainstorms. "You'll never belong to anyone," she said to the bald girl in the mirror.

Tree Spirit

The chain saws were buzzing like giant razors. Witch Baby pressed her palms over her ears.

"What is going on?" Coyote cried, padding into the cottage.

Witch Baby had hardly ever heard Coyote raise his voice before. She curled up under the clock, and he knelt beside her so that his long braid brushed her cheek. She saw the full veins in his callused hands, the turquoise-studded band, blood-blue, at his wrist.

"Where is everyone, my little bald one?" he asked gently.

"They went to the street fair."

"And they left you here with the dying trees?"

"I didn't want to go with them."

Coyote put his hand on Witch Baby's head. It fit perfectly like a cap. His touch quieted the saws for a moment and stilled the blood beating at Witch Baby's naked temples. "Why not?" he asked.

"I get lonely with them."

94

"With all that big family you have?"

"More than when I'm alone."

Coyote nodded. "I would rather be alone most of the time. It's quieter. Someday I will live in the desert again with the Joshua trees." He took a handkerchief out of his leather backpack and unfolded it. Inside were five seeds. "Joshua tree seeds," he said. "In the blue desert moonlight, if you put your arms around Joshua trees and are very quiet, you can hear them speaking to you. Sometimes, if you turn around fast enough, you can catch them dancing behind your back."

Coyote squinted out the window at the falling branches, the whirlwind of leaves, blossoms and dust.

"Now I'm going to do something about those tree murderers." He went to the phone book, found the number of the school across the street, and called.

"I need to speak to the principal. It's about the trees."

He waited, drumming his fingers. Witch Baby crept up beside him, peering over the tabletop at the sunset desert of his face.

"Is this the principal? I'd like to ask you why you are cutting those trees down. I would think that a school would be especially concerned. Do you know how long it takes trees to grow? Especially in this foul air?"

The saws kept buzzing brutally while he spoke. Witch Baby thought about the jacaranda trees across the street. Coyote had told her that all trees have spirits, and she imagined women with long, light-boned limbs and falls of whispery green hair, dark Coyote men with skin like clay as it smooths on the potter's wheel. Some might even be hairless girls like Witch Baby—the purple-eyed spirits of jacaranda trees.

Finally, Coyote put the phone down. He and Witch Baby sat together at the window, wincing as all the trees in front of the school became a woodpile scattered with purple blossoms.

Coyote is like My Secret and me, Witch Baby thought, feeling the warmth of his presence beside her. But he recognizes that I am like him and My Secret doesn't see.

Witch Baby's almost-family came home and saw them still sitting there. Weetzie invited Coyote to stay for dinner but he solemnly shook his head.

"I couldn't eat anything after what we saw today," he said.

That night, when everyone else was asleep, Witch Baby unfolded the handkerchief she had stolen from Coyote's backpack and looked at the five Joshua tree seeds. They seemed to glow, and she thought she heard them whispering as she crept out the window and into the moonlight. In the soil from which the jacaranda trees had been torn, Witch Baby knelt and planted Coyote's five seeds, imagining how one day she and Coyote would fling their arms around five Joshua trees. If she was very quiet she might be able to hear the trees telling her the secrets of the desert.

"Where are they?"

Coyote stood towering above Witch Baby's bed. She blinked up at him, her dreams of singing trees passing away like clouds across the moon, until she saw his face clearly. His hair was unbraided and fell loose around his shoulders.

"Where are my Joshua tree seeds, Witch Baby?"

Witch Baby sat up in bed. It was early morning and still quiet. There was no buzzing today; all the trees were already down.

"I planted them for you," she said.

Coyote looked as if the sound of chain saws were still filling his head. "What? You planted them? Where did you plant them? Those were special seeds. My Secret Agent Lover Man brought them to me from the desert. I told him I had to take them back the next time I went, because Joshua trees grow only on sacred desert ground. They'll never grow where you planted them."

"But I planted them in front of the school because of yesterday. They'll grow there and we'll always be able to look at them and listen to what they tell us."

"They'll never grow," Coyote said. "They are lost."

Witch Baby spent the next three nights clutching a flashlight and digging in the earth in front of the school for the Joshua tree seeds, but there was no sign of them. Her fingers ached, the nails full of soil, the knuckles scratched by rocks and twigs. She was kneeling in dirt, covered in dirt, wishing for the tree spirits to take her away with them to a place where Joshua trees sang and danced in the blue moonlight.

Stowawitch

It was Dirk who found Witch Baby digging in the dirt. He was taking a late-night run on his glowing silver Nikes when he noticed the spot of light flitting over the ground in front of the school. Then he saw the outline of a tree spirit crouched in the darkness. He ran over and called to Witch Baby.

"What are you doing out here, Miss Witch?"

Witch Baby flicked off the flashlight and didn't answer, but when Dirk came over, she let him lift her in his beautiful, sweaty arms and carry her into the house. She leaned against him, limp with exhaustion.

"Never go off at night by yourself anymore," Dirk said as he tucked her into bed. "If you want, you can wake me and we can go on a run. I know what it's like to feel scared and awake in the night. Sometimes I could go dig in the earth too, when I feel that way."

Before Witch Baby fell asleep that night she looked at the picture she had taken of Dirk and Duck at the party. Dirk, who looked even taller than he was because of his

Mohawk and thick-soled creepers, was pretending to balance a champagne glass on Duck's flat-top and Duck's blue eyes were rolled upward, watching the glass. Almost anyone could see by the picture that Dirk and Duck were in love.

Dirk and Duck are different from most people too, Witch Baby thought. Sometimes they must feel like they don't belong just because they love each other.

When Dirk and Duck announced that they were going to Santa Cruz to visit Duck's family, Witch Baby asked if she could go with them.

"I'm sorry, Witch Baby," Dirk said, rubbing his hand over the fuzz that had grown back on her scalp. "Duck and I need to spend some time alone together. Someday, when you are in love, you will understand."

"Besides, I haven't seen my family in years," Duck said. "It might be kind of an intense scene. We'll bring you back some mini-Birkenstock sandals from Santa Cruz, though."

But Witch Baby didn't want Birkenstocks. And she already understood about spending time with the person you love. She wanted to go to Santa Cruz with Dirk and Duck, especially since she could never go anywhere with Raphael.

I'll be a stowaway, Witch Baby thought.

Dirk and Duck put their matching surfboards, their black-and-yellow wet suits, their flannel shirts, long underwear, Guatemalan shorts, hooded mole-man sweatshirts, Levi's and Vans and Weetzie's avocado sandwiches into Dirk's red 1955 Pontiac, Jerry, and kissed everyone good-bye—everyone except for Witch Baby, who had disappeared.

"I hope she's okay," Weetzie said.

"She's just hiding," said My Secret Agent Lover Man.

"Give the witch child these." Duck handed Weetzie a fresh box of Fig Newtons. He did not know that Witch Baby was hidden in Jerry's trunk, eating the rest of the Newtons he had packed away there.

On the way to Santa Cruz Dirk and Duck stopped along the coast to surf. They stopped so many times to surf and eat (they finished the avocado sandwiches in the first fifteen minutes and bought sunflower seeds, licorice, peaches and Foster's Freeze soft ice cream along the way) that they didn't get to Santa Cruz until late that night. Duck was driving when they arrived, and he pulled Jerry up in front of the Drake house where Duck's mother, Darlene, lived with her boyfriend, Chuck, and Duck's eight brothers and sisters. It was an old house, painted white, with a tangled garden and a bay window full of lace and crystals. In the driveway was a Volvo station wagon with a "Visualize World Peace" bumper sticker.

Dirk and Duck sat there in the dark car, and neither of them said anything for a long time. Witch Baby peeked out from the trunk and imagined Duck playing in the garden as a little Duck, freckled and tan. She imagined a young Duck running out the front door in a yellow wet suit with a too-big surfboard under one arm and flippers on his feet.

"I wish I could tell my mom about us," Duck said to

Dirk, "but she'll never understand. I think we should wait till morning to go in. I don't want to wake them."

"Whatever you need to do," Dirk said. "We can go to a motel or sleep in Jerry."

"I have a better idea," said Duck.

That night they slept on a picnic table at the beach, wrapped in sweaters and blankets to keep them warm. Duck looked at the full moon and said to Dirk, "The moon reminds me of my mom. So does the sound of the ocean. She used to say, 'Duck, how do you see the moon? Duck, how do you hear the ocean?' I can't remember how I used to answer."

When Dirk and Duck were asleep, Witch Baby climbed out of the trunk, stretched and peed.

I wish I could play my drums so they sounded the way I hear the ocean, she thought, closing her eyes and trying to fill herself with the concert of the night.

Then she looked up at the moon.

How do I see the moon? I wish I had a real mother to ask me.

The next morning, while Witch Baby hid in Jerry's trunk, Dirk and Duck hugged each other, surfed, took showers at the beach, put on clean clothes, slicked back their hair, hugged each other and drove to the Drake house.

Some children with upturned noses and blonde hair like Duck's and Birkenstocks on their feet were playing with three white dogs in the garden. When Dirk and Duck came up the path, one of the children screamed, "Duck!" All of them ran and jumped on him, covering him with kisses. Then three older children came out of the house and jumped on Duck too.

"Dirk, this is Peace, Granola, Crystal, Chi, Aura, Tahini and the twins, Yin and Yang," Duck said. "Everybody, this is my friend, Dirk McDonald."

A petite blonde woman wearing Birkenstocks and a sundress came out of the house. "Duck!" she cried. "Duck!" She ran to him and they embraced.

Witch Baby watched from the trunk.

"We have missed you so much," Darlene Drake said. "Well, come in, come inside. Have some pancakes. Chuck'll be home soon."

Duck looked at Dirk. Then he said, "Mom, this is my friend, Dirk McDonald."

"I'm very happy to meet you, Mrs. Drake," Dirk said, putting out his hand.

"Hi, Dirk," said Darlene, but she hardly glanced at him. She was staring at her oldest son. "You look more like your dad than ever," she said, and her eyes filled with tears. "I wish he could see you!"

Dirk, Duck, Darlene and the little Drakes went into the house. Witch Baby climbed out of Jerry's trunk and sat in the flower box, watching through the window. She saw Darlene serve Duck and Dirk whole-wheat pancakes full of bananas and pecans and topped with plain yogurt and maple syrup. A little later the kitchen door opened and

103

a big man with a red face came in.

"Chuck, honey, look who's here!" Darlene said, scurrying to him.

"Well, look who decided to wander back in!" Chuck said in a deep voice. He started to laugh. "Hey, Duck-dude! We thought you drowned or something, man!"

"Chuck!" said Darlene.

Duck looked at his pancakes.

"I'm just glad he's here now," Darlene said. "And this is Duck's friend . . ."

"Dirk," Dirk said.

"Do you surf, Dirk?" Chuck asked.

"Yes."

"Well, me, you and Duck can catch some Santa Cruz waves. And I'll show you where the No-Cal babes hang," Chuck said.

"Chuck!" said Darlene.

"Darlene hates that," Chuck said, pinching her.

"Stop it, Chuck," Darlene said.

Witch Baby took a photograph of Duck pushing his pancakes around in a pool of syrup while Dirk glanced from him to Chuck and back. Then she climbed in through the window, hopping onto a plate of pancakes on the kitchen table.

"Oh my!" Darlene gasped. "Who is this?"

"Witch Baby!" Dirk and Duck shouted. "How did you get here?"

"I stowed away."

"I better call home and tell them," Duck said. "They're probably going crazy trying to find you." He got up to use the phone.

"Oh, you're a friend of Duck's," Darlene said as Duck left the room. "Well, stop dancing on the pancakes. You must be hungry; you're so skinny." She pointed at Witch Baby's black high-top sneakers covered with rubber bugs. "And we should get you some nice sandals."

Witch Baby thought of her toes curling out of a pair of Birkenstocks and looked down at the floor.

"They were worried about you, Witch Child," Duck said when he came back. "Weetzie bit off all her fingernails and My Secret Agent Lover Man drove around looking for you all night. Never run away like that again!"

Did they really miss me? she wondered. Did they even know who it was who was gone?

Duck turned to his brothers and sisters, who were staring at Witch Baby with their identical sets of blue eyes. "This is my family, Peace, Granola, Crystal, Chi, Aura, Tahini and Yin and Yang Drake," Duck said. "You guys, this is Witch Baby. She's my . . . she's our . . . well, she's our pancake dancer stowawitch!"

Witch Baby bared her teeth and Yin and Yang giggled. Then all Duck's brothers and sisters ran off to play in the garden.

Duck Mother

In Santa Cruz, Dirk, Duck and Darlene went for walks on the beach, hiked in the redwoods, marketed for organic vegetables and tofu and fed the chickens, the goat and the rabbit. Witch Baby followed along, taking pictures, whistling, growling, doing cartwheels, flips and imitations of Rubber Chicken and Charlie Chaplin and throwing pebbles at Dirk, Duck and Darlene when they ignored her. Sometimes, when a pebble skimmed her head, Darlene would turn around, look at the girl with the fuzzy scalp and sigh.

"Where did you find her?" she said to Dirk. "I've never seen a child like that." Then she would link arms with Duck and Dirk and keep walking.

"Mom, don't say that so loud!" Duck would say. "You'll hurt her feelings."

But Witch Baby had already heard. She poked her tongue out at Darlene and tossed another pebble.

Clutch mother duck!

That evening, Dirk, Duck and Darlene were walking

the dogs. Witch Baby was following them, watching and listening and sniffing the sea and pine in the air.

"Dirk, you are such a gentleman," Darlene said. "Your parents did a good job of raising you."

"I was raised by my Grandma Fifi," Dirk said. "My parents died when I was really little. I don't even remember them. They were both killed in a car accident."

Darlene's eyes filled with tears. "Like Duck's dad," she said.

That night she gave both Dirk and Duck fisherman sweaters that had belonged to Duck's dad, Eddie Drake. She didn't give Witch Baby anything.

Witch Baby kept watching and listening and nibbling her fingernails. She hid in the closet in Duck's old bedroom, with the fading surf pictures on the walls and the twin beds with surfing Snoopy sheets, and heard Duck and Dirk talking about Darlene's boyfriend, Chuck.

"He is such a greaseburger!" Duck told Dirk.

"Tell me about your dad, Duck," Dirk said. He had asked before, but Duck wouldn't talk about Eddie Drake.

"He was a killer Malibu surfer," Duck said. "I mean, a *fine* athlete. He had this real peaceful look on his face, a little spaced out, you know, but at peace. They were totally in love. She was Miss Zuma Beach. They fell in love when they were fourteen and, like, that was it. They had all of us one right after the other. Me while they were into the total surf scene when we lived in Malibu, Peace and Granola during their hippie-rebel phase, and then they got more into Eastern philosophy—you know, the twins, Yin and Yang. But then he died. He was surfing." Duck blinked the tears out of his eyes. "I still can't talk about it," he said.

"Duck." Dirk touched his cheek.

"I remember, later, my mom trying to run into the water and I'm trying to hold her back and her hair and my tears are so bright that I'm blind. I knew she would have walked right into the ocean after him and kept going. In a way I wanted to go too."

"Don't say that, puppy," Dirk whispered.

Witch Baby tried to swallow the sandy lump in her throat.

"But who the hell is Chuck?" Duck said. "I couldn't believe she'd be with a greaseburger like that, so I left. Plus, I knew they'd never understand about me liking guys."

Dirk kissed a tear that had slid onto Duck's tan and freckled shoulder and he drew Duck into his arms, into arms that had lifted Witch Baby from the dirt the night she had been searching for the Joshua tree seeds.

Just then, Witch Baby stepped out of the closet, holding out her finger to touch Duck's tears, wanting to share Dirk's arms.

"What are you doing here, Witch?" Duck said, startled.

"Go back to bed, Witch Baby," said Dirk, and she scampered away.

Later, curled beneath the cot that Darlene had set up for her in Yin and Yang's room, Witch Baby tried to think of ways to make Dirk and Duck see that she understood them, she understood them better than anyone, even better than Duck's own mother. Then they might let her stay with them and see their tears, she thought.

The next day Duck and Darlene were walking through the redwood forest. Witch Baby was following them.

"Duck!" Witch Baby called, "Do you know that all trees have spirits? Maybe your dad is a tree now! Maybe your dad is a tree or a wave!"

Duck glanced at Darlene, concerned, then turned to Witch Baby and put his finger on his lips. "Let's talk about that later, Witch. Go and play with the twins or something," he said, and kept walking.

"Duck, why did you go away?" Darlene asked, ignoring Witch Baby. "What have you been doing with your life?"

Duck told Darlene about the cottage and his friends. He told her about the slinkster-cool movies they made, the jamming music they played and the dream waves they surfed. The Love-Rice fiestas, Chinese moon dragon celebrations and Jamaican beach parties.

"You sound very happy," Darlene said. "Do you have a girlfriend to take care of you?"

"My friends and I take care of each other," Duck said. "We are like a family."

"That's good," said Darlene. "They sound wonderful. The little witch is a little strange, but I really like Dirk."

Just then Witch Baby jumped down on the path in front of Duck and Darlene. She was covered with leaves and grimacing like an angry tree imp.

"That's good," she said. "That you like Dirk. Because Duck likes Dirk a lot too. They love each other more than anyone else in the world. They even sleep in the same bed with their arms around each other!"

"Witch Child!" Duck tried to grab her arm, but he missed and she escaped up into the branches of a young redwood.

Darlene stood absolutely still. The light through the ferns made her blonde hair turn a soft green. She looked at Duck.

"What does she mean?" Darlene asked. And then she began to cry.

She cried and cried. Duck put his arms around her, but no matter what Duck said, Darlene kept crying. She cried the whole way along the redwood path to the car. She cried the whole way back to the house, never saying a word.

"Mom!" Duck said. "Please, Mom. Talk to me! Why are you crying so much? I'm still me. I'm still here."

Darlene kept crying.

Back at the house Chuck was barbecuing burgers. Dirk and the kids were playing softball.

"What is it, Darlene?" Chuck asked.

Darlene just kept crying. Dirk came and stood next to Duck.

"I'm gay," Duck said suddenly.

Chuck and all Duck's brothers and sisters stared. Even Darlene's sobs quieted. Dirk raised his eyebrows in surprise. Duck's voice had sounded so strong and clear and sure.

There was a long silence.

"Better take a life insurance policy out on you!" Chuck said, laughing. "The way things are these days."

"Chuck!" Darlene began to sob again.

"You pretend to be so liberal and free and politically correct and you don't even try to understand," Duck said. "We're leaving."

"Clutch pigs!" said Witch Baby. "You can't even love your own son just because he loves Dirk. Dirk and Duck are the most slinkster-cool team."

Duck ran into the house to pack his things, and Dirk and Witch Baby followed him.

A little while later they all got into Jerry and began to drive away.

"Wait, Duck!" his brothers and sisters called. "Duck, wait, stay! Come back!"

Darlene hid her ex-Zuma-Beach-beauty-queen face in her hands. Chuck was flipping burgers. Dirk looked back as he drove Jerry away but Duck stared straight ahead. Witch Baby hid her head under a blanket.

On the way home from Santa Cruz, Dirk and Duck stopped to walk on the beach. They were wearing their matching hooded mole-man sweatshirts. Witch Baby walked a few feet behind them, hopping into their footprints, but they hardly noticed her. It was sunset and the sand looked pinkish silver.

"There are places somewhere in the world where colored sparks fly out of the sand," Dirk told Duck, trying to distract him. "And I've heard that right here, if you stare at the sun when it sets, you'll see a flash of green."

Duck was staring straight ahead at the pink clouds in the sky. There was a space in the clouds filled with deepening blue and one star.

"I want to let go of everything," Duck said. "All the pain and fear. I want to let it float away through that space in the clouds. That is what the sky and water are saying to do. Don't hold on to anything. But I can't let go of these feelings."

"Let go of everything," Witch Baby murmured.

Dirk put his arms around Duck.

"How could she be with him?" Duck asked the sky.

"She must have been lonely," Dirk said.

"If I ever lost you, no amount of loneliness or anything could drive me into the arms of another!" Duck said. "Especially not into the arms of a greaseburger like Chuck!"

Witch Baby felt like burying herself headfirst in the sand. She knew that if she did, Dirk would not lift her in his arms like a precious plant, as he had done that night in front of the school. She knew that Duck would never share his tears with her now.

Dirk and Duck gazed at the ocean.

"How do you hear the water?" Dirk asked Duck.

Dirk and Duck and Witch Baby didn't arrive at the cottage for three days because they stopped to camp along the coast. The whole time Dirk and Duck ignored Witch Baby. She wished she had her drums to play for them so that they might understand what she felt inside.

When they got home, they smelled garlic, basil and oregano as they came in the door. They entered the dining room and Duck practically jumped out of his Vans. There at the table with Weetzie, My Secret Agent Lover Man, Cherokee and Raphael sat Darlene, Granola, Peace, Crystal, Chi, Aura, Tahini and Yin and Yang Drake.

Darlene didn't have tears in her eyes. She and Weetzie were leaning together over their candle-lit angel hair pasta and laughing.

"Duck!" Darlene leaped up and ran to him. "I need to talk to you."

Darlene and Duck went out onto the porch. The crickets chirped and there were stars in the sky. The air smelled of flowers, smog and dinners.

"Duck," Darlene said. "After you told me, I went to everyone—my acupuncturist, my crystal healer and my sand-tray therapist. Then I went for a long walk and thought about you. I realized that it wasn't you so much as me, Duck. My femininity felt threatened. I don't know if you can understand that, but that's how it was. I felt that if my oldest son rejects women, he's rejecting me. That somehow I made him—you—feel bad about women. Ever since your dad died, I've been so vulnerable and confused about everything."

"This is crazy!" Duck said. "You are such a beautiful

woman. And how I feel about Dirk has nothing to do with your femininity. I love Dirk. It just is that way."

"I don't understand," Darlene said. "But I'll try. I am worried about your health, though."

"Everyone has to be careful," Duck said. "Dirk and I believe there will be a cure very soon. But we are safe that way, now."

"I love you, Duck," said Darlene. "And your friend Dirk is darling. Your father would be proud of you."

"I miss him so much," said Duck putting his arms around her. "But he's still guiding us in a way, you know? When I'm surfing, especially, I feel like he's with me."

Suddenly there was the click and flash of a camera and Duck turned to see Witch Baby photographing them.

A few days later, after Darlene and the little Drakes had left, Duck found a new photograph pasted on the moon clock. The picture on the number eleven showed Weetzie, My Secret Agent Lover Man, Dirk, Duck, Cherokee, Raphael, Valentine, Ping, Coyote, Brandy-Lynn and Darlene. Their arms were linked and they were all smiling, cheese. It looked as if everyone except Witch Baby were having a picnic on the moon.

Angel Wish

No one at the cottage paid much attention to Witch Baby when she got back from Santa Cruz. They didn't even mention how worried they had been when she had disappeared. Everyone was too busy working on My Secret Agent Lover Man's new movie, *Los Diablos*, about the glowing blue radioactive ball.

So Witch Baby skated to the Spanish bungalow where Valentine and Ping Chong Jah-Love lived. Raphael lived with them, but he was almost always at the cottage with Cherokee.

Wind chimes hung like glass leaves from the porch, and the rosebush Ping had planted bloomed different colored roses on Valentine's, Ping's and Raphael's birthdays— one rose for each year. Now there were white roses for Ping. Inside, the bungalow was like a miniature rain forest. Valentine's wood carvings of birds and ebony people peered out among the ferns and small potted trees. Ping's shimmering green weavings were draped from the ceiling.

Witch Baby sat in the Jah-Love rain forest bungalow watching Ping with her bird-of-paradise hair, kohl-lined eyes, coral lips, batik sarong skirt and jade dragon pendants, sewing a sapphire blue Chinese silk shirt for Valentine.

"Baby Jah-Love," Ping Chong sang. "Why are you so sad? Once I was sad like you. And then I met Valentine in a rain forest in Jamaica. He appeared out of the green mist. I had been dreaming of him and wishing for him forever. When I met Valentine I wasn't afraid anymore. I knew that my soul would always have a reflection and an echo and that even if we were apart—and we were for a while in the beginning—I finally knew what my soul looked and sounded like. I would have that forever, like a mirror or an echoing canyon."

Ping stopped, seeing Witch Baby's eyes. She knew Witch Baby was thinking about Raphael.

"Sometimes our Jah-Love friends fool us," she said. "We think we've found them and then they're just not the one. They look right and sound right and play the right instrument, even, but they're just not who we are looking for. I thought I found Valentine three times before I really did. And then there he was in the forest, like a tree that had turned into a man."

Witch Baby wanted to ask Ping how to find her Jah-Love angel. She knew Raphael was not him, even though Raphael had the right eyes and smile and name. She knew how he looked—the angel in her dream—but she didn't know how to find him. Should she roller-skate through

116

the streets in the evenings when the streetlights flicker on? Should she stow away to Jamaica on a cruise ship and search for him in the rain forests and along the beaches? Would he come to her? Was he waiting, dreaming of her in the same way she waited and dreamed? Witch Baby thought that if anyone could help, it would be Ping, with her quick, small hands that could create dresses out of anything and make hair look like bunches of flowers or garlands of serpents, cables to heaven. But Witch Baby didn't know how to ask.

"Wishes are the best way," said a deep voice. It was the voice of Valentine Jah-Love. He had been building a set for *Los Diablos* and had come home to eat a lunch of noodles and coconut milk shakes with Ping.

Valentine sat beside Ping, circling her with his sleek arm, and grinned down at Witch Baby. "Wish on everything. Pink cars are good, especially old ones. And stars of course, first stars and shooting stars. Planes will do if they are the first light in the sky and look like stars. Wish in tunnels, holding your breath and lifting your feet off the ground. Birthday candles. Baby teeth."

Valentine showed his teeth, which were bright as candles. Then he got up and slipped the sapphire silk shirt over his dark shoulders.

"Even if you get your wish, there are usually complications. I wished for Ping Chong, but I didn't know we'd have so many problems in the world, from our families and even the ones we thought were our friends, just because my skin is dark and she is the color of certain lilies. But still you must wish." He looked at Ping. "I think Witch Baby might just find her angel on the set of *Los Diablos*," he said, pulling a tiny pink Thunderbird out of his trouser pocket. It came rolling toward Witch Baby through the tunnel Valentine made with his hand.

Niña Bruja

On the set of *Los Diablos*, My Secret Agent Lover Man and Weetzie sat in their canvas chairs, watching a group of dark children gathered in a circle around a glowing blue ball. Valentine was putting some finishing touches on a hut he had built. Ping was painting some actors glossy blue. Dirk and Duck were in the office making phone calls and looking at photos.

Witch Baby went to the set of *Los Diablos* to hide costumes, break light bulbs and throw pebbles at everyone. That was when she saw Angel Juan Perez for the first time.

But it wasn't really the first time. Witch Baby had dreamed about Angel Juan before she ever saw him. He had been the dark angel boy in her dream.

When the real Angel Juan saw Witch Baby watching him from behind My Secret Agent Lover Man's director's chair, he did the same thing that the dream Angel Juan had done—he stretched out his arms and opened his hands. She sent Valentine's pink Thunderbird rolling toward his feet and ran away.

"Niña Bruja!" Angel Juan called. "I've heard about you. Come back here!"

But she was already gone.

The next day Witch Baby watched Angel Juan on the set again. Coyote was covering Angel Juan's face with blue shavings from the sacred ball. They sat in the dark and Angel Juan's blue face glowed.

When the scene was over, Angel Juan found Witch Baby hiding behind My Secret Agent Lover Man's chair again.

"Come with me, Niña Bruja," he said, holding out his hand.

Witch Baby crossed her arms on her chest and stuck out her chin. Angel Juan shrugged, but when he skateboarded away she followed him on her roller skates. Soon they were rolling along side by side on the way to the cottage.

They climbed up a jacaranda tree in the garden and sat in the branches until their hair was covered with purple blossoms; climbed down and slithered through the mud, pretending to be seeds. They sprayed each other with the hose, and the water caught sunlight so that they were rinsed in showers of liquid rainbows. In the house they ate banana and peanut butter sandwiches, put on music and pretended to surf on Witch Baby's bed under the news-paper clippings.

"Where are you from, Angel Juan?" Witch Baby asked.

"Mexico."

Witch Baby had seen sugar skulls and candelabras in the shapes of doves, angels and trees. She had seen white dresses embroidered with gardens, and she had seen paintings of a dark woman with parrots and flowers and blood and one eyebrow. She liked tortillas with butter melting in the fold almost as much as candy, and she liked hot days and hibiscus flowers, mariachi bands and especially, now, Angel Juan.

Angels in Mexico might all have black hair, Witch Baby thought. I might belong there.

"What's it like?" she asked, thinking of rose-covered saints and fountains.

"Where I'm from it's poor. Little kids sit on the street asking for change. Some of them sing songs and play guitars they've made themselves, or they sell rainbow wish bracelets. There are old ladies too—just sitting in the dirt. People come from your country with lots of money and fancy clothes. They go down to the bars, shoot tequila and go back up to buy things. It's crazy to see them leaving with their paper flowers and candles and blankets and stuff, like we have something they need, when most of us don't even have a place to sleep or food to eat. Maybe they just want to come see how we live to feel better about their lives, or maybe they're missing something else that we have. But you're different." He stared at Witch Baby. "Where did you come from?"

Witch Baby shrugged.

"Niña Bruja! Witch Baby! Cherokee and Raphael told

me about you. What a crazy name! Why do they call you that? I don't think you're witchy at all."

"I don't know why."

"Who are your parents?"

Witch Baby shrugged again. She thought Angel Juan's eyes were like night houses because of the windows shining in them.

He sat watching her for a long time. Then he looked up at her wall with the newspaper clippings and said, "You need to find out. That would help. I bet you wouldn't need all these stories on your wall if you knew who you were."

Witch Baby took out her camera and looked at Angel Juan through the lens. "Can I?" she asked.

"Sure. Then I've got to go." Angel Juan winked at the camera and slid out the window. "*Adios*, Baby."

But Angel Juan came back. He and Witch Baby sat in the branches of the tree, whistling and chirping like birds. They went into the shed and he played My Secret Agent Lover Man's bass while Witch Baby jammed on the drums she hadn't touched for so long. Fireworks went off inside of her. Their lights came out through her eyes and shone on Angel Juan.

How could I not play? she wondered.

"They should call you Bongo Baby," Angel Juan said. "What does it feel like?"

"All the feelings that fly around in me like bats come together, hang upside down by their toes, fold up their wings, and stop flapping and there's just the music. No bat feelings. But sometimes the bats flap around so much that I can't play at all."

"Don't let them," said Angel Juan. "Never stop playing."

They made up songs like "Tijuana Surf," "Witch Baby Wiggle," and "Rocket Angel," and sometimes they put on music and danced—holding hands, jumping up and down, hiphopping, shimmying, spinning and swimming the air. They went to the tiny apartment where Angel Juan lived with his parents, Gabriela and Marquez Perez, and his brothers and sisters—Angel Miguel, Angel Pedro, Angelina and Serafina—and played basketball until it got dark, then went inside for fresh tortillas and salsa. The apartment was full of the lace doilies Gabriela crocheted. They looked like pressed roses covered with frost, like shadows or webs or clouds. Hanging on the walls and stacked on the floor were the picture frames that Marquez made. Some were simple wood, others were painted with blue roses and gold leaves; there were elaborately carved ones with angels at the four corners. Angel Juan and his brothers and sisters had drawn pictures to put in some of the frames, but most were empty. Everyone in the Perez family liked to hold the frames up around their faces and pretend to be different paintings. The first time Witch Baby came over and held up a frame, Angel Juan's brothers and sisters laughed in their high bird voices. They squealed at her hair and her name and her toes, but they always laughed at everyone and everything, including themselves, so she laughed too.

123

"Take our picture, Niña Bruja!" they chirped from inside one of Marquez's frames when they saw her camera.

The pictures of Angel Juan were always just a dark blur. "Why do you move so fast?" she asked him. "You are even faster than I am."

"I'm always running away. Come on!" He took Witch Baby's hand and they flew down the street.

They flew. It felt like that. It was like having an angel for your best friend. An angel with black, black electric hair. It didn't even matter to Witch Baby that she didn't know who she was. At night she put pictures of an Angel Juan blur on her wall before she fell asleep.

Weetzie smiled when she saw the pictures. "Witch Baby is in love," she told My Secret Agent Lover Man. "Maybe she'll stop being obsessed with all those accidents and disasters, all that misery. It's too much for anyone, especially a child."

"Witchy plus Angel Juan!" Cherokee sang from inside her tepee. "Witch hasn't put up one scary picture for two weeks."

Witch Baby ignored Cherokee. She was wearing a T-shirt Angel Juan had given to her. Gabriela Perez had embroidered it with rows of tiny animals and it smelled like Angel Juan—like fresh, warm cornmeal and butter. The smell wrapped around Witch Baby as she drifted to sleep.

"My pain is ugly, Angel Juan. I feel like I have so much ugly pain," says Witch Baby in a dream.

"Everyone does," Angel Juan says. "My mother says that
pain is hidden in everyone you see. She says try to imagine it like
big bunches of flowers that everyone is carrying around with
them. Think of your pain like a big bunch of red roses, a beautiful thorn necklace. Everyone has one."

Witch Baby and Angel Juan made gardens of worlds.
They were Gypsies and Indians, flamenco dancers and
fauns. They were magicians, tightrope walkers, clowns,
lions and elephants—a whole circus. They spun My Secret
Agent Lover Man's globe lamp and went wherever their
fingers landed.

"We live in a globe house."

"Our house is a globe."

"I am a Sphinx."

"I am a bullfighter who sets the bulls free."

"I am an African drummer dancing with a drum that is
bigger than I am."

"I am a Hawaiian surfer with wreaths of leaves on my
head and ankles."

"I am a dancing goddess with lots of arms."

"I am a Buddha."

"I am a painter from Mexico with parrots on my
shoulders and a necklace of roses."

And then one day Angel Juan wasn't on the set of *Los
Diablos*, where Witch Baby always met him.

Somehow she knew right away that something was

wrong. She hurled herself past Dirk and Duck's trailer, among the children Ping was painting, under the radiant blue archways that Valentine was building. The whole set and everyone on it seemed to pulse with blue, the blue of fear, the blue of sorrow.

"Angel Juan!" Witch Baby called. She jumped up and down at Valentine's feet. "Have you seen Angel Juan?"

Valentine shook his head.

"Angel Juan!" cried Witch Baby, tugging at Ping's sarong.

"I haven't seen him today, Baby Love," said Ping.

Dirk and Duck opened the door of their trailer. They didn't know where Angel Juan was either.

My Secret Agent Lover Man was directing the scene in which Coyote was dying of radiation in a candle-lit room. Witch Baby pulled on the leg of My Secret Agent Lover Man's baggy trousers with her teeth.

"Cut!" he said.

Coyote sat up and opened his eyes.

My Secret Agent Lover Man scowled. "I'm busy now, Witch Baby. This is a very important scene. What do you want?"

"Angel Juan!"

"Angel Juan didn't come to the set today. I don't know where he is."

Witch Baby put on her skates and rolled away from the blue faces and archways as fast as she could. When she got to the Perez apartment, she felt as if a necklace of thorns had suddenly wrapped around her, pricking into her flesh.

Angel Juan was not there.

Angel Miguel, Angel Pedro, Angelina and Serafina were not playing basketball in the driveway. There weren't any baking smells coming from Gabriela's kitchen and there was no sound of Marquez's hammering. There was only a "For Rent" sign on the front lawn.

"Angel Juan!"

Witch Baby pressed her face against a window. The apartment was dark, with a few frames and doilies scattered on the floor, as if the Perez family had left in a hurry.

"I'm always running away," Angel Juan had said. Witch Baby heard his voice in her head as she skated home, stumbling into fences and tearing her skin on thorns.

Weetzie was talking on the phone and biting her fingernails when Witch Baby got there.

"Witch Baby!" she called, hanging up. "Come here, honey-honey!" She followed Witch Baby into her room and sat beside her on the bed while Witch Baby pulled off her roller skates.

"Where is Angel Juan?" Witch Baby demanded. On her wall the pictures of Angel Juan were all running away— blurs of black hair and white teeth.

Weetzie held out her arms to Witch Baby.

"Where is Angel Juan?"

"I just got a call from My Secret Agent Lover Man. He found out that the immigration officers were looking for the Perez family because they weren't supposed to be here anymore. They went back to Mexico."

Witch Baby leaped off the bed and out the window.

She wanted to run and run forever, until she reached the border. She imagined it as an endless row of dark angel children with wish bracelets in their hands and thorns around their necks, sitting in the dirt and singing behind barbed wire.

My Secret

Witch Baby was crying. Witch babies never cry, snapped a voice inside, but she couldn't stop. Angel Juan had been gone for two days.

Weetzie had never seen Witch Baby cry before and went to hug her, but Witch Baby curled up like a snail in the corner of the bed, burying her face in the embroidered animal T-shirt Angel Juan had given her. It hardly smelled like him anymore. Weetzie saw that the tears streaking Witch Baby's face were the same color as her eyes.

"Come on," Weetzie said, scooping her up.

Because Witch Baby was limp from the tears and the effort of trying to find Angel Juan in the T-shirt, her kicks and kitten bites did not prevent Weetzie from carrying her into the pink bedroom.

My Secret Agent Lover Man was in bed, reading the paper. He had never seen Witch Baby cry before either.

"What is it?" he asked gently, moving aside so Weetzie and Witch Baby could sit on the warm place. He reached out to stroke Witch Baby's tangles, but she shrank away from him, baring her teeth and clinging to the T-shirt.

"She wants to understand about Angel Juan," Weetzie said. "I thought you could explain."

My Secret Agent Lover Man scratched his chin.

"The Perez family came here to work, to make beautiful things. But our government says they don't belong here and sent them back again. It doesn't make a lot of sense. I'm sorry, Witch Baby. I wish there was something I could do. Maybe with my movies, at least."

"Angel Juan belongs anywhere he is," Witch Baby said. "Because he *knows* who he is."

"He is lucky then," said My Secret Agent Lover Man. "And he will be okay."

"Will I see him again?" Witch Baby whispered.

"I don't know, Baby. There are barbed wire fences and high walls to keep the Perez family and lots of other people from coming here."

Witch Baby crawled under the bed and began to cry loud sobs that shook the mattress. She felt like a drum being beaten from the inside.

My Secret Agent Lover Man got down on his hands and knees and tried to reach for her, but she was too far under the bed. She looked at him through a glaze of amethyst tears.

"Who am I?" she asked, clutching Angel Juan's T-shirt to her chest. "I need to know. You tell me."

My Secret Agent Lover Man turned to Weetzie, who was kneeling beside him and she reached out and took his hand. Then he looked at Witch Baby again. His face was dusky with worry.

"I didn't want to tell you because I was afraid you would be ashamed of me," he began. "I'm sorry, Witch Baby. I should have told you before. See, I've always thought the world was a painful place. There were times I could hardly stand it. So when Weetzie wanted a baby, I said I didn't want one. I didn't want to bring any baby angel down into this messed-up world. It seemed wrong. But Weetzie believed in good things—in love—and she went ahead and made Cherokee with Dirk and Duck. Or maybe Cherokee is mine. We'll never be sure who her dad really is. Well, you know all that.

"But then I got jealous and angry because of what Weetz had done, so I went away.

"While I was away I met a woman. She was a powerful woman named Vixanne Wigg and I fell under her spell. I didn't know what I was doing. Then something happened that woke me up and I left. I found Weetzie again, but I had been through a very dark time.

"One day Vixanne left a basket on our doorstep. There was a baby in it. She had purple tilty eyes.

"The only good thing about what happened with Vixanne Wigg was that we had made you, Witch Baby. I didn't want to tell you about it because I wasn't sure you would understand. But you're mine, Witch Baby. Not only because I love you but because you are a part of me. I'm your real father."

"And we all love you as if you were our real child," Weetzie added. "Dirk and Duck and I. You belong to all of us."

Witch Baby searched My Secret Agent Lover Man's face for her own, as she had always done. But now she knew. Tassellike eyelashes, delicate cheekbones, sharp chins. When he reached for her again, she let him bring her out from under the bed.

My Secret Agent Lover Man held Witch Baby against his heart, and she felt damp with tears and almost boneless like a newborn kitten. She closed her eyes.

She is holding on to the back of his black trench coat that has the fragrance of Drum tobacco from Amsterdam deep in the folds. His back is tense and bony like hers but his shoulders are strong. She is strong too, even though she is small—strong from playing drums—he has told her that. He will take her with him down arrow highways past glistening number cities, telling her stories about when she was a baby.

"My baby, my child that lay on the doorstep smoldering. For such a young child—it frightened us to see that strength and fire. But I knew you. I remembered the way I'd seen the world when I was young. I'd seen the smoke and the pain in the streets, heard the roaring under the earth, felt the rage beneath the surface of everything, most people pretending it wasn't there. Only those who are so shaken or so brave can wear it in their eyes. The way you wear it in your eyes."

They are both dressed in Chaplin bowler hats and turned-out shoes as they ride My Secret Agent Lover Man's motorcycle around a clock that is a moon.

Witch Hunt

The next morning Witch Baby woke at dawn and ran around the cottage naked, crowing like a rooster and dragging Rubber Chicken along behind her. Cherokee climbed out of her tepee and stood in the hallway rubbing her eyes.

"Witch, why are you crowing?"

"My Secret Agent Lover Man is my real dad," Witch Baby crowed.

"He is not," Cherokee said. "I know! He and Weetzie found you on our doorstep."

"He told me he's my real dad! He went away and met my mom and she had me and brought me here."

"He is *not* your dad!"

"Yes he is. He's my real dad but maybe not yours. You'll never be sure who your real dad is!"

Cherokee began to cry. "My Secret Agent Lover Man and Dirk and Duck are all my dads. None of them are yours!"

"My Secret Agent Lover Man is," said Witch Baby. "You have three dads but it's like not having any. You're a brat bath mat bat."

Cherokee ran to My Secret Agent Lover Man and Weetzie's bedroom. Her face and cropped hair were wet with tears.

"Witch says I'm a brat mat because I have three dads!"

My Secret Agent Lover Man took her in his arms. "Cherokee, you've known about that all your life. Why are you so upset now?"

"Because Witch says you're her real dad. I want one real dad if she has one."

"Honey-honey," Weetzie said, "My Secret Agent Lover Man is Witch Baby's real dad, but you get to live with your real dad and two other dads even if you aren't sure which is which. Witch Baby doesn't even get to meet her real mom. Think what that must be like."

Cherokee stopped crying and caught a tear in her mouth. She snuggled between My Secret Agent Lover Man and Weetzie, her hair mingling with Weetzie's in one shade of blonde.

None of them knew that Witch Baby was hiding at the doorway and that she had heard everything.

I'll meet my real mom! she told herself. I'll have two real parents and I'll know who I am more than Cherokee knows who she is.

The next morning Witch Baby put her baby blanket, her rubber-bug sneakers, her camera, Angel Juan's T-shirt and some Halloween candy she stole from Cherokee's hoard into her bat-shaped backpack, and she skated away on her cowboy-boot roller skates.

135

Later Weetzie and My Secret Agent Lover Man woke up and lay on their backs, holding hands and listening for the morning wake-up crow. But this morning the house was quiet and Rubber Chicken lay limply by the bed.

"Where is Witch Baby?"

They looked at each other, looked at the globe lamp on the bed table, looked at each other again and jumped out of bed. They ran through the cottage, checking under sombreros and sofas, behind surfboards and inside cookie jars, but they couldn't find Witch Baby. They woke Dirk and Duck, who were surfing in their sleep in their blue bedroom, and told them that Witch Baby was missing. Cherokee came shuffling in, holding the puppy Tee Pee wrapped up like a papoose.

Duck pushed his fingers frantically through his flat-top. "I bet the witch child ran away!" he said.

Cherokee began to cry. "I've been so clutch to her."

"Let's go!" Dirk said, pulling on his leather jacket and Guatemalan shorts.

My Secret Agent Lover Man took the motorcycle, Duck took his blue Bug, Dirk took Jerry, Weetzie called Valentine and Ping who got in Valentine's VW van. They drove in all directions looking for Witch Baby. They went to the candy stores, camera stores, music stores, toy stores and parks, asking about a tiny, tufty-headed girl. Cherokee and Raphael ran to Coyote's shack on the hill, chanting prayers to the sun and looking in the muddy, weedy places that Witch Baby loved. Brandy-Lynn stayed with Weetzie by the phone, while Weetzie called everyone she knew and peeled the Nefertiti decals off her fingernails.

Weetzie and Brandy-Lynn waited and waited by the phone for hours. Finally, Weetzie's fatigue swept her into a dream about a house made of candy. Inside was a woman with a face the color of moss who warmed her hands by a wood-burning stove. A suffocating smoke came out of the stove and there was a tiny pair of black high-top sneakers beside it.

Weetzie woke crying and Brandy-Lynn held her until the sobs quieted and she could speak.

"Witch Baby is in danger," Weetzie said.

"Come on, sweet pea," said Brandy-Lynn. "I'll make you some tea. Chamomile with milk and honey like when you were little."

They sat drinking chamomile tea with milk and honey by the light of the globe lamp and Weetzie stared at the milk carton with a missing child's face printed on the back. She read the child's height, weight and date of birth, thinking the numbers seemed too low. How could this missing milk-carton child be so new, so small? Weetzie imagined waking up day after day waiting for Witch Baby, not knowing, seeing children's faces smiling blindly at her from milk cartons while she tried to swallow a bite of cereal. Seeing a picture of Witch Baby on a milk carton.

"Where do you think she could be?" Weetzie asked her mother. "Would she just run away from us? Last time she was with Dirk and Duck."

Brandy-Lynn was staring at the clock on the wall and the pictures Witch Baby had taken. There they all were—the family—bigger and bigger groups of them circling the clock up to the number eleven. They were all laughing, hugging, kissing. In one picture, Weetzie and Brandy-Lynn were displaying their polished toenails; in one, Weetzie and Cherokee wore matching feathered headdresses; Ping was playing with Raphael's dreadlocks; Darlene was messing up Duck's flat-top. There were pictures of My Secret Agent Lover Man, Dirk, Valentine and Coyote. But there was no picture on the number twelve.

"Look at all those beautiful photographs," Brandy-Lynn said. "And Witch Baby isn't even on the clock. No matter how much we love her, she doesn't feel she belongs. You have me, Cherokee has you, but Witch Baby still doesn't know who her mother is."

"I've been a terrible almost-mother," said Weetzie. "I won't just stop and pay attention when someone is sad. I try to make pain go away by pretending it isn't there. I should have seen her pain. It was all over her walls. It was all in her eyes."

"It takes time," Brandy-Lynn said, fingering the heart locket with the shadowy picture of Charlie Bat. "I didn't want to let you be the witch child you were once. I couldn't face your father's death. And even now darkness scares me." She set down the bottle of pale amber liqueur she was holding poised above her teacup, and pushed it away from her. "I didn't understand those newspaper clippings on Witch Baby's wall."

"How will I ever be able to tell Witch Baby what she means to us?" Weetzie cried. "She isn't just my baby, she's my teacher. She's our rooster in the morning, she's . . . How will I ever tell her?" she sobbed, while Brandy-Lynn stroked her hair. But Weetzie could not say the other thought. Would she be able to tell Witch Baby anything at all?

Vixanne Wigg

When she left the cottage, Witch Baby skated past the Charlie Chaplin Theater and the boys in too-big moon-walk high-tops playing basketball at the high school. She passed rows of markets where old men and women were stooped over bins of kiwis and cherries. They lived in the rest homes around the block, where ambulances came almost every day without using their sirens. One old woman with a peach in her hand stared as Witch Baby took her photograph and rolled away.

At Farmer's Market she skated past stalls selling flowers, the biggest fruits she had ever seen, New Orleans gumbo, sushi, date shakes, Belgian waffles, burritos and pizzas—all the smells mingling together into one feast. At the novelty store she saw pirate swords, beanies and vinyl shoppers covered with daisies. There were mini license plates and door plaques with almost every name in the world printed on them. But there was nothing with "Witch Baby" or "Vixanne" on it. Witch Baby knew she wouldn't find her mother here, eating waffles and drinking espresso in the sunshine. So she caught a bus to the park above the sea.

Under palm trees that cast their feathery shadows on the path and the green lawns, Witch Baby photographed men in ragged clothes asleep in a gazebo, and a woman standing on the corner swearing at the sun. Near the woman was a shopping cart packed with clothes, blankets, used milk cartons, newspapers and ivy vines. Witch Baby took a picture and put some of her Halloween candy into the woman's cart. Two young men were walking under the palms. They looked almost like twins—the way they were dressed and wore their hair—but one was tanned and healthy and one was fragile, limping in the protection of the other man's shadow over a heart-shaped plot of grass. Because of the palm trees, for a moment, the healthy man's shadow looked as if it had wings. Witch Baby took a picture and skated to the pier lined with booths full of stuffed animals.

She rode a black horse on the carousel, made faces at the mechanical fortune teller with the rolling eyeballs and bought a hot dog at the Cocky Moon. Nibbling her Cocky Moon dog, she stood at the edge of the pier and looked down at the blue-and-yellow circus tent in the parking lot by the ocean. Weetzie and My Secret Agent Lover Man had taken Witch Baby and Cherokee to the tent to see the clowns coming out of a silvery-sweet, jazzy mist. The silliest, tiniest girl clown hid behind a parasol and was transformed into a golden tightrope walker.

Witch Baby thought of the old ladies and the basket-ball boys, the street people and the clowns, the tightrope walker goddess and the man who could hardly walk. She remembered the globe lamp burning with life in the magic shop. She remembered Angel Juan's electric black-cat hair.

This is the time we're upon.

She skidded down to the sand, took off everything except for the strategic-triple-daisy bikini Weetzie had made for her and jumped into the sea. Oily seaweed wrapped around her ankles and a harsh smell rose up from the waves, only partly disguised by the salt. Witch Baby thought of how Weetzie, My Secret Agent Lover Man, Dirk, Duck and Coyote had once walked all the way from town to bless the polluted bay with poems and tears. She got out of the water and built a sand castle with upside-down Coke cup turrets and a garden full of seaweed, cigarette butts and foil gum wrappers. Then she took pictures of surfer boys with peeling noses, blonde surfer girls that looked like tall Cherokees, big families with their music and melons, and men who lay in pairs by the blinding water.

When evening came Witch Baby had a sunburned nose and shoulders and she was starving. After she had eaten the sandy candy corn and Three Musketeers bars from her bat-shaped backpack, she was still hungry and it was getting cold.

I won't find my mother here, she thought, getting back on a bus headed for Hollywood.

She found a bus stop bench in front of the Chinese Theater and curled up under the frayed blanket in her backpack, the same blanket that had once covered her in the basket when Weetzie, My Secret Agent Lover Man, Dirk and Duck had found her on their doorstep. Shivering with cold, she finally slept.

The next morning Witch Baby waited until the tourists started arriving for the first matinee. She rolled backward, leaping and turning on her cowboy-boot skates over the movie-star prints in the cement all day, and some people put money in her backpack. Then she went to see "Holly-wood in Miniature," where tiny cityscapes lit up in a dark room. Hollywood Boulevard was very different from the clean, ice-cream-colored miniature that didn't have any people on its tiny streets.

If there were people in "Hollywood in Miniature," they'd be dressed in white and glitter and roller skates, with enough food to eat and warm places to go at night, Witch Baby thought, watching some street kids with shaved heads huddling around a ghetto blaster as if it were a fire.

That was when she saw a piece of faded pink paper stapled to a telephone pole. The blonde actress in the pic-ture pressed her breasts together with her arms and opened her mouth wide, but even with the cleavage and lips she looked small and lost.

"Jayne Mansfield Fan Club Meeting," said the sign. "Free Food and Entertainment! Candy! Children Wel-come!" and there was an address and that day's date.

So Witch Baby ripped the pink sign from the telephone pole and took a bus up into the hills under the Hollywood sign.

Witch Baby skates until she comes to a pink Spanish-style house half hidden behind overgrown-pineapple-shaped palm trees and hibiscus flowers. Some beat-up 1950's convertibles are parked in front. Witch Baby takes off her skates, goes up to the house and knocks.

The door creaks open. Inside is darkness, the smell of burning wood and burning sugar. Witch Baby creeps down a hallway, jumping every time she glimpses imps with tufts of hair hiding in the shadows, and breathing again when she realizes that mirrors cover the walls. At the end of the hallway, she comes to a room where blondes in evening gowns sit around a fire pit roasting marshmallows and watching a large screen. Their faces are marshmallow white in the firelight and their eyes look dead, as if they have watched too much television.

One of the women stands and turns to the doorway where Witch Baby hides. She is a tall woman with a tower of white-blonde hair and a chiffon scarf wound around her long neck.

"We have a visitor, Jaynes," the woman says.

Witch Baby feels herself being drawn into the firelit room. She stares into the woman's tilted purple eyes, a purple that is only found in jacaranda tree blossoms and certain silks, knowing that she has come to the right place.

"Are you Vixanne?"

"Who are you?" The woman's voice is carved—cold and

hard. The necklace at her throat looks as if it is made of rock candy.

"Witch Baby Wigg, your daughter."

All the people in the room begin to laugh. Their voices flicker, as separate from their bodies as the shadows thrown on the walls by the flames.

"So this is Max's little girl. I wonder if she's as quick to come and go as her father was. Did Max and that woman tell you all about how he left me, Witch Baby?" Vixanne asks. Then she turns to the people. "Do you think my daughter resembles me, Jaynes?" She reaches up and removes her blonde wig, letting her black hair cascade down, framing her fine-boned porcelain face.

"Let's see how my baby witch looks as a Jayne blonde," she says, putting the wig on Witch Baby. "You need a wig with that hair, Witch Baby!" The people laugh again.

"Now you can be a part of the Jayne Club." Vixanne leads Witch Baby over to the screen. Jayne Mansfield flickers there, giggles, her chest heaving.

"Sit here and have some candy," says someone in a deep voice, delicately patting the seat of a chair with two manicured fingers. Witch Baby can't tell if the thick, pale person in the wig and evening gown is a man or a woman.

Witch Baby sits up all night, gnawing on rock candy and divinity fudge, drinking Cokes, which aren't allowed at the cottage, and watching Jayne Mansfield films. After a while she feels sick and bloated from all the sugar. Lipstick-smeared mouths loom around her. Her eyes begin to close.

"I'll put you to bed now, Witch Baby Wigg," Vixanne says, lifting Witch Baby up in her powdery arms.

There is something about being held by this woman. Witch Baby feels she has fallen into an ocean. But it is not an ocean of salt and shadows and dark-jade dreams. Witch Baby's senses are muffled by pale shell-colored, spun-sugar waves that press her eyelids shut, pour into her nostrils and ears, swell like syrup in her mouth. A sea of forgetting.

Vixanne carries Witch Baby up a winding staircase to a bedroom and tucks her beneath a pink satin comforter on a heart-shaped bed. Then she sits beside her and they look at each other. They do not need to speak. Without words, Witch Baby tells her mother what she has seen or imagined—families dying of radiation, old people in rest homes listening for sirens, ragged men and women wandering barefoot through the city, becoming ghosts because no one wanted to see them, children holding out wish bracelets as they sit in the gutter, the dark-haired boy who disappeared. What do I do with it all? Witch Baby asks with her eyes. Vixanne answers without speaking.

We are the same. Some people see more than others. It gets worse. I wanted to blind myself. You must just not look at it. You must forget. Forget everything.

And Witch Baby falls into a suffocating sleep.

In the morning, Witch Baby is too weak to get up. Vixanne comes in dressed in perfumed satin and carries Witch Baby's limp body downstairs. The others, the "Jaynes," are already gathered around the screen, eating candy and watching Jayne Mansfield waving from a convertible. Witch Baby sits propped *up among them, wearing a long blonde wig. Her eyes are glazed like sugar cookies; her throat, no matter how many sodas she is given, is parched.*

Late that night she wakes in her bed. "How will I ever be able to tell her what she means to us?" says a voice. Weetzie's voice. "Weetzie," she whispers.

She stumbles out of the room to the top of the stairs and looks down. Vixanne and the Jaynes are still watching the screen and charring marshmallows over the fire pit. A soft chant rises up. "We will ward off pain. There will be no pain. Forget that there is evil in the world. Forget. Forget everything." Vixanne is holding herself, rocking back and forth, smiling. Her eyes are closed.

Witch Baby goes back into her room and packs her bat-shaped backpack. For a moment she stops to look at the pictures she has taken on her journey. The floating basketball boys. The old woman with the peach. The hungry men in the gazebo. The dying young man and his angel twin. A picture of a child with tangled tufts of hair and mournful, tilted eyes. She leaves the pictures on the heart-shaped bed, hoping that Vixanne will look at them and see.

Then she slips downstairs, past the Jaynes and out the front door. She sits on the front step, tying her roller skates, clearing her lungs of smoke, gathering strength from the night.

The mint and honeysuckle air is chilly on her damp face, awake on the nape of her neck as Witch Baby Wigg skates home.

Black Lamb Baby Witch

When Witch Baby tiptoed into the cottage, she saw Weetzie and My Secret Agent Lover Man holding each other and weeping in the milky dawn light. They looked as pale as the sky. She stood beside them, close enough so that she could feel their sobs shaking in her own body.

Weetzie lifted her head from My Secret Agent Lover Man's shoulder and turned around. Blind with tears, she held out her arms to the shadow child standing there. Only when Witch Baby was pressed against her, My Secret's arms circling them both, did Weetzie believe that the child was not a dream, a vision who had stepped from the milk-carton picture.

Beneath the pink feather sweater Weetzie was wearing, Witch Baby felt Weetzie's heart fluttering like a bird.

"Will you tell everyone she's home? I need to be alone with her," Weetzie said to My Secret Agent Lover Man. She turned to Witch Baby. "Is that okay with you, honey-honey?"

Witch Baby nodded, and Weetzie put on her pink

Harlequin sunglasses and carried Witch Baby out into the garden. The lawn was completely purple with jacaranda blossoms.

"Are you all right? We were so worried. Where did you go? Are you okay?" Witch Baby nodded, not wanting to move her ear away from the bird beating beneath Weetzie's pink feathers.

They were silent for a while, listening to the singing trees and the early traffic. Weetzie stroked Witch Baby's head.

"When I was little, my dad Charlie told me I was like a black lamb," Weetzie said. "My hair is really dark, you know, under all this bleach, not like Brandy-Lynn's and Cherokee's. I used to feel like I had sort of disappointed my mom. Not just because of my hair, but everything. But my dad said he was the black sheep of the family, too. The wild one who doesn't fit in."

"Like me."

"Yes," said Weetzie. "You remind me of a lamb. But you know what else Charlie Bat said? He said that black sheeps express everyone else's anger and pain. It's not that they have all the anger and pain—they're just the only ones who let it out. Then the other people don't have to. But you face things, Witch Baby. And you help us face things. We can learn from you. I can't stand when someone I love is sad, so I try to take it away without just letting it be. I get so caught up in being good and sweet and taking care of everyone that sometimes I don't admit when people are really in pain." Weetzie took off her pink sunglasses. "But I think you can help me learn to not be afraid, my black lamb baby witch."

When they went back into the cottage everyone was waiting to celebrate Witch Baby's return. My Secret Agent Lover Man, dressed like Charlie Chaplin, was riding his unicycle around the house. Dirk was preparing his famous homemade Weetzie pizza with sun-dried tomatoes, fresh basil, red onions, artichoke hearts and a spinach crust. Darlene Drake, who had arrived the day before, was helping Duck twist balloons into slinkster dogs. Valentine and Ping Chong presented Witch Baby with film for her camera. Brandy-Lynn lifted her up onto Coyote's shoulders.

"I think I saw five little Joshua tree sprouts coming up across the street," Coyote said, parading with Cherokee, Raphael, Slinkster Dog, Go-Go Girl and the puppies following him.

Then Coyote put Witch Baby down and knelt in front of her, like a sunrise, warming her face. "I'm sorry about the seeds. Even if they never came up, I shouldn't have been angry with you. We are very much the same, Witch Baby."

Everyone else gathered around.

"We want to thank you," My Secret Agent Lover Man said. "I've been remembering that night when the article and the globe lamp appeared, and I realized that they must have been from you." He scratched his chin. "I don't know how I didn't see that before. They are beautiful gifts, the best gifts anyone has ever given me. Gifts from my daughter."

"And I want to thank you, too," Darlene Drake said shyly, placing a slinkster dog balloon at Witch Baby's feet. "You knew more about love than I knew. You helped me get my son back again."

"Without you, Miss Pancake Dancer Stowawitch, we might never have really known each other," said Duck, stooping to kiss Witch Baby's hand.

"Welcome home, Witch," Cherokee said. "I don't even mind my haircut anymore. I deserve it, I guess, since I did the same thing to you once. And besides, I look more like Weetzie now!"

Witch Baby snarled just a little.

"And thank you for helping me and Raphael find each other," Cherokee went on. "While you were away, Raphael told me it was your drumming I heard that day. You are the most slinkster-cool jamming drummer girl ever, and we hope you will play for us again even though we are clutch pigs sometimes."

"Yes, play!" everyone said.

My Secret Agent Lover Man set up the drums.

"I had them fixed for you," he said. "My daughter, a drummer. I knew it!"

So Witch Baby played. Tossing her head, sucking in her cheeks and popping up with the impact of each beat. Thrusting her whole body into the music and thrusting the music into the air around her. She imagined that her drums were planets and the music was all the voices of growth and light and life joined together and traveling into the universe. She imagined that she was playing for Angel Juan, turning the pain of being without him into music he could hear, distilling the flowers of pain into a perfume that he could keep with him forever.

Everyone sat in the candlelight, watching and listening and imagining they smelled salty roses in the air. Some of their mouths fell open, some of their eyes filled with tears, some of them bounced to the beat until they couldn't stand it anymore and had to get up and dance. Weetzie put her palms over her heart.

When Witch Baby was finished, everyone applauded. Weetzie kissed her face.

"And now it is time for a picture," Weetzie announced.

Witch Baby started to get her camera, but someone had set it up already.

"Come here, Baby," My Secret Agent Lover Man said. "You are as good a photographer as a drummer, but you aren't taking this one. This picture is of all of us."

He put her on his lap and they all gathered around. Weetzie set the timer on the camera and then hurried back to the group.

The picture was of all of them, as My Secret Agent Lover Man had said—himself and Weetzie, Dirk and Duck and Darlene, Valentine and Ping, Brandy-Lynn and Coyote, Cherokee and Raphael and Witch Baby.

"Twelve of us," said Weetzie. "So the twelve on the clock won't be empty anymore."

"Once upon time," Witch Baby said.

At dinner that night, Witch Baby looked up at the globe lamp in the center of the table. Suddenly, as if a genie had touched it, the lamp bloomed with jungles and forests, fields and gardens, became shining and restless with oceans and rivers, burned with fires, volcanoes and radiation, sparkled with deserts, beaches and cities, danced with bodies at work in factories and on farms, bodies in worship, playing music, loving, dying in the streets, flesh of many colors on infinite varieties of the same form of bones. And there—so tiny—Witch Baby saw their city.

This is the time we're upon.

Witch Baby looked around the table. She could see everyone's sadness. Her father was thinking about the movie he was making—the village where everyone is poisoned by something they love and worship. Witch Baby knew he was haunted with thoughts about the future of the planet. Dirk and Duck prayed that a cure would be found for the disease whose name they could not speak. Brandy-Lynn had never gotten over the death of Weetzie's father, Charlie Bat, and Darlene was with Chuck because she could not face another loss like the loss of Eddie Drake. Coyote mourned for the sky and sea, animals and vegetables, that were full of toxins. Some people hated to see Ping and Valentine together, because they weren't the same color, and Cherokee and Raphael might have to face the same hatred. Cherokee would never know for sure who her real dad was. There was Weetzie with her bitten fingernails,

153

taking care of all these people, showing them the world she saw through pink lenses. Somewhere in Mexico, separated from Witch Baby by walls and barbed wire, floodlights and blocked-off trenches, was the Perez family—Marquez, Gabriela, Angel Miguel, Angel Pedro, Angelina and Serafina, and Angel Juan—Angel Juan who would always be with Witch Baby, a velvet wing shadow guarding her dreams. And there was Vixanne trying to deny the grief she saw, trying to keep it from entering her body through eyes that were just like Witch Baby's eyes.

Witch Baby saw that her own sadness was only a small piece of the puzzle of pain that made up the globe. But she was a part of the globe—she had her place. And there was a lot of happiness as well, a lot of love—so much that maybe, from somewhere, far away in the universe, the cottage shone like someone's globe lamp, Witch Baby Secret Agent Black Lamb Wigg Bat thought.

BOOK THREE

Cherokee Bat
and the
Goat Guys

Wind Song

The black Snake Wind came to me;
  The Black Snake Wind came to me,
Came and wrapped itself about
  Came here running with its songs.

Pima Indian

Dear Everybody,

We miss you. Witch Baby is burying herself in mud again. But don't worry. Coyote is taking care of us the way you said he would. He is going to help me make Witch Baby some wings. Coyote is teaching me all about Indians. I am a deer, Witch Baby is a raven and Raphael is a dreaming obsidian elk. I hope the film is going well. We love you.

Cherokee Thunderbat

Wings

Cherokee Bat loved the canyons. Beachwood Canyon, lined with palm trees, hibiscus, bougainvillea and a row of candles lit for the two old ladies who had been killed by a hit-and-run, led to the Hollywood sign or to the lake that changed colors under a bridge of stone bears. Topanga Canyon wound like a river to the sea past flower children, paintings of Indian goddesses and a restaurant where the tablecloths glowed purple-twilight and coyotes watched from among the leaves. Laurel Canyon had the ruins of Houdini's magic mansion, the country store where rock stars like Jim Morrison probably used to buy their beer, stained-glass Marilyn Monroes shining in the trees, leopard-spotted cars, gardens full of pink poison oleander and the Mediterranean villa on the hill where Joni Mitchell once lived, dreaming about clouds and carousels and guarded by stone lions. It also had the house built of cherry wood and antique windows where Cherokee lived with her family.

Cherokee always felt closer to animals in the canyons.

Not just the stone lions and bears but the real animals—silver squirrels at the lake, deer, a flock of parrots that must have escaped their cages to find each other, peacocks screaming in gardens and the horses at Sunset Stables. Cherokee dreamed she was a horse with a mane the color of a smog-sunset, and she dreamed she was a bird with feathers like rainbows in oil puddles. She would wake up and go to the mirror. She wanted to be faster, quieter, darker, shimmering. So she ran around the lake, up the trails, along winding canyon roads, trying not to make noise, barefoot so her feet would get tougher or in beaded moccasins when they hurt too much. Then she went back to the mirror. She was too naked. She wanted hooves, haunches, a beak, claws, wings.

There was a collage of dead butterflies on the wall of the canyon house where Cherokee lived with her almost-sister Witch Baby and the rest of their family. At night Cherokee dreamed the butterflies came to life, broke the glass and flew out at her in a storm, covering her with silky pollen. When she woke up she painted her dream. She searched for feathers everywhere—collected them in canyons and on beaches, comparing the shapes and colors, sketching them, trying to understand how they worked. Then she studied pictures of birds and pasted the feathers down in wing patterns. But it wasn't until Witch Baby began to bury herself that Cherokee decided to make the wings.

Witch Baby was Cherokee's almost-sister but they were very different. Cherokee's white-blonde hair was as easy to comb as water and she kept it in many long braids; Witch Baby's dark hair was a seaweed clump of tangles. It formed little angry balls that Witch Baby tugged at with her fingers until they pulled right out. Cherokee, who ran and danced, had perfect posture. Witch Baby's shoulders hunched up to her ears from years of creeping around taking candid photographs and from playing her drums. Cherokee wore white suede moccasins and turquoise and silver beads; Witch Baby's toes curled like snails inside her cowboy-boot roller-skates and she wore an assortment of whatever she could find until she decided she would rather wear mud.

One day, Witch Baby went into the backyard, took off all her clothes and began to roll around in the wet earth. She smeared mud everywhere, clumped handfuls into her hair, stuffed it in her ears, up her nostrils and even ate some. She slid around on her belly through the mud. Then she slid into the garden shed and lay there in the dark without moving.

Cherokee and Witch Baby's family, Weetzie Bat and My Secret Agent Lover Man, Brandy-Lynn Bat and Dirk and Duck, were away in South America shooting a movie about magic. They had left Cherokee and Witch Baby under the care of their friend Coyote, but Cherokee hated to bother him. He lived on top of a hill and was always very busy with his chants and dances and meditative rituals. So Cherokee decided to try to take care of Witch Baby by herself. She went into the shed and said, "Witch Baby, come out. We'll go to Farmer's Market and get date shakes and look at the puppies in the pet store there and figure out a way to rescue them." But Witch Baby buried herself deeper in the mud.

"Witch Baby, come out and play drums for me," Cherokee said. "You are the most slinkster-jamming drummer girl and I want to dance." But Witch Baby shut her eyes and swallowed a handful of gritty dirt.

Cherokee heard Witch Baby's thoughts in her own head.

I am a seed in the slippery, silent, blind, breathless dark. I have no nose or mouth, ears or eyes to see. Just a skin of satin black and a secret green dream deep inside.

For hours, Cherokee begged Witch Baby to come out. Finally she went into the house and called the boy who had been her best friend for as long as she could remember—Raphael Chong Jah-Love.

Raphael was practicing his guitar at the house down the street where he lived with his parents, Valentine and Ping Chong Jah-Love. Valentine and Ping were away in South America with Cherokee and Witch Baby's family working on the movie.

"Witch Baby is buried in mud!" Cherokee told Raphael when he answered the phone. "She won't come out of the shed. Could you ask her to play drums with us?"

"Witch Baby is the best drummer I know, Kee," Raphael said. "But she'll never play drums with us."

Raphael and Cherokee wanted to start a band but they needed a bass player and a drummer. Witch Baby had always refused to help them.

"Just ask her to play for you then, just once," Cherokee begged. "I am really worried about her."

So Raphael tossed his dreadlocks, put on his John Lennon sunglasses, and rode his bicycle through sunlight and wind chimes and bird shadows to Cherokee's house.

He found Cherokee in the backyard among the fruit trees and roses knocking at the door of the shed. Witch Baby had locked herself in.

"Come out, Witch Baby," said Raphael. "I need to hear your drumming for inspiration. Even if you won't be in our band."

Cherokee kissed his powdered-chocolate-colored cheek. There was still no sound from inside the shed.

Cherokee and Raphael stood outside the shed for a long time. It got dark and stars came out, shining on the damp lawn.

"Let's go eat something," Raphael said. "Witch Baby will smell the food and come out."

They went inside and Cherokee took one of the frozen homemade pizzas that Weetzie had left them when the family went away, and put it in the oven. Raphael played an Elvis Presley record, lit some candles and made a salad. Cherokee opened all the windows—the stained-glass roses, the leaded glass arches, the one that looked like rain—so Witch Baby would smell the melting cheese, hear it sizzle along with "Hound Dog" and come out of the mud shed. But when they had finished their pizza, there was still no sign of Witch Baby. They left two big slices of pizza in front of the shed. Then they set up Cherokee's tepee on the lawn, curled into their sleeping bags and told ghost stories until they fell asleep.

In the morning, the pizza looked as if it had been nibbled on by a mouse. Cherokee hoped the mouse had tangled hair, purple tilty eyes and curly toes, but the door of the shed was still locked.

Witch Baby would not come out of the mud shed. Cherokee finally decided she would have to ask Coyote what to do. With his wisdom and grace, he was the only one who would know how to bring Witch Baby out of the mud.

Early that morning, Cherokee took a bus into the hills where Coyote lived. She got off the bus and walked up the steep, winding streets to his shack. He was among the cactus plants doing his daily stretching, breathing and strengthening exercises when she found him. Below him the city was waking up under a layer of smog. Coyote turned his head slowly toward Cherokee and opened his eyes. Cherokee held her breath.

"Cherokee Bat," said Coyote in a voice that reminded her of sun-baked red rock, "are you all right? Why have you come?"

"Witch Baby is burying herself in mud," Cherokee told him. "She won't come out of the shed. We keep trying to help her but nothing works. I didn't know what else to do."

Coyote walked to the edge of the cactus garden and looked down at the layer of smog hovering over the city.

He sighed and raised his deeply lined palms to the sky.

"No wonder Witch Baby is burying herself in mud," he said, looking out at the city drowning in smog. "There is dirt everywhere, real filth. We should not be able to see air. Air should be like the lenses of our eyes. And the sea . . . we should be able to swim in the sea; the sea should be like our tears and our sweat—clear and natural for us. There should be animals all around us—not hiding in the poison darkness, watching with their yellow eyes. Look at this city. Look what we have done."

Cherokee looked at the city and then she looked down at her hands. She felt small and pale and naked.

Coyote turned to Cherokee and put his hand on her shoulder. The early sun had filled the lines of his palm and now Cherokee felt it burning into her shoulder blade.

"The earth Witch Baby is burying herself in is purer than what surrounds us," Coyote said. "Maybe she feels it will protect her. Maybe she is growing up in it like a plant."

"But Coyote," Cherokee said. "She can't stay there forever in the mud shed. She hardly moves or eats anything."

Coyote looked back out at the city. Then he turned to Cherokee again and said softly, "I will help you to help Witch Baby. You must make her some wings."

A strong wind came. It dried the leaves to paper and the paper to flames like paint. Then it sent the flames through the papery hills and canyons, painting them red. It knocked over telephone poles and young trees and sent trash cans crashing in the streets. The wind made

Cherokee's hair crackle with blue electric sparks. It made a kind of lemonade—cracking the glass chimes that hung in the lemon tree outside Cherokee's window into ice and tossing the lemons to the ground so they split open. It brought Cherokee the sea and the burning hills and far-away gardens. It brought her the days and nights early; she smelled the smoky dawn in the darkness, the damp dark while it was still light. And, finally, the wind brought her feathers.

She was standing with Coyote among the cactus and they were chanting to the animals hidden in the world below them, "You are all my relations." It was dawn and the wind was wild. Cherokee tried to understand what it was saying. There was a halo of blue sparks around her head.

"Wind, bring us the feathers that birds no longer need," Coyote chanted. "Hawk and dove. Tarred feathers of the gull. Shimmer peacock plumes. Jewel green of parrots and other kept birds. Witch Baby needs help leaving the mud."

The wind sounded wilder. Cherokee looked out at the horizon. As the sun rose, the sky filled with feathery pink clouds. Then it seemed as if the clouds were flying toward Cherokee and Coyote. The rising sun flashed in their eyes for a moment, and as Cherokee stood, blind on the hill-top, she felt softness on her skin. The wind was full of feathers.

Small, bright feathers like petals, plain gray ones, feathers flecked with gleaming iridescent lights like tiny tropical waves. They swirled around Cherokee and Coyote, tickling their faces. Cherokee felt as if she could lift her arms and be carried away on wings of feathers and wind. She imagined flying over the city looking down at the tiny cars, palm trees, pools and lawns—all of it so ordered and calm—and not having to worry about anything. She imagined what her house would look like from above with its stained-glass skylights and rooftop deck, the garden with its fruit trees, roses, hot tub and wooden shed. And then she remembered Witch Baby slithering around in the mud. That was what this was all about—wings for Witch Baby.

The wind died down and the feathers settled around Cherokee and Coyote. They gathered the feathers, filling a big basket Coyote had brought from his shack.

"Now you can make the wings," Coyote said.

Cherokee looked at her hands.

Cherokee took wires and bent them into wing-shaped frames. Then she covered the frames with thin, stiff gauze, and over that she pasted the feathers the wind had brought. It took her a long time. She worked every day after school until late into the night. She hardly ate, did her homework or slept. At school she finally fell asleep on her desk and dreamed of falling into a feather bed. The dream-bed tore and feathers got into her nostrils and throat. She woke up coughing and the teacher sent her out of the room.

"What is wrong, Cherokee?" Raphael asked her on the

phone when she wouldn't come over to play music with him. "You are acting as crazy as your sister."

But she only sighed and pasted down another feather in its place. "I can't tell you yet. Don't worry. You'll find out on Witch Baby's birthday."

The rain was like a green forest descending over the city. Cherokee danced in puddles and caught raindrops off flower petals with her tongue. Her lungs didn't fill with smog when she ran. She loved the rain but she was worried, too. She was worried about Witch Baby getting sick out in the shed.

Cherokee brought blankets and a thermos of hot soup and put them outside the door. Witch Baby took the blankets and soup when no one was looking, but she didn't let Cherokee inside the shed.

When Witch Baby's birthday came, Cherokee and Raphael planned a big party for her. They made three kinds of salsa and a special dish of crumbled corn bread, green chiles, artichoke hearts, cheese and red peppers. They bought chips and soda and an ice-cream cake and decorated the house with tiny blinking colored lights, piñatas, big red balloons and black rubber bats. All their friends came, bringing incense, musical instruments, candles and flowers. Everyone ate, drank and danced to a tape Raphael had made of African music, salsa, zydeco, blues and soul. It was a perfect party except for one thing. Witch Baby wasn't there. She was still hiding in the shed.

Finally, Raphael got his guitar and began to play and

sing some of Witch Baby's favorite songs—"Black Magic Woman," "Lust for Life," "Leader of the Pack" and "Wild Thing." Cherokee sang, too, and played her tambourine. Suddenly, the door opened and a boy came in. He was carrying a bass guitar and was dressed in baggy black pants, a white shirt buttoned to the collar and thick black shoes. A bandana was tied over his black hair. Everyone stopped and stared at him. Cherokee rubbed her eyes. It was Angel Juan Perez.

When Witch Baby was very little, she had fallen in love with Angel Juan, but he had had to go back to Mexico with his family. He still wrote to Witch Baby on her birthday and holidays and she said she dreamed about him all the time.

"Angel Juan!" Cherokee cried. She and Raphael ran to him and they all embraced.

"Where've you been?" Raphael asked.

"Mexico," said Angel Juan. "I've been playing music there since my family and I were sent back. I knew someday I'd get to see you guys again. And how is . . .?"

"Witch Baby isn't so great," said Cherokee. "She won't come out of the shed in back."

"What?" said Angel Juan. "Niña Bruja! My sweet, wild, purple-eyes!"

"Come and play some music for her," said Raphael. "Maybe she'll hear you and come out."

Witch Baby, huddling in the mud shed, smelled the food and saw colored lights blinking through the window.

She even imagined the ice cream cake glistening in the freezer. But nothing was enough to make her leave the shed until she heard a boy's voice singing a song.

"Niña Bruja," sang the voice.

Witch Baby stood up in the dark shed, shivering. Mud was caked all over her body, making her look like a strange animal with glowing purple eyes. It was raining when she stepped outside, and the water rinsed off the mud, leaving her naked and even colder. The voice drew her to the window of the house and she stared in.

Cherokee was the only one who noticed Witch Baby clinging to the windowsill and watching Angel Juan through the rain-streaked stained-glass irises. Cherokee ran and got a purple silk kimono robe embroidered with dragons, went out into the rain, slipped the robe on Witch Baby's hungry body, pried her fingers from the windowsill and took her hand. Hiding behind her tangled hair, Witch Baby followed Cherokee into the house as if she were in a trance.

Cherokee handed Witch Baby a pair of drumsticks and helped her tiptoe past everyone to the drums they had set up for her behind Raphael and Angel Juan. Witch Baby sat at her drums for a moment, biting her lip and staring at the back of Angel Juan's head. Then she lunged forward with her body and began to play.

Everyone turned to see what was happening. The drumming was powerful. It was almost impossible to believe it was coming through the body of a half-starved young girl who had been hiding in the mud for weeks. As Witch Baby played, a pair of multicolored wings descended from the ceiling. They shimmered in the lights as if they were in flight, reflecting the dawns and cities and sunsets they passed, then rested gently near Witch Baby's shoulders. Cherokee attached them there. The wings looked as if they had always been a part of Witch Baby's body, and the music she played made them tremble. Angel Juan turned to stare. Once everyone had caught their breath, they tossed their heads, stamped their feet, shook their hips, and began to dance. Cherokee got her tambourine and joined the band.

When the song was over, Cherokee brought out the ice-cream cake burning with candles and everyone sang "Happy Birthday, dear Witch Baby." It was hard for Cherokee to recognize her almost-sister. Glowing from music, and magical in the Cherokee wind-wings, Witch Baby was beautiful. Angel Juan could not take his eyes off her.

After she had blown out all the candles, he came up and took her hand. "Niña Bruja," he said, "I've missed you so much."

Witch Baby looked up at Angel Juan's smooth, brown face with the high cheekbones, the black-spark eyes. The last time she had seen him, he was a tiny blur of a boy.

"Dance with me," he said.

Witch Baby looked down at her bare, curly toes. There was still mud under her toenails, but the wings made her feel safe.

"Dance with me, Niña Bruja," Angel Juan said again.

173

He put his hands on Witch Baby's shoulders, hunched tightly beneath the wings, and she relaxed. Then he took one of her hands, uncurling the fingers, and began to dance with her in the protective shade of many feathers. Witch Baby pressed her head of wild hair against Angel Juan's clean, white shirt.

Everyone clapped for them, then found partners and joined in. Cherokee stood watching. She remembered how Witch Baby and Angel Juan had played together when they were very young, how Witch Baby had covered her walls with pictures she had taken of him, how she never bit her nails or pulled at her snarl-balls or hissed or spit when he was around. Then he had had to leave so suddenly when his family was sent back to Mexico.

Now, seeing them dancing together, the nape of Angel Juan's neck exposed as he bent to hold Witch Baby, the black flames of her hair pressed against his chest, Cherokee felt like crying.

Raphael came up to Cherokee and took her hands. For almost their whole lives, Cherokee and Raphael had been inseparable, but tonight Cherokee felt something new. It was something tight and slidey in her stomach, something burning and shivery in her spine; it was like having hearts beating in her throat and knees. Raphael had never looked so much like a lion with his black eyes and mane of dreadlocks.

"The wings are beautiful, Kee," Raphael said. "They are the best gift anyone could give to Witch Baby." He lifted

Cherokee's hands into the light and examined them. "How did you do it?" he asked.

"Love."

"You are magic," Raphael said. "I've known that since we were babies, but now your magic is very strong. I think you are going to have to be careful."

"Careful?" said Cherokee. "What do you mean?"

"Never mind," said Raphael. "I just got a funny feeling. I just want things to stay like this forever." And he stroked Cherokee's long, yellow braids, but he didn't put his arms around her the way he had always done before.

Song of Encouragement

Within my bowl there lies
Shining dizziness,
Bubbling drunkenness.

There are great whirlwinds
Standing upside down above us.
They lie within my bowl.

A great bear heart,
A great eagle heart,
A great hawk heart,
A great twisting wind—
All these have gathered here
And lie within my bowl.

Now you will drink it.

Papago Indian

Dear Everybody,

Witch Baby is fine! Angel Juan came back. He got here on Witch Baby's birthday! That was her best present but I also gave her some wings Coyote helped me make. She looks like she will fly away. Angel Juan moved in with Raphael and Witch Baby is still sleeping in the garden shed but she isn't doing the mud thing anymore. We started a band called The Goat Guys. We are going to play out soon, I think. Raphael is the most slinkster-cool singer and guitar player. We all send our love.

Cherokee

Haunches

After Witch Baby's birthday, Cherokee, Raphael, Witch Baby and Angel Juan decided to form a band called The Goat Guys. Every day, when Angel Juan got home from the restaurant where he worked and the others from school, they practiced in Raphael's garage with posters of Bob Marley, The Beatles, The Doors and John Lennon and a velvet painting of Elvis on the walls around them. Witch Baby sat at her drums, her purple eyes fierce, her skinny arms pounding out the beat; Angel Juan pouted and swayed as he played his bass, and Raphael sang in a voice like Kahlúa and milk, swinging his dreadlocks to the sound of his guitar. Cherokee, whirling with her tambourine, imagined she could see their music like fireworks—flashing flowers and fountains of light exploding in the air around them.

One night, Cherokee and Raphael were walking through the streets of Hollywood. Because it had just rained and was almost Christmas, a twinkling haze covered the whole city.

They passed stucco bungalows with Christmas trees shining in the windows and roses in the courtyard gardens. They stopped to catch raindrops off the rose petals with their tongues.

"What does this smell like?" Cherokee asked, sniffing a yellow rose.

"Lemonade."

"And the orange ones smell like peaches."

Raphael put his face inside a white rose. "Rain," he said.

They walked on Melrose with its neon, lovers, frozen yogurt and Italian restaurants, Santa Monica with its thin boys on bus-stop benches, lonely hot dog stands, auto repair shops where the cars glowed with fluorescent raindrops, Sunset with its billboard mouths calling you toward the sea, and Hollywood where golden lights arched from movie palace to movie palace over fake snow, pavement stars, ghetto blasters, drug dealers, pinball players and women in high-heeled pumps walking in Marilyn's footprints in front of the Chinese Theater.

Cherokee and Raphael made shadow animals with their hands when they came to bare walls. They stopped for ice-cream cones. Cherokee heard Raphael's voice singing in her head as she sucked a marshmallow out of her scoop of rocky road.

"We are ready to play out," she told him. They were hopping from star to star on Hollywood Boulevard.

"I don't know. I'm not sure I want to deal with the whole nightclub scene," he said.

"But it would be good for people to hear you." She looked at him. Raindrops had fallen off some of the roses they had been smelling and sparkled in his dreadlocks. He was wearing a denim jacket and jeans and he stepped lightly on his toes as if he weren't quite touching the ground.

He shrugged. "I don't think it's so important. I like to just play for our friends."

"But other people need our music, too. Let's just send the tape around," Cherokee said. She looked up and pointed to the spotlights fanning across the cloudy sky. "I think you are a star, Raphael. You're my star. I'll send the tapes for us."

He shook his head so his hair flew out, scattering the drops of rain. "Okay, okay. You can if you really want to."

Let's not be afraid, Cherokee thought. Let's not be afraid of anything that can't really hurt us. She grabbed his wrist and they ran across the street as the red stoplight hand flashed.

Cherokee sent Goat Guy tapes to nightclubs around the city. She put a photograph that Witch Baby had taken of the band on the front of the cassette. Zombo of Zombo's Rockin' Coffin called her and said he could book a show just before Christmas.

When Cherokee told Raphael, he got very quiet. "I'm not sure we're ready," he said, but she kissed him and told him they were a rockin' slink-chunk, slam-dunk band and that it would be fine.

On the night of the first show, Raphael lit a cigarette.

"What are you doing?" Cherokee said, trying to grab it out of his hand. They were sitting backstage at the Coffin. Raphael coughed but then he took another hit.

"Leave me alone." He got up and paced back and forth.

Angel Juan and Witch Baby came with Witch Baby's drums.

"What's wrong, man?" Angel Juan asked, but Raphael just took another puff of smoke.

Cherokee had never seen him look like this. There were dark circles under his eyes and his skin seemed faded. And he had never told her to leave him alone before.

Cherokee kissed Raphael's cheek and went to the front of the club. It was decorated with pieces of black fabric, sickly-looking cupids, candles and fake, greenish lilies. The people seated at the tables had the same coloring as the flowers. They were slumped over their drinks waiting for the music to begin.

Cherokee turned to see a short, fat man in a tuxedo staring at her. His chubby fingers with their longish nails were wrapped around a tall glass of steaming blue liquid.

"Aren't you a little young to be in my club?"

"I'm in the band," Cherokee said.

"You sure don't look like a Goat Guy." He eyed her up and down and wiped his mouth with the back of his hand.

Cherokee glared at him.

"Sorry to stare. I always stare at how girls do their

184

makeup. It's a business thing. I like that blue line around your eyes."

She started to edge away.

"I used to be an undertaker before I opened this place. Still got family in the business. Maybe you could come with me sometime and make up a few faces. You did your eyes real nice."

Cherokee could smell Zombo's breath. Her stomach churned and tumbled. "I better go get ready," she said, feeling him watching as she walked backstage.

When the band came on, Cherokee saw Zombo leering up at her with his hands in his pants pockets. She saw the rest of the hollow-eyed audience lurched forward on their elbows and guzzling their drinks. Standing there in the spotlight, she felt an icy wave crash in her chest and she knew that she was not going to be able to play or sing or dance. She could tell that the rest of The Goat Guys were frozen too. Witch Baby lost a drumstick right away and started to jump up and down, gnashing her teeth. When Angel Juan played the wrong chords, he frowned and rolled his eyes. But it was Raphael who suffered more than anyone that night. He stood trembling on the stage with his dreadlocks hanging in his face. His voice strained from his throat so that Cherokee could hardly recognize it.

The Coffin crowd began to hiss and spit. Some threw cigarette butts and maraschino cherries at the stage. When a cherry hit Raphael in the temple, he looked helplessly around him, then turned and disappeared behind the black curtain. Witch Baby thrust her middle finger into the air and waved it around.

"Clutch pigs!" she shouted.

Then, she, Cherokee and Angel Juan followed Raphael backstage, ducking to miss the objects flying through the air at them.

Raphael hardly spoke to anyone after Zombo's Coffin. He didn't want to rehearse or play basketball, surf or talk or eat. He lay in his room under the hieroglyphics he and Cherokee had once painted on his wall, listened to Jimi Hendrix, Led Zeppelin and The Doors and smoked more and more cigarettes. Cherokee came over with chocolates and oranges and strands of beads she had strung, but he only glared at her and turned up the volume on his stereo. She didn't know what to say.

When Christmas came, Cherokee, Witch Baby and Angel Juan planned a party to cheer Raphael up and keep them all from missing their families. Angel Juan drove his red pickup truck downtown at dawn to a place by the railroad tracks and came back with a pink snow-sugared tree that Witch Baby and Cherokee decorated with feathers, beads, and miniature globes; Kachina, Barbie, and Japanese baby dolls; and Mexican skeletons. They filled the rooms with pine branches, red berries, pink poinsettias, tiny white lights, strands of colored stars and salsa and gospel music. They baked cookies in the shapes of hieroglyphics and

Indian symbols and breads in the shapes of angels and mermaids.

On Christmas Eve they made hot cinnamon cider, corn bread, yams, salad and cranberry salmon and invited Raphael over. The table was an island of candles and flowers and cascading mountains of food floating in the dark sea of the room.

And we are the stars in the sky, Cherokee thought, seeing all their faces circling the table.

Raphael was hunched in his chair playing with his food. She had never seen him look so far away from her.

After dinner they opened presents in front of the fire. Big packages had arrived from their families—leather backpacks, woven blankets, painted saints and angels, mysterious stones, beaded scarves and candelabra in the shapes of pink mermaids and blue doves. Coyote, who had been invited but did not want to leave his hilltop, had painted Indian birth charts for everyone—Cherokee the deer, Witch Baby the raven, Raphael and Angel Juan the elks. Everyone loved their presents except for Raphael. He didn't seem to care about anything.

"Raphael," Cherokee whispered, "what do you want me to give you for Christmas?"

The fire crackled and embers showered down. The air smelled of pine and cinnamon.

Raphael just stared at her body without saying anything, his eyes reflecting the flames, and Cherokee was glad she was wrapped in one of the woven blankets her family had sent.

The next day Cherokee went to see Coyote. He was watering the vegetables he grew among his cactus plants

"Our first show was terrible," she told him.

"Yes?"

"Raphael is very upset. I don't know what to do."

"You must practice."

"He won't even pick up his guitar."

"What did you come to me for, Cherokee?"

"I was wondering," she said, "if maybe you would help me make something for Raphael. The wings helped Witch Baby so much."

Coyote squinted at the sun. "And what do you think would help Raphael?"

"Not wings. Maybe some goat pants would help. Then he'd feel like a Goat Guy and not be so scared on stage. He's really good, Coyote. He just gets stage fright."

Coyote sighed and shook his head.

"Please, Coyote. Just one more gift. I am really worried that Raphael will hurt himself. It's kind of hard for him with his parents away and everything."

Coyote sighed again. "I did promise all your parents I would help you," he said. "But I must think about this. Go now. I must think alone."

So Cherokee went to Raphael's house, where she found him lying on his bed in the dark listening to Jimi Hendrix and smoking a cigarette. She sat cross-legged beside him.

The moonlight fell across the blankets in tiger stripes.

"What?" he growled.

"Nothing. I just came to be with you."

Raphael turned his back, and when she tried to stroke his shoulder through the thin T-shirt, he jerked away.

"Come on, Raphael, let's play some music."

"I am playing music," he said, turning up the volume on the stereo.

"We can't just give up."

"I can."

Cherokee wanted to touch him. She felt the tingling sliding from her scalp down her spine and back again. "We need practice, that's all. That club wasn't the right place anyway." As she spoke, she loosened her braids, tossing her gold hair near his face like a cloud of flowers.

He stirred a little, awakened by her, then smashed his cigarette into an Elvis ashtray. She noticed how thick the veins were in his arms, the strain in his throat, the width of his knees in his jeans. He seemed older, suddenly. The small brown body she had grown up with, sprawled beside on warm rocks, painted pictures on, slept beside in her tepee, was no longer so familiar. He reached out and barely stroked the blonde bouquet of her hair with the back of his hand. Then, suddenly, he grabbed her wrists and pulled her toward him. Cherokee didn't recognize the flat, dark look in Raphael's eyes. She pulled away, twisting her wrists so they slipped from his hands.

"I have to go," she said.

"Cherokee!" His voice sounded hoarse.

"I'll talk to you tomorrow." Cherokee backed out of the room. When she got outside she heard howling and the trees looked like shadow cats ready to spring. She thought there were men hiding in the dark, watching her run down the street in her thin, white moccasins.

The next day, after school, Cherokee went to see Coyote again. He was standing in his cactus garden as if waiting for her, but when she went to greet him he didn't say anything. He turned away, shut his eyes and began to hum and chant. The sounds hissed like fire, became deep water, then blended together, as hushed as smoke. Cherokee felt the sounds in her own chest—imagined flames and rivers and clouds filling her so that she wanted to dance them. But she stayed very still and listened.

Cherokee and Coyote stood on the hillside for a long time. Cherokee tried not to be impatient, but an hour passed, then another, and even Coyote's chants were not mesmerizing enough to make her forget that she had to find a way to make goat pants or something for Raphael. It was getting dark.

Coyote turned his broad face up to the sky and kept chanting. It seemed as if the darkening sky were touching him, Cherokee thought, pressing lightly against his eyelids and palms, as if the leaves in the trees were shivering to be near him, even the pebbles on the hillside shifting, and then she saw that pebbles were moving, sliding down; the leaves were shaking and singing in harsh, throaty voices.

Or something was singing. Something was coming.

The goats clambered down sideways toward Cherokee and Coyote. A whirlwind of dust and fur. Their jaws and beards swung from side to side; their eyes blinked.

"I guess these are the real goat guys," Cherokee said.

Coyote opened his eyes and the goats gathered around his legs. He laid his palms on each of their skulls, one at a time, in the bony hollow between the horns. They were all suddenly very quiet.

Coyote turned and the goats followed him into his shack, butting each other as they went. Cherokee stood in the doorway and watched as Coyote lit candles and sheared the thick, shaggy fur off the goat haunches. They did not complain. When he was done with one, the next would come, not even flinching at the buzz of the electric shears. The dusty fur piled up on the floor of the shack, and when the last and smallest goat had been shorn, they all scrambled away out the door, up the hillside and into the night.

Cherokee watched their naked backsides disappearing into the brush. She wanted to thank them but she didn't know what to say. How do you thank a bare-bottomed goat who is rushing up a mountain after he has just given you his fur? she wondered.

Coyote stood in the dim shack. Cherokee noticed that his hair was even shinier with perspiration. She had never seen him sweat before. He frowned at the pile of fur.

"Well, Cherokee Bat," Coyote said, "here is your fur.

Use it well. The fur and the feathers were gifts that the animals gave you without death, untainted. But think of the animals that have died for their hides, and for their beauty and power. Think of them, too, when you sew for your friends."

Cherokee gathered the fur in bags and thanked Coyote. She wanted to leave right away without even asking him how to go about making the haunches. There was a mute, remote look on his face as if he were trying to remember something.

When Cherokee got home, she thought of Coyote's expression and blinked to send the image away. It frightened her. She washed the fur, pulling out nettles and leaves, watching the dark water swirl down the drain. The next day she dried the fur in the sun. But she did not know what to do next.

For nights she lay awake, trying to decide how to make haunches. She dreamed of goats dancing in misty forest glades, rising on their hind legs as they danced, wreathed with flowers, baring their teeth, drunk on flower pollen, staggering, leaping. She dreamed of girls too—pale and naked, being chased by the goats. The girls tried to cover their nakedness but the heavy, hairy goat heads swung toward them, teeth chewing flowers, eyes menacing, the forest closing in around, leaves chiming like bells.

Cherokee woke up clutching the sheets around her body. The room smelled of goat, and she got up to open the windows. As she leaned out into the night, filling herself with the fragrance of the canyon, she thought of Raphael's heavy dreadlocks, the cords of hair like fur. She had spent hours winding beads and feathers into his hair and her own. Now she loosened her braids.

She knew, suddenly, how she would make the pants.

Cherokee braided and braided strands of fur together. Then she attached the braids to a pair of Raphael's old jeans. She put extra fur along the hips so the pants really looked like shaggy goat legs. She made a tail with the rest of the fur. When she was finished, Cherokee brought the haunches to Raphael's house and left them at the door in a box covered with leaves and flowers.

That night he called her: "I'm coming over," and hung up.

She went to the mirror, took off her T-shirt and looked at her naked body. Too thin, she thought, too pale. She wished she were dark like the skins of certain cherries and had bigger breasts. Quickly she dressed again, brushed her hair and touched some of Weetzie's gardenia perfume to the place at her throat where she could feel her heart.

When Raphael came to the door, Cherokee saw him through the peephole at first—silhouetted against the night with his long, ropy hair, his chest bare under his denim jacket, his fur legs.

Cherokee opened the door and he walked in heavily, strutting, not floating. The tail swung behind him as he went straight to Cherokee's room and turned off the light. She hesitated at the door.

"They look good," she said.

Raphael stared at her. "Things are different now." His voice was hoarse. "Come here."

His teeth and eyes flashed, reflecting the light from the hallway. He was like a forest creature who didn't belong inside.

Cherokee tried to breathe. She wanted to go to him and stroke his head. She wanted to paint red and silver flowers on his chest and then curl up beside him in her tepee the way she used to do. But he was right. Things were different now.

Then, without even realizing it, she was standing next to him. They were still almost the same height. She could smell him—cocoa, a light basketball sweat. She could see his lips.

All their lives, Cherokee and Raphael had given each other little kisses, but this kiss was like a wind from the desert, a wind that knocks over candles so that flowers catch fire, a wind, or like a sunset in the desert casting sphinx shadows on the sand, a sunset, or like a shivering in the spine of the earth. They collapsed, their hands sliding down each other's arms. Then they were reeling over and over among the feathers and dried flowers that covered Cherokee's floor. She remembered how they had rolled down hills together, tangling and untangling, the smell of crushed grass and coconut sun lotion and barbecue smoke all mixed up in their heads. Then, when she had rolled against him, she hardly felt it—they were like one body. Now each touch stung and sparkled. He grasped her hair in his hand and kissed her neck, then pressed his face between her breasts as if he were trying to get inside to her heart.

"White Dawn," he whispered. "Cherokee White Dawn."

Suddenly she couldn't swallow—the air thick around her like waves of dark dreadlocks—and she pushed him away.

Raphael put his hands on his stomach. He glared at her. "What are you doing?"

Cherokee ran out of the room, out of the house, to the garden shed where Witch Baby was practicing her drums. Cherokee leaned her head against the wall, feeling the pounding go through her body.

"What's wrong with you?" Witch Baby asked when she had finished playing.

"Can I stay here tonight?"

"Why? Is Raphael being a wild thing?"

"I just don't feel like being in the house," Cherokee said.

"*Sure!*" said Witch Baby. "I bet it's because of Raphael. I just hope you use birth control like Weetzie told us."

Cherokee frowned and started to turn away.

"I guess you can stay if you want," Witch Baby said.

Cherokee curled up next to Witch Baby but she didn't sleep all night. She lay awake with the moon pouring over her through the shed window, bleaching her skin even whiter. Sometimes she thought she heard Witch Baby's hoarse voice singing her a mysterious lullaby, but she wasn't sure.

After that, Cherokee was afraid to see Raphael, but he called her a few days later and said there would be a rehearsal at his house the next day. It was the first time he had suggested that they play music since Zombo's Coffin.

Raphael wore the fur pants. He didn't say much to Cherokee but he sang and played better than ever. When they were done, he said, "I booked a gig for us."

"Where at?" Angel Juan asked, peering over the top of his sunglasses.

"I thought you didn't want to play," Witch Baby said.

"It's at The Vamp. We'd be opening for The Devil Dogs."

"Sounds kind of creepy!" Cherokee said, but she was glad that Raphael wanted to play again.

"The owner, Lulu, heard our tape. She is really into us." Raphael stomped over to the mirror, puffed out his chest and modeled the fur pants. "The Goat Guys are ready for anything now."

Lulu was tall and black-cherry skinned with waves of dark hair and large breasts. She moved gracefully in her short red dress.

"How do you like the club?" Lulu asked Raphael, brushing his arm with her fingertips.

The Vamp was dark with black skull candles burning and stuffed animal heads on the walls. Cherokee shivered.

"It's a great setup. Thanks, a lot," he said, looking at

Lulu's lips as if he were in a trance.

Lulu smiled. "I think you'll be just great here, honey. Let me know if you need anything."

She walked away, shifting her hips precisely from side to side. Raphael watched her go.

"Raphael!" Cherokee said. A stuffed deer head had its glass eyes fixed on her.

"Let's do a sound check," Raphael said to his cigarette.

Maybe it was the fact that they had been rehearsing or that after the first show it just got easier, or maybe it was the goat pants. Or maybe, Cherokee thought, it was the anger Raphael felt toward her after the night in her bedroom—the power of that. Whatever the reason, Raphael was not the frightened boy who had left the Rockin' Coffin stage before the first song was over.

He strutted, he staggered, he jerked, he swirled his dreadlocks and his tail. He bared his teeth. He touched his bare chest. His sweat flew into the audience.

The audience howled, panted and crowded nearer to the stage, their faces bony as the wax skull candles they held above their heads. The flame shadows danced across Raphael's face.

With the heat pressing toward them and Raphael's bittersweet voice and reeling body moving them, Angel Juan, Witch Baby and Cherokee began to play better than they had ever played before. Cherokee felt as if the band were becoming one lashing, shimmery creature that the room full of people in leather wanted to devour. Someone reached up and pulled at her skirt, and she whirled away from the edge of the stage. The room was spinning but even as she felt hunted, trapped, about to be devoured by the crowd at the foot of the stage, she also felt free, flickering above them, able to hypnotize, powerful. The power of the trapped animal who is, for that moment, perfect, the hunter's only thought and desire.

When the set was over, the band slipped backstage away from the shrieks and the bones and the burning. Raphael turned to Cherokee, drenched and feverish. She was afraid he would turn away again but instead he took her face in his hands and kissed her cheeks.

"Thank you, Cherokee White Dawn," he murmured.

Then they were running, holding hands and running out of the club. They ran through the streets of Hollywood but Cherokee hardly noticed the fallen stars, the neon cocktail glasses. They could have been anywhere—a forest, a desert—running in the moon-shadow of the sphinx, a jungle where the night was green. They could have been goats, horses, wildcats. They could have been dreaming or running through someone else's dream.

They ran to Raphael's house. Cherokee felt a metallic pinch between her eyes, something hot and wet on her upper lip. She touched her nose and looked at her fingers. "I'm bleeding."

Raphael helped her lie down on his bed. He brought

a wet cloth and pressed it against her nose. "Keep your head back."

"I get too excited, I guess."

As he cradled her head in one hand, he began kissing her throat, the insides of her elbows and wrists for a long time. Then he kissed her forehead and temples. "Is it better?"

She moved the cloth away and sat up. It was dark in the room but the animals, pyramids, eyes and lotus flowers glimmered on the moonlit wall. Cherokee and Raphael were both sweaty and tangled. She could smell his chocolate, her vanilla-gardenia, and something else that was both mingling together.

"Coyote told me about Indian women who fell in love with men because of their flute playing and got nosebleeds when they heard the music because they were so excited," Cherokee said.

"Does it work with a guitar?"

"It works when I look at you."

He touched her face. "You're okay now, I think. . . . I miss you, Cherokee. I want to wake up with you in the morning the way we used to. But different. It's different now."

It was different. It was light-filled red waves breaking on a beach again and again—a salt-stung fullness. It was being the waves and riding the waves. The bed lifted, the house and the lawn and the garden and the street and the night, one ocean rocking them, tossing them, an ocean of liquid coral roses.

Afterward, Cherokee was washed ashore with her head on his chest. She could hear the echo of herself inside of him.

Song of the Fallen Deer

At the time of the White Dawn;
  At the time of the White Dawn,
I arose and went away.
  At Blue Nightfall I went away.

I ate the thornapple leaves
  And the leaves made me dizzy.
I drank the thornapple flowers
  And the drink made me stagger.

The hunter, Bow-Remaining,
  He overtook and killed me,
Cut and threw my horns away.
  The hunter, Reed-Remaining,
He overtook and killed me,
  Cut and threw my feet away.

Now the flies become crazy
  And they drop with flapping wings.
The drunken butterflies sit
  With opening and shutting wings.

Pima Indian

Dear Everybody,

The Goat Guys played at a club called The Vamp and we jammed. I wish you could have seen us. I made Raphael these cool fur pants so he really looks like a Goat Guy. It's getting warm and I'm having a little trouble concentrating on school. But don't worry. We're all doing our work and we only play in clubs on weekends mostly. Thanks for your letter.

Love,
Cherokee Goat-Bat

Horns

Cherokee noticed that the air was beginning to change, becoming powder-sugary with pollen as if invisible butterfly wings and flower petals were brushing against her skin. It was getting warmer. The light was different now—dappled greenish-gold and watery. After school, The Goat Guys would run, bicycle and roller-skate home to play basketball or, when Angel Juan got back from the restaurant wearing his white busboy shirt that smelled of soup and bread and tobacco, they would all ride to the beach in his red truck and surf or play volleyball on the sand until sunset. At night they rehearsed. It was hard for them to think about homework or studying when they were getting so many calls to play in clubs. Everyone wanted to see the wild goat singer, the winged witch drummer, the dark, graceful angel bass player and the spinning blonde tambourine dancer.

After rehearsals, or on weekends after the shows, Cherokee and Raphael stayed together in his bed or her tepee. She hardly slept. There was a constant tossing and tangling of their bodies, a constant burning heat. She remembered how she had slept before—a caterpillar in a cocoon, muffled and peaceful. Now she woke up fragile and shaky like some new butterfly whose wings are still translucent green, easy to tear and awaiting their color. All day she smelled Raphael on her skin. Her eyes were stinging and glazed and her head felt heavy. A slow ache spread through her hips and thighs.

"Cherokee and Raphael are doing it!" Witch Baby sang. Cherokee tried to ignore her.

"Aren't you? Aren't you doing it?"

"Shut up, Witch."

"You are! I hear you guys. And you look all tired all the time."

"Stop it, Witch. You shouldn't talk. Why would you want to move out into the shed? I bet I know what you and Angel Juan do out there."

Witch Baby was quiet. She gnawed her fingernails and pulled at a snarl-ball in her hair. Right away, Cherokee wished she hadn't said anything. She realized that Witch Baby wouldn't tease her if Witch and Angel Juan were doing the same thing.

Witch Baby bared her teeth at Cherokee. "I'm writing to Weetzie and telling!" she said as she roller-skated away.

Cherokee watched Angel Juan and Witch Baby more closely after that. She saw how Angel Juan tousled Witch Baby's hair and picked her up sometimes. But he did it like an older brother. When Witch Baby looked at Angel Juan, her tilty eyes turned the color of amethysts and got so big that her pointed face seemed smaller than ever.

One day, while The Goat Guys were rehearsing, Raphael went over and touched Cherokee's hair. It was only a light touch but it was so charged that tiny electric sparks seemed to flare up. Witch Baby stopped drumming. Angel Juan's eyes were hidden behind his sunglasses. Witch Baby looked at him. Then she got up and ran out of the room.

Cherokee followed her into the garden. "What is it, Witch?" she asked.

Witch Baby didn't answer.

"I see how he looks at you when you wear your wings and play drums for him. I think he's just afraid of his feelings."

Witch Baby shrugged and chewed her fingernails.

"Tell me about Angel Juan."

Witch Baby didn't say anything about Angel Juan out loud, but Cherokee could tell what she was thinking.

He is a dangerous flamenco shadow dancer and a tiny boy playing music in the gutter. His soul sounds like my drums and looks like doves. He is fireworks. He is the black-haired angel playing his bass on the top of the tree, on the top of the cake. I want him to see the flowers in my eyes and hear the songs in my hands.

After a show at The Vamp, some girls followed Raphael backstage. They wanted to stroke his fur pants, they told him, giggling. One kept flicking out her tongue like a snake.

They wore black bras and black leather miniskirts.

Cherokee stood with her arms crossed on her chest, watching them. Then she noticed that Angel Juan was standing in the same position with a frown on his face that matched her own. He turned and stalked out of the club, and Witch Baby came and stood beside Cherokee.

"All the girls pay attention to Raphael but Angel Juan is a slinkster-cool bass player and beautiful, too," Cherokee said.

"Ever since you made Raphael those goat pants, he's been acting like the only person in the band," Witch Baby said. Then she added, "You never made anything for Angel Juan."

Cherokee wished the girls would leave Raphael alone, take their hands off his hips and their breasts away from his face. But she thought he was happier lately than he had ever been and he would hold her in the tepee that night and sing songs he had made up about her until the images of the girls drifted out of her head and she fell into a sleep of running animals and breaking lily-filled waves. But what about Witch Baby? She would be curled up in the shed under the bass drum, alone. She would dream of Angel Juan's obsidian hair and deer face, reach for him and find a hollow drum. What about Angel Juan? Cherokee thought. He would be waiting outside for them by his red truck with a frown on his face. He would drive home with swerves and startling stops. He would not look at any of them, especially Witch Baby. He was the only Goat

Guy Cherokee had not made a present for.

What should I do for Angel Juan? Cherokee wondered. I will ask Coyote.

Cherokee, Witch Baby, and Raphael went out to meet Angel Juan at his truck.

"We were hot tonight," said Raphael.

Angel Juan turned to him. "What makes you think you are such a star all of a sudden, man?"

"I said *we*. I can't help it if the girls like me," Raphael said, tossing his dreadlocks back over his bare shoulders.

"They might like me too if I shook my hips at them like some stripper chick."

"Maybe they would." Raphael grinned and swiveled his hips in the goat pants. "Why don't you, man? Too freaked out?"

That was when Angel Juan made a fist and hit Raphael in the stomach under his ribs. Raphael staggered backward, staring at Angel Juan as if he weren't quite sure what had just happened.

Cherokee put her arms around Raphael. I will have to go back to Coyote, she thought.

Cherokee asked Coyote if she could go running with him around the lake. It was a morning of green mist, and needles of sun were coming through the pines. Cherokee had to run at her very fastest pace to keep up with Coyote's long legs. She glanced over at his profile—the proud nose, the flat dreamy eyelids, the trail of blue-black hair.

"Coyote . . ." Cherokee panted.

"We are running, Cherokee Bat," Coyote said. "Keep running. Think of making your legs long. Think of deer and wind."

When they had circled the lake twice, Cherokee leaned against a tree to catch her breath. She felt as if Coyote had been testing her, forcing her forward.

"Coyote," she said. "I have to ask you something."

Coyote was tall. He never smiled. He had chosen to live alone, to work and mourn and see visions, in a nest above the smog. The animals came to him when he spoke their names. He was full of grace, wisdom and mystery. He had seen his people die, wasted on their lost lands. Cherokee had never seen his tears but she thought they were probably like drops of turquoise or liquid silver, like tiny moons and stars showering from his eyes. She knew that he had more important things to do than give her gifts. But still, she needed him. And she had gone this far.

"Coyote, Angel Juan is jealous of Raphael. He's shy around girls—even Witch Baby, and I know he loves her. Witch Baby is jealous of how Raphael is with me. She wants Angel Juan to treat her the same way. Angel Juan is the only one of The Goat Guys I haven't made anything for," Cherokee blurted out. Then she stopped. Coyote was eyeing her.

"Cherokee Bat," he said. "The birds have given you feathers for Witch Baby. The goats have given you fur for

Raphael Chong Jah-Love. What do you want now?"

"I want the horns on your shelf for Angel Juan," Cherokee whispered.

She was braced against the tree, and she realized that she was waiting for something, for thunder to crack suddenly or for the ground to shake. But nothing happened. The morning was quiet—the early sun coaxing the fragrance from the pines and the earth. Coyote did not even blink. He was silent for a while. Then he spoke.

"My people are great runners, Cherokee. They go on ritual runs. Before these they abstain from eating fatty meat and from sexual relations. These things can drain us."

Cherokee looked down at the ground and shrugged. "What do you mean?"

"You know what I mean. You are very young still. So is Raphael. Angel Juan and Witch Baby are both very young. You must be careful. While your parents are away, I am responsible. Use your wisest judgment and protect yourself."

"We do. I do," Cherokee said. "Weetzie told me and Witch Baby all about that stuff. But this is about Angel Juan. We all have what we want, but it's been harder for him his whole life and now he's the only one without a present."

"There is power, great power," Coyote said. "You do not understand it yet."

"I am careful," Cherokee insisted. "Besides, if I haven't been responsible, it doesn't have to do with you or with

211

the wings and haunches. I just want the horns for Angel Juan so he won't feel left out."

"I cannot do any more for you. You'll have to make something else for Angel Juan. I cannot give you the horns."

"Coyote . . ."

"I want you to try to get more sleep," Coyote said. "If you want to find the trail, if you want to find yourself, you must explore your dreams alone. You must grow at a slow pace in a dark cocoon of loneliness so you can fly like wind, like wings, when you awaken."

I'm awake now, Cherokee wanted to shout. I'm a woman already and you want to keep me a child. You want us all to be children.

But instead she turned, jumped on Raphael's red bicycle and rode down the hill, away from the lake, away from Coyote.

Cherokee could not stop thinking about the horns. Why was Coyote so afraid of giving them to her? She had always known inside that the wings and the haunches were not just feathers and fur. The horns must have even greater power.

Cherokee rode home and found Witch Baby practicing her drums in the shed.

"I tried to get a present for Angel Juan," Cherokee said. "But Coyote won't help me. I don't know what to do."

"What about those goat horns you were talking about?"

Cherokee played with one of her braids. "Coyote said

the horns have a lot of power. He's afraid to give them to us."

Witch Baby crunched up her face. "It's not fair. Coyote helped you get presents for me and Raphael." She was quiet for a moment. "I wonder what's so special about the horns," she said. "I want to find out."

"Witch, don't do anything creepy," Cherokee said. "Coyote is like a dad to us and he is very powerful."

Witch Baby pulled a tangle-ball out of her hair, looked at it and growled. Watching her, Cherokee wished she hadn't said anything about the horns. Witch Baby might do something. But at the same time Cherokee was curious. What would happen to The Goat Guys if they had the magic horns?

I don't need to know, Cherokee told herself. I'll think of something else for Angel Juan. And Witch Baby is only a little girl. She won't be able to do anything Coyote doesn't want her to do.

Witch Baby was little. She was so small that she was able to slip in through the window of Coyote's shack one night. Witch Baby was very quiet when she wanted to be, and very fast—so quiet and fast that she was able to take the goat horns off a shelf and leave with them in her arms while Coyote slept. Witch Baby was very much in love. She had convinced Angel Juan to drive her up to Coyote's shack late at night and wait for her because, she said, Coyote had a present for them. Witch Baby was so in love

213

that all she cared about was getting the horns. She didn't even think about how Coyote would feel when he woke a few moments after the red truck had disappeared down the hillside and saw that the familiar horn shadow was not falling across the floor in the moonlight.

When Witch Baby and Angel Juan got back to Witch Baby's house, they sat in the dark truck.

"Well, aren't you going to let me see?" Angel Juan asked.

Witch Baby took the horns out from under her jacket and gave them to him.

"Oopa! Brujita!"

"They're for you. I asked Coyote if I could have them for you."

Angel Juan held the horns up on his head and looked at himself in the rearview mirror. His eyes shone, darker than the lenses of the sunglasses he almost always wore.

"Thank you, Baby. This is the coolest present. I feel like a real Goat Guy now."

Witch Baby looked down to hide the flowers blooming in her eyes, the heat in her cheeks. Angel Juan leaned over and kissed her face. Bristling roughness and shivery softness, heat and cool, honeysuckle and tobacco and fresh bread and spring. The horns gleaming like huge teeth in Angel Juan's lap. Then Witch Baby leaped out of the car.

"Wait! Baby!" Angel Juan leaned his head out the window of the truck and watched her run into the shed. The horns were cool, pale bone.

Angel Juan attached them to a headband so he could wear them when he played bass. The next night, backstage at The Vamp, he put them on and admired himself in the mirror. He looked taller, his chin more angular, and he thought he noticed a shadow of stubble beginning to grow there. He took off his sunglasses and turned to Witch Baby.

"Hey, what do you think?"

"You are a fine-looking Goat Guy, Angel Juan."

Cherokee and Raphael came through the door. Raphael and Angel Juan hadn't been speaking since the fight, but now, wearing his horns, Angel Juan forgot all about it. And Raphael was so impressed by the horns that he forgot too.

"Cool horns," he said, swinging his tail.

Cherokee gasped and pulled Witch Baby aside.

"What did you do?" She dug her nails into Witch Baby's arm. "Coyote will kill us!"

"Let go, clutch! I did it because I love Angel Juan. Just like you got goat pants for your boyfriend."

"I didn't go against anyone's rules."

"You and your stupid clutchy rules!"

"We have to give them back! Witch!"

Witch Baby jammed her hand into her mouth and began gnawing on her nails. Cherokee looked over at Angel Juan. He was very handsome with his crown of horns and he was smiling.

Maybe it would be okay just this once, Cherokee thought. We could play one show with the horns. Angel Juan would feel so good. And maybe the horns are really magical. Maybe something magical will happen.

Angel Juan was still showing Raphael the horns. He looked over at Witch Baby. "That niña bruja got them for me. Pretty good job, hey?" He grinned.

Cherokee sighed. "Listen, Witch," she whispered. "We'll play one gig with the horns and then we'll tell Angel Juan that Coyote has to have them back. We'll get him another present. But we can't keep them."

Witch Baby didn't say anything. It was time to go on.

If the crowd had loved The Goat Guys before, had loved the Rasta boy with animal legs, the drummer witch with wings and the dancing blur of blonde and fringe and beads that was Cherokee, then tonight they loved the angel with horns.

Angel Juan's horns glowed above everything, pulsing with ivory light. His body moved as if he were the music he played. When he slid to his knees and lifted his bass high, the veins in his arms and hands were full.

We are a heart, Cherokee thought.

After the set, she watched Angel Juan pick Witch Baby up in his arms and swing her around. Cherokee had never seen either of them look so happy. She hated to think about taking the horns back to Coyote.

But Angel Juan has the confidence he needs now even without the horns, she told herself. We all do.

So at dawn the next morning, Cherokee untangled herself from Raphael, crawled out of the tepee and tiptoed across the wet lawn to the garden shed. She saw Witch

Baby and Angel Juan lying together on the floor, their dark hair and limbs merged so that she could not tell them apart. Only when they moved slightly could she see both faces, but even then they wore the same dreamy smile, so it was hard to tell the difference. Then Cherokee saw the horns gleaming in a corner of the shed. She lifted them carefully, wrapped them in a sheet and carried them away with her.

Cherokee got on Raphael's bicycle and started to ride to Coyote's shack. But at the foot of Coyote's hill Cherokee stopped. She took the horns from the basket on the front of the bicycle and stroked them, feeling the weight, the smooth planes, the rough ridges, the sharp tips. She thought of last night on stage, the audience gazing up at The Goat Guys, hundreds of faces like frenzied lovers. It had never been like that before. She thought of the witch and angel twins, wrapped deep in the same dream on the floor of the garden shed.

Cherokee did not ride up the hill to Coyote's shack. Goat Guys, she whispered, turning the bike around. Beatles, Doors, Pistols, Goat Guys.

When Cherokee got home, the horns weighing heavy in the basket on the front of Raphael's bicycle, the sun had started to burn through the gray. Some flies were buzzing around the trash cans no one had remembered to take in.

Cherokee felt sweat pouring down the sides of her body and the sound of Raphael's guitar pounded in her head as she walked up the path.

Witch Baby was waiting in the living room eating Fig Newtons. She glared at Cherokee. "Where are they?"

Cherokee handed over the horns. Then she turned and went to her tepee, pulled the blanket over her head and fell asleep.

The wind blew a storm of feathers into her mouth, up her nostrils. Goats came trampling over the earth, stirring up clouds of dust. Horns of white flame sprang from their heads. And in the waves of a dark dream-sea floated chunks of bone, odd-shaped pieces with clefts in them like hooves.

At the next Goat Guy show, the band came on stage with their wings, their haunches, their horns. The audience swooned at their feet.

Cherokee spun and spun until she was dizzy, until she was not sure anymore if she or the stage was in motion.

Afterward two girls in lingerie and over-the-knee leather boots offered a joint to Raphael and Angel Juan. All four of them were smoking backstage when Cherokee and Witch Baby came through the door.

Witch Baby went and wriggled onto Angel Juan's lap. He was wearing the horns and massaging his temples. His face looked constricted with pain until he inhaled the smoke from the joint.

"Are you okay?" Witch Baby asked.

"My head's killing me."

Angel Juan offered the burning paper to Witch Baby.

She inhaled, coughed and gave it to Raphael, who also took a hit.

"Want a hit, Kee?" he asked.

The girls in boots looked at each other, their lips curling back over their teeth.

"No thanks," Cherokee said. She went and stood next to Raphael and began playing with his hair.

The girls in boots crossed and uncrossed their legs, then stood up.

"We'll see you guys later," said one, looking straight at Raphael. The other smiled her snarl at Angel Juan. Then they left.

"Ick! Nasty!" Witch Baby hissed after them.

"I saw that one girl in some video at The Vamp," said Raphael. "She had cow's blood all over her. It was pretty sick." He took another hit from the joint and gave it back to Angel Juan.

"Let's get out of here," Cherokee said, wrinkling her nose at the burned smell in the air.

But the next time Raphael offered her a joint, she smoked it with him. The fire in her throat sent smoke signals to her brain in the shapes of birds and flowers. She leaned back against his chest and watched the windows glow.

"Square moons," she murmured. "New moons. Get it? New-shaped moon."

Later, in the dark kitchen, lit only by the luminous

refrigerator frost, they ate chocolate chip ice cream out of the carton and each other's mouths.

But in the morning Cherokee's throat burned and her chest ached, dry. There were no more birds or flowers or window-moons, and when she tried to kiss Raphael he turned away from her.

The band played more and more shows. Cherokee's skull was full of music, even when it was quiet. Smoke made her chest heave when she tried to run. She remembered drinks and matches and eyes and mouths and breasts coming at her out of the darkness. She remembered brushing against Witch Baby's wings, feeling the stage shake as Raphael galloped across it; she remembered the shadow of horns on the wall behind them and Angel Juan massaging his temples. When she woke in the morning, she felt as if she had been dancing through her sleep, as if she had been awake in the minds of an audience whose dreams would not let her rest. And she did not want any of it to stop.

Some days, Angel Juan would drive Cherokee, Raphael and Witch Baby to school and then go to work. But more and more often they all just stayed home, piled in Weetzie's bed, watching soap operas and rented movies, eating tortilla chips and talking about ideas for new songs. At night they came to life, lighting up the house with red bulbs, listening to music, drinking beers, taking hot tubs on the deck by candlelight, dressing for the shows. At night they were vibrant—perfectly played instruments.

Sometimes Cherokee wanted to write to her family or visit Coyote, but she decided she was too tired, she would do it later, her head ached now. They would be out of school soon anyway, so what did it matter if they missed a few extra days, she told herself, running her hands over Raphael's thigh in the haunch pants. And they were doing something important. Lulu from The Vamp had told Raphael that she thought they could be the next hot new band.

Angel Juan and Witch Baby were kissing on the carpet. Through the open windows, the evening smelled like summer. It would be night soon. There would be feathers, fur and bone.

Omen

By daylight a fire fell. Three stars together it seemed: flaming, bearing tails. Out of the west it came, falling in a rain of sparks, running to east. The people saw, and screamed with a noise like the shaking of bells.

Aztec Indian

Dear Everybody,

I know the film is very important but sometimes I wish you were home. Maybe The Goat Guys can be in your next movie.

Love,
Cherokee

Hooves

Summer came and the canyon where Cherokee lived smelled of fires. Sometimes, when she stood on the roof looking over the trees and smog and listening to the sirens, she saw ash in the air like torn gray flesh. She wondered what Coyote was thinking as the hills burned around him. If lines had formed in his face when he had discovered that the horns were gone. Lines like scars. She had not spoken to him in weeks.

That summer there was dry fragile earth and burning weeds, buzzing electric wires, parched horns and the thought of Coyote's anger-scars. There was Cherokee's reflection in the mirror—powder-pale, her body narrow in the tight dresses she had started to wear. And there were the shows almost every night.

The shows were the only things that seemed to matter now. More and more people came, and when Cherokee whirled for them she forgot the heat that had kept her in a stupor all day, forgot the nightmares she had been having, the charred smell in the air and what Coyote was thinking.

People were watching her, moving with her, hypnotized. And she was rippling and flashing above them. On stage she was the fire.

And then one night, after a show, The Goat Guys came home and saw the package at the front door.

"It says 'For Cherokee.'"

Witch Baby handed over the tall box and Cherokee took it in her arms. At first she thought it was from her family. They were thinking of her. But then she saw the unfamiliar scrawl and she hesitated.

"Open it!" said Angel Juan.

"You have a fan, I guess," said Raphael.

Cherokee did not want to open the box. She sat staring at it.

"Go on!"

Finally, she tore at the tape with her nails, opened the flaps, and removed the brown packing paper. Inside was another box. And inside that were the hooves.

They were boots, really. But the toes were curved, with clefts running down the front, and the platform heels were sharp wedges chiseled into the shape of animal hooves. They were made of something fibrous and tough. They looked almost too real.

"Now Cherokee will look like a Goat Guy too!" Angel Juan said.

"Totally cool!" Raphael picked up one of the boots. "I wish I had some like this!"

Cherokee sniffed. The hooves smelled like an animal. They bristled with tiny hairs.

"Put them on!"

She took off her moccasins and slid her feet into the boots. They made her tall; her legs were long like the legs of lean, muscled models who came to see The Goat Guys play. She walked around the room, balancing on the hooves.

"They are hot!" Raphael said, watching her.

They were fire. She was fire. She was thunderbird. Red hawk. Yellow dandelion. Storming the stage on long legs, on the feet of a horse child, wild deer, goat girl . . .

"Cherokee! Cherokee!"

They were calling her but she wasn't really listening. She was dancing, thrusting. Her voice was bells. Her tambourine sent off sparks. The Vamp audience reached for her, there at the bottom of the stage, there, beneath her hooves.

She spun and spun. She had imagined she was the color of red flame but she was whiter than ever, like the hottest part of the fire before it burns itself out.

Later, someone was reaching down her shirt. She called for Raphael but he was not there. Witch Baby came and pulled her away. Feathers were flying in a whirlwind. Her feet were blistering inside the hoof boots.

Then they were back at the house. Raphael had invited Lulu over and he, Lulu and Angel Juan were on the couch sharing a joint. Candles were burning. Raphael touched Lulu's smooth, dark cheek with the back of his hand. Or had Cherokee imagined that? Her feet hurt so much and in the candlelight she could have been mistaken.

"Help me take these off," she said to Witch Baby. "Please. They hurt."

Witch Baby pulled at one boot. Every part of her body strained, even the tendons in her neck. Finally she fell backward and Cherokee's foot was free, throbbing with pain. Witch Baby pulled on the other boot until it came off too.

"It cut me! Nasty thing!"

"What?"

"Your boot cut me." There was blood on Witch Baby's hand.

"Let's wash it off."

They went into the bathroom and Cherokee held on to the claw-footed tub for balance. She felt as if she were going to be sick and took a deep breath. Then she helped clean the cut that ran across Witch Baby's palm like a red lifeline.

"I want to stop, Witch Baby," she whispered.

Witch Baby stood at the sink, her wings drooping with sweat and filth, her eyes glazed, blood from her hand dripping into the basin. "Tell that to our boyfriends out there on the couch," she said. "Tell that to Angel Juan's horns."

But what did Angel Juan's horns tell Angel Juan?

The next night The Goat Guys smoked and drank tequila before the show. On stage they were all in a frenzy. Cherokee, burning with tequila, could not stop whirling, although her toes were screaming, smashed into the hooves. Witch Baby was playing so hard that the wings seemed to be flapping by themselves, ready to fly away with her. Raphael leaped up and down as if the fur pants were scalding him. Finally, he leaped into the audience and the people held him up, grabbing at matted fur, at his long dreadlocks, at his skin slippery with sweat.

While Raphael was thrashing around in the audience trying not to lose hold of his microphone, Angel Juan pumped his bass, charging forward with his whole body like a bull in a ring. He swung his head back and forth as if it were very heavy, crammed full of pain and sound. He slid to his knees. Something flashed in his hand. Cherokee thought she could hear the audience salivating as they yelled. They saw the knife before she did. They saw Angel Juan make the slash marks across his bare chest like a warrior painting himself before the fight. They reached out, hoping to feel his blood splash on them.

It was only surface cuts; The Goat Guys saw that later when they were at home cleaning him. But Cherokee's hands were trembling and her stomach felt as if she had eaten a live thing. She took the horns off Angel Juan's head.

He sat in a chair, his eyes half closed. Witch Baby was kneeling at his feet with a reddened washcloth in her hands. Raphael stood by himself, smoking a cigarette. They all watched Cherokee as she put the horns on the floor and backed away from them.

"We have to give them back to Coyote," she said.

231

"What are you talking about?"

"The horns. They don't belong to us. Coyote was here while we were out." Cherokee reached into her pocket and held out three glossy feathers she had found tied to the front door. "We have to give back the horns."

"You can't do that now," Witch Baby said. "Tomorrow night we'll have at least two record companies at our house! We need the horns!"

"Yeah, Cherokee, cool out," Angel Juan said. "You're just uptight about tomorrow."

"Look at you!" She pointed to his chest.

"He's all right. Lots of rock stars get carried away and do stuff like that. And we won't drink anything tomorrow," Raphael promised her.

She wanted him to hold her but lately they almost never touched. After the shows they were always too exhausted to make love and collapsed together, chilled from their sweat and smelling of cigarettes, when they got back.

"And we're not even playing at a club. It'll be like my birthday party," Witch Baby said.

"Better! We're so much hotter now. Bob Marley, Jimi Hendrix, Jim Morrison, Elvis."

"I'm not doing any more shows 'til we give back the horns," Cherokee said. "Don't you see? We have to stop!"

"Don't worry," Raphael said. "Coyote gave us the horns. Why are you so afraid?"

Witch Baby began gnawing her cuticles, her eyes darting from Cherokee to Raphael. When Cherokee saw her,

232

she just shook her head silently at Raphael. She couldn't tell him and Angel Juan the truth about the horns because she was afraid they wouldn't be able to forgive her and Witch Baby for what they had done.

When she fell asleep that night, Cherokee dreamed she was in a cage. It was littered with bones.

The night of the party, the house was crammed with people. They wore black leather and fur and drank tall, fluorescent-colored drinks. Some were in the bedrooms snorting piles of cocaine off mirrors. They were playing with the film equipment, pretending to surf on the surfboards, trying on beaded dresses and top hats, undressing the Barbie dolls and twisting the Mexican skeleton dolls' limbs together. There were some six-foot-tall models with bare breasts and necklaces made of teeth. Men with tattooed chests and scarred arms. The air was hot with bodies and smoke.

Before The Goat Guys played live, Raphael put on their tape—his own loping, reggae rap, Angel Juan's salsa-influenced bass, Witch Baby's rock-and-roll-slam drums, Cherokee's shimmery tambourine and backup vocals. A few people were dancing, doing the "goat." They rocked and hip-hopped in circles, butting each other with imaginary horns.

Cherokee was drinking from a bottle of whiskey someone had handed her when she saw Lulu go over to Raphael. Lulu was wearing a very short, low-cut black dress, and she leaned forward as she spoke to him. Cherokee could not hear what they were saying, but she saw Raphael staring down Lulu's dress, saw Lulu take his hand and lead him away. On the stereo, Raphael's voice was singing.

"White Dawn," Raphael sang. It was a song he had written when the band first started, a name he never used anymore.

Cherokee followed Raphael and Lulu into Weetzie's bedroom. She watched Lulu bend her head, as if she were admiring her reflection in a lake, and inhale the white powder off a mirror. She watched Raphael stand and flex his bare muscles. Lulu put her hands on Raphael's hips.

That was when Cherokee turned and ran out of the room.

First, she found Raphael's haunches lying in her closet. The hot, heavy fur scratched her arms when she lifted the pants. Next, she found Angel Juan's horns and Witch Baby's wings strewn on the floor of the living room among the bottles and cigarette butts, dolls, surf equipment and cannisters of film. Cherokee was already wearing the hooves.

She took the armload of fur and bone into the bathroom, pulled off her clothes, and stared at her reflection— a weak, pale girl, the shadows of her ribs showing bluish through her skin like an X ray.

I am getting whiter and whiter, she thought. Maybe I'll fade all the way.

But the hooves and haunches and horns and wings were not fragile. Everything about them was dark and full, even the fragrance that rose from them like the ghosts of the animals to whom they had once belonged. Cherokee had seen her friends transformed by these things, one at a time. She had seen Witch Baby soar, Raphael charge, Angel Juan glow. She had felt the wild pull of the hooves on her feet and legs. But what would it be like to wear all this power at once, Cherokee wondered. What creature could she become? What music would come from her, from her little white-girl body, when that body was something entirely different? How would they look at her then, all of them, those faces below her? How would Raphael look at her, how would his eyes shine, mirrors for her alone? He would look at her.

Cherokee stepped into the haunches. They made her legs feel heavy, dense with strength. Her feet in the boots stuck out from the bottom of the hairy pants as if both hooves and haunches were really part of her body. She fastened Witch Baby's wings to her shoulders and moved her shoulder blades together so that the wings stirred. Then she attached Angel Juan's horns to her head. In the mirror she saw a wild creature, a myth-beast, a sphinx. She shut her eyes, threw back her head and licked her lips.

I can do anything now, Cherokee thought, leaving the bathroom, passing among the people who had taken over the house so that she hardly recognized it anymore. Angel Juan was on the couch, surrounded by girls, their limbs flailing, but Cherokee didn't see Witch Baby anywhere.

Then Cherokee passed the room where Raphael and Lulu were sitting on the bed, staring at each other. Raphael did not take his eyes off Lulu as Cherokee walked by.

I don't need Raphael or Weetzie or Coyote or anybody, Cherokee told herself. She kept her eyes focused straight ahead of her and paraded like a runway model.

Cherokee climbed up the narrow staircase and out onto the roof deck, into the night. She could see the city below, shimmering beyond the dark canyon. Each of those lights was someone's window, each an eye that would see her someday and fill with desire and awe. Maybe tonight. Maybe tonight each of those people would gaze up at her, at this creature she had become, and applaud. And she wouldn't have to feel alone. Even without her family and Coyote. Even without the rest of The Goat Guys. Even without Raphael. She would fly above them on the wings she had made.

Cherokee swayed at the edge of the roof, gazing into the buoyant darkness. She felt the boots blistering her feet, the haunches scratching her legs, the horns pressing against her temples; but the wings, quivering with a slight breeze, would lift her away from all that, from anything that hurt. The way they had lifted Witch Baby from the mud.

Cherokee spread out her arms, poised.

And that was when she felt flight. But it was not the flight she had imagined.

Something had swept her away but it was not the wings carrying her into air. Something warm and steady and strong had swept her to itself. Something with a heart-beat and a scent of sage smoke. She was greeted, but not by an audience of anonymous lights, voices echoing her name. She recognized the voice that drew her close. It was Coyote's voice.

"Cherokee, my little one," Coyote wept. They were not the tears of silver—moons and stars—she had once imag-ined, but wet and salt as they fell from his eyes onto her face.

Dream Song

Where will you and I sleep?
At the down-turned jagged rim of the sky
you and I will sleep.

Wintu Indian

Dear Cherokee, Witch Baby, Raphael
and Angel Juan,

   We are coming home.

                    Love,
                    Weetzie

Home

The first things Cherokee saw when she woke were the stained-glass roses and irises blossoming with sun. Then she shifted her head on the pillow and saw Raphael kneeling beside her.

"How are you feeling?" he whispered, his eyes on her face.

She nodded, trying to swallow as her throat swelled with tears.

"We're all going to take care of you."

"What about you?"

"Don't worry, Kee. Coyote said he is going to help all of us. I'm going to quit drinking and smoking, even. And he called Weetzie. They're all on their way home."

"What about Angel Juan's headaches?"

"Coyote is going to get some medicine together." He pressed his forehead to her chest, listening for her heart. "I'm so sorry, Cherokee."

"I just missed you so much."

"Me too. Where were we?"

Cherokee looked down at herself, small and white beneath the blankets. "Do you like me like this?" she asked. The tears in her throat had started to show in her eyes. "I mean, not all dressed up. I'm not like Lulu. . . ."

Raphael flung his arms around her and she saw the sobs shudder through his back as she stroked his head. "You are my beauty, White Dawn."

Coyote, Witch Baby and Angel Juan came in with strawberries, cornmeal pancakes, maple syrup and bunches of real roses and irises that looked like the windows come to life. They gathered around the bed scanning Cherokee's face, the way Raphael had done, to see if she was all right.

"What happened?" Cherokee asked them.

"Witch Baby saw how you were acting at the party and she went to get Coyote," Angel Juan said, squinting and rubbing his temples.

"She told me all about the horns," Coyote said. "Forgive me, Cherokee."

"*I'm* sorry," Cherokee said. "About the horns."

"It's my fault!" said Witch Baby. "I should never have taken those clutch horns."

"Yes," said Coyote, "we were all at fault. But I am supposed to care for you and I failed."

"Did you know we had the horns?" Cherokee asked.

"I could have guessed. I turned my mind away from you. Sometimes, there on the hilltop, I forget life. Dreaming of past sorrows and the injured earth, I forget my friends and their children who are also my friends."

244

"What are we going to do?"

"I called your parents and they will be home in a few days."

"But will you help us now?" Cherokee asked. She looked over at Witch Baby, who was gazing at Angel Juan as if her head ached too. "Will you help take away Angel Juan's headaches and help Raphael stop smoking?"

The lines running through Coyote's face like scars were not from anger but concern. He took Cherokee's cold, damp hands in his own that were dry and warm, solid as desert rock. "I will help you," Coyote said.

After they had scrubbed the house clean, glued the broken bowls, washed the salsa- and liquor-stained table-cloths, waxed the scratched surfboards, and fastened the dolls' limbs back on, Coyote, Cherokee, Raphael, Witch Baby and Angel Juan gathered in a circle on Coyote's hill.

Coyote lit candles and burned sage. In the center of the circle he put the tattered wings, haunches, horns and hooves. Then he began to chant and to beat a small drum with his flat, heavy palms.

"This is the healing circle," Coyote said. "First we will all say our names so that our ancestor spirits will come and join us."

"Angel Juan Perez."

"Witch Baby Wigg Bat."

"Raphael Chong Jah-Love."

"Cherokee Bat."

"Coyote Dream Song."

Coyote Dream Song chanted again. His voice filled the evening like the candlelight, like the smoke from the sage, like the beat of his heart.

"Now we will dance the sacred dances," Coyote said, and everyone stood, shyly at first, with their hands in their pockets or folded on their chests. Coyote jumped into the air as he played his drum, and the music moved in all of them until they were jumping too, leaping as high as they could. Then Coyote began to spin and they spun with him, circles making a circle, planets in orbit, everything becoming a blur of fragrant shadow and fragmented light around them.

"And we will dance our animal spirit," Coyote said, crouching, hunching his shoulders, his eyes flashing, his face becoming lean and secretive. The circle changed, then. There were ravens flying, deer prancing, obsidian elks dreaming.

Finally, the dancing ended and they sat, exhausted, leaning against each other, protected by ancestors who had recognized their names, and glowing with the dream of the feathers and fur they might have been or would become.

"This is the healing circle," Coyote said. "So you may each say what it is you wish to heal. Or you may think it in silence." And he put his hand to his heart, then reached to the sky, then touched his heart again.

"The children in my country who beg in gutters and

the hurt I gave to Witch Baby," Angel Juan said.

"My Angel Juan's headaches and all broken hearts," Witch Baby said.

"Cherokee's blistered feet and anything in the world that makes her sad," Raphael murmured.

"Our damaged earth. Angel Juan's headaches. Raphael's desire for smoke. Witch Baby's sweet heart. Cherokee's pain," Coyote said.

Wings, haunches, horns and hooves, thought Cherokee Bat. Wings, haunches, horns, hooves, home. Then, "All of you," she said aloud.

Coyote put his hand to his heart, reached to the sky, then touched his heart again.

That was when the wind came, a hot desert wind, a salt crystal wind, ragged with traveling, full of memories. It was wild like the wind that had brought Cherokee the feathers for Witch Baby's wings, but this time there were no feathers. This wind came empty, ready to take back. Cherokee imagined it extending cloud fingers toward them, toward the circle on the hill, imagined the crystalline gaze of the wind when it recognized Witch Baby's wings made from the feathers it had once brought.

The wings also recognized the wind and began to flap as if they were attached to a weak angel crouched in the center of the circle. They flapped and flapped until they began to rise, staggering back and forth in the dust. Cherokee, Raphael, Witch Baby, Angel Juan and Coyote stared in silence as the wind reclaimed the wings and carried them off, flapping weakly into the evening sky.

Witch Baby stood and reached above her head, watching the wings disappear. Then she collapsed against Angel Juan and he held her.

"You don't need them," he whispered. "You make me feel like I have wings when you touch me." And as he spoke, one fragile feather, glinting with a streak of green, drifted down from the sky and landed upright in Witch Baby's hair.

Meanwhile, Raphael was inching toward the haunches that lay in front of him. Cherokee could see by his eyes that he wasn't sure if he was ready to give them up. But it was too late.

The goat had come down the hill. One old goat with white foamy fur and wet eyes. Unlike the goats who had come before, to give their fur to Coyote and Cherokee, this goat was quiet, so quiet that when he had gone, dragging the haunches in his mouth, Coyote and The Goat Guys were not sure if he had been there at all. Raphael started to stand, but Cherokee touched his wrist. He reached for her hand and they turned to see the goat being swallowed up by the hillside, a wave vanishing back into the ocean.

Cherokee knew what she had to do. Coyote was standing, facing her with a shovel in each hand. He held one out. Together, Cherokee and Coyote began to dig a hole in the dirt in the center of the circle. Dust clouds rose, glowing pink as the sun set, and the pink dust filled Cherokee's eyes and mouth.

The hooves were much heavier than they looked, heavier, even, than Cherokee remembered them, and the bristles poked out, grazing her bare arms. The hooves smelled bad, ancient, bitter. She dropped them into their grave. Then she and Coyote filled the grave up with earth and patted the earth with their palms. The dust settled, the sun slipped away, darkness eased over everything.

Coyote built a fire on the earth where the hooves were buried. The flames were dancers on a stage, swooning with their own beauty.

Angel Juan was staring into these flames. His horns lay at the edge of the fire and Cherokee remembered her dream of flame horns springing from goat foreheads. She watched Angel Juan stand and pick up the horns. Then Coyote held out his arms and Angel Juan went to him, placing the horns in Coyote's hands. Coyote set the horns down in the fire and embraced Angel Juan. Like a little boy who has not seen his father in many years, Angel Juan buried his head against Coyote's chest. All the pride and strength in his slim shoulders seemed to fall away as Coyote held him. When he moved back to sit beside Witch Baby, his forehead was smooth, no longer strained with the weight or the memory of the horns.

Later, after Cherokee, Raphael, Witch Baby and Angel Juan had left, looking like children who have played all day in the sea and eaten sandy fruit in the sun and gone home sleepy and warm and safe; later, when the fire had gone out, Coyote took the horns from the log ashes and brushed them off. Then Coyote Dream Song carried the horns back inside.

When Cherokee and Raphael got back to the canyon house, they set up the tepee on the grass and crept inside it. They lay on their backs, not touching, looking at the leaf shadows flickering on the canvas, and trying to identify the flowers they smelled in the warm air.

"Honeysuckle."

"Orange blossom."

"Rose."

"The sea."

"The sea! That doesn't count!"

"I smell it like it's growing in the yard."

They giggled the way they used to when they were very young. Then they were quiet. Raphael sat up and took Cherokee's feet in his hands.

"Do they still hurt?" he asked, stroking them tenderly. He moved his hands up over her whole body, as if he were painting her, bringing color into her white skin. As if he were playing her—his guitar. And all the hurt seemed to float out of her like music.

They woke in the morning curled together.

"Remember how when we were really little we used to have the same dreams?" Cherokee whispered.

"It was like going on trips together."

"It stopped when we started making love."

"I know."

"But last night . . ."

"Orchards of hawks and apricots," Raphael said, remembering.

"Sheer pink-and-gold cliffs."

"The sky's wings."

"The night beasts run beside us, not afraid. Dream-horses carry us . . ."

"To the sea," they said together as they heard a car pull into the driveway and their parents' voices calling their names.

At the end of the summer, The Goat Guys set up their instruments on the redwood stage their families had helped them build behind the canyon house. Thick sticks of incense burned and paper lanterns shone in the trees like huge white cocoons full of electric butterflies. A picnic of salsa, home-baked bread still steaming in its crust, hibiscus lemonade and cake decorated with fresh flowers was spread on the lawn. Summer had ripened to its fullest—a fruit ready to drop, leaving the autumn tree glowing faint amber with its memory as the band played on the stage for their families and friends.

Cherokee looked at the rest of The Goat Guys playing their instruments beside her. Even dressed in jeans and T-shirts, Raphael and Angel Juan could pout and gallop and butt the air. Witch Baby seemed to hover, gossamer, above her seat. The music moved like a running creature, like a creature of flight, and Cherokee followed it with her mind. She was a pale, thin girl without any outer layers of fur or bone or feathers to protect or carry her. But she could dance and sing, there, on the stage. She could send her rhythms into the canyon.

BOOK FOUR

Missing Angel Juan

Angel Juan and I walk through a funky green fog. It smells like hamburgers and jasmine. We don't see anybody, not even a shadow behind a curtain in the tall houses. Like the fog swirled in through all the windows, down the halls, up the staircases, into the bedrooms and took everybody away. Then fog beasties breathed clouds onto the mirrors, checked out the bookshelves, sniffed at the refrigerator—whispering. We hear one playing drums in a room in a tower.

Angel Juan stops to listen, slinking his shoulders to the beat. "Not as good as you," he says.

I play an imaginary drum with imaginary sticks. I am writing a new song for him in my head.

He sees something on the other side of a wall and picks me up. I feel his arms hard against the bottom of my ribs. Jungle garden. Water rushes. Dark house. Bright window. A piano with the head of Miss Nefertiti-ti on top.

"You look like her," he says. "Your eyes and your skinny flower-stem neck."

"But she doesn't have my snarl-ball hair or my curly toes." My toes curl like cashew nuts.

He puts me down and messes up my messy hair the way he used to do when we were little kids. Before he ever kissed me.

A black cat with a question-mark tail follows us for blocks. He has fur just like Angel Juan's hair. Angel Juan crouches down to stroke him and I stroke Angel Juan. We are all three electric in the fog. The cat keeps following us. I hear him wailing for a long time after he disappears into the wet cloud air. Angel Juan has one arm around me and is holding my inside hand with his outside hand. It is our brother grip. We are bound together. My outside hand is at his skinny hips, quick and sleeky-sleek like a cat's hips. I could put one finger into the change pocket of his black Levi's.

I want to take his photograph with his hand at the cat's throat, his eyes closed, feeling the purr in his fingers. I want to take his picture naked in the fog.

The shiny brown St. John's bread pods crack open under our feet and their cocoa smell makes me dizzy and hungry.

Then Angel Juan stops walking. It's so quiet. Nothing moves. There's a shiver in the branches like a cat's spine when you stroke it. The green druggy fog.

I remember the first time he ever kissed me. I mean really kissed me. We had just finished a gig with our band The Goat Guys and he put his hands on my shoulders. His hair was slicked back and it gleamed, his lips were tangy and his fingers were callusy and we were both so sweaty that we stuck together. Our eyelashes brushed like they would weave together by themselves turning us into one wild thing.

I say, "I think I missed you before I met you even."

"Witch Baby," he says. He never calls me that. Niña Bruja or Baby or Lamb but never Witch Baby. I start to feel a little sick to my stomach. Queased out. Angel Juan's eyes look different. Like somebody else's eyes stuck in his head. Why did I say that about missing him? I never say clutchy stuff like that.

"I'm going to New York."

New York. We were going to go there. We were going to play music on the street. What is he saying? He just told me I looked like Nefertiti. He just had his arms around me in our brother grip.

"You're always taking pictures of me and writing songs for me but that's not me. That's who you make up. And in the band. I feel like I'm just backing up the rest of you. I've got to play my own music."

"Just go do it with her," I say.

"There's no her. I don't even feel like sex at all. Nothing feels safe."

For the last few weeks we've been snuggling but that's about it. I've been telling myself it's just because Angel Juan's been tired from working so much at the restaurant.

"But we've only ever been with us."

257

"Do we want to be together just because we think it's safer? I need to know about the world. I need to know me."

Safer? I've never even thought of that.

My heart is like a teacup covered with hairline cracks. I feel like I have to walk real carefully so it won't get shaken and just all shatter and break.

But I start to run anyway. I run and run into the fog before Angel Juan can go away.

By the time I get back to the house with the antique windows, I feel the jagged teacup chips cutting me up. I go into the dark garden shed. The doglet Tiki-Tee who has soul-eyes like Angel Juan's and likes to cuddle in the bend of my knees at night whimpers and skulks away when he sees me. Skulkster dog. I must look like a beastly beast with a cracked teacup for a heart. I lie on the floor listening for the broken sound inside like when you shake your thermos that fell on the cement.

We used to lie here hugging with a balloon between us. Angel Juan's body floating on the balloon, his body shining through its skin. Then the balloon popped and we giggled and screamed falling into each other, all the sadness inside of us gone into the air.

All over the walls are pictures I took of Angel Juan. Angel Juan plays his bass—eyelash-shadow, mouth-pout, knee-swoon. Angel Juan kisses the sky. Angel Juan the blur does hip-hop moves. There's even one of us together in Joshua Tree standing on either side of our cactus Sunbear. It's like Sunbear's our kid or something. We're holding hands behind him. You can see our grins under our suede desert hats and our skinny legs in hiking boots. I never let anybody take my picture unless it's Angel Juan or I'm with Angel Juan. If you saw this picture you'd probably think that Angel Juan Perez and Witch Baby Secret Agent Wigg Bat will be together forever. They will build an adobe house with a bright-yellow door in a desert oasis and play music with their friends all night while the coyotes howl at the moon. That's what you'd think. You'd never think that Angel Juan would go away.

That's why I like photographs.

And that's why I hate photographs.

I want to smash the lens of my camera. I want to smash everything.

When I feel like this I play my drums. But I don't want to play my drums. I want to smash my drums. So I'll never write or play another song for Angel Juan. "Angel Boy," "Funky Desert Heaven," "Cannibal Love." I wish I could smash the songs and the feelings the way you smash a camera lens or put your fist through the skin of a drum.

Some native Americans believe that the drum is the heart of the universe. What happens to the rest of something when you smash its heart?

Then I hear a noise outside and my heart starts going to the beat of "Cannibal Love." It's him. It's him. Him. Him. Him. Hymn.

"Witch Baby," he whispers on the other side of the door. I don't say anything.

"I still love you," he says. "I'm sorry." His voice sounds different, like somebody else is inside of him using his voice.

I don't move. It's hard to breathe. Afraid the broken pieces cutting.

"Let me in," he says. "Please. I leave tomorrow."

I sit up like electric shocked. I start ripping the pictures of Angel Juan off my walls. Tomorrow.

"Go away now!" I growl, shredding the picture of us in the desert, shredding Angel Juan. Shredding myself.

After all the pictures are gone I slam my arms against the wall of the shed again, again, and crumple down into a shred-bed of eyes and mouths and bass guitars and cactus needles. I am not going to let myself cry.

When I wake up I reach for him—his hair crisp against my lips, his hot-water-bottle heat. I crawl clawing and sliding over the torn photographs to the door. Out in the empty garden it is already tomorrow.

I don't go to school. I lie in the bed of ruined pictures for hours. The shed is dark. Smells of soil and sawdust. Blue and yellow sunflower bruises bloom on my arms.

I remember the time when I was a kid and I first met the little black-haired boy named Angel Juan. He was the first person that made me feel I belonged—like I wasn't just some freaky pain-gobbling goblin nobody understood. Then he had to go back to Mexico with his parents, Marquez and Gabriela Perez, and his brothers and sisters,

Angel Miguel, Angel Pedro, Angelina and Serafina. I didn't see him for years. But it was okay. I had myself. I knew that I could feel things. Not just smashing anger and loneliness. But love too. It was inside of me. And then on my birthday a few years later Angel Juan came back.

Now it's different because he doesn't *have* to go away. He wants to. And also we've done it—the wild love thing. So I feel like I need him to put me back together every night. After his kisses and hugs it feels like without them my body will fall apart into pieces.

I get up and take the shoe boxes out from under the bed. They are filled with newspaper clippings I used to have on my walls—before Angel Juan. "Whales Die in Toxic Waters." "Beautiful Basketball God Gets Disease." "Family Burned in Gas Explosion." "Murderer Collects Victims' Body Parts." Even after Angel Juan I cut them out when we had a fight or something but I'd always hide them under my bed. Pictures of all the pain I could find. A pain game.

"What a world!" says the Wicked Witch in *The Wizard of Oz* before she melts.

The only way I used to be able to stand being in this world was to hold it in my hands, in front of my eyes. That way I thought—it can't get me or something. But when I had Angel Juan I only wanted to touch and see *him*. He was the only way I've ever really been able to escape.

Now it's the pain game again.

Night.

261

Across the garden my family is together eating vegetarian lasagna, edible flower salad and fruit-juice-sweetened apple pie. They are laughing in the beeswax candlelight, talking about the next movie they are going to make and looking out over the ruins of the magician's castle through stained-glass flowers. I wonder if they wonder where I am. They probably think I'm having a picnic at the beach in the back of Angel Juan's red pickup truck. Or maybe by now they all know that Angel Juan is gone. Maybe he told them before me.

There is a knock on my door.

It's him. He's back. I made this whole thing up. He is here with his pickup truck full of blankets and Fig Newtons for a moonlight picnic.

But then I hear my almost-mom Weetzie Bat's voice.

"Honey-honey," she says. "Aren't you going to eat tonight?"

I don't move. It's like I'm a statue of me.

Weetzie opens the door slow. I didn't lock it this morning. Should have. She's carrying the lamp shaped like a globe that I gave to my dad a long time ago. She plugs it in and the world lights up.

Weetzie looks around at the torn-up pictures of Angel Juan and the scattered newspaper clippings. Then she sits down next to me on the floor. The blue oceans make her shine.

Suddenly remember. Lifted into the light. Somebody playing piano. Vanilla-gardenia. Weetzie's white-gold halo hair. It's the day I was left in a basket on the doorstep and Weetzie found me like those changeling things in stories, the ones that fairies leave in baskets, strange kids with some mark on them or the wrong color eyes. My eyes are purple. In a way I want Weetzie to lift me up into the light again. But more I want to sink back into the darkness where I came from. I want to drown under the newspaper pain and the shreds of Angel Juan.

"Go away," I growl at Weetzie. But she knows me too well by now. And I feel too old and weak to bite and scratch the way I did when I was a little kid before Angel Juan came. So she just sits there with me not touching, not talking for a long time. I wonder if she can see the bruises on my arms.

Finally she says, "I wanted to bring you something magic that would make everything okay." She must have already heard about Angel Juan. "But now I know that magic's not that simple. I wish I could give you a lamp with a genie in it to make all your wishes come true. But you're a genie. Your own genie. Just believe in that."

Supposedly a long time ago Weetzie wished on her genie lamp and that's how she met my dad and how her best friend Dirk McDonald met his true love Duck Drake and how they all ended up living together. Weetzie thinks life's so slinkster-cool as she would say because all her wishes came true.

But right now I don't believe in that magic crap. I don't believe in anything. All I want is to find Angel Juan.

"I want to go to New York," I say. My voice sounds gritty. My throat hurts like my voice is made of broken glass.

"To find him or to find you?" Weetzie asks

Why is she asking me stuff like this like she thinks she knows so much? I want her to leave me alone.

I look at the globe lamp. If somebody said to me, You can go all over the world by yourself looking at everything—all the death and all the love—or you can sleep inside the globe lamp with the echo of the oceans as your lullaby and the continents floating around you like blankets with Angel Juan beside you, I would choose to sleep with Angel Juan in a place he can never leave.

To find him.

Niña Bruja,

The building on the front of this card looks like a firefly tree at night.

The acoustics in the subways are good for playing music. I close my eyes underground to try to see you jammin' on your drums, your hair all flying out like wild petals, beat pulsing in your flower-stem neck.

I have breakfast in Harlem. You would love the grits. You eat like a kitten dipping your chin.

I built a tree house in the park. I think the trees have spirits living in them but the one in this tree doesn't seem to mind me being here.

Being in the trees helps me see outside of myself. So does riding the Ferris wheel at Coney Island. Coney Island is closed in the winter but I met a man who knows how to get in.

I saw a saint parade with all these little girls wearing wings. Remember the wings you used to wear? I thought the little girls were all going to float off their floats into the sky. Afterwards one came over to me and handed me this little silver medal with St. Raphael on it. He is a wound healer. He is riding on a fish. I hope he watches over you.

In Mexico people wear hummingbird amulets around their necks to show they are searching for love. Here people pretend that they aren't. Searching.

I hope that you are being sweet to yourself. I wish that I could comb the snarl-balls out of your hair and hear you purr.

I don't have an address yet but I'll write to you again soon.

I love you.

Angel Juan

Dear Angel Juan,

You used to guard my sleep like a panther biting back my pain with the edge of your teeth. You carried me into the dark dream jungle, loping past the hungry vines, crossing the

265

shiny fish-scale river. We left my tears behind in a chiming silver pool. We left my sorrow in the muddy hollows. When I woke up you were next to me, damp and matted, your eyes hazy, trying to remember the way I clung to you, how far down we went.

Was the journey too far, Angel Juan? Did we go too far?

School's out pretty soon. Can't wait. I hardly talk to anybody there. Sometimes I feel like I come from another planet. Planet of the Witch Babies where the sky is purple, the stars are cameras, the flowers are drums and all the boys look like Angel Juan. When I'm at school I wish I came from my own planet. And I want to go back.

I've got some money from *The Goat Guys*, the movie my dad directed about the slam-jam band my almost-sister Cherokee and her soul-love Raphael and me and Angel Juan are in. Were in—before. In the movie we all played us.

The angel medallion that came in the mail sleeps in the hollow part of my neck. I can't send a letter telling that or anything else to Angel Juan.

I don't know where he is. But I'm going to look for him.

The only thing is where to stay in New York. So I ask Weetzie about Charlie Bat's place.

Weetzie's dad Charlie Bat died a long time ago before I was born. But Weetzie begged her mom Brandy-Lynn not to let go of his old apartment in the Village. It's like she doesn't want to admit that he's dead.

Weetzie is sitting in the room with the dried roses and painted fans all over the walls and the stained-glass pyramid-palm-tree windows that look out on the canyon. From here you can see a few blue pools like the canyon's eyes and the waves of palm, eucalyptus and oleander like the canyon's swirly green hair. The canyon talks in different voices. In the day she growls with traffic, but real early or late at night she sings with mockingbirds and you can hear her wind-chime jewelry. Angel Juan and I used to sneak over garden walls and swim in the pool eyes at night. We used to climb the trees, tangling in the braids of leaves, and Angel Juan told me he was going to build us a tree house someday. His dad Marquez, who makes frames and furniture, taught him how to build tree houses.

In our house that feels like a tree house sometimes—deep in the canyon, nested in leaves—Weetzie's working on the script for the next movie she and my dad are making. It's a ghost story.

"I'm going to New York," I say. "Could I stay at Charlie Bat's?"

"Are you sure you want to go to New York, honey?"

"I'm going to New York," I say. I start to nibble at my fingernails, chew my cuticles.

Weetzie goes over to her 1920's dressing table with the round mirror and the lotus-blossom lights. The little genie lamp is sitting there—still gold but empty of genies and wishes now. Weetzie takes an old photo album out of a dressing table drawer. It's so old that almost all the pile of the pink velvet has worn down around the gold curlicues and cupids. It's so old that it was probably red velvet once, a long time ago. Weetzie sits on her seashell-shaped love seat that is the same velvet pink as the photo album and pats it for me to sit next to her. I climb up the side and perch, looking over her shoulder instead. Inside the photo album is a picture of a tall skinny man with sunken eyes and bones like the guys in those old black-and-white silent movies. Kind of like Valentino but a lot thinner and not so healthy-looking. The man has his arm around a little blonde woman with a big lipsticky smile and slidey gold mules on her feet. They seem really in love standing in front of this cherry yellow T-bird clinking champagne glasses: Weetzie's mom and dad when they were young. Before Brandy-Lynn and Charlie and the champagne glasses and the T-bird got smashed. Before Brandy-Lynn kicked Charlie out and he went to New York and died there.

Weetzie shows me a picture of her and her real daughter, my almost-sister Cherokee, with Charlie from the time when they went to visit him just before he died. It was taken in one of those photo booths. Cherokee was just a baby then with little tufts of white hair like a Kewpie doll or something. Weetzie looks exactly the same as she does now—elf mom—maybe a little skinnier and her hair was a little shorter, kind of spiky. But Charlie doesn't look much like a silent-movie star anymore. He looks more like a ghost. There's a spooky light around his head and his eyeballs are rolled up. Weetzie has her arm around him really tight and her fingers pressed into his shoulder.

She's never held on to me like that.

Not that I'd let her.

"I think people leave here before we think they're gone," Weetzie whispers as she looks at the picture. "And when you're with them you know it. Part of you knows it—that they've left. But you don't let yourself really accept it. And then later you think about it and you know you knew."

I can see her going back to that time, trying to find her dad.

"We had to walk up nine flights of stairs to his apartment in the dark and every time he whistled 'Rag Mop' to us—you know, 'R-A-G-G M-O-P-P Rag Mop doodely-doo' to make us laugh. But that time he was quiet. When we got to the apartment he went and stood by the window and shut his eyes, listening to the echoes of kids playing outside way down there in the distance, and he said, 'It sounds like when I was a little boy in Brooklyn and we ran around the streets in the twilight, hoping it would never get all the way dark so we'd have to go in. Kids playing sound the same wherever you are. They sound so happy. They don't know what's in store for them.'

"I said it could still be happy, like kids playing in the street before they have to go in for dinner. My friends and I, we live like that. Come live with us. But he was far away already." Weetzie closes her eyes. It's real quiet for a minute and I can hear the canyon tossing her hair and her wind-chime earrings clinking like Charlie and Brandy-Lynn's champagne glasses in the photograph.

I wonder what it would be like to talk to Charlie Bat. I bet he would get it. He died from drugs all alone. He was an artist but he didn't make pretty things. Weetzie says he wrote movies and plays about monsters, but they were really about the monster feelings inside.

"I miss him so much. But I can't even dream about him," Weetzie says.

What she says reminds me of Angel Juan. Sometimes it almost feels like Angel Juan is dead too.

It's like Weetzie's reading my mind for a second. "You really need to look for him, don't you?"

I am busy with my cuticle gnaw. "Can I go see Charlie Bat?" I mumble.

Weetzie stares at me like she's seen a ghost. "Lanky lizards," she whispers.

"I mean Charlie *Bat's*—his place," I say.

Weetzie nods, looking at her photo album.

In a way I'm glad she's into letting me go. But another part of me wishes she didn't want me to. It seems like she's thinking more about Charlie Bat than about me.

Dear Angel Juan,

Why haven't you written again? It's been three weeks one day and three hours since the last time I saw you in the fog.

I try to dream about you but I can't. The harder I try to find you, the farther away you get. Instead I dream about my real mother Vixanne Wigg.

There's a knock on the shed door and I think—Angel Juan—and open it. But it's a tall lanky lanka in a blonde wig. She has purple crazy eyes. And they are the same as mine. She's my mother. I try to close the door but she shoves herself inside. Her wig falls off. Long black hair pours down wrapping me up like vine arms. She forces apples down my throat and needles into my fingers.

I wake up choked, prickly. It's one thing to read fairy tales when you are a regular kid but what about when your mother is a real witch? Or maybe it's the same for all kids these days. People really do inject apples with needles full of poison and hand them out at doorways. The good thing about fairy tales, though, is that there is always a fairy god-mother and/or a prince to take the curse away.

Sometimes when this same dream used to wake me up in the middle of the night, you said, "The curse is broken," and put me back to sleep with lullaby kisses.

Maybe Vixanne can help me find you.

I get up, put on my cowboy-boot roller skates and go out into a fog as green as the fog was green on the night before Angel Juan left.

I haven't been to the big pink house in the hills for years but somehow I know exactly how to get back there.

The way our dog Tiki-Tee keeps going back to where he was born, the place my family uses as a studio now. He slinks out and trots through the canyon down the street named for the newest moon all the way to the cottage. Whenever he's missing, we know we'll find him there curled up in between the stone gnomes under the rosebushes.

Just like Tiki-Tee finds the cottage, I find the place where I was born. It blooms out of the fog. It's all falling apart now. The driveway is empty and the windows are caked with dust. Maybe Vixanne moved away.

I take off my skates, creep up to the door and knock. No one answers. The door swings open by itself and I slip in, skidding on my socks.

There's the hallway lined with mirrors where I freaked myself once. Now I know they're me but I want to smash my reflections. So in the mirror I'll look like I feel. Pieces. But if you break a mirror there are just more whole little yous in every piece.

I go into the dusty sunken room. Empty. Cold air burns in the empty fireplace. There are squished tubes of paint and canvases everywhere. And lots of big portraits of Vixanne Wigg in colors like tropical flowers—almost glow-in-the-dark.

Vixanne powdery-pink and sparkle-platinum as Jayne Mansfield chomp-gnawing off a cluster chunk of crystally-white dry-ice rock candy. Vixanne lounging in a fluorescent green jungle tied up in her own jungle-green writhe-vine hair. Dressed in milky apple blossoms and holding a

272

grimacy shrively monkey-face apple. Wreath of giant blue and orange butterflies around her head. With a rainbow-jewel-scaled mermaid tail. A ripple-haunched horse from the waist down. Vixanne with black roses tattooed on her naked chest. All of the Vixannes staring at me with purple eyes.

I go up to the one with the tattoo. Pain-ink flowers. Meat-eating roses in a demony garden. The paint is rich and smooth like batter. I wish Vixanne would paint me:

Angel Juan's name tattooed on my heart in a wreath of black roses.

Something rustles. Heavy crunched silk. I turn around.

"You've been gone a long time," says a voice. She sounds tired.

Vixanne's long dark hair that she used to wear under the Jayne Mansfield wig is hacked short and kind of uneven like she did it herself. It reminds me of me when Cherokee cut off my hair with toenail scissors when we were babies. Vixanne wears a black silk dress with watery patterns in it. She is so different from the glam lanka I remember.

"Remember those photographs you gave me?" she says.

When I found her the first time, I gave her some pictures I took. An old woman shaking her fist and screaming at the sun. A man who was too young to be dying. Me looking like a little lost loon waif thing. I wanted my mother to have something when I left. I wanted her to see.

"At first I put them away and didn't look at them but

273

I kept thinking about you. You were so little skating around with that camera seeing all the pain."

Her eyes roll in her head. I want to leave but instead I sit down and start playing with the paints on the table. It feels good to squeeze the tubes of paint. Smell the stinkster turpentine. Vixanne sits down next to me. I want to paint a picture of Angel Juan. As big as life. A boy that will never leave.

"I like to be alone," Vixanne says. "I've started painting. I'm not anyone's slave now."

I listen to the sound of her voice and feel all the twilight purple eyes watching me while my hand moves by itself in the shadowy room.

Maybe hours go by.

"I look things right in the eye now. That's the best way. Right in the eye and without anything to make it easier," says Vixanne.

I look down and drop my paintbrush. It skids across the floor. Instead of Angel Juan I've made a picture of a man with big teeth eating a cake that drips icing all over his face and hands. It gives me a creepy-crawly-heebee-jeebee feeling.

I pretend the goose bumps studding my arms are 'cause I'm cold.

I take black paint and wipe out the man with the cake like he was never there. "I don't want to look at anything or anybody except for Angel Juan."

Vixanne shakes her head. Then she says, "You have

to leave now, Witch Baby. You can come back after your journey."

She goes to the door with me and I put on my skates. I wonder how I will ever make it home and then all the way to New York. The parts of my body feel held together by strings you could cut with a scissors.

"Remember to look in the eye. That's what you taught me," Vixanne says. "Look at your own darkness."

I leave my mother all complete in a gnarly snarly forest of herself, and the puppet parts of my body skate away into the fog.

I am going to leave.

I think that Weetzie misses her dead dad more than she will miss me.

Vixanne is busy painting pictures of her own face.

The rest of my family is working on their movie. It's about ghosts but if anybody knows about being haunted it's me.

In the shed by the light of the globe lamp I pack up my bat-shaped backpack. Angel Juan has taken my mind and my heart away and his ghost is trapped in the empty places that are left. Not so I feel like he's with me. Just like always remembering that he's not. So it's not like I can just sit around here waiting. I have to go find him.

∽❧

I am going to take a cab to the airport because everybody's too busy to drive me. My dad is in the desert by himself meditating about the new movie. Weetzie has a yoga class that she hates to miss.

Just before I leave I go into the kitchen. Blue and yellow handpainted sunflower tiles. Stained-glass sunflower skylight. Reminds me of the bruises I gave myself when Angel Juan left.

Weetzie puts out a glass of honey lemonade and a stack of pumpkin pancakes for me but I can't eat anything.

"New York makes my nerves feel like this," she says, sliding something down the butcher-block table to me. "Maybe if you wear it yours won't."

It's a skeleton charm bracelet. I pick it up and the skeletons click their plastic bones. Weetzie usually gives people stuff with cherubs, flowers and stars. I guess witch babies get bone things.

"I'm sorry I can't take you to the airport," she says. "Are you sure you'll be all right?"

I roll my eyes and don't talk. I'm afraid I'll start to cry like some watery-knee weaselette.

"Well, remember, Mr. Mallard and Mr. Meadows will give you the key to the apartment and they'll help you if you need anything."

The cab is honking outside. Weetzie tries to kiss me but I am out the door already. Maybe she should have been a little more clutch like in that picture of her and her dad Charlie Bat where she looks like she'll never let go.

Dear Angel Juan,

I'm on a plane. I imagine you out there on a cloud, playing your bass and grinning at me, wearing chunky black shoes and Levi's with rips at the knees. I imagine the rest of the band and it is one heavenly combo—Jimi and Jim and John and Bob and Elvis—all the dudes you are into.

All those guys are dead.

So I think about you down on the ground with me.

We are at the movies. The air-conditioned air on our bare arms and the crackle and smell of the popcorn and the crackle of the film in between the previews that is the same sound as the popcorn almost. And we're holding hands and we know we'll hold hands on the way to the truck and even while we're driving home in between clutch shifting and then we'll get into bed together and hold each other in our sleep and wake up together in the morning and slurp fruit shakes and munch jammy peanut-butter-banana sandwiches.

It's summer. We're on the wooden deck. We've been in the sun all day and just had a hot tub. You're playing bass and I'm playing my drums. Our music weaves together like our bodies in the night. The lanterns are lit and the air smells like honeysuckle, barbecue smoke and incense. The dark canyon is rustling with heat around us.

We're in Joshua Tree. We sit on a huge flat rock still warm from the day and you comb the tangles out of my hair and it doesn't even hurt. We eat honey-nut Guru Chews and

277

watch the full moon rise. The moon makes my insides stir.
Then we hear something. You stop combing my tangles.
Music. Pouring from somewhere in the empty desert. It's like
fountains in the sand or sky islands. "Celestial music," you
say. No one else hears it.

I tell myself I have to stop thinking words like celestial
and heavenly. And angel. But that last one is hard.

I load the cab with the globe lamp, my camera, my roller
skates and my bat-shaped backpack. The angel medallion
is around my neck. As the cab drives along the highway
from the airport into Manhattan I shake my wrist so that
the skeletons on my charm bracelet do their bone jig.
Looking up at all the big buildings and seeing the crowd
scurrying along, I know what Weetzie meant about her
nerves and the skeletons. New York is not a Weetzie-city.
Weetzie is a kid of the city where movies are made and it's
always sunny, where Marilyn's ghost rises up out of her
spiky birdy footprints to dance on beams of light with red
lacquer dragons in front of the Chinese Theater, and James
Dean's head star-watches with you at the observatory like
a fallen star somebody found and put on a pedestal; a city
where you can only tell the seasons by the peonies or
pumpkins or poinsettias at the florists'.

But me, maybe I fit in a place like this. Maybe the cold
inside of me will seem less cold in this winter. Maybe the
tall buildings will make the brick walls I build for myself

seem smaller. Maybe the noises in my head will quiet down in the middle of all the other noises. Or maybe my cold and walls and noise will get worse.

It looks frosty out and the store windows are filled with red velvet bows, white fur, plastic reindeer with long eyelashes and flaming Christmas trees and for the first time I realize that I won't be with my almost-family for the holidays. I was so busy thinking about finding Angel Juan that I didn't even realize that before.

"Where are you from?" the driver asks after a while. He has a beautiful island voice and it makes me feel warmer just hearing it. For a second I think about Angel Juan and me sharing a ginger beer on the rocks behind a fall of see-through water and ruby-red flowers that he keeps catching and sticking in my tangles.

Another cab swerves into our lane and my driver slams the brakes. I'm jolted out of Jamaica.

"Los Angeles."

"Oh, Angel City. You won't be finding too many of those here. Especially in the meat district."

I look out the window at the meat-packing plants lining the cobblestone streets by the river. Men are unloading marbly sides of beef from a truck. There isn't much sign of Christmas out here.

"Of what?" I ask.

"Angels," he says.

"I just need to find one," I say.

We pull up to the brownstone building where Charlie

Bat lived and died. The driver says, "Well, if you're looking for angels in New York, at least this is a good place."

"What?"

"I've heard things about that building, that's all," he says, helping me unload. "Magic stuff. Good luck."

I zip up my leather jacket and hand him his money. "Thanks," I say, thinking he is just trying to be nice about the angel thing. But when I see how he is staring up at the brownstone I wonder what he meant. He has this look on his face—kind of wonder or something. Charlie's building doesn't look magic to me though. Just old and ready to crumble. A few of the windows are cracked. It reminds me of an old vaudeville guy who wears baggy dirty suits and can't dance anymore, and somebody beat him up and smashed his glasses.

I stand on the curb and watch the cab drive away. It's dark now. When did that happen? No time for sunset here. Just a fast change of backdrop like in a store window display.

Some dancer girls colt by. They look like their feet hurt but they don't care because they've been dancing. A woman holds on to her kid in a different way from how parents hold kids where I come from. She is gripping the little mittened hand and the kid's face looks pale and almost old. Two men in tweed coats and mufflers go into the building. One walks with a cane and wears sunglasses even though it's night and the other is carrying a bag of groceries. I can see French bread and flowers sticking out of the top. The flowers look like they are wondering what they are doing in this city like they flew here by mistake and saw these two men and decided that their bag was probably the best place to land.

I want to take photographs for the first time since Angel Juan left. But I don't. I won't use my eyes for anything except finding Angel Juan.

I try to picture Weetzie coming here, a long time ago with Cherokee tucked in her arms, all excited to show her new baby to her dad. She must have felt kind of weird though, standing in front of this building in the middle of the meat-packing district. Maybe that's when she decided to stop eating meat when she saw the dead cows unloaded from the trucks. She must have been freaked about Charlie living here all alone. I wish I got to come meet Charlie too. I wonder if he would have thought I was his real granddaughter like Cherokee.

Inside the lobby is dark and musty-dusty. There is an elevator but it has an "Out of Order" sign on it so I find the stairs.

The stairs are even darker. As I walk up I think I hear somebody whistling a tune. What is it? Sort of silly but also sad, like whoever is whistling wants to stop but can't or like a circus clown with a smile painted on.

I stop on the third floor and knock. A gray-haired slinkster man answers. He is one of the men in the tweed coats I saw on the street.

"I'm Witch Baby."

"Witch Baby! Come in. Weetzie has been calling all day to see if you've arrived. Come in."

The little warm apartment is covered—floor, walls, ceiling—in faded Persian pomegranate-courtyard-garden carpets. There are lots of velvety loungy couches and chairs that make me feel like curling up like Tiki-Tee does in the bend of my knees, lots of overstuffed tapestry pillows and bookshelves stuffed with old leather books. See-through veils hanging from the ceiling. Tall viny iron candlesticks blooming big candles frosted with dripped wax. What it makes me think about mostly is crawling inside that genie lamp Weetzie has at home—what it would be like in there.

The man who walked with a cane is arranging the flowers in a golden vase that almost looks like the genie lamp.

"Meadows, Charlie Bat's grandchild has arrived," says the first man. The man named Meadows comes over and holds out his hand. He has a sweet boy-face even though he is probably almost as old as the other man and he is still wearing his dark glasses.

"That's Meadows and I'm Mallard," the first man says. "For some reason your mother thought that my name was funny. Something to do with ducks. I didn't get it."

In my family duck means a pounceable guy who likes guys, which is what Mallard is—a very grown-up gray duck—but I don't know how to explain it. "In my family names are a kind of weird thing," I say.

"I can tell," says Mallard. "Now where did they come

up with Witch Baby? You are much too pretty for that. She looks like a skinny, boyish, young Sophia Loren hiding under a head full of tangles." He turns to Meadows, who smiles and nods.

I sure don't think I look like any gorgeous Italian actress with a big chest. "Weetzie tried to name me Lily but it never stuck," I say.

"Lily sounds right for you," says Meadows. "May we call you Lily?"

"Sure."

Mallard says, "You must be exhausted, Lily. Would you like to sleep on our couch? It might be more comfortable than your grandfather's apartment. There isn't any furniture there."

"He wasn't really my true grandfather," I say. "He was my almost-grandfather. He's Weetzie's dad and she met my dad when she was working at Duke's because she had wished for him on the genie lamp that Dirk—that's her best friend—Dirk's grandma Fifi gave her and she also wished for a duck for Dirk and a house for them to live in and Fifi died and Dirk met Duck and Weetzie and My Secret Agent Lover Man—that's my dad's name—all moved into Fifi's cottage but then Weetzie wanted a baby and my dad didn't want one so she had Cherokee with Dirk and Duck and my dad left and met Vixanne Wigg who is a lanka witch and stayed with her but then he came back to Weetzie and one day Vixanne brought me and left me on the doorstep in a basket and Weetzie and my dad and Dirk

283

and Duck made me like part of the family but in a way
I'm not."

"Very confusing," says Mallard. "Sometime you must
draw us a family tree."

"Okay. But I'll be okay at Charlie's."

"What have you brought with you?" Mallard is looking
at the globe lamp.

"Weetzie thinks it'll be good luck."

Meadows nods all solemn. "Apotropaic."

"What?"

"It means something to ward off evil. You will be comfortable wherever you sleep. Can you have dinner with us
tomorrow night?"

"Sure."

Mallard hands me a set of keys on a big silver ring. My
wrist is so skinny it could almost be a bracelet.

"We know a macrobiotic place with the best tofu pie,"
Meadows says.

Soybean-curd pie doesn't sound so great to me but I
don't say anything.

"Meanwhile, you must take some of our groceries."
Mallard goes to the kitchen and comes back with a paper
bag full of food.

"That's okay."

"You must. You have to eat and it's not a great idea
to be running around alone at night. I'll show you up to
Charlie's place."

I say good-bye to Meadows and walk up seven flights

of stairs with Mallard, the keys, the food and a stack of blankets to Charlie Bat's apartment.

Mallard opens the door and lets me in. "No one's lived here for a long time," he says. "We take care of it and we tried to make it as nice as possible for you but still . . ."

The apartment is smaller than the one downstairs and it's cold and empty except for an old trunk thing made out of leather. The paint on the walls is peeling. But there is a view of the city, not a speck of dust-grunge anywhere and a Persian rug like the ones downstairs on the floor. Suddenly I feel so tired I want to fall into the garden of the rug, just keep falling forever through pink leaves.

"Now you'd better eat something and get right to bed," Mallard says, putting down the blankets. "We thought you'd be safe and comfortable on the rug. There's no phone but you just run downstairs anytime if you need anything."

He hands me the groceries. "Remember dinner tomorrow. Good night."

As he closes the door I feel loneliness tunnel through my body. I look inside the bag of food and there's granola, milk, strawberries, bananas, peanut butter, bagels, mineral water and peppermint tea. I sit on the old trunk and eat a banana-and-peanut-butter bagel sandwich to try to fill up the tunnel the loneliness made. Then I try to open the trunk but it's locked. I go stand by the window.

New York is like a forbidden box. I am looking down into it. There's the firefly building on Angel Juan's card and the dark danger streets. All these sparkling electric treasures and all these strange scary things that shouldn't have been let out but they all were. And somewhere, down there, with the angels and the demons, is Angel Juan.

I plug in the globe lamp and lie down on Mallard and Meadows's carpet under the blankets in a corner.

"Apotropaic," Meadows said.

I hold on to the globe like it is my heart I am trying to hold together. But my heart isn't solid and full of light like the lamp. It's cracked and empty and I just lie there not trying to hold it together anymore, letting my dry no-tear sobs break it up into little pieces, wanting to dream about Angel Juan—at least that.

But when I do fall asleep it's like being buried with nothing except dirt filling up my eyes.

Morning. Strawberry sky dusted with white winter powder-sugar sun. And nobody to munch on it with.

I drink some tea, get my camera and go out into the bright cold.

As soon as I start skating I get the sick empty feeling in my stomach again. But it's worse this time. How am I ever supposed to find Angel Juan in this city? It is the clutchiest thing I have ever tried to do. What made me think I could find him? Here is this whole city full of monuments and garbage and Chinese food and cannolis and steaks and drug dealers and paintings and subways and cigarettes and mannequins and a million other things and I am looking for one kind-of-small boy who left me. As if I know where he would be. As if he wanted me to find him. Why am I here at all?

I see men crumple-slumped in the gutters like empty coats and women who hide their bodies and look like their heads hurt. I see couples of men that look older and thinner than they should and kids that look harder than everybody pretends kids look. Everything vicious and broken and my eyes ache dry and tearless in my sockets. I can't even take pictures.

Subway.

In Angel Juan's letter: *I close my eyes underground to try to see you jammin' on your drums, your hair all flying out like petals, beat pulsing in your flower-stem neck.*

I go down, tilting my roller-skate wheels into the steps and holding on to the rail so I don't free-fall.

The trains are all I can hear burning through the emptiness inside of me like acid on a cut—no music. There aren't any boys playing guitars down here, their eyelashes grazing their cheekbones to protect them from the fluorescent light, their bodies shivery like guitar strings.

I get on a train and stand in between all the padded people with puffy faces and blind eyes.

I climb up the subway stairs with my skates still on, using my arms to hoist me.

On the street I see a scary-looking girl with jungle-wild hair and eyes and then I see it's me reflected in a stained

287

oval mirror that's propped against some trash cans. I drag
the mirror back to the apartment holding it away from me
so I don't have to see my face.

I'm thrashed and mashed—starving and ready to cry
again. My arms and legs are shaking and I can hardly make
it up to the ninth floor carrying the mirror, even with my
skates off. My head is full of wound-pictures, my camera is
empty and I feel farther away from Angel Juan than ever.

On the door of Charlie Bat's apartment is a note.

*Lily: Meet us in the lobby for dinner at 6:00. Your benevo-
lent almost-almost uncles, Meadows and Mallard.*

I would rather collapse in the pomegranate garden
of the Persian carpet and go to sleep forever, but I make
myself wash my face and go downstairs.

Mallard and Meadows are waiting for me in the lobby
wearing their tweed coats.

"How was your day?" Mallard asks.

I shrug.

"You look tired. Did you eat anything?"

"We are going to buy you a nice big dinner," Meadows
says.

They walk on either side of me like tweedy angels or
like halves of a pair of wings as we go through the streets
past the meat-packing plants. Meadows's cane taps on the
cobblestones. Some six-foot-tall skulkster drag queens wait
in the shadows flashing at the passing cars. Mallard picks a

wildflower that grows up between the stones. It's a strange-looking lily and I wonder why it's growing here in the middle of the meat and dark.

The restaurant is hidden on a narrow winding side street. We come in out of the cold.

This place is like somebody's enchanted living room. There's flowered paper on the walls. If you look close you can see tiny mysterious creatures peering out from between the wallpaper flowers and the lavender-and-white frosted rosette-shaped glass lights strung around the ceiling blink on and off, making it look like the creatures are dancing. On every table there are burning towers of wax roses that give off a honey smell. The music isn't like anything I ever heard before. It's crickety and rivery. The waitress has a dreamy-face, long blonde curls and a tiny waist. She is wearing a crochet lace dress. She serves us tea that smells like a forest and makes my headache go away. Then she brings huge mismatched antique floral china plates heaped with brown rice and these vegetables that I've never seen before but taste like what goddesses would eat if they ate their vegetables. Miso-oniony, golden-pumpkiny, sweety-lotusy, sesame-seaweedy. The food makes me stop shaking.

"How did you find this place?" I ask.

"We try everything but this is the best," says Meadows.

"This food helps us write better," says Mallard. "We commune better when we aren't digesting animals."

"What do you write?" I ask.

Mallard looks at Meadows. Then he says, "We write about . . . phenomena. Supernatural phenomena."

"Ghosts," says Meadows.

"Like what my family's movie is about."

"Really?" says Mallard. "That must be why they sent you here."

"I don't think so."

"Maybe they thought you'd find a ghost here." Mallard chuckles.

"But you won't," Meadows says. "We haven't found a single ghost in our building."

The waitress brings more tea and a cart of desserts that she says are made without any sugar or milk stuff. Mallard and Meadows and I share a piece of creamy you-wouldn't-believe-it's-soy-curd tofu pie, a piece of scrumptious yam pie and a dense kiss piece of caroby almond cake. The carob reminds me of the walk Angel Juan and I took before he left when we stepped on the St. John's bread pods and they cracked open and smelled like chocolate.

Why aren't you here? I think. Why aren't you here, Angel Juan?

We're sitting on cushions in Mallard and Meadows's apartment listening to Indian sitar music. If I close my eyes I can see a goddess with lots of arms and almondy eyes moving her head from side to side like it's not part of her neck, hypnotizing a garden of snakes. Maybe she's hiding behind the veils that hang from the ceiling.

"Feel better?" Meadows asks.

"Yes, thanks for dinner. I'll take you guys out tomorrow night."

"We have to go on a trip, Lily," Mallard says. "We leave tonight."

"It's for our book," says Meadows. He turns his head to me. He isn't wearing his glasses and suddenly his eyes catch the light. I have this feeling that he can see. "We are visiting a house in Ireland where a woman's father keeps appearing."

"Except he's dead," says Mallard.

"Except he's about this big," says Meadows, holding his hands a few inches apart. "Sitting on her teacup."

"If you want you can stay at our place instead of upstairs while we're away," says Mallard. "It might be more comfortable."

He looks very serious and I wonder if he's thinking about how Charlie Bat died up there. I hadn't even thought about it last night because I'd been so tired and crazed about Angel Juan: Charlie Bat probably OD'd in the same corner where I slept. But I kind of like being in my almost-grandpa's place.

I try not to show how I feel about my new friends going away, how I know tonight with its macro-heaven dinner and goddess music will fade, leaving me just as empty as before, loneliness attacking all my cells like a disease.

"Thanks but I'll be okay," I say.

"Did you sleep all right last night?" Meadows asks.

"I didn't even dream."

"We'll leave keys to our place," says Mallard. "In case you change your mind. Use the phone anytime and whatever is in the fridge." Then he goes, "I'm sorry we won't be with you for Christmas."

"But we'll be back New Year's Eve day," says Meadows.

When I leave he hands me the meaty white lily Mallard picked.

I carry the lily in front of me up the dark staircase like it is a lantern. And then a creepster thing happens. Light *does* start coming out of the flower. At first I think from the flower but then the light starts jumping all over the walls in front of me lighting the way. Someone is whistling somewhere. No, the *light* is whistling.

I get to the top of the stairs on the tenth floor. The light goes out and the whistling stops. I must have imagined it because I'm tired. Maybe I'm going crazy.

I think that all of me is broken. Not just my heart which cracked the night Angel Juan told me he was going away. Not just my body slammed with the sadness I see with no one there to put me back together in bed at night. Now it feels like my mind too.

In Charlie's apartment I put the flower in a teacup and look at myself in the mirror I found on the street. I can hardly stand to see my face. Pinchy and hungry-looking. I don't need a hummingbird around my neck for people to see I am searching for love.

I wrap the mirror in a sheet and hit it with a hammer I found in a kitchen drawer. Feeling the smooth whole thing turn into sharp jags shifting under the sheet, spilling out all bright and broken. I don't even care about seven years' bad luck.

But then I look into the jags and there I am—still all one scary-looking Witch Baby in every piece.

I just want to disappear. Everything to stop.

That's when the whistling flower lights up again. I sit staring as the light jumps out of the flower, all around the apartment and lands inside the globe lamp, making it day all over the world. And instead of whistling the light starts singing a song—soft and snap-crackly like an old reel of film.

"R-A-G-G M-O-P-P, Rag Mop doodely-doo."

Lanky lizards, as Weetzie would say. Maybe I am cracking up.

"Who are you?"

The voice doesn't answer. Only keeps on singing— "R-A-G-G M-O-P-P."

Why would somebody write a whole song about a mop made out of rags? And why would they spell it?

The light dances out of the globe lamp and all over the walls to the tune it is whistling. It's jiggling doing a jig.

Then it flashes in a piece of broken mirror and I go

over to look but instead of me I see this guy.

He's black and white and flickery like an old movie; he's wearing a rumpled black suit and a top hat like a spooky circus ringmaster. Light is filling him up like he swallowed it and it is coming through his pores, making him kind of fidget-dance around in the mirror like one of the plastic skeletons on my charm bracelet. His eyes are ringed with dark shadows like the negatives of two moons before a rain. He wrinkles his forehead, moves his hands and opens and closes his mouth.

"Who are you?" I ask.

Finally he coughs, clears his throat and says, "You're my baby's witch baby and you are witnessing a spectacular spectral spectacle sort of."

I try to look deeper in the mirror but it's like a smog-mirage in L.A. when the heat ripples and blurs like water or like looking into the Pacific Ocean so dull with crud it's like a smoggy sky. I can't see too well but I know it's him.

Charlie B., Chucky Bat, C. Bat, Mr C. Bbbbb-b-Bat. My almost-grandpa-Bat Charles.

He's a lot like he was in the pictures Weetzie showed me but if he didn't look healthy then he really doesn't look so well now and he's not in color anymore.

What do you say to a ghost? "I'm not Weetzie's real kid."

"You look real to me."

"I don't feel like it lately."

"Neither do I." He laughs soft. I think about the pop

in the film before a Charlie Chaplin movie starts. "We have some things in common."

"Yeah. I mean besides the unreal thing. I take pictures which is kind of like making movies. And you made things up in your head." I stop. Do you say made or make to a ghost?

"Make," says Charlie, smiling a little.

"*Make*. I do that."

"Something else, Witch Baby." I wonder if he has curly toes. But he says, "I was by myself a lot too. I played the pain game."

So am I going to end up like him, alone and losing it because I don't find Angel Juan? I wonder. I remember the made/make thing. I hope he can't always read my mind.

"You don't have to," he says. "End up like me." Oh well for secrets.

All of a sudden I wish he was real. I wish he was my real grandfather or even my almost-grandfather but alive with his heart beating and sending warmth through his body—warmth that would turn into hugs and those plays he wrote. I wish he could pick me up and hold me. I'd smell coffee and cigarettes on his collar. We'd eat hot cinnamon-raisin bagels together and walk all over the city. I'd play my drums for him. He'd make everything okay.

"Do Mallard and Meadows know about you?" I ask.

"They are very nice gentlemen but they ignore the ghost closest to them."

"They'd get a kick out of you. Right in this city. In their building."

"They travel all over but this city is full of its own surprises," Charlie says. "Things pop out of the darkness like elves and fairies in a rotten wood or ghosts in a ruined house. I could show you if you want, the way I showed Weetzie and Cherokee." His voice cracks on their names and his face fades a little in the mirror.

"I am here to look for somebody," I say.

"Well you've found me. And I've found you."

"No. I mean I'm here to look for my boyfriend Angel Juan. He went away and wrote me one letter and . . ."

But Charlie twinkles out of the mirror—a light again.

"Charlie?"

The light disappears inside a crack in the old leather trunk.

I try to open the trunk—tugging at the straps and wedging my gnawed fingertips against the buckles. It's still all locked up. Charlie is gone.

What a slam-a-rama dream!

But it wasn't. Or I'm still dreaming now. Because the first thing I hear when I wake up at almost noon is that singing again. This time it's "Witch Baby, Baby" to the tune of "Louie, Louie": "We gotta go now."

Go where? "Charlie?"

The light is by the window. "Take a picture," he says.

"Of what?"

"Of me."

I reach for my camera and focus on the light. But through the lens I see all of Mr. Bat again like in the mirror. He is looking out the window at the gray day, one bony hand pressed against the cloudy glass. He's so so thin, his jacket and pants just hanging on him like if you dressed one of my charm-bracelet skeletons in a suit. He turns and grins at me but only with his mouth not his eyes. His shoulders are hunched like two people at a funeral.

"Do you know how many versions of 'Louie, Louie' there are? It's unbelievable. Hundreds. No one knows what the real lyrics are."

Oh.

"You don't have much to eat here," he says.

"You eat?"

"No, but it's the idea. Like when I used to write about people traveling in space and battling monsters. We should go out."

"I'm going to go look for Angel Juan in Harlem today. He wrote me that he ate breakfast there."

"Sylvia's is in Harlem. That was Weetzie's favorite. Come on," Charlie says on the other side of my camera lens. "How often do I have the chance to watch my grandchild eat breakfast? Sweet-potato pie. Grits."

Maybe it's him calling me his grandchild or the grits like in Angel Juan's card or maybe just his moons-before-the-rain eyes but how can I not go with Charlie Bat? I put down my camera and he's a light again, ready to lead me out into the city.

We go down into the subway. It's so different today. Charlie—he's a dazzle at my shoulder like rhinestones splitting up the sun—whispers in my ear which way to skate.

An old woman with a shopping cart full of fish and bursting flowers made out of bright-colored rags. She's sitting on a bench sewing like she's in her living room or her little shop, sewing fast like she can't stop, more and more tropical finned flower fish and exotic polka-dot flowers, like if she stopped the subway would turn real.

Three boys with guitars. One has a blonde bristle flattop, one is small with a long braid, one is tall with brown skin and ringlets. They are all wearing white T-shirts, torn jeans, steel-toed boots and strands of beads and amulets—peace signs, ankhs, crystals, scarabs. Their music reminds me of what Angel Juan and I heard in Joshua Tree. Celestial. Turning the subway into an oasis or a church. I wonder if they have wings, matted feathers folded up under their T-shirts.

A little farther along the air shimmers with the silver steel drum slamster sound. Some Rasta men with long swinging dreadlocks play. Makes my whole body ache for my drums for the first time since Angel Juan left.

The train comes, biting up the music. They should

make subway trains that sound like steel drums.

Charlie and I get on. No music here or flowers or fish. I hang on to the hand rail feeling my skate wheels roll at every stop and start like they want to take off, slam me down the aisles. What if I let go and let them? Would anybody even look up?

I use one hand to look at Charlie through my camera. He's sitting next to me jiggling his legs. The woman on the other side of him sneers. I guess she thinks I'm taking her picture. She's already growly 'cause I wouldn't let her sit in Charlie's seat. Charlie starts to whistle like trying to calm me down.

What song it it? Not "Rag Mop."

"'Papa's gonna buy you a hummingbird,'" Charlie sings. I don't think those are the right words. But the way he sings them is like a real grandfather would to a baby they love.

Harlem.

One thing good about Charlie being a ghost and not a guy is he can keep up with me on my skates and I'm jamming through the crowds of people like a hell bat. I feel like the whitest white-thing around except for Charlie, and he's a vapor.

I remember how I always wanted to slip inside of Angel Juan's brown skin. It seemed safer than mine. Now especially.

299

The sky is still gray and flat like stone, but when we go inside Sylvia's, sun pours through the windows. Sylvia's is warm and glinty with tinsel and it smells like somebody's kitchen.

"I brought Weetzie here," Charlie says.

"You talk about her a lot," I say. A woman at the next table rolls her eyes at her friend and I remember who I'm talking to and cough.

"She ate everything on the whole menu. And she was such a skinny bones. I don't think her mother fed her properly when she was growing up. How is she, Witch Baby? What's your life like now?"

I whisper so nobody takes me away for talking to myself. "We built a house in the canyon out of windows we collected. We play music and make movies. We eat a lot. Vegetarian. Weetzie's happy I think mostly. She misses you though."

"I wish I had talked to her about more things before I died. She shouldn't be missing me so much anymore. It's been a long time. But I miss her too," he says. "Maybe it's my fault."

The waitress comes over. I wish I was her color—maple-sugar-brown, darker than Angel Juan. And I wish I was big like that. The kind of body people want to snuggle with, not dangle on a plastic bracelet with other dancing skeletons.

"Yes?" the waitress says.

300

My stomach feels scratchy like it's filled with gravel so I just order coffee.

"That's it?" she says. "A little white child coming all the way to Harlem just for coffee?"

"That's it?" says Charlie.

"I'm not hungry."

"Not hungry? At Sylvia's? Smell." I can almost see Charlie sniffing the air like when Tiki-Tee sticks his nose out the window of Angel Juan's pickup truck on the way to the sea.

I remember what he said about the idea of eating. And the air does smell like browning butter and maple. "Okay, okay. I'll have eggs, grits and sweet-potato pie," I say. I look at the spark of Charlie-light. "Is that enough for you, Mr. Bat?" The waitress cocks her head at me and squints.

It's the best breakfast I've ever had and my stomach feels better. Every once in a while I pick up my camera to see Charlie. He's sitting across the booth dreamy in a halo of breakfast steam, his eyes half closed.

The waitress comes over to bring the bill and fill my coffee cup. She looks at me different for a few seconds, thinking. "You okay?" she asks.

I want to show her a picture of Angel Juan but they are all ripped up so I just say, "I'm looking for somebody. A cute Hispanic boy? He dresses like this." I am wearing my hooded mole-man sweatshirt with the hood sticking out of my leather jacket and a red bandana around my head.

301

"That sounds familiar." The woman squints again, this time at the shine of sunlight on tinsel which is really Charlie. "He liked my grits."

Angel Juan's card is in the pocket next to my heart. The part about the grits and how I eat like a kitten dipping my chin. "That's him," I say.

"Well, a lot of people like my grits. If it was him he hasn't been here for a few weeks."

She walks away. I wish I had on sunglasses. I can tell my eyes are turning darker, bruise-purple with tears I won't let escape. It's like all of a sudden Angel Juan is so close and more gone than ever.

But the waitress stops and turns around. "There was one thing kind of strange." She looks at me and shrugs like, *This child talking to herself in my booth won't mind strange.* "He had leaves in his hair. I told him and he laughed and said it was 'cause he was living in the trees."

Living in the trees. "Come on, Charlie."

Outside.

It's overcast again. I look for trees where Angel Juan might be living but there aren't too many around here.

I skate past the Apollo Theatre and Charlie whistles for me to stop. I look into the glass of the ticket booth, Charlie reflected next to me. He takes off his top hat, rests it on his chest and bows his head.

"I used to make pilgrimages here from Brooklyn when I was a little boy. I wanted to move in," he says. "All the greatest of the greats played the Apollo. James Brown.

302

Josephine Baker dressed up like a chandelier or a peacock. Weetzie's mother was always dressing up in things
like that when I met her. And then Weetzie started with the
feathers."

I look at the theater. I try to imagine the music steaming out and the people rushing in, the dancing, sweating,
the lights like jewel rain glossy on everybody's skin. But
it just looks like a run-down theater to me. I wonder if
Angel Juan saw the Apollo, if he felt sad or if he could
imagine everything the way it was. Maybe he doesn't need
me around to see beauty the way I need him to see it.

"Charlie, I need to go now."

Some little girls are sucking on pink sticky candy and
playing hip-hop-hopscotch in front of the theater to the
ghetto blaster blasty blast.

"That might make a good picture," Charlie says.

I hold up my camera not really planning on taking
anything. But through my lens I see they are mini flygirls
with skin like a dark pony's velvetness. They are doing the
Running Man and Roger Rabbit, Robocop and Typewriter
in the chalk squares. There is something so complete about
them. Like they don't need anything or anyone else in the
world. I wish I felt like that.

"Go ahead," Charlie says.

I take their picture and they give me dirty looks at first
but then they start getting into it showing off their moves.

"Hey," they say. "Hey. Yo." And I snap more and more
hip hop-hopscotch shots. Sometimes I can see Charlie

workin' it in the background looking kind of gawky and funny and rhythmless trying to dance with them.

"You going to make us famous?" one of the girls asks.

"Maybe so," I say.

After a while they stop and stand around me. They're as tall as I am. One stares at my hair.

"You could have some white-girl dreads if you wanted," she says. My hair is so tangled it does almost look like dreadlocks sometimes.

"What are you doing up here?" another says.

I've forgotten for a little while. It was so cool watching them. "I was looking for somebody."

"Can you dance?"

I look down at my feet in the roller skates.

"Any kid who can skate like you can dance," Charlie says. "Come on, Witch Baby."

I give him a grumpy scowly scowl. But the girls are waiting with their arms crossed. I take off my skates, hand one of them my camera and hip-hop into the chalk squares while Neneh Cherry raps on the ghetto blaster. The girls jump around laughing. When I get to the end of the hopscotch I do it backwards. I feel better. I feel almost free.

"Miss Thing! Now you can forget Homes, girlfriend," one of the girls says, giving me my camera. "He'll come back on his own. Just get yourself some tunes and a piece of chalk."

I put my skates back on. "I'll send you the pictures."

One of the girls writes her address on the back of my hand.

And I skate away, Charlie next to me, leaving them hip-hopscotching like maybe the next funky Josephines.

By the time we get downtown it's dusk.

"I want to go look in the trees," I say.

"We'll look tomorrow," says Charlie. "It's too dark now. Are you hungry?"

"Charlie, I ate all that food before."

"Witch Baby, that was hours and hours ago and you danced a long time. This is the best market in town."

"Were you always so into food?"

He's quiet for a minute doing dips and circles in the air like a firefly. "Actually no. But if I were to do life again I'd probably enjoy everything a lot more. For instance, I never used to dance."

I could have guessed that. "Weetzie said you were kind of a grumpster."

"Grumpster? Maybe. You learn things."

The little market has piles of fruit out in front lit up so they almost don't look real. Inside, the market's warm and bright and jammed with single people buying their dinners. There's a wild salad bar with Christmas lights all around and flowers frozen in the ice between the food. Charlie is flickering from the rainbow pastas to the stuffed grape leaves, from the egg rolls to the greens, between the beans, seeds, nuts, cheese, dried figs and dates and pineapple, muffins, corn bread, carrot cake, pastel puddings, fruit, cookies. He wants me to get everything but I just take a pink sushi roll and a fortune cookie.

In the window of the store next door there are things like huge ostrich eggs and snakeskins and skulls. I press my face up to the glass to look at a human skull, trying to imagine what my own skull looks like inside my head and what Angel Juan's looks like and if our bones look the same.

"Thoughts like that will mess you up," Charlie says in my ear. I keep forgetting about this mind-reading thing.

We cross the street to get to the subway. But I see a boutique—all chrome with high windows—and I want to stop. Boy and girl mannequins in black leather are kneeling around a man mannequin. He's wearing a white coat with the collar turned up and white gloves. He has white hair and pale no-color glass eyes and girl's lips.

I feel so cold. I feel like one of those flowers in the salad bar frozen in ice. But I don't want to move away from the window.

"Witch Baby," Charlie calls. "Come on." His voice sounds nerve urgent. Maybe that mannequin freaks him out too.

"You have to be careful," he says. "There's some nastiness around."

We go down into the subway where the noise and the dark are better than that plastic face.

❧

"How does it taste?"

"Good."

"I mean really how does it taste?"

I am eating my pink sushi roll on the carpet at Charlie's place by the light of the globe lamp. I sigh. I wish he'd just let me alone to think about Angel Juan's bone structure.

"Seaweed, sesame, spinach, carrot, radish sprouts."

"Witch Baby, remember I'll never get to eat another thing."

"Okay okay." I close my eyes to get the tastes better. "The avocado's silky and the rice is sweetish—that might be pink sugar or something. The ginger's got like a tang. The horseradish burns right through my nostrils to my brain."

"Thank you," he says. He sighs like he's just eaten a big meal.

Later he goes, "What about dessert?"

I crackle open my fortune cookie and slip out the strip of paper from the tight glazed folds.

Make your own wishes come true.

Oh, really helpful. I crunch the cookie in my mouth and spread out the fortune so Charlie can read it. I sit cross-legged on the carpet.

"Do you believe in genies?" Charlie asks.

"Genies?"

"Weetzie tried to tell me once, something about three wishes and a genie? I believed in my monsters but not

307

creatures that take care of you and grant wishes."

"Weetzie says people can be their own genies," I tell him.

"Well, you do look like a genie child to me. What would you do if you were a genie?"

Make Angel Juan come back.

"I think if you were a genie you'd live in your globe lamp and you'd ride this carpet everywhere taking pictures. You could get some pretty amazing shots from a magic carpet. You could go to Egypt and take pictures of kids riding the Sphinx. In Mexico you'd take pictures of kids in Day of the Dead masks running through the graveyards. And in exchange for letting you take their pictures you could grant their wishes."

That doesn't sound too sludgy. But it would have to be me and Angel Juan together.

Charlie laughs his crackle laugh. It reminds me of the sound of me eating the fortune cookie. "You should see yourself sitting there cross-legged," he says. "You look about to take off. Is there a mirror in here?"

We both look at the broken pieces.

"I was never into mirrors either," he says.

"Now you're *only* in mirrors."

"Maybe you could put that one back together again so you could see me. Don't you have some glue with you?"

I roll my eyes. Is he a clutch or what? How is gluing a mirror together going to help? But I get the glue from my

308

bat-shaped backpack, pick up all the pieces from the mirror and start sticking them to the wall like a big starburst
thing. It takes a while. Charlie whistles the theme to *I
Dream of Jeannie*. Mr. Goof.

I look into the glass. Like that—all close together—the
pieces break me up into a shattered Witch Baby the way
I wanted last night.

"But you're not," Charlie says. "You're all one Witch
Baby. And you are very beautiful, you know."

And there he is hovering just a little above me in the
pieces of mirror. I think about the mannequin in white
and Charlie calling me away, twinkling ahead of me as we
went down into the subway dark.

"Good night, Witch Baby," Charlie says. He leaves the
mirror, turns back into light and flash-dashes into his
leather trunk.

"Good night, Charlie." My voice echoes—ghosts of
itself—in the empty room.

I wake up to horns honking, tires screeching, snarling and
yelling in the street.

At home Angel Juan and I used to wake up to the tartest
summer-yellow smell of lemons and the whisper of the
slick lemon leaves and the singing birds in the tree outside
the shed. We named the birds Hendrix, Joplin, Dylan, Iggy,
Ziggy and Marley. But here I haven't heard a bird the whole

time. Not even a Boone bird or a Humperdink bird or a Neil Sedaka bird.

I want to go someplace where there are trees today. And mostly a boy living in the trees.

"I'm going to the park," I say.

"I took Weetzie and Cherokee to the park," says the only sunbeamer in the city flying out of the trunk in the corner. He always has to talk about Weetzie and Cherokee, Weetzie and Cherokee.

But then he says so soft and sweet, like he's talking to Josephine Baker or Weetzie or something, "May I escort you?"

In Central Park the trees are scratchy from winter. But they are trees at least. I follow the paths for a while—Miss Snarly Skate Thing—while Charlie flies around in the branches—Star Helicopter on Speed.

"Weetzie loved it here," he says. "It was spring. Weetzie took Cherokee running with her in a stroller. I thought they were like the flower goddesses bringing spring to the city. I couldn't keep up with them. Weetzie thought that kids who grow up seeing the world from a running stroller would be less anxious."

I wish Weetzie had taken me running in a stroller through Central Park with Charlie panting behind us, probably wearing his oxfords, baggy pants, his shirttails flying out. The world rushing by. Flowers in our hair. Leaves on the trees then. Ducks in the pond that's frozen now. People rolling on the grass 'til their jeans turned green. Maybe I wouldn't have shredded fingernails now if I had been in that stroller with Cherokee.

It looks more fun up there where Charlie is and easier to see what's happening so I take off my skates, hide them in between some roots and shimmy up.

"Where'd you learn to do that?" he asks from the branches. Mr. Flash.

"I've been climbing since I was little."

"*Since* you were little? What are you now?"

"You know what I mean."

"Since you were knee high to a grasshopper? A rug ratter? A baby witch baby?"

Where does he come up with this stuff?

"Aren't your feet cold?"

Is he kidding? My curly toes are furling up even more than ever in my socks. "Yes."

"Do you want to go back and get some shoes?"

"No."

I can almost hear him shrug. "Well, you could probably get some good shots from up here."

I look through my lens and there's Charlie perched on a branch clutching with his fingers. He doesn't seem too at home. He lets go for a second with one hand and points to the ground.

A woman with a baby on her back is looking through a trash can. The light is chilly and the color of lead. Even if I had color film it would be this black and white.

"Are you going to take a picture of her?" Charlie asks.

I dangle my legs and freezy feet over the branches and look down at the path. The woman is going through another trash can. I hold up my camera and she looks different all of a sudden. Or maybe it's just 'cause I feel different looking at her. I feel hungry, dizzy with hungry, sick with hungry even though I had breakfast this morning. I take my lunch—the loaf of French bread and the piece of cheese wrapped in a clean red bandana—and toss it down. It lands on the scraggly grass by the woman's feet. She turns and picks it up, peeks inside and slips it into her jacket like she doesn't want anybody to see and then she goes away with her baby. I press my face against tree bark feeling the rough edges ridging my skin.

I follow Charlie over a bridge of branches into the next tree—a small gray one. I feel strong holding on to the limbs full of sap like blood. I think about Ianka love goddesses with lots of arms. I want to hold on forever.

"Have you ever seen a tree spirit?" Charlie asks me and I shake my head.

"But I've thought about them. I used to look at trees and try to make up what their spirits were like."

"If you were one you'd be the spirit of those Weetzie-trees—you know, the ones with the purple flowers that get all over everything in the spring in L.A? They fell in the T-bird when the top was down but my little girl liked it. She said it made the T-bird like a just-married-mobile."

"I bet the spirit of this tree is an old woman—real

smart—who talks to the squirrels and the moon," I say. I want him to come back, pay attention to me.

"Hey," Charlie says. "Look. Way up there."

I don't see anything.

"Through your camera."

In the highest branches a pair of legs swing back and forth. A woman with bird bones and skin like autumn leaves. She blinks her milky opal-sky eyes. Then she's gone.

Did I see that?

"You were right," Charlie says. "What about that one?" He points to a big muscle tree.

"A warrior dude with a hawk nose and raven-wing hair."

Just when I say it I spot somebody through my camera in the strong tree. A dark sleekster guy with tangly snarl-ball nests full of birds on his bare chunkster shoulders. He disappears into the top branches.

"Pretty good," says Charles.

"Let's follow him."

I have to go down on the ground to scramble back up into the next tree, and by the time I get there tree man is gone. Then I see something dangling in the branches hidden by the few leaves that are still clinging on. It's a rope ladder slinking from a square cut in some wooden boards. I hoist myself up behind Charlie into a serious kick-down tree house.

There's a rope hammock and an old cracked piece of glass fit into one window. And around the window frame somebody started to carve rough roses.

The kind that you carve on picture frames. The kind that Angel Juan's father taught Angel Juan to carve.

I feel like I'm still on the rope ladder. I feel like I *am* a rope ladder trembly in a wind storm. I grab onto the hammock but it swings and I stumble against the tree house wall. A ghost is here with me and I've seen two tree spirits, but finding this is the most slamminest thing of all.

Angel Juan told me that someday he would build a tree house for us in the lemon tree looking out over the canyon. And the lady at Sylvia's told me that a boy who loved her grits and wore a mole-man sweatshirt and a bandana had leaves in his hair and said he lived in the trees.

"Charlie," I say all shaky. "We have to stay here. I have to wait for him to come back."

"It's too cold to stay here now. You don't have any shoes on."

"I don't care. He was here."

"If he was here I don't think he's coming back, Witch Baby."

"What are you talking about?"

"None of his things are here. And it's too cold."

I sit on the splintery floor of the tree house. I want to live here with Angel Juan. We could just go down to play music and make a little money, buy some food and come back, stay here all the time. In the spring we'd eat raspberries and kiss right in the hug of the branches, the stars shifting through the leaves like sparkles in a kaleidoscope. We'd wake up to a neighborhood of birds' nests right

314

outside and the world far away down below. Sometimes Charlie Bat and the tree spirits would come over for dinner—or to watch us eat dinner I guess. We'd hardly ever have to leave.

I pick up a dried leaf and an acorn, with its little beanie cap, lying on the tree house floor. I try to bend the leaf to make it into an elf's coat for the acorn head but it crumbles in my hand. I look down through cracked glass at the winter park, the scattered people with maybe nowhere else to be.

Everybody should have their own tree house. Maybe Angel Juan and I could help build houses in every tree. If the tree spirits wouldn't mind. If I ever find Angel Juan again.

Someone is standing under the house looking up. Who wears white in New York city in the middle of winter except for maybe mannequins in store windows? All of a sudden I feel frosty, stiff and naked like a winter branch.

"Who's that?" I whisper to Charlie.

"He doesn't look like a tree spirit," Charlie says.

I swing down the rope ladder into the lower branches to see better but the snow-colored-no-colored man has disappeared.

I feel Charlie behind me. "I think we should leave now," he says.

On the way home Charlie stops in front of a glassed-in courtyard with a big twinkling tree, little tables underneath, heat lamps all around.

"What are those lights in the tree?" I ask.

"Fireflies."

"Fireflies in New York city? They look like a whole lot of guys like you."

"Let's go in and eat," says Charlie.

I don't feel like eating. I want to pad around in a circle on the carpet at Charlie's place like Tiki-Tee making his bed in the dirt and then I want to curl up there and sleep and sleep and have at least one dream about melting into Angel Juan. But I follow Charlie anyway. Maybe because Angel Juan and I used to eat samosas bursting peas and potatoes at an Indian restaurant in L.A. that looked like a camera on the outside. Maybe because of the fireflies.

I sit near a heat lamp that takes the cold ache out of my knobby spine. A man with incense-colored skin and a turban comes over. He has a liquid-butter voice. Ghee they call it on the menu he gives me.

Charlie tells me to order saffron-yellow vegetable curry with candy-glossy chutney, rice and lentil-bread. The food is so hot it scalds the taste right out of my mouth but it's so good I keep eating to get the taste back again. When I'm finished I stop to look through my camera at Charlie. He seems like he rocked on watching the meal about as much as I did eating it.

"Do you think that would make a good picture?" Charlie asks, pointing.

"Maybe *you* should start taking pictures." I'm sick of him telling me what to take all the time. "I want to go home now." But I look. Of course I look.

Across the courtyard are two tall beautiful lankas and a little girl. The little girl has red pigtails and freckles, wide-apart amber-colored eyes and gaps between her teeth. She looks just like one of the lanks. She keeps getting up from her chair and running around the tree squealing at the fire-flies. The lankas take turns chasing after her, catching her, hugging her and sitting her down again, trying to get her to eat her rice. There is something about the three of them eating their dinner under the firefly tree that burns inside of me more than the food burning my mouth. They keep touching each other and laughing, sharing their tandoori chicken.

The red-haired lanka notices I'm staring at them and she smiles at me. She has the same gap-tooth grin as the little girl. Her friend gets up to catch the little girl who is off in another firefly frenzy.

I'm feeling sort of high from the hot food. "Can I take your picture?" Usually I don't ask—just do it—but it seems like with them I should.

"It's okay with me." Her voice is deep and rich like the ambery color of her eyes. "Honey," she says to the other one, "she wants to take our picture. Grab Miss Pigtails."

The friend has black hair and a diamond in her nose. She comes back with Miss Pigtails squirming in her arms. That squirmy-wormyness reminds me of me when I was little but I never giggled like that.

The lankas put their arms around each other and the

little girl wriggles in between them still giggling. Through my camera lens I see their love even more. It's almost like a color. It's like a firefly halo. I also see that one of the lanks is beautiful in the strong way that only real androgynous ones are. She has really broad shoulders and long muscles and glamster legs. She laughs with a deep voice and if you look close you can see an Adam's apple.

I think one was probably once a man. That little girl's mom was probably once her dad. But it doesn't matter because she is about the happiest kid I've ever seen.

"I'll send you one if you want," I say. I don't want to take any more pictures of them. I feel like maybe I saw a little too much.

But they're just smiling like they don't mind what anybody sees or thinks. They give me their address on a book of matches and I get up to leave.

The little girl is off again firefly chasing.

She points up into the trees. "I want one."

I would like to catch some too, put them in a jar. Put the jar in the tree house so Angel Juan would be able to read at night when he and I live there in the spring.

The red-haired lanka kneels next to the little girl. She plays with her pigtails and says, "They'd die in a jar. But you can have them all the time in the tree." The little girl looks into her eyes and nods.

I look through my camera at the firefly tree. For just a second I think I see a ghost-a-rama—a whole bunch of them, like they jumped out of some black-and-white movie except for their sparkly golden eyes—sitting in the branches.

I am huddling in a corner holding my letter thinking about being right where Angel Juan was living and not finding him.

Charlie is doing spin-dive-dips in the air and humming that song "Green Onions," trying to make me laugh but I don't want to laugh. I wish he'd just shut up and go back into his trunk. I want to think about Angel Juan. How we went surfing 'til the sun set on a beach where the sand was all polished black rocks. I cut my feet on the rocks and he put Band-Aids on them. We were changing out of our bathing suits behind the truck and saw each other naked under our towels and climbed into the back of the pickup truck and didn't leave 'til morning. Angel Juan pretended the salt water he dripped onto my cheeks when he kissed me was from the ocean but I knew it was his tears.

Finally Charlie settles on the trunk, stops humming and says, "Tomorrow I want to take you to the place I was born. I never got to take Weetzie there. I think about it all the time."

"Charlie, I have to find Angel Juan. I'm not here on vacation."

"Well, where are you going to go look?"

"I wanted to go to Coney Island but I think it's closed in winter."

"I can get you in. And I grew up right near there. We can stop on the way back."

This is the train to Coney Island. This is the darkness roaring around me that seems like it will never end. This is what it might be like to be dead.

And then the train comes up into the light. And everywhere for as far as I can see are hunched gnome tombstones. I think about what my tombstone will look like. Wonder if I'll be buried next to Angel Juan.

This is the darkness again.

This is the light.

This is Coney Island.

"I used to work here when I was a kid," Charlie says. "I learned how to run the Ferris wheel." He shows me a hole in a fence and we sneak through—well I sneak, Charlie's light just kind of glides.

An amusement park in winter is like when you go to the places where you went with the person you love but they're not with you anymore. Everything rickety and cold and empty. If you had cotton candy it would burn your lips and cut your throat like spun pink glass. If you rode the roller coaster you'd have to hold on tight to the bar to keep your whole body from being lifted right off the seat with nobody there to hang on to you except maybe a ghost. You used to always want to go fast—speed monster—faster than anybody but now if you rode the roller coaster you'd just keep wishing for it to be over. The bathroom is filthy, stinky so you don't go, and you have to walk around holding it in. The booths are empty. No fur beasties for sale. Why are you here? You remember the card in your pocket. Your friend the ghost wants to cheer you up and runs the Ferris wheel while you ride it all by yourself thinking about the one on the West Coast where you and your pounceable boyfriend made the cart you were in swing and swing while you kissed and kissed above the ocean and the pier and the carousel, drenched in sunset, lips salty with popcorn and sticky sweet with ice cream, not sick at all. This Ferris wheel is different. Here you are on the most coupley kind of ride in the world all by yourself. You never knew you were scared of heights before. You just grip the bar and wish you were down. If you thought you were empty inside from being alone you know that you for sure have a stomach anyway but it doesn't want to stay in there. You also for sure have a heart which is beating hard and doesn't want to stay where it is either. You look down trying to think about something else and you can see popcorn bags, scarves, mittens and some rotting stuffed beasties in the weeds below where they must have fallen when the wheel turned last summer. You hold on tight to the card in your pocket and the angel around your neck and the camera in your lap. You remember how the card said that thing about riding the Ferris wheel to get outside of yourself. You try to look out over the park and up into the sky. You try to get outside of yourself to someplace where you don't feel so alone. The carnival booths are not tombstones, you tell yourself. But you think about the tombstones you saw from the train and how Charlie Bat is really dead and Angel Juan is gone. Then the plastic skeleton bracelet slips off your wrist. You watch it fall down into the thing-graveyard under the Ferris wheel.

When the ride is over you and the ghost go down to the weedy muddy slushy place and grope around in the dirt. You kick and pick through some stuff and after a while your friend spotlights the string of skeletons all quiet in the weeds. You pick them up and they start to shimmy, and underneath them you see what you probably most want in the whole world—or a picture of what you want most in the whole world anyway: his face three times in black and white. The boy you love caught in three photo-booth clicks. He looks very serious and older. And something else. There's a man sitting next to him. You can only see the man's mouth and chisel chin and his white shirt—the rest of him is cut off. You wonder who the man is and how you could have found this and what it means. You look into the dark of your angel's sunglasses like they are his eyes trying to see clues but there aren't any. You put the strip of pictures of his face into your pocket along with the card.

You see a photo booth and for a second you have the crazy thought that the boy whose face is in your pocket three times might be in there, sitting behind the dark curtain waiting for the shot.

You throw back the curtain with a negative of his smile flashing behind your eyes. But it's empty.

You sit down. "This is where Weetzie and Cherokee and I took our picture," says the ghost. "Maybe you could send her this one." He sits next to you reflected in the glass but you both know there will just be empty space when the photo comes out.

Three. In one you smile sickly sweet as cotton candy. In one you grimace like a little grumpster demon. In one you are just you—Witch Baby—looking straight out at yourself.

This is Brooklyn. This is the station and these are the people walking with their heads down and their hands in their pockets.

The rows of brownstones all look kind of the same at first until I notice the little piece of lace in a window, cat on a piano, the Big Wheel bike on the front step, the raggedy dead geranium plant waiting for spring. Some bearded guys in long black coats and fur hats walk by separate from the rest of the world like prayers in a book. Kids playing basketball, slammin' the way kids do, into it, not thinking about anything except the game. Pregnant teenagers with strollers.

I think about what it would be like if I had got pregnant with Angel Juan. Brown baby twins with curly cashew nut toes and purple eyes. Kid Niblett and Señorita Deedles. With no dad now.

Charlie's been quiet this whole time. Now he goes, "Would you like to see how it was?"

"Charlie, I just want to go home," I grunt. "Every time I get closer to Angel Juan you want to take me off in some other direction."

"I'm not taking you in any other direction. You tell me where we should go next."

"I don't know!"

"We'll go home soon. I really want to show you this. Over here."

He turns onto an empty street, looking like a sunbeam that decided to hang out a little longer than the rest. It's creepy-quiet and I wonder where everybody is. The sky is starting to get purplish.

"Look through your camera," Charlie says.

I look. But instead of him I see this little boy wearing short pants, bruised knees sticking out. He's black and white, shadows and light like Charlie.

"This is me when I was a kid," he says in a kid's voice.

"How'd you do that?"

"It's one of the things I can do now. Like climbing trees and walking through fences and dancing."

I hope he can't read my mind about the dancing.

"Besides, I used to be a special effects man," he says. "Come on."

I cross the street and stand next to him in front of a chunkster brownstone with dead rosebushes clinging to the sides. One time Angel Juan and I stole roses from the neighbors' gardens and put them on a cake we made but nobody would eat the cake because they were afraid of the bug spray (not 'cause of the stealing—they thought we asked) so we ate it all ourselves and got high maybe from the sugar or maybe from the bug spray or maybe because it was our special secret stolen thing.

Charlie points to a window on the top floor.

"That's where we lived when I was growing up."

"Hey, Charlie."

I turn around and hold up my camera. A little girl is standing in the street but she's not a real little girl. She's like Charlie, like her own movie without a projector.

"That's my sister Goldy," I hear Charlie say. He runs over to her and they start throwing a shadow ball back and forth. Then after a while I hear somebody calling their names from the window. I can't see anything but a champagne-colored glow until I hold my camera up and then I see the flickery face of a woman.

"That's my mother." Charlie's voice clicks a little. "She makes hats."

Charlie and Goldy run inside the building and I follow their echoing laughter upstairs into a deserted apartment that looks like nobody but maybe skulky rats have lived in for a long time.

"Look through your camera," Charlie says.

The apartment changes. It's suddenly warm and full of ghosty chairs and couches printed with cabbagy roses, crochet blankets, lamps with slinky silk fringe. There's a table covered with laces and ribbons, a sewing machine and a bunch of mannequin heads wearing huge hats decorated with flowers, fruits and vegetables, tiny birds' nests, butterflies, fireflies. I can smell onions cooking. The door opens and a man comes in. He's tall and his eyebrows grow together making him look kind of scary.

"That's my father," Charlie says to me. "He came from Poland on a ship when he was a little boy. They couldn't understand his name so they put down 'Bat' because of his eyebrows. His father was a fisherman. In Poland in the spring they filled their cottage with lilacs and covered the floor with white sand."

Charlie's dad goes over to where Charlie's mom is setting the table with china plates and he puts his arms around her. She pushes him away like playing but he spins her and lifts her up onto his wing-tip shoes and starts dancing with her like that, two grainy black-and-white images twirling like they got bored of staying inside their movie.

"Not tonight." Charlie's mom is out of breath. "It's the sabbath. Now stop that." She tries not to giggle.

Charlie and Goldy dance too, like the ghosts in the haunted house at Disneyland. Angel Juan's favorite. He wanted to dance in the ballroom with me and see if the ghosts would go through our bodies.

"Now stop," Charlie's mom says.

She pulls away from their grinning goofster dad and straightens her apron. She goes over to the table and puts a piece of lace on her head. Everybody else sits down while

Charlie's mom lights some candles. She says a prayer with sounds from deep inside her throat. Then she serves baked chicken, peas, carrots and pearl onions. I've never seen a movie that smells this good.

"We light the candles for your grandparents in a few days." Charlie's mother passes a loaf of braided bread.

"When does the angel visit?" asks Goldy.

"Elijah doesn't come until Passover," Charlie's father says.

"And he'll drink the wine out of Papa's cup," says Goldy.

"Maybe someday Charlie will write a play about angels," Charlie's mother says.

"Charlie just writes about monsters," Goldy says. "He scared me again today, Papa."

"It was just a mask." Charlie holds up a rubber monster face. Goldy screams.

"Charlie, don't scare your sister," his father says. "Your mother's idea is good. You could write something about Elijah."

Charlie whispers to me, "The candles we lit once a year for the dead didn't mean much to me then. Until my mother got sick and then she died and the candles meant something and nothing at all. I decided when I grew up I wouldn't fast, light candles for the dead or pour wine for angels since none of it helped her stay alive."

Then he gets up from the table and goes over to his mother. He throws his arms around her all of a sudden so clutch tight. Even though he's a kid he's almost bigger than she is.

"Charlie?" she says. "What is it, *bubela*?"

Charlie just keeps holding on. Then he kisses her cheek, lets go and sits down again.

"They're all gone now," he whispers.

I look at Charlie's hat-making braided-bread-baking beautiful phantom mom. I think about how it must have been for him when she died. And for his sister and his father with the bat eyebrows. Now they're all dead. And I feel like it's hard for me to unclutch Angel Juan!

The Bat family is starting to fade. So is all the furniture in the room and the dinner smells. I press my eye to my camera trying to keep the picture but it's almost all gone. And then it is—gone. Just a deserted apartment about to be filled with night.

"Charlie!" I almost shout. Scared he's going to leave with them. I put down my camera searching for the light. "I'm sorry. I'm sorry I didn't want to come here with you." I look at the photo booth strip of me and not-Charlie.

Then, "Over here, honey," calls a voice from the doorway. Honey like salt in my throat making me want to cry. He's here. "We'd better go," he says.

We're back in the Village. I am sitting on the floor eating a rice cake.

"Couldn't you put something on that thing?" Charlie says. "It tastes—I mean it looks like you are eating cardboard."

I shrug. "I like it plain."

"You're getting so skinny."

Because I want him to enjoy my meal a little I go and get some peanut butter.

"Charlie, how did you deal when your mom died?" I ask.

"I wrote. I was okay as long as I was writing. Whenever anything hurt me I wrote, but after a while I couldn't anymore. I just stopped. It was like the sadness stopped filling me up with stuff to turn into art. I was just empty."

"That's how I feel."

"Make yourself keep taking pictures and the pictures will start filling you up again. And isn't there something else you like to do? Come on."

We go out of his apartment into the silent, shadowy hall. It seems like nobody else even lives in the whole building. We start down the stairs.

That's when I hear them. There on the ninth floor. The drums.

The sound makes me want to play so bad I have to stop and chew my nails. It's African drums in waves breaking again and again taking me out of my body.

A door is open and inside lit by pale winter sun from a big window dancers move in tides toward the drummers. The dancers wear batik sarongs—burnt-orange skies, jade-green jungles, violet-blue flowers—and shell belts that shiver on their hips. Their feet beat the floor like hands on a drum and their hands are bound by invisible ropes

329

behind their backs, then turn into birds as they leap free. There are two little girls, and a woman with braids to her waist and a high dark gloss queen's forehead holds their hands and leads them down the room, her solid feet talking each step so that even though the kids probably just started walking a little while ago they are getting it. The drummers are men with bare chests and rainbow ribbons around their muscly arms. Some have dreads. Everybody in the room is sweating like it's summer and the music is setting free their souls into the air so I feel like I can almost see them.

All I want to do is play drums. I know the dances from when my dad filmed some African dancers and I got to jam with them.

When they take a break Charlie says, "Go ask him."

"I can't."

"Go on. How often do I have the chance to hear my witch baby play drums!"

Why do I listen to this crazy ghost? I don't know.

My witch baby.

I go over to the head drummer—a tall man wearing full batik pants. His dreadlocks must be as old as he is, thick and wired with his power. I feel like a pale weasel baby staring up at him.

"Can I sit in?" I ask.

He looks down at me frowning like, *How can this will-o'-the-wisp white child think she can hang with this?* "Can you play?"

"I know *Fanga, Kpanlogo, DunDunBa, Kakilamba* . . ."

He raises his eyebrows. "This is a fast class. If you're not good it will be bad for everybody."

"You're good," Charlie whispers.

"I'm good," I say.

The man's still frowning but he points over to a little drum. It's perfect. A little heart of the universe.

They start again and it's a dance to heal sick spirits. The women throw spirits out of their chests, tossing back their heads with each fling of their hands. Their backs ripple like lanky lizards while their arms reach into the air and pull the healing spirits down into them. It's my favorite dance and so strong that while I play the drum I feel pain smacked out of me.

When the class is over the head drummer shakes my hand in his big callused hand. Him doing that is like having a medicine man pull out any other evil spirits that might be left over.

Charlie is waiting at the doorway, a pulsing golden light. "Yes!" he says. "Phenomenal. You are a beautiful drummer!"

I feel glowy all over, almost as bright as he is.

We go outside. I look up at Charlie's building. I wish I could take off the front of it and look into all the rooms like you do with a dollhouse. From out here it seems almost deserted like you'd never guess that magic-carpet-collecting ghost chasers live here and a whistling ghost in a top hat and that dancers and drummers are flinging bad spirits out of their bodies in one of the rooms.

I just wonder what my bad spirits look like and where all the flung-out bad spirits go.

All up and down the avenue shivering junkies are selling things. Ugster vinyl pumps, Partridge Family records, plastic daisy jewelry, old postcards. Where do they get this stuff? It's a magpie Christmas market.

"Look at that man," Charlie says.

I see a hungry face.

"No. With your camera."

I look through my camera at the man and I can almost feel the veins in my own arms twitch-switching with wanting. In a way the junkies aren't so much different from me or maybe from everybody.

I guess in a way Angel Juan is my fix and I've been jonesing for him. If he were a needle I'd be shooting up just like these jittery junkies. I'd be flooding my veins with Angel Juan. When we made love it felt like that.

And doing it can be about as dangerous as shooting up if you think about it.

And I wasn't the only one sad and lonely and freaked. There was a whole city of people. Some had to sell other people's postcards on the street just to buy a needle full of junk so they wouldn't shatter like the mirror I smashed with a hammer in Charlie Bat's apartment.

"Hey," the man shouts, "I've got something for you."

The man's sunken eyes are like Charlie's. I go over to his table and he holds up a pair of droopy soiled white angel wings. I touch the medallion in the hollow of my neck and think about the saint parade Angel Juan wrote about in his card. The little girls in feathers. I want those wings.

"How much?"

"Ten dollars."

"Five," Charlie whispers.

"Five."

"Eight and I'll throw this in." He waves a wrinkled postcard in front of his face. It has a picture of two Egyptian mummies on it. They remind me of my walk with Angel Juan when we saw the head of Nefertiti-ti on the piano in the window in the fog once upon time. I wonder if that king and queen ever screamed at each other and cried in the night with pain and desire or if they always looked so sleek and lazy-lotus-eyed.

I give the man eight dollars I was going to spend on food and he stuffs the bills into his pocket and licks his lips like he's already feeling what it's going to be like when the needle hits the vein. He could be a writer like Charlie Bat or a painter or a musician. He could have a kid like Charlie had Weetzie. And all people see is a junkie selling lost wings.

I flip over the postcard and it's like the dream I keep waiting to have but better because it's real. Is it real? Those slanty letters scrunching up toward the bottom like all of a sudden realizing there's no more space. I know those letters.

It can't be.

But there it is—his name.

Yo Te Amo, Angel Juan.

Dearest Niña Bruja,

I go to the museum and look at the Egypt rooms. The goddesses remind me of you. There are jars with cats' heads that hold the hearts of the dead.

This city is like an old forest or house that you think's just rotting away and then you see there's magic inside. I try to remember that about life and about my heart in me. I think by being by myself I am learning how to love you more and not be so afraid.

Yo Te Amo, Niña,

Angel Juan

"Where did you get this?" I ask the man, almost screeching.

"I don't know. Found it."

"Where did you find it?" I growl, pulling feathers out of the wings.

He shrugs. Then he says, "Somewhere down on Meat Street. It was lying in the gutter like somebody dropped it on the way to the mail."

334

"Meat Street?"

"The meat-packing district. Somewhere around there."

I know I'm not going to get anything else out of him. But here in my hand is a postcard from the Metropolitan Museum addressed to Witch Baby Wigg Bat, stamped, ready to be mailed and written by Angel Juan Perez.

I know where I'm going tomorrow.

I slip the postcard into the pocket next to my heart with the other card and the photo booth strip, sling the wings over my shoulder and try to skate the shakes out of my knees. Charlie twinkles near my ear like a whistling diamond earring.

Today Charlie and I go up the steps where people from all over the world are huddling in their coats with Christmas shopping at their feet. They're eating hot dogs and salt-crystaled soft pretzels. The pretzels smell good. Buttery, doughy. But I'm not going to spend any money on food today even though Charlie keeps telling me I am too skinny and I have to eat.

We go into the big entry that's high and bright like a church. Perfume and flowers. Voices echo. Warm bodies. Cool marble.

Egypt first.

There is so much here I feel like, How am I supposed to even start? Rooms and rooms of glass cases. Mummies.

Real bodies inside there. High lotus foreheads. Painted tilted fish-shaped eyes. Smooth flat jewel-collared chests. Lanky limbs. Long desert feet. I bet inside they don't look like that. Jars with the heads of baboons or cats or jackals for holding the organs like Angel Juan said.

Cases and cases of tiny things. Secret scarab beetles. Why did the Egyptians have this thing about dung beetles? Mud love. Sludge and mud. It reminds me of me when I was a little kid covering myself with dirt. Slinky cats with golden hoops in their ears. Chalky blue goddesses missing their little arms or legs. Where did the lost parts of them go? Maybe they reminded Angel Juan of me because they're broken.

"You know, you look like a little Egyptian queen," Charlie says. His reflection ripples like water next to mine in the glass case.

We come out of the dim tomb rooms and at first I can't see—it's so flood-bright. The glass walls let in the park and the ceiling lets in the sky. And in the center is this whole temple—this huge white Egyptian palace with the lotus-head people carved on the sides and a shallow pool of water all around full of penny wishes.

Charlie sighs. "This was Weetzie's favorite place in the whole city. She did like the dancing chicken in Chinatown too."

Could you please stop bat-chattering about when Weetzie visited you.

I think it and I don't even care if he can read my mind.

336

"I'm sorry, Baby. I'm trying not to be such a clutch pig. Isn't that what you say? A lankster lizard?"

I sit down on a bench facing the temple and pretend that I'm in Egypt. I wear a tall headdress, a collar of blue and gold beads and a long sheer pleated tunic. I pray in a gleamy white temple. I ride on the Nile in a barge and play drums. I carve pictures of my family on stone walls. I have a slinkster cat with a gold hoop in its ear that sits on my shoulder and helps me understand mysteries. When I die I'll be put in a tomb and my organs will be put in jars. If somebody finds me centuries later they will know exactly where my heart is.

On the way back through, Charlie leads me into a tiny room. Nobody else is here. I'm blind after the brightness of the temple. The darkness feels like it's seeping into me, drugging me like spooky smoke, mystery incense taking me into an ancient desert.

Then I see the hipster king and queen from the post-card standing together with their organ jars next to them, staring out at me like, *Hello, we are perfect twins and who are you?*

"*Hello, we are perfect twins and who are you?*"

"Did you say something, Charlie?"

"*Not me.*"

"Well don't tell me *they* said it." I lower my voice, hiss-whisper. "Charlie, what's going on?"

"Maybe you should introduce yourself."

"Oh *right*. Okay. My name is Witch Baby. I shouldn't be

surprised that statues are talking to me. I've already seen tree spirits and my best friend almost-grandpa is a ghost. This is Charlie."

"Hello, Witch Baby. Charlie." Two voices—a drum and a flute, one song.

I look at the pair of statues with their matching smooth golden faces, high eyebrows, far-apart eyes, small noses, graceful necks. Part of me wishes that that was me and Angel Juan—together forever with our hearts in jars. Better than not knowing where his heart is.

No. Shut your clutch thoughts up, Witch Baby. You don't wish that.

"You are alive. Remember. As long as you are alive you'll know where his heart is. It will be in you."

"Like Charlie will always be alive in Weetzie and me?"

"Yes."

"Charlie, did those statues really talk to me?"

"I'm not in a good position not to believe that, being myself a . . . well you know. Anyway, you heard what you needed to hear. Maybe I did too.

"Shall we try China?"

In China there is a room full of beamy-faced people doing yoga. They make a wreath around me, flower children breathing peace. The Egyptians were so much in the world with all their gold and stuff but these guys are like from some other world. They don't have wings but they remind me of angels.

338

In a room with a high ceiling I stand at the solid feet of a massive Buddha dude. His stone robes are covered with petals and they fall like silk. His hands are gone. I wonder what happened to them.

He has a topknot, droopy earlobes and a gentle mouth. He is gazing down at me like, *Everything will be all right, Baby, no problem.*

"*Everything will be all right.*"

"Charlie!"

"If any statue could talk it would probably be him. Why don't you ask him something?"

"Why are your earlobes like that?"

"Witch Baby, that might not be the best question."

"Well it's hard to think."

"*I used to wear big earrings when I valued material wealth.*"

"What am I supposed to do about Angel Juan?"

"*Let go.*"

All of a sudden I know just how his hands would be if they were there. One would be held up with the thumb and third finger touching and the pinky in the air. One palm would be open.

Next Charlie and I go to Greece. In the airy echoing room of dessert-colored marbles we stand in front of a pale boy, so beautiful on his pedestal but so white. The marble muscles mold marble flesh. There are even marble tendons, ridges of marble veins, so real they look like if you pressed on them they'd flatten out for a second. I wonder how the real boy who posed for the statue felt. If he felt like the statue took his soul away, like all that mattered was his pretty body.

The statue seems to be looking at me like . . .

Yes, it's happening again:

"Your friend needs to go make music by himself."

"You mean he needs to not just be my pounceably beautiful boyfriend who I take pictures of and write songs about."

"Yes."

"It might be even hard for him to be made into stuff by me until he starts making stuff of his own."

"Yes."

I take the strip of photos out of my pocket and try to look into Angel Juan's eyes behind the sunglasses.

While I'm standing in front of the pedestal boy looking at Angel Juan I hear something behind me.

"Do you wish that you could turn him into stone? Make him a mummy? Keep his heart in a jar?"

Another talking statue? But this time the voice makes me feel cold like marble. I turn around.

No statue but that man—the one in the white coat, the one from the park.

He slithers behind a wall painted with flower garlands and demon masks.

I run after him.

"Witch Baby!" Charlie calls.

I don't stop. My footsteps echo through the rooms. The

blank eyeless marble eyes are all around.

But when I get to the lobby the man is gone and I am still marble-slab cold.

"Who was that ghoulie guy?" I ask the Bat Man back at the apartment.

"I don't know," he says. "But you shouldn't go chasing after that kind of people. Maybe you should take some pictures."

"Of what. Of you?"

"I'm not very photogenic. You're going to take pictures of you."

"What?"

"Look in the trunk."

I jiggle the lock and the leather trunk opens right up. I choke on stink-a-rama mothballs and dust.

Inside is a bunch of stuff. Clothes. Wigs. Masks. I figure either Charlie got off dressing up weird when he was alive or they were for his plays. Either way the trunk is filled with stuff to make me into all my dreams and all my nightmares.

I turn into Nefertiti in a gold paper headdress and collar with cool kohl eyes and a pout of my lips.

I wear a curly blonde wig, a wreath of plastic leaves and a toga sheet and do a Greek-dude-statue-on-a-pedestal thing.

I keep on the wig and attach the magpie-market wings

to my back for a Cupid look holding a rickety bow and arrow from the trunk.

I put my hair in a topknot and wear an old silk kimono and be Buddha cross-legged and meditating.

I find a really ugster monster rubber monster mask. I don't even want to touch it. It looks like some leper-monster's shed skin all shreddy at the edges. Just like the one Charlie had in Brooklyn. But I put that on too and take a picture of my face with the eyes staring out of two holes gouged in the rubber.

I slick back my hair, put on my dark glasses, bandana, hooded sweatshirt, leather jacket, Levi's and chunky shoes.

Me as Angel Juan.

Click. Click. Click.

I stay up all night. The sky is starting to get pale.

The black top hat that Charlie was wearing when we first met is in the trunk too and I put that on with a black tuxedo jacket, dark eyeliner circles under my eyes: the ghost of Charlie Bat.

"Do I look like you, Charlie?"

"You are a lot like me, especially the way I used to be. Even without the costume. You're more like me than Weetzie and Cherokee. I think you are my real blood granddaughter."

I wonder if he knows how slink that makes me feel. How I feel warm for the first time since I've been in this city, I mean really warm. From the inside out.

I hear his crackly voice. "We both believe in monsters. But all the ghosts and demons are you. And all the angels and genies are you. All the kings, queens, Buddhas, beautiful boys. Inside you. No one can take them away."

"So then that means nobody can take you away from Weetzie and me even though you're—"

"Yes, I guess you're right."

Why doesn't he let me finish?

"You should get some sleep now," he says.

Suddenly I'm so tired. I collapse onto the carpet with all the costumes all around me.

Dear Angel Juan,

I dream about you for the first time since you left. You are wearing the magpie-market angel wings and standing on a street corner playing your guitar, singing for a crowd of people. You look so happy and free.

But who's that? There is someone hiding in the crowd watching you that shouldn't be there. Someone in the rubber monster mask from Charlie's trunk. They want you to belong to them. They want to lock you up in a tomb so you can't breathe, so no one else can ever touch you, so you can't sing anymore.

I wake up with a cold. One of those bad almost flu-y things where you feel all your nerve endings splitting on the surface of your skin and your ears ring like you've been playing a tough gig at a loud smoky club all night. I've slept for hours—it's dark. When I go to turn on the globe lamp nothing happens. I try the bathroom switch. Nothing. Electricity out. And you know what it is? Christmas Eve.

In Los Angeles my family is all together feasty-feasting in a house lit with red and green chili-pepper lights. There is a big blazing tree. After they eat they are going to make home movies of each other dancing and opening their presents.

I wish I was home with all of them and Angel Juan having a jammin' jamboree, playing music and sharing a stolen-roses cake in front of the fireplace.

"Charlie?" I say.

No song. No light.

I light candles and wrap up in my sleeping bag and some of Mallard and Meadows's blankets on the carpet. I remember that my heart is a broken teacup. I remember the feeling of my own heart shredding me up from the inside out. I think about the dream.

"Charlie!"

"Are you all right?" he asks flickering in a corner.

"I had a bad dream about Angel Juan. I have to go out and look for him." I try to stand up but I have Jell-O knees.

"You look like you have a fever," Charlie says. "You can't go out."

"But Charlie, I think that man in the museum wants to hurt Angel Juan."

344

"Just rest now, Baby." His voice is like a lullaby.

I feel creepy-crawly. I shiver back into a fever-sleep.

When I wake up this time my skin feels sore—like it's been stretched too tight or something—and hot. Outside the firefly building is shining in the night.

Then I remember my dream again and I feel splinters of ice cracking in my chest. Now what? All I know is that I have to go out no matter what Charlie thinks. I'm so sick of him telling me what to do, keeping me from finding Angel Juan. And he's hiding in his trunk now anyway. There is something I have to do.

I get up and dress in baggy black. I put my hair back under a black baseball cap, grab my camera and roller skates.

When I get down to the street I put on my skates and take off into the darkness. My hands are frozen inside my mittens and my frozen toes keep slamming against the pointed cowboy-boot toes. My nose is running and my chest aches. Fog is coming in and the air smells salty and fishy. A few glam drag queens in miniskirts and high heels are strutting in the shadows cooing and hollering. Sometimes a car drives by, stops and picks one up.

It's freaky. I kind of know exactly where I'm going. Or I don't know but the roller skates do. They just seem to carry me along over the cobblestones. I can feel every stone jolting my spine but not enough to jolt the fear out of me.

Driving it deeper in.

The place where the roller skates want to take me is the meat-packing district down by the river.

Meat Street, I think, remembering what the junkie said.

In between the big meat warehouses on the cobble-stone pavement is a little fifties-style hot-dog-shaped stainless-steel diner-type place lit with tubes of buzzing red neon that make the shadows the color of raspberry syrup. The neon sign reads "Cake's Shakin' Palace."

And standing there in the window of the empty diner is Angel Juan!

I think it is really him. Not so much because I feel tired and spooked and sick but because I just want it to be. I want him to be all right.

But this is a mannequin. It has Angel Juan's nose and cheekbones and his chin, his dark eyes and hair and even the tone of his brown skin under the raspberry-syrup light. He's dressed like a waiter with a white shirt and a bow tie and a little cap and there's a tray with a plastic milk shake and burger in one hand. I am standing here on a dark street in New York in the middle of the night in front of a window looking up at my boyfriend offering me a hamburger but his body would be cold if I touched it and if I held a mirror up to his face no breath would cloud it. His eyes are blind. But for some reason I have the feeling that this really *is* Angel Juan. I can't explain the feeling except that it is the scariest thing I have ever felt. I think I will be sick right here on the street, dry heaves because my stomach is empty.

Then I hear something behind me and I turn around shivering like somebody just slid some ice inside my shirt down my spine. There's this guy standing there.

He is tall and he has white hair and you can almost see the blood beating at his temples because his skin is so thin and white. He has those eyes that look like cut glass and those pretty lips and he's wearing that white coat. He is probably the most gorgeous human being I have ever seen in real life and the most nasty-looking at the same time.

He's the mannequin in the boutique window and the man in Central Park and at the museum.

"It's kind of late for you to be here, isn't it?" he says. He has a very soft voice. Something about his voice and the dry sweet smoky powdery champagne-y smell of his cologne and the way his hands look in his white gloves makes me want to sleep. "I don't open for a few more hours."

"I was just kickin' around," I say.

He glances up at Angel Juan in the window of the diner. "Would you like something to eat?" he asks me. "You look hungry."

I know it is stupid to be standing here talking to this freaky beautiful man but somehow I can't split.

"I make great hamburgers." He smiles. His teeth look really yellow next to his white skin, which is weird because the rest of him is so perfect. "Or milk shakes if you are a grass-eating *vegetarian*."

This is his place—the diner. And in the diner is a

mannequin of Angel Juan. So what am I supposed to do? I stand watching him take out a set of keys like they are something that a hypnosis guy swings in front of your face to put you to sleep and I follow him inside.

He puts on some lights and the spotless curved silver walls of the diner shine. The floor is black-and-white squares and the counter and swivel chairs are mint green. There are mirrored display cabinets on the walls full of fancy cakes that look like they are going to slide right down into your mouth. I feel a blast of sleepy heat filling the place.

"Sit down," he says. "What would you like?"

"I'm okay," I say. I don't want to eat but all of a sudden my stomach starts making noises like I haven't had food in it for weeks. Then I remember I really haven't eaten anything except some rice cakes in a while.

He smiles like Miss Shy Girl Thing. He goes behind the counter and takes off his gloves. I can see the blue veins in his hands. Then he starts scooping and mixing and whirring until he has made this amazing thick frosty snowy whipped-cream-topped vanilla milk shake. He puts it in a tall parfait glass, plops on one of those poison red candied cherries Weetzie won't let us eat, sinks in a straw and sets it on the counter. Then he presses raw meat into a patty and slaps that onto the sizzling grill. I haven't eaten a hamburger in a long time because no one at my house is into meat anymore but that meat smells pounceable. I feel dizzy. I skulk over to the milk shake on the counter and take a sip. You know those cold-headaches you get from eating ice cream too fast when you are a kid? That happens. But the sweet milkiness is like warm kisses at the same time so I just keep inhaling on that straw even with my head and chest frozen and hurting.

The man finishes the hamburger, slides it onto a fat sourdough bun, adds lettuce and onions and a juicy slab of tomato, stabs the whole thing with a toothpick and sets it in front of me on a plate. I almost fall on top of it. I can taste the meat before my teeth plunge in.

The man puts on the jukebox and it plays "Johnny Angel." I am so drugged by my meaty hamburger that it takes me a while to realize that Johnny Angel and Angel Juan are the same song. Same name. The voice singing "Johnny Angel" seems to be laughing at me, the whole jukebox shaking with laughter like, *Look at this crazy girl following some stranger into his diner trying to save her boyfriend who isn't even her boyfriend anymore because of some weird creepster dream.*

This is how people die. This is how kids are murdered. This is how you lose your mind and then your body and maybe this is how you lose your soul. Johnny Angel.

The man puts on a white waiter's cap like the one Angel Juan is wearing in the window and he leans over the counter staring at me with his no-color eyes.

"I am Cake," the man says.

He looks up at the neon-rimmed clock on the wall.

"I'm late," he says like the White Rabbit in *Alice in*

349

Wonderland, putting his gloves back on. "Come on. I have something to show you."

I don't know why I get up and go with him. But I keep thinking about my dream and the Angel Juan mannequin in the window.

Cake kneels on the floor behind the counter and lifts up one of the tiles. There's a dark staircase going down. Cake moves his hand for me to go first. Cake smiles and he looks like a guy in one of those sexy jeans ads but all bleached-out.

I hear music coming from down below and I think I recognize it. It sounds like the tune to "Niña Bruja," which is the song that Angel Juan wrote by himself when he was in Mexico. It has a kind of psychedelic sixties sound. I look up at Cake. Behind him, in the window of the diner, I can see the back of the Angel Juan mannequin's head.

Then I take off my roller skates and squeeze down through the trapdoor.

Cake follows me but it is more like I am following him even though I go first.

We walk down a few flights of stairs. Every once in a while there is a gold hand sticking out of the wall holding a neon candelabra with neon-tipped candles and you can see that the walls are red velvet but it is mostly pretty dark. I can still hear the music and I start to smell the sweet smoky smell, like what Cake is wearing only stronger and coming from ahead of us. I can feel Cake smiling behind me.

When we get to the bottom of the stairs there's a door. I can hear the music jamming louder now, making the door shudder but it isn't Angel Juan's song anymore. It still has a psychedelic sound though. Cake opens the door.

Here's this room with walls paneled in gold paint, mirrors and white velvet, white marble floors with red veins running through and huge red neon candles everywhere and all these kids sitting really still like statues. They are of all different races but they look kind of the same, I'm not sure why. They're all in white. All their eyes are really big and their cheeks are sunken and the girls look like boys and the boys look like girls. Then I realize they *are* statues like the mannequin of Angel Juan upstairs in the diner, which seems so far away now. One of these mannequins is sitting on a big overstuffed red velvet thing shaped like a mushroom and he's holding a long neon pipe. Real smoke is coming out of the pipe and filling the room and I wonder if the smoke is why I'm feeling drowsy. It smells like Cake. There're these other mannequins sitting at a long table. On one end is this guy with a really big droopy red velvet top hat that covers his eyes and at the other end there's this girl with white hair and buck teeth and in the middle of the table there's this huge teacup about the size of a baby bed which is what it is I guess because there's a baby mannequin sitting in it. Then there's a dark-skinned boy curled up on the floor and grinning so big and hard it looks like it hurts him even if he is a mannequin, which he is. The whole thing is too much for me and I think how I can get out of here when Cake comes up and puts his gloved hand on my shoulder.

"This is Cake's *real* shakin' palace," he says. "What's your name, sweetie?"

I don't say anything.

"Are you a runaway?"

I shake my head. It's hard to talk.

He smiles, pressing his lips together and nodding like—*right*. "I see kids on the streets like you. It's a crime the way they live. I feed them upstairs and then we come down here to play. They're like my family." He takes off his white coat. He is wearing a white double-breasted suit. "Will you dance with me?"

Before I know it I'm letting him twirl me around. I feel like one of those ballerinas on music boxes going around and around like I can't stop. My baseball cap flies off and my hair snakes out. I want to stop but Cake is still twirling me. Finally I fall against his white suit. I have a flash of dancing with Angel Juan at my birthday party once a long time ago. Feeling so safe inside those arms. Nothing could hurt.

"Don't be afraid, little lamb," Cake whispers. Lamb. Angel Juan used to call me that. "You're home now. Cake will take good care of you."

When I wake up I'm lying in the softest bed hung with white silk. I might be dead. Everything is so soft and quiet. The whole room is covered in white silk.

I feel sore and muffled from my cold, which is a full-on flu by now. I try not to think about who put me in this bed. Then I remember Cake and the mannequin kids. I've got to get out of here.

That's when I hear the whistling. I have never loved that goofster song so much in my whole life. Whatever it means. "R-A-G-G M-O-P-P Rag Mop doodely-doo."

Charlie B., Chuck Bat, the Bat Man. The glowy glow is hovering like a hummingbird. I get up and reach for a huge heavy silver hand mirror by the bed.

And there he is looking at me and waving his hands around all frantic.

"What is it, Charlie?" I ask. "Are you okay?"

He's not okay. I mean even for a ghost. His eyes aren't just sad. They're like tormented. I think he wants to tell me something.

"Do you want to tell me something?"

He points at me, puts his finger to his lips, points to the door. Then he turns slowly in the mirror so his back is to me. Stuck to his back are the wings I bought on the street! He looks at me over his shoulder.

"Angel?" I mouth.

Charlie turns back around and points to his heart. Then he clasps his hands together. I think about the brother grip.

353

"Angel Juan."

Charlie puts his finger to his lips again. I look toward the door. When I look back there's an ugster monster in the mirror. It takes me a second to get that it's Charlie wearing the rubber monster mask from the trunk. He takes it off and looks at me with those crazed eyes again.

Charlie's face in the mirror starts to blur. Then he flies out of the mirror like a comet. Out the door. I follow him.

We go down a maze of red-veined white marble hallways that seem like they don't lead anywhere. We pass mannequins half dressed in silk flowers and vines, sitting on garden swings that swing back and forth from the ceiling. Blonde boy mannequins on skateboards balanced on marble ramps. A glittery girl with blonde cotton-candy hair and a wand like Glinda's from *The Wizard of Oz*. A huge fish tank with mermaid mannequin children and tropical fish. A tall angel with a very young glowy face riding on a statue of a fish with plastic kids kneeling all around him. And somewhere, behind one of these doors we pass—my grandpa's ghost and me trying to be that quiet—is Cake sleeping with his pale eyes open. I hope Cake is sleeping. And maybe behind one of the doors ahead is Angel Juan.

I'm out of breath. I lean against the icy-veined marble wall and it makes my bones ache. I feel like I'm in a tomb. I wipe my forehead. My whole body is pounding with fever-fear.

Charlie's light is doing the nerve-jig so I keep following him through the maze and into a room made of mirrors.

And there in the mirror, jiggling like a puppet made of light, like the plastic charm-bracelet skeletons, like a life-sized Day of the Dead doll, is Charlie. He waves his hands all excited, his face scrunched with worry, and I figure out he wants me to press on one of the mirror panels and it opens. Out of the mirror he turns into a light again and we go down a staircase. At the bottom is a metal chamber room. It's so small and crowded with naked mannequins that I feel like I can't breathe, like the mannequins are hogging up all the air. A mannequin falls against me, hitting me with its jointed plastic arm and I look at its face and I see that it is Angel Juan. He's bald but it's him. I try not to scream but I jump back and bump into another mannequin and that one is Angel Juan too. I start slamming around and they're all falling on me and every single one has Angel's face. This is a room full of Angel Juans. What does this Cake want? What is happening here?

Then I notice the Charlie glow lighting up a corner of the room.

I touch the silvery angel that sleeps in the hollow part of my neck.

A boy is slumped against a wall with the mannequins all around him and a guitar with the Virgin Mary in a wreath of roses painted on it leaning against his chest. His hair is long and falling in his face and he looks like he hasn't eaten much in a while but even though he's changed a lot I know right away who he is. And it's like I understand stuff all of a sudden.

Dear Angel Juan,

Do you know when they say soul-mates? Everybody uses it in personal ads. "Soul-mate wanted." It doesn't mean too much now. But soul-mates—think about it. When your soul—whatever that is anyway—something so alive when you make music or love and so mysteriously hidden most of the rest of the time, so colorful and big but without color or shape—when your soul finds another soul it can recognize even before the rest of you knows about it. The rest of you just feels sweaty and jumpy at first. And your souls get married without even meaning to—even if you can't be together for some reason in real life, your souls just go ahead and make the wedding plans. A soul's wedding must be too beautiful to even look at. It must be blinding. It must be like all the weddings in the world—gondolas with canopies of doves, champagne glasses shattering, wings of veils, drums beating, flutes and trumpets, showers of roses. And after that happens you know—that's it, this is it. But sometimes you have to let that person go. When you're little, people, movies and fairy tales all tell you that one day you're going to meet this person. So you keep waiting and it's a lot harder than they make it sound. Then you meet and you think, okay, now we can just get on with it but you find out that sometimes your soul brother partner lover has other ideas about that. They want to go to New York and write their own songs or whatever. They feel like you don't really love them but the idea of them, the dream you've had since you were a kid about a

356

panther boy to carry you out of the forest of your fear or an
angel to make love and celestial music with in the clouds or
a genie twin to sleep with you inside a lamp. Which doesn't
mean they're not the one. It just means you've got to do
whatever you have to do for you alone. You've got to believe
in your magic and face right up to the mean nasty part of
yourself that wants to keep the one you love locked up in a
place in you where no one else can touch them or even see
them. Just the way when somebody you love dies you don't
stop loving them but you don't lock up their souls inside you.
You turn that love into something else, give it to somebody
else. And sometimes in a weird way when you do that you
get closer than ever to the person who died or the one your
soul married.

I run over and fall down next to him and put my arms
around him and he looks up like his head is almost too
heavy to lift and his jaw drops but he doesn't say anything.
He almost looks as blind as those mannequins himself.
But his heart is beating and he's not made of plastic and
I have my arms around him. He is in my arms.

Charlie-light starts doing his nervous dance like he
wants us to hurry.

I try to get Angel Juan to stand up but it's like he's too
weak or something—he just slumps down again, his fingers catching in my sweater and bringing me down with
him. I try to think of what to do but every time I see the
plastic mannequin faces staring at me and the plastic

smiles made from my boyfriend's lips and teeth I just go blank. I just keep thinking over and over again, What is Cake trying to do? How could this be? How can anything I do save us from this kind of a ghoulie demon thing?

And then we hear something that sounds like glass shattering. For a second I think of how I smashed that mirror in Charlie Bat's apartment and how stupid that was and that I'll be lucky if I'm around long enough to get seven years of any kind of luck at all. And then before any of us can move, the Cake demon comes storming into the room, pushing over the mannequins. He has blood on his hand. Maybe he cut himself on the mirror he broke in the mirror room. The blood is so red against his white hand and dripping onto his white silk robe. It almost seems like he wouldn't have red blood because he is so white. Like he'd have white icing coming out of him or something. But it's blood. I just stare at it. Then I see that he's holding something wrapped in a sheet and his blood is getting all over that too.

"What are you doing down here?" he says in his very soft voice. "Who said you could come down here?" He is King Clutch Warthog.

"I was just kickin'."

"Well, it's all right," Cake says. "I have something for you anyway."

He starts to unwrap the thing he's carrying. I see that it's another mannequin and it's smaller than the Angel Juan mannequins. I see the back of its head and it reminds me of the time when I shaved off all my hair with my dad's razor. Then I realize that the reason I'm thinking that is because this mannequin's head looks exactly like the shape of my head without any hair. Cake spins the mannequin around and there's me, Witch Baby—it's my face with the pointed chin and the tilty eyes. I hold on tight to Angel Juan's hand.

"When?" I say.

"I made her while you were sleeping. You've been sleeping for a few days. I'm going to put you inside of her."

"Why?" I say.

"Do you know about mummies? It's a little like that. I give you a place to sleep. All the children that I find. It's like you are immortal." Cake strokes the cheek of one of the Angel Juan mannequins. "Usually I just make one. But he is so beautiful. I just keep wanting to make more of him. Now I guess I'll have to put you both away for good." He looks at us with his pale-crystal eyes.

He comes toward me and puts out his hand—the one that's not bleeding. I want to go to him. I feel drowsy. I wish I had the globe lamp Weetzie gave me to ward off evil.

But:

Believe in your *own* magic, Weetzie said. Maybe my own magic gave me Charlie Bat.

Look stuff right in the eye, Vixanne Wigg said. Look at your own darkness. Maybe Cake is that. Maybe Cake is me. The part that wants to keep Angel Juan locked in my life.

359

All the ghosts and demons are just you, Charlie said. Look stuff right in the eye.

But I can't look in Cake's eyes. I'll be under his spell. So I take my camera and look at him through that.

My own magic. Maybe magic is just love. Maybe genies are what love would be if love walked and talked and lived in a lamp. The wishes might not come true the way you think they will, not everything will be perfect, but love will come because it always does, because why else would it exist and it will make everything hurt a little less. You just have to believe in yourself. Look your demons right in the eye. Set your Angel Juans free to do the same thing themselves.

I snap a picture of creepster Cake with the last shot in my camera. There is a flash like lightning.

My wishes are: my beloved Angel Juan is free, Charlie Bat finds peace, Cake becomes who he really is. These are my wishes.

Cake starts to shake. He is a white blur. Then he gets very still.

Angel Juan's limp fingers wake up in my hand. "Niña Bruja," he says. I look at him. We are both crying like babies. I feel my fever break into clean sweat. Angel Juan takes my hand and presses it to his lips. We put our arms around each other in our brother grip. And we watch Cake seal up inside himself, becoming a bleached plastic manne- quin man without a breath or a heartbeat. He's not any different from before really. This is who he really is.

We can leave.

Charlie's light leads us out of the chamber, down the halls. Angel Juan doesn't ask about the light that looks like it's coming from an invisible flashlight. He leans against me, holding my hand.

We get to the gold-and-white room with the manne-quin smoking a pipe and the family having a tea party and the grinning boy. None of them will ever leave. They look so real that it seems like we could wake them and take them with us but I know if I shook one of them the only sound would be the clatter of bones against plastic. Angel Juan knows what I'm thinking. He holds my hand tighter as we go through the door that leads back to our life.

It's dark when Charlie, Angel Juan and I come up into the empty diner. The jukebox is still playing "Johnny Angel" like it never stopped. My dirty dishes are still on the counter. But the Angel mannequin isn't in the window anymore.

I put on my skates. We go outside and it's so cold that Angel Juan and I can see the ghosts of our breath on the air. We put our arms around each other in our perfect-fit brother grip. We stumble-shake-skate back to the apart-ment following Charlie's light.

If Charlie's building reminded me of a beat-up old vaudeville guy when I first saw it, now I think all the rooms are like songs he still remembers in his head. And the best song is on the tenth floor in the Rag Mop room.

361

There is a note on the door.

Dear Lily,

We are home. The ghost is at peace. We hope you don't mind but we let ourselves in to give you a few things. Come by as soon as you can. We are worried about you. Love from your benevolent almost-almost uncles, Mallard and Meadows.

We go in. Charlie flies right over to his trunk and slips inside.

I look in the cupboards and the refrigerator. Mallard and Meadows filled them with food—apples, oranges, scones, bagels, oatmeal, raisins, almond butter, strawberry jam, tea and honey. Angel Juan and I chomp-down lap-up almost everything and fall onto the Persian carpet wrapped in each other like blankets.

"Thank you, Niña Bruja," he whispers, taking me in his arms. "You set me free, Miss Genie."

His eyelids flicker closed and I can hear his breathing getting deeper. I get up and go over to the trunk.

"Come on, Charles," I say.

I look into the mirror pieces. "Grandpa Bat?"

Slowly, like when ripply water in a pool gets still so you can see yourself, his face floats up out of the murky murk of the mirror.

"I'll miss you, Witch Baby." His voice fortune-cookie crackles, old-movie pops.

"You can come back with me to L.A. Weetzie would rock."

"I can't."

"Well then I'll visit you."

"No. I'm going to leave now. I needed to finish some things and now I'm done."

"Finish what?"

"I wanted to stay and meet you, little black lamb. And make sure you would be all right. I wanted to help you but I messed up and really you helped me."

"You didn't mess anything up."

"I didn't help you find Angel Juan."

"You helped me find me. You helped me rescue Angel Juan."

"I guess I did. I did something right finally. Something besides Weetzie."

"What did I do for you?"

"You made me see how I was—what is it you guys say—clutching? Onto Weetzie. Onto you so you couldn't do what you had to do. Clutching on life."

"How did I do that? I just hung out with you. You're the one who showed me all around."

"I saw you learning how to let go. And I have to remember I'm not alive anymore, honey."

"What am I supposed to do now?"

"Take your pictures, play your drums. I should have kept writing my plays."

"Don't go away, Charlie."

"Good-bye, Baby. Send my love to everyone. Especially Weetzie. I love you."

"Charlie. Grandpa."

But Charlie Bat smiles. It is strange and slow-mo. Real peaceful like the Buddha. It seems like his eyes are smiling along with his mouth now for the first time, the pupils almost disappearing into a crinkle of lines, just shining out a little. He lifts his hand and waves it back and forth, long fingers leaving a trail of light. Then he disappears into the darkness like a candle blown out. The shiny restless whistling whirr of energy that was my grandfather ghost is quiet now. All I see in the mirror is a kind-of-small girl. Maybe she looks a little like an Egyptian queen.

I open the window and look out. Blast of cold air makes my snarl-ball hair stand up on my scalp. There are stars, electric light bulbs, candles, fireflies. There are a million flickers, glimmers, shimmers, flashes, sparkles, glows. None of them will sing "Rag Mop" to me. None of them will take me through the city. None of them will tell me that we have the same blood. But in all of them is some Charlie Bat.

"Good-bye, Grandmaster Rag Mop Man," I whisper, lying down to sleep next to Angel Juan.

Dear Angel Juan,

I dream we are inside the globe lamp. But this time we just sleep there for a little while like two genies. In the morning we will fly out of the lamp. We will be able to travel all

around the world on our magic carpets, you and I, seeing
everything—sometimes parting, sometimes meeting again.

It's almost the next night when we wake up, shy like we've
never touched each other before or something.

I get the rest of the food and we munch it sitting on the
carpet talking about the things we've seen. Angels and fireflies, temples and flea markets. How I found his photo
booth pictures and his lost postcard. We don't talk about
Cake though.

"I started playing my songs on the streets," Angel Juan
says. "People give me money."

"Can I hear?"

And Angel Juan plays the song on his guitar.

Panther girl you guard my sleep
bite back at my pain with the edge of your teeth
carry me into the jungle dark
lope easy past the eyes that watch
stride the fish-scale river shine
and the pumping green-blood vines
we will leave my tears behind
in a pool that silver chimes
we will leave behind my sorrow
leave it in the rotting hollows
when I wake you are beside me
damp and matted from the journey

365

your eyes hazy as you try to know
how far down we tried to go
and the way I clung to you
all my tears soaking through
fur and flesh, muscle, bone
like a child blind, unborn
whose dreams caress you deep inside
are my dreams worth the ride?

In all the time we've made music together I have almost never heard his voice by itself without the rest of our band. It's a little scratchy and also sweet. I look at him and think, he's not a little boy anymore. He can go into the world alone and sing by himself. I am so hypnotized that at first I don't realize that the words are almost the same as the letter I wrote to him and never sent.

"How did you know?" I say when he is done. I am out of breath.

"What?"

"You just know me so much. How do you know me so much?"

He grins. "Do you like it?"

I don't have to say anything. He can see in my face.

"Baby, I missed you," he says.

"Do you need to stay in New York still?" I ask it looking right at him trying not to crampy-cram up inside.

He looks back into my eyes and nods. "I think so. A little while longer."

"Aren't you scared?"

"It's okay now. It's over."

It is.

"Maybe you could stay with me," he says.

"I have to go back to school and everything."

"Do you want me to go home with you?"

I look out the window. I think about Angel Juan playing his music down there in the streets. I think about the crowds rushing past. Some of the people stopping. Breathing in his music like air. Feeling it warm their skin and take them to places where it is green and gold and blue. Taking them into their dreams. Suddenly they can remember their dreams and walk through the city streets wearing their dreams. They turn into panthers, fireflies, trees, fields of sunflowers, oceans, avalanches, fireworks. It's all because of Angel Juan and his guitar.

"No," I say. "You stay. You can stay in Charlie's apartment."

"Niña . . ."

I put my finger to his lips. They press out firm and full and a little dry against the pad of my fingertip. I can feel my own lips buzz.

"I don't think I should stay in your family's place," he says.

"Weetzie would want you to."

"Only if you ask her."

"Angel Juan," I say, "I found your tree house."

He looks at me, his eyes so sparkly-dark. "Niña," he says. "Only you could do that."

"Were you with anybody else?" I ask.

"No, Baby. I thought about you all the time."

"What about that thing you said about us being together just 'cause we're scared of getting sick."

"I'm so sorry I said that shit. It scared me that you were the only person I've ever loved like this."

"Who was that man?"

"He was our fear," says Angel Juan. "My fear of love and yours of being alone. But we don't need him anymore."

I feel the tight grainy cut-glass feeling in my throat and my eyes fill up. Crying for the mannequin children and how we had to learn.

"Don't cry," Angel Juan says, but it looks like he is too. "You'll get tears in your ears. Don't cry, my baby. You saved me."

Then I feel Angel Juan's lips on mine like all the sunsets and caresses and music and feasty-feasts I have ever known.

It's the best feeling I've ever had. But it's not the only good feeling. I kiss Angel Juan back with all the other good feelings I can find inside of me, all the magic I have found.

When we go downstairs to see Mallard and Meadows it's kind of late.

Mallard throws open the door letting out steamy, fresh-baked-bread-and-cinnamon-incense-air into the hall.

"There you are," he says. "Meadows, she's fine."

"This is Angel Juan," I say as we come inside to the candlelit apartment lined with magic carpets.

Mallard and Meadows shake his hand. "Happy New Year," they say.

Happy New Year? Angel Juan and I look at each other. When did that happen?

"We lost track of time," I say.

"Well, it's New Year's," says Meadows. He smiles. "And Christmas too."

Mallard points to some packages. "They came for you in the mail."

We sit on the carpet eating cranberry bread while I open my packages.

There's film for my camera.

I take a picture of Mallard and Meadows on either side of Angel Juan in front of a wall with a magic carpet on it.

There's also a big black cashmere sweater and warm socks that I make Angel Juan take for himself.

From Weetzie there's a collage she made and put in a gold-leaf frame painted with pink and blue roses. The collage has pressed pansies, rose petals, glitter, lace, tiny pink plastic flamingos and babies, gold stars, tiny mirrors and hand-colored cutout photographs of my family. In the center there's a picture of me and a picture of Charlie Bat goofing in his top hat and it looks like we're holding hands. Something about our smoky eyes and skinny faces makes us look like a real grandfather and granddaughter.

There's a letter from Weetzie too.

Dear Witch Baby,

Happy Holidays! We all miss you so much. We're send-
ing you a ticket to come home on the second. I hope you
have found everything you are looking for.

After you left I thought a lot about why I couldn't dream
about Charlie. I think it was because I was holding on and
trying too hard. But somehow knowing you were in his
apartment bringing new life there I could let go of him. I
realized how I miss you, honey, and I can <u>see</u> you. Charlie's
gone. I made this collage of you and him and that night I
dreamed about him. He seemed very peaceful and happy in
the dream and it was so real.

I'm also sending you this other package that came in the
mail.

We are all going to be there to pick you up from the
airport.

We love you.

Weetzie

The other package is from Vixanne. I know right away
but I don't know how I know. I open it.

The girl is staring with slanted dark-violet eyes under
feathery eyelashes. Her hair is black and shiny with purple

370

lights, every strand painted so you can almost feel it. Her neck and shoulders are bare and small painted with creamy paint and there is a hummingbird hanging around her throat. She's in a jungle. Thick green vines and leaves. You can almost hear the sound of rushing water and feel the air all humid. On the girl's left shoulder is a black cat with gold eyes. On her right shoulder is a white monkey with big teeth bared. The scary clutch monkey is playing with her hair. Perched on top of her head are butterflies with wings the color and almost shape of her eyes.

"It's you," says Angel Juan.

It's weird because I guess it really does look like me but I didn't recognize myself. The girl is strange and wild and beautiful.

I think about Charlie like the black cat and Cake like the white monkey and how they are both parts of me and about butterflies shedding the withery cocoons, the prisons they spun out of themselves, and opening up like flowers.

Angel Juan just puts his arms around me. Mallard pours all of us some sparkling apple cider.

"How was your ghost?" I ask.

"He's fine now. His daughter and he just had to let each other go. She had to believe . . ."

"That he's inside her?"

"In a way. You know, Lily, you might make a good ghost hunter someday."

371

I just smile and we clink our glasses watching the tiny fountains of amber bubbles.

"Happy New Year."

Outside the window is New York city with its subways and shining firefly towers, its genies and demons. It is waiting for Angel Juan to sing it to sleep.

I look at Angel Juan. My black cashmere cat, my hummingbird-love, my mirror, my Ferris wheel, King Tut, Buddha Babe, marble boy-god. Just my friend. I know I'll be leaving him in the morning.

At home I'll skate to school and take lots of pictures. I'll take pictures of lankas, ducks, hipsters and homeboys. When I look through my camera at them I'll see what freaks them out and what they really jones for, what they want the most in the whole world and then I'll feel like they're not so different from me. I'll send copies of my New York pictures to the hip-hopscotch girls, the beautiful lanks and their Miss Pigtails, the African drum-dancers. I'll take more pictures of me too, dressed up like all the things I am scared of and the things I want. One will be of genie-me in a turban doing yoga next to the globe lamp with smoke all around me. Maybe Vixanne would like to see my pictures.

I'll play drums with The Goat Guys and write songs about New York and my family and me. I'll help with my family's movie about ghosts. I think they should call it *The Spectacular Spectral Spectacle*. It could be about a ghost of a man who helps a girl free herself from an evil demon ghoulie ghoul and how the girl lets go of her dad and sets *his* spirit free.

I might not see Angel Juan for a while. But we'll see each other again. Meet to dream-rock-slink-slam it-jam in the heart of the world.

Like we always do.

BOOK FIVE

Baby Be-Bop

PART I

Dirk and Fifi

Dirk had known it since he could remember.

At nap time he lay on the mat, feeling his skin sticking to brown plastic, listening to the buzz of flies, smelling the honeysuckle through the faraway window, tasting the coating of graham cracker cookies and milk in his mouth, wanting to be racing through space. He tried to think of something he liked.

He was on a train with the fathers—all naked and cookie-colored and laughing. There under the blasts of warm water spurting from the walls as the train moved slick through the land. All the bunching calf muscles dripping water and biceps full of power comforted Dirk. He tried to see his own father's face but there was always too much steam.

Dirk knew that there was something about this train that wasn't right. One day he heard his Grandma Fifi talking to her canaries, Pirouette and Minuet, in the teacup-colored kitchen with honey sun pouring through the windows.

"I'm afraid it's hard for him without a man around, Pet," Fifi said as she put birdseed into the green dome-shaped cage.

The canaries chirped at her.

"I asked him about what the men and ladies on his toy train were doing, Mini, and do you know what he said? He said they were all men taking showers together."

The canaries nuzzled each other on their perch. Pet did a perfect pirouette and Mini sang.

"I guess you're right. It's something all little boys go through. It's just a phase," Fifi said.

Just a phase. Dirk thought about those words over and over again. Just a phase. Until the train inside of him would crash. Until the thing inside of him that was wrong and bad would change. Until he would change. He waited and waited for the phase to end. When would it end? He tried to do everything fast so it would end faster. He got A's in school. He ran fast. He made his body strong so that he would be picked first for teams.

That was important—being picked first. The weak, skinny, scared boys got picked last. They got chased through the yard and had their jeans pulled up hard. Sometimes other kids threw food at them. Sometimes they went home with black eyes, bloody noses or swollen lips. Dirk knew that almost all the boys who were treated this way really did like girls. It was just that girls didn't like them yet. Dirk also knew that some of the boys that hurt them were doing it so they wouldn't have to think about liking boys themselves. They were burning, twisting and beating the part of themselves that might have once dreamed of trains and fathers.

Dirk knew that the main thing was to keep to himself and never to seem afraid.

Every Saturday afternoon his Grandma Fifi took him to see a matinee, where he could hide, dreaming, in crackling popcorn darkness. They saw James Dean in *Rebel Without a Cause*. That was who he wanted to be. He practiced squinting and pouting. He turned up his jacket collar and rolled his jeans. He slicked back his hair, carefully leaving one stray piece falling into his eyes. James Dean was beautiful because he didn't seem afraid of anything, but when Dirk looked into his eyes he knew that he secretly was and it made Dirk love him even more.

Grandma Fifi had two friends named Martin and Merlin who were afraid in a way Dirk didn't want to be. They were both very handsome and kind and always brought candies and toys when they came over for tea and Fifi's famous pastries. But as much as Dirk liked Martin and Merlin he knew he was different from them. They talked in voices as pale and soft as the shirts they wore and they moved as gracefully as Fifi did. Their eyes were startled and sad. They had been hurt because of who they were. Dirk didn't want to be hurt that way. He wanted to be strong and to love someone who was strong; he wanted to meet any gaze, to laugh under the brightest sunlight and never hide.

Dirk especially didn't want to hide from Grandma Fifi

but he wasn't sure how to tell her. He didn't want to disturb the world she had made for him in her cottage with the steep chocolate frosting roof, the birdbath held by a nymph and the seven stone dwarfs in the garden. There were so many butterflies in that garden that when Dirk was a little boy he could stand naked in a crowd of them and be completely covered. Jade-green pupas hung from the bushes like earrings. Fifi showed Dirk the gold sparks that would later become the butterflies' orange color. Then the pupa darkened and stretched and finally a fragile monarch bloomed. Fifi and Dirk put flower nectar or a mixture of honey and water on their fingertips and the newborn butterflies crawled onto them, all ticklish, and practiced fanning wings that were like amber stained glass in the sun. In the garden there were also little butterflies that looked like petals blown from the roses with the almond scent. There were peaches with pits that also smelled and looked like almonds when you cracked them open. Fifi showed Dirk how to pinch the honeysuckle blossoms that grew over the back gate so that sweet drops fell onto his tongue. She showed him how to pinch the snapdragons' jaws to make them sing. If Dirk ever cut himself playing, Fifi broke off a piece of the thick green aloe vera plant she called Love and a gel oozed out like Love's clear, thick blood. Fifi put the gel onto Dirk's cut and stuck a Peanuts Band-Aid over it; the cut always healed by the next day, skin smooth as if it had never been broken.

Fifi had a cat named Kit who had arrived through the window one evening while an Edith Piaf record was playing and never left. Kit had pinkish fur like the tints Fifi put in her white hair. If Dirk or Fifi ever had an ache or a pain, Kit would come and sit on the part of the body that hurt them—just sit and purr. She was very warm, and after a while the soreness would disappear.

"Kit is a great healer in a cat's body," Fifi said.

Kaboodle the Noodle was Fifi's dog. He had a valentine nose, long Greta Garbo lashes and a tiny shock of hair that stood straight up. When you were sad he kissed your hand and winked at you.

Dirk and Fifi and Kaboodle went shopping at the fruit stands on Fairfax that were covered with pink netting to keep out the flies. Kaboodle sat out in front and waited. Fifi bought bags of asparagus and bananas, kiwis and radishes, persimmons and yams. There was a little Middle Eastern market where she bought bottles of rose water and coffee beans as dark as chocolate. Fifi made pastries shaped like shells, ballet slippers and moons, and salads full of vegetables cut into the shapes of flowers.

Dirk knew that Fifi wanted great-grandchildren someday. She wanted to make pastries for them and teach them about how peach pits smelled like almonds, about butterflies that looked like flowers and about talking snapdragons. He knew he was her only chance. Worst of all, he knew she wanted him to be happy and how could he be happy in this world, he wondered, if what he knew about himself was true? So Dirk didn't tell Fifi. He didn't tell anyone. He kept to himself. He waited for the phase to end. Until the day he met Pup Lambert.

Dirk and Pup

The air smelled like lemon Pledge, sweet jasmine and mock orange. Bougainvillea grew thick up the fences like walls of paper flowers. Morning glories glowed neon purple, twining among the pink oleander. Nasturtiums shimmered along the ground like fallen sunlight.

As Dirk walked home from school he heard a whistle, and he looked up into an olive tree. In the branches sat a boy. He had brown hair with leaves in it, freckles on his turned-up nose and a Cheshire cat grin.

"Hey," the boy said.

"Hey," said Dirk.

"Want to shoot some baskets?" the boy asked.

"Sure."

The boy jumped out of the tree, landing lightly on the white rubber soles of his baby-blue Vans deck shoes.

Dirk and the boy shot baskets in the driveway of the pale yellow house with the pink camellias growing in front. Dirk was taller, but the boy was light on his feet and had perfect aim. Dirk's heart was beating fast like the basketball hitting the pavement again and again; he was sweating.

When a car pulled into the driveway the boy grabbed the basketball and took off down the street.

"Come on," he shouted.

Dirk stood still, looking at the boy and then into the car. A heavyset man got out. Dirk just had time to wonder how such a big man could have such a quick and slender son when the man said, "Scram! I told you not to hang around here anymore! I'll call the cops!"

Dirk ran after the boy. When he caught up with him, at the edge of a field of wildflowers, he was out of breath. The sweat was getting into his eyes.

"I thought that was your house," Dirk said.

The boy grinned. "Nope."

They stood under the shifting sunlight, laughing. Dirk thought their laughter would look like sunlight through leaves if he could see it. A flock of poppies, with their faces toward the sun, moved in the breeze as if they were laughing too. Dirk noticed that the boy's ears came to slight points at the top.

"I'm Pup," the boy said.

"Dirk."

"Hey, Dirk. Next time we'll borrow someone's swimming pool."

Two days later Pup jumped out of the tree again. He and Dirk climbed the fence of an ivy-covered Spanish house with a terra-cotta roof, and stripped down to their underwear. Then they took turns diving into the aqua water. Pup did more and more elaborate dives—cannonballs and flips and flailing-in-the-air things—and Dirk tried to imitate him. They stayed in the pool until the tips of their fingers looked crinkled and crushed, and then they dried out on the hot cement. Pup had freckles on his shoulders and a gold dusting of hair on his arms and legs. With his wet hair slicked back Dirk thought he looked like James Dean.

"Are you hungry?" Dirk asked Pup.

"Starving."

Dirk and Pup went to Farmer's Market where the air smelled like tropical fruit, chilled flowers, Cajun corn bread, Belgian waffles, deli meats and cheeses, coffee and the gooey sheets of saltwater taffy that spun round and round behind glass. The light filtered softly through the striped circus tent awnings. Wind chimes and coffee cups sang. Dirk looked for Pup but couldn't find him. Then he heard a whistle. He followed the sound to a corner table where Pup was sitting behind a huge banana cream pie. He handed Dirk a fork.

"Want some?"

"Where'd you get that?" Dirk asked.

Pup grinned his Cheshire grin.

Nothing had ever tasted so good to Dirk as that frothy concoction—peaks of meringue and melts of banana— that Pup had lifted so slyly from the pie counter. But the next day Dirk asked Grandma Fifi to make a pie so Pup wouldn't have to steal and invited his friend over for dinner.

After school they went to Fifi's cottage through the backyards of houses, leaping fences and climbing walls, patting dogs and dodging the lemons that one woman threw at them. Pup gathered avocados, roses and sprigs of cherry blossoms as he ran so that by the time he met Grandma Fifi at the front door he had almost more presents than he could carry.

"This is Pup," Dirk told her.

"Pleased to meet you, Pup," said Grandma Fifi. "Thank you for the alligator pears and the flowers."

"This is my Grandma Fifi," Dirk said.

"Hi," said Pup. He seemed suddenly shy. He shook the tips of his hair out of his eyes. He lowered his eyelashes.

"Come in for some snacks," said Fifi.

She brought out guava cream cheese pastries and a pitcher of lemonade. Pup gulped and swallowed as if he hadn't had food in days.

Then Dirk showed Pup the comics that he drew. They were about two boys who turned into the superheroes Slam and Jam when there was danger.

"You're serious," Pup said.

They lay on the floor of Dirk's room reading comics until the room turned jacaranda-blossom-purple with evening and the glow-in-the-dark constellations that Fifi had pasted on the ceiling began to come out.

"Superheroes aren't afraid of anything," Pup said softly, his voice fading with the light.

Kit jumped off the windowsill where she had been gazing at the blur of a hummingbird in the bottlebrush bush and sat on Pup's chest, over his heart. Kaboodle licked between his fingers.

"You don't seem afraid of much," said Dirk.

"I'm afraid of everything. That's why I do stuff. My mom is afraid of everything too but she just stays inside. She's afraid to go to the market, even."

"You can come over and eat with us when you want," Dirk said. "My grandma would like it."

"Thanks," said Pup.

He stayed for chicken pot pie with carrots and peas and peach pie for dessert. When you asked Fifi for pie you got it.

While they ate their dessert Fifi played an old record.

"Chills run up and down my spine / Aladdin's lamp is mine," the singer crooned, and Dirk felt silvery chills, saw, beneath his eyelids, the glinting lamp of love.

"This is cool music," Pup said.

"Do you dance, Pup?" Fifi asked.

"Not really," Pup said. "But I'm willing to have some lessons."

Fifi blushed. "Oh, I'm not very good anymore."

"That's not true," Dirk said. "She's a cool dancer."

"Show me," Pup said.

He stood and offered Fifi his hand. She took it, putting his other arm around her waist. Dirk watched as Fifi led Pup around the room so skillfully that it appeared he was leading her. But that was also because Pup was a natural dancer. Dirk watched how he held his head, proud on his straight strong neck, the way his shoulders curved.

"Your turn now, Dirk," Fifi said.

Dirk wasn't embarrassed the way he would have been around anyone else except Pup. Fifi felt light in his arms as they danced over the garlands of roses on the carpet. Pirouette and Mini did a waltz in their cage. Kaboodle sat up on his hind legs and offered Pup his paws. While Pup danced with Kaboodle, Kit watched them all from the mantelpiece.

When the record ended Pup insisted on skateboarding home although Fifi tried to offer him a ride. He and Dirk planned to meet in the quad at school the next day at lunch.

That morning Dirk told Fifi he was especially hungry so when he opened his lunch there was one sandwich with cheese, avocado, lettuce, pickles, artichoke hearts, olives, red onion and mustard and one with peanut butter, raspberry jam, honey, bananas and strawberries, both on home-baked bread.

"She always does that," Dirk said, pulling out the sandwiches and shaking his head. "Would you eat one of these, Pup?"

"Are you sure?"

"She acts all hurt when I bring one home but she keeps giving them to me."

Every day after that Fifi put two sandwiches in Dirk's lunch. She never asked her grandson why he had started to eat twice the normal amount. She just beamed at him and said, "You are growing so tall and strong. And so is your friend Pup Lambert. When I first met him I was sad to see how thin he was."

"I love you, Fifi," said Dirk.

"I love you, Dirk," Fifi said.

After school Pup and Dirk listened to music in Dirk's room. They could play it loud because Fifi was a bit hard of hearing. On the wall was a chalk drawing Dirk had made of Jimi Hendrix.

"That is hell of cool," said Pup. "You are a phenomenal artist, man."

Dirk tried to concentrate on keeping his ears from turning red.

"My mom went out with this gross trucker guy once," Pup told him. "He saw the Jimi poster in my room and goes, `That nigger looks like he's got a mouth full of cum.' I wanted to kill him. I told my mom I would if she didn't stop seeing him."

"Did she?"

"Yeah. But I don't think that's why. Her next boyfriend saw my Bowie poster and started calling him a fag. My mom said if I ever dressed like that she'd kick me out of the house."

Dirk and Pup looked up at Jimi burning his guitar. It flamed beneath the steeple of his hands, between his legs. Jimi had said it was like a sacrifice. He loved his guitar. He was giving up something he loved. Dirk wondered if Jimi had felt that way about life.

"We should start a band," Dirk said.

"Can you play?" asked Pup.

"A little. I mess around with my dad's guitar."

Dirk got out the guitar that he kept hidden in the closet. Pup stroked it. Dirk had never seen him touch anything with such concentrated love except for Kit and Kaboodle. Just like Kit and Kaboodle, the guitar seemed to love Pup. Dirk imagined he could hear it singing in Pup's arms although Pup's fingers never touched the strings.

"It's beautiful," Pup said. "Your dad was cool."

"I don't remember him," Dirk said.

"What happened?"

"My mom and dad died in a crash."

Pup looked up at the picture Dirk had drawn of his hero standing with his hands in his jeans pockets, shoulders hunched, feet rolling out.

"Like James Dean?"

"Kind of."

Pup's eyes got big. "I bet your dad looked like James Dean," he said. "'Cause you do."

Dirk picked up the guitar and bent to tune it so that Pup wouldn't see that his ears were turning red. He felt almost as if Pup had put his arm around him and said,

"I'm so sorry about your parents, Dirk. I wish they were alive."

Pup took a cigarette out of his pocket.

"Where did you get that?" Dirk asked.

"I steal them from my mom."

He lit the cigarette and handed it to Dirk. Dirk hesitated. He didn't want Pup to see him cough like someone who had never smoked before.

"You know I still cough sometimes," Pup said as if he could read Dirk's mind. "And I've been smoking for a year."

Dirk inhaled. He could feel where Pup's lips had been, moist on the paper end. Pup was unscrewing one of the large brass balls on Dirk's bedposts. "This is perfect," he said.

"For what?" Dirk coughed.

"For a tobacco stash," said Pup, depositing another cigarette inside the ball.

After he met Pup, Dirk's room became full of secrets. The cigarettes in the bedposts. The stolen Three Musketeers bars in the dresser drawer. The *Playboy* magazines under the bed. And the real secret that had always been there grew larger and larger each day until Dirk thought it would burst out licking its lips and rolling its eyeballs and telling everyone that Dirk McDonald wasn't normal.

Dirk looked at the *Playboys* that Pup brought, trying to feel something. All he could think of was that the giant breasts must keep the women safe somehow, protected. As if the breasts were padding for their hearts. His own was so close to the surface of his chest. He was afraid Pup might be able to see it beating there.

Dirk's heart sent sparks and flares through his veins like a fast wheel on cement when he was with Pup. They rode their bikes and skateboards, popping wheelies, doing jumps and flips. Dirk wanted to do wilder and wilder things. It wasn't so much that he was competing with Pup or showing off for him; he wanted to give the tricks to Pup like offerings. He wanted to say, neither of us has to be afraid of anything anymore. Their knees and elbows were always speckled with blood and gritty dirt from falling but Fifi treated them with gel from Love's leaves.

Every morning Pup came by on his skateboard or his bike. He never let Dirk meet him at his house. Dirk wondered what Pup's room was like, what his mother was like.

"You wouldn't want to know," Pup said. "She's just all sad and scared."

Dirk didn't push Pup. It didn't matter anyway where Pup came from as long as they were together. At school they met for lunch. Dirk always had two sandwiches—sometimes he even had peanut butter and jam on waffles, which was Pup's favorite. Dirk rolled his eyes and acted as if Fifi had always given him two sandwiches. He and Pup didn't talk much at school, just sat eating and scowling into the sun. Sometimes girls walked by giggling in their pastel T-shirts, matching tight jeans and pale suede platform Corkees sandals. Pup winked at them, and they tossed their winged hair, smacked their lip-glossed lips. Dirk was glad the girls were too shy to do much more than that. Even the tough boys never approached Dirk and Pup although Dirk was always braced for it, a tension in his shoulders that never went away. It seemed Pup was braced too. His muscles were a man's already, as if his fear had formed them that way to make up for his small size. So the tough boys never bothered them. Together they were invincible. You couldn't find anything nasty to say. They were brown all year long, lean and strong, good at sports, smart; they smoked cigarettes and skateboarded. They wore Vans and their Levi's were always ripped at the knees. The most popular girls dreamed about them.

They shot baskets in strangers' driveways and swam in neighbors' pools and picked flowers and fruits from gardens for Fifi. Sometimes they borrowed dogs from backyards and took them on walks for a while, bringing them home before their owners returned.

It was not just Kaboodle—Pup loved all dogs and all dogs loved Pup. They came running up to him with worshipping eyes and licked his fingers, immediately flopping onto their backs like hot dogs to let him pet their bellies. He always had scraps of bread in his pockets for them.

"What do you think dogs dream about?" Pup asked Dirk one day as Kaboodle lay stretched on top of his Vans, long eyelashes curling as if he had styled them that way.

"I've never really thought about it."

"I think dogs dream about wind and light and leaves

395

and squirrels and birds and when they cry they are dreaming about wolves and freeways. I wish I dreamed about those things."

"What do you dream about?"

"I don't know," Pup said.

Dirk was glad that Pup didn't ask him what he dreamed.

Dirk dreamed about Pup.

He dreamed they were the superheroes Slam and Jam—skateboarding in the sky over the city, rescuing hurt children and animals. The clouds were the shape and color of giant flowers. In Dirk's dream, he and Pup held each other in the center of a purple orchid cloud.

In the summer Dirk and Pup took the bus to the beach with Pup's two surfboards. Dirk never asked where he had gotten the boards but he thought Pup might have stolen them on one of his runs through the neighbors' backyards. As they waxed the boards with Mr. Zogg's Sex Wax to make them glide through the water, Pup told Dirk that surfing wasn't much different from skateboarding.

"You'll be a pro." He looked out at the horizon, measuring the swells.

Dirk followed Pup into the water with the board under his arm. All around him the ocean was blindingly bright, the color of water on a map. Through the sparkles of wet light Dirk saw Pup's smile before Pup paddled out on the surfboard, climbed onto it and was carried away like a part of the wave. Thinking about giving Pup his surfing like an embrace, Dirk plunged into the water with the board, steadying his body as the waves filled and fell beneath and around him.

Afterward they raced up the hot sand and collapsed belly-first onto their towels. They lay there until their hair was dry and the sun and salt water made their skin feel taut against their bones. Then they used the outdoor showers, peeling their trunks away from their bodies, feeling the granules of scratchy sand rinse off from between their legs in the cold water. Pup wrapped his towel around his waist and pulled off his trunks from underneath. Dirk tried not to look. He wrapped his towel the same way and tried to get out of his trunks as smoothly as possible while Pup pulled up his jeans under the towel.

Sometimes after they'd been surfing they sat at The Figtree Cafe on the Venice boardwalk drinking smoothies, eating blueberry muffins and watching the parade. There were velvet and tie-dye women who read tarot cards. Dirk never even wanted them to look at him, afraid they would guess his secret. There were kids break dancing and bulky bronze bodybuilders, a carnival of half-naked roller women, bicycle magician trickster boys, a clown who painted faces, a mocha-colored, electric blue-eyed man in a white turban who played electric guitar and warbled electric songs like a skating genie. There was an accordion-playing devil with a circus cart drawn by mangy stuffed

animals on bicycles. More animals dangled from a miniature carousel, and there was a real stuffed taxidermy dog,
rigid and nightmarish. Sometimes, to get away from all
of it—especially that dog carcass—Dirk and Pup walked
under the arcade of pastel Corinthian columns decaying in
the salt air, past the vine-covered wood-frame houses and
rose-jasmine gardens on the canals and the ducks flapping
their feet through the streets like little surfers.

One day after they'd been surfing Dirk started to get
on the bus but Pup put his sun-warmed hand on Dirk's
surf-sore biceps.

"I know a faster way."

Pup stuck out his thumb. With the freckles on his nose
and his bare feet he reminded Dirk of Huckleberry Finn,
his Huckleberry friend. Fifi had told Dirk never to hitch-
hike but Dirk didn't want to be afraid of anything, and
besides Pup looked so cute standing there with his thumb
out, so defiant and twinkly holding his surfboard, one hip
a little higher than the other, behind him the sky turning
as pink as the skin on his shoulders where his tan was
peeling.

Two girls in a white convertible Mustang stopped. Dirk
recognized them—it was Tracey Stace and Nancy Nance,
two of the most popular girls from their school.

"Don't you know it's dangerous to pick up hitchhikers?"
Pup teased.

"You guys aren't dangerous. You're too cute," Tracey
Stace said. "Besides, you go to Fairfax."

She had dimples and her hair was almost white in the sun, her breasts straining her crocheted bikini top. She was wearing cutoffs ripped the whole way up the sides to show her sleek tan thighs. Nancy Nance was a smaller, less dimpled, less cleavaged version of Tracey Stace. She flopped over into the backseat, and Dirk sat next to her. Pup sat in front with Tracey Stace.

"Want to come over?" she asked. "My mom's out of town."

Tracey Stace lived in a modern house in the hills, all wood and glass. There was a Jacuzzi in the backyard. She told Pup and Dirk to test the water while she and Nancy got what she called "refreshments." Pup slipped in. Dirk followed him, feeling big and awkward. The blasts of hot water massaged deep into the muscles of his lower back. Tracey and Nancy came out in their bikinis, carrying cold beers and a joint. Their bodies hardly made a ripple as they slid into the Jacuzzi. The moon was full, reflecting the whole of the sun. Lit up with it, the flowers in the garden looked like aliens with glowing skins. The palm trees shook in the Santa Ana winds like the hips of Hawaiian hula girls. Dirk thought about how Fifi called them palmistrees. She said she wondered if you could read their fortunes from above in the sky. He was glad that no one here could read his fortune.

Dirk watched how Pup held the joint and sucked in, narrowing his eyes. He did it too. The smoke burned sweetly in his throat and chest, releasing the place in his shoulders that was always tight, ready to react, to fight back, if someone found out his secret.

Tracey smacked some pink bubblegum-scented gloss from a fat stick onto her lips and moved closer to Pup. Then Dirk watched Pup lean over, just like that, not even thinking, not even trying, and kiss Tracey Stace's mouth. Seeing Pup like that, kissing the most beautiful girl in school, made Dirk want to weep—not just because it was Tracey Stace and not Dirk who Pup was kissing but because of the beauty of it, the way Pup's hand looked against Tracey Stace's back and the way his eyes closed, the long lashes clumping together, the moonlight washing over everything like the waves that Dirk still felt pulling his body and seething beneath him although they were now miles and hours away.

Dirk turned to Nancy Nance, who looked very delicate, like a little girl. He was afraid he might crush her. Her lashes were like flickers of moonlight on her cheek.

"You're so pretty," Dirk said. He wanted her to know that if something went wrong it wasn't because of that. She smiled shyly at him and he reached out for her, eyes closed, pressing his lips against hers.

Nancy did all the work after that. Dirk's beauty was all he had to give her although he would have given her more if he could. When he felt as if she would guess his secret he looked over at Pup and Tracey Stace. Pup had his legs around her and their bodies were moving up and down in the water.

Then Pup looked at Dirk. When Dirk saw what was in Pup's eyes his heart contracted with tiny pulses, the way Nancy Nance's body was trembling near his. Dirk knew then that Pup loved him too. But mixed with Pup's love was fear and soon it was just fear sucking the love away. Pup closed his eyes and there wasn't even fear anymore. There was just a beautiful boy with pointed ears kissing a girl in a Jacuzzi, a boy who hardly knew that Dirk existed.

After what had happened with Tracey Stace and Nancy Nance, Dirk knew that everything had changed. Before Dirk and Pup had kissed the girls they were still safe in their innocence, little Peter Pans never growing old, never having to explain. Now Dirk's love for Pup raged through him bitterly. It burned his shoulders like the sun, blistering as if it could peel off layers of skin. It stung like shards of glass embedded in a wound. It jolted him awake like an electric shock.

Tracey Stace and Nancy Nance picked Pup and Dirk up at Fifi's cottage. The girls were wearing tight white jeans that laced up front and back and lace-up T-shirts.

"Where we going?" Pup asked, kissing Tracey Stace's cheek.

"A dance club in the valley," Tracey said.

"We don't dance," Pup said. "We hate disco."

"It's not a disco place. They play KROQ music."

"We still don't dance," said Pup.

Dirk was glad he hadn't told them about dancing with Fifi in the kitchen.

"You can watch us," Tracey said and Nancy giggled.

Dirk and Pup sat behind the dj booth watching Tracey's and Nancy's blond hair change colors under the strobe lights as they danced to Adam and the Ants, Devo, and the Go-Gos. Pup lit up a cigarette. Dirk waited for Pup to hand it to him but instead Pup held out the pack. Dirk took his own cigarette. It was the first time they hadn't shared.

"I scored a whole pack this time," Pup said, as if he were explaining it.

Dirk looked at Pup, far away behind a cloud of blue smoke, moving farther and farther away. Tracey and Nancy were twisting, snaking, shaking and skanking all over the floor. When "Los Angeles" by X came on they butted heads and collided into each other, working their elbows and knees in all directions.

"Punk rock," Tracey shrilled.

Punk rock, Dirk thought as a boy jumped off the carpeted bench along the mirrored wall and began slamming with invisible demons. With his stiff sunglass-black Mohawk, rows of earrings and black leather boots, the sweat and strength of his body, he made Tracey and Nancy's version look like hopscotch.

Dirk could almost feel Pup's heart slamming inside of him as he watched the boy. Dirk knew, seeing that dancer, alone and proud, tormented and beautiful, that he had

found something he wanted to be. The boy reminded Dirk
of Wild Animal Park.

When he was little Fifi had taken him on the wild
animal safari. You had to keep the windows rolled up so
the animals couldn't get in. Dirk wanted to get out of the
car and run around with them. They were fierce and wise
and easy in their skins. That was what the dancing boy
reminded Dirk of.

"That dude has some hell of cool boots," Pup said,
flicking ashes.

Tracey and Nancy danced over. "She told you this
wasn't a disco," Nancy said.

"I think punk is gross," said Tracey.

When they left the club that night Dirk saw Mohawk
and three other boys with short hair and black clothes
leaning against a turquoise-blue-and-white '55 Pontiac in
the parking lot, smoking.

"My grandmother drives a car like that," Dirk said.
"A red-and-white one."

He looked back at the boys as Tracey Stace drove away.

"Want to come over?" Tracey asked.

"I'm feeling kind of burnt," Dirk said. "You can just
drop me off."

Pup didn't come by Dirk's house the next day. Dirk felt
like his stomach was a roller coaster as he rode his skateboard to school. At lunchtime he looked for Pup. He was
sitting with Tracey Stace and Nancy Nance.

"What's up?" Dirk asked.

"Not much," Pup said. "You should have hung with us last night. We drove up to Mulholland."

"Where were you this morning?" Dirk asked.

He saw Pup's upper lip curl slightly. "Tracey gave me a ride. We were out all night."

For three days Pup didn't come by Dirk's house. When Dirk finally called and asked him what he was doing that night Pup said, "I'm seeing Tracey." That was all. He didn't ask Dirk to join them.

Dirk saw Pup and Tracey walking on campus with their hands in the back pockets of each other's jeans and knew that he had to do something. If he didn't tell Pup his feelings he thought he might go slamming through space, careening into everything until there was nothing left of him but bruises wilting on bone. He caught up with Pup in the hall after school.

"Are you free today, man?" Dirk asked.

Pup looked like a startled animal caught in the beam of headlights in the middle of a road.

"I'm seeing Tracey," he said. It didn't sound mean, just sad, Dirk thought.

"Just meet me at the tree this afternoon." Dirk walked away.

He didn't really expect Pup to be at the tree where they had first met. It was a warm day but he kept his Wayfarer sunglasses on, kept his sweatshirt on. He practiced skate-

board tricks on the sidewalk under the olive tree where Pup
and he had put their footprints once when the cement
was wet. He was skateboarding over the black stains of
smashed olives and the footprints when he heard the thud
of rubber Vans soles on cement, and there was Pup with
leaves in his hair just like the first day.

"Hey," Pup said.

"Hey," said Dirk, flipping his skateboard into the air and
catching it. He gestured with his head and started walking.
Pup walked much more slowly than usual. Dirk could smell
his scent—clean like salt water and honeysuckle and grass.

"Want to stop by the house?" Dirk asked.

Pup shrugged. They were silent the whole way to the
cottage.

Jimi Hendrix on the stereo. Pup slouched on the floor
in Dirk's room while Dirk unscrewed the bedpost and took
out what he had hidden there. He shook the pot into the
paper and rolled and licked the way the boy who had sold
it to him had done. Then he lit the joint and handed it
to Pup. Pup took a deep hit and handed it back. Dirk
breathed in smoke like the green and golden afternoon
light. Maybe it would make him brave.

"Nancy really likes you," Pup said after his second hit.
"She's a babe."

"She is," said Dirk.

"You should've gone with us up to Mulholland."

Dirk wanted a magical plant to grow inside of him,

405

making him proud and at ease. He and Pup smoked some more. Jimi's guitar burned with music.

"I just wanted to tell you. I've been pretending my whole life. I'm so sick of it. You're my best friend." Dirk looked down, feeling the heat in his face.

"Don't even say it, Dirk," said Pup.

Dirk started to reach out his hand but drew it back. He started to open his mouth to explain but Pup whispered, "Please don't. I can't handle it, man."

He got up and pushed his hair out of his eyes. "I love you, Dirk," Pup said. "But I can't handle it."

And then before Dirk knew it, Pup was gone.

That night Dirk stood in the bathroom looking at his reflection. He didn't see the fine angles of his cheekbones, the delicate bridge of his nose, the tenderness of his lips. He didn't see the sparkle of his dark eyes that seemed to shine up from the deepest, brightest place. He saw a scared boy who was in love with Pup Lambert and who hated himself.

Dirk took a razor and began to shave the sides of his scalp. The buzz vibrated into his brain. How thin was the skin at his temples, Dirk thought. Just skin stretched over pulse. He thought about the punk rock boy at the dance club. There was something about that boy that no one could touch. Dirk took the hair that was left on his head and dyed it with black dye so that it was almost blue. Then he formed it into a spikey fan. He smoothed it with Fifi's gel and sprayed it with her Aqua Net so it stood

straight up like the hair on top of Kaboodle's head.

At school Dirk wore all black and his Mohawk. Everyone turned and stared. But no one had questions in their eyes about what it was all hiding underneath. The disguise worked. There was some fear, some admiration, some jealousy, but no one despised Dirk the way he knew they would if he revealed his secret.

Also, no one questioned why Dirk and Pup didn't share a lunch on the same bench anymore, why they didn't play basketball together. It all seemed because of the Mohawk, the big boots Dirk had started to wear, the Germs and X buttons on his collar. That seemed like enough. No one knew that it was because of a glance in a Jacuzzi, a joint shared like a kiss and then turned to ash, a shock of love.

Dirk and the Tear Jerks

Fifi watched Dirk and his Mohawk more closely now. Her blue eyes looked always ready to spill. Dirk wanted to tell her, how he wanted to tell her, but what if the tears spilled, blue onto her cheeks? What if he hurt the one person who had loved him his whole life? What if she said, "It's just a phase," and he had to tell her, "It's not just a phase, Grandma Fifi. It's who I am."

And why did he have to tell? Boys who loved girls didn't have to sit their mothers down and say, "Mom, I love girls. I want to sleep with them." It would be too embarrassing. Just because what he felt was different, did it have to be discussed?

On Dirk's sixteenth birthday Fifi called him into the kitchen.

"Where's Pup?" Fifi asked. "I thought you were going to invite him over."

"He's busy," Dirk said. "You know that. You ask me every day."

Kit came and sat on Dirk's lap. Kaboodle covered his

eyes with his paws. Pet and Mini did a tragic ballet in their cage.

Fifi had baked Dirk a chocolate raspberry kiwi cake. The candles made her shine like the Christmas tree angel she put on her pink-flocked tree each year. Dirk closed his eyes and blew the candles out. He didn't make a wish. There were no wishes inside of him anymore.

"I have something for you, sweetie," Fifi said.

Kaboodle winked at him and licked frosting off his fingers.

Dirk followed Fifi outside, Kaboodle bouncing at their feet so that his tongue swung with each step. Fifi's red-and-white 1955 Pontiac convertible was parked in the driveway. It had a huge red ribbon tied around its middle.

"I know it's nothing you haven't seen before," Fifi said. "I would have gotten you a new car if I could have."

"You're giving me your car!"

He stroked the cherry red, the vanilla white, the silver chrome. It was like a sundae, like a valentine, like a little train, a magic carpet.

"Well, if you want it. Now that you can drive I thought it would be a good present. It's very safe. They made those things sturdy back then. And I'm getting a little too old to drive."

"I'll be your chauffeur. I love it, Grandma," Dirk said.

Then he noticed something different about the car. Mounted on the front was a golden thing.

"What's that?"

"It's a family heirloom. A lamp. It comes off the car, but for now I thought it looked splendid as a hood ornament."

"What's it for?"

"When you are ready you can tell your story into it," Fifi said. "You can talk about Pup—whatever you want to say. Secrets. Things you can't tell anyone."

"I don't have anything to say."

"Someday you may. Someday it might help."

Dirk looked at the golden thing. He was afraid of it. He wanted Fifi to take it back. But what could he do? Anyway, he had the car and that's what mattered. With the car he didn't need Pup; he didn't need anybody. He could drive through the canyons with the top down, race along Mulholland's precarious curves, looking at the city glistering below. He could feel the breeze kissing his naked temples, more tender than any lover. Go to punk gigs by himself. Slam in the pit with the boys until the pain sweated out of him, let the pain-sweat dry up and evaporate in the night air as he drove and drove.

But Dirk didn't go out that night. Instead he lay alone in the darkness. His hands kept wandering over his body wanting to touch himself the way someone would rub a magic lamp in a fairy tale to make a genie appear. But Dirk pulled his hands away. He wanted to cut them off. He wanted to turn off his mind. He tried to think about Nancy Nance but all he could see was Pup Lambert.

Dirk remembered what Fifi had said to him. How could he tell his story, he wondered? He had no story.

And if he did no one would want to hear it. He would be laughed at, maybe attacked. So it was better to have no story at all. It was better to be dead inside.

He looked up at the billboard models looming above like hard angels in denim as he drove down the Sunset Strip one night. I would rather have no story at all, Dirk decided. I want to be blank like a model on a billboard. I want to be untouchable and beautiful and completely dead inside. But he thought of the stuffed dog he and Pup had seen on the Venice boardwalk, so long ago it seemed now—a rigor mortis display. Without a story of love would he become only that?

Dirk was going to see X at the Whiskey A-Go-Go. He had a fake ID he had made himself using his new driver's license. He had a black leather motorcycle jacket covered with zippers that he had found at a musty dusty cobwebs-and-lace thrift store for only ten dollars. He had his warrior Mohawk. Kaboodle was sitting next to him on the front seat with gel in his shock of hair and his big paw resting on Dirk's leg.

The dark club was full of pierced, painted boys with shaved heads. They were slamming in the pit in front of the stage, throwing their bodies against each other in a wild-thing rumpus. Dirk felt that he fit in here much better than at school. Exene wove around with her two-tone hair hanging over her eyes and her arms and legs sticking out of her little black dress like the limbs of a doll that had been thrown around too much. John Doe's face looked even

411

whiter against his black hair as he twisted it into expressions of torture and ecstasy, baring his teeth or pouting like James Dean. Billy Zoom's platinum ice devil smile never left his lips as he played his guitar at crotch level. The music made Dirk think of black roses on fire. He wanted to leap onstage and dive into the crowd the way some of the boys were doing. He wanted to play music that would make the boys in the pit sweat like that. Maybe that was how those boys cried, Dirk thought. Maybe he would start a band called the Tear Jerks. For a moment he remembered sitting in his room with Pup, Pup holding the guitar, but he let the drums beat the thought away. His own band. Dirk and the Tear Jerks. Tear Jerk Dirk.

His throat and heart felt tight, constricted with dryness, so he bought a beer and gulped it down. Then he went and stood at the edge of the slammers. Some boys behind him were moving up and down in place, jostling him forward. Finally he flung himself into the writhing body mass. It was like surfing in a way, fighting to stay up above seething waters that wanted to consume you, part of you wanting to be consumed, to vanish into radiance.

"The world's a mess it's in my kiss," X sang.

Dirk felt the bitterness and anguish making his lips tingle. He raged arms and legs akimbo into the fury. He was carried forward by the whirlpools of the crowd to the stage. On the stage. Blinded sweat tears lights. Howling. Panic. Pandemonium. Pan, hooved horned god. Flinging himself off into space. Waiting for the fall, the hard smack, unconsciousness.

No. Buoyed up. Thrilling sweat-slick biceps. Cradled for a moment. Father. Father. Objects in flight around the room. Fragments of poetry. Lost eyes far away. Eyes like boats drifting farther and farther away.

He was back on his feet again. The crowd had caught him. He had felt their respect and admiration. He wiped off sweat with the back of his hand and went to get another beer. As he walked through the crowd he felt some bodies move back to give him room, witness his strength, others brush against him to feel it. The lights caught zipper metal and raven hair. Sweat on tan skin like beer drops brown glass glisten.

After the show Dirk gave Kaboodle some water and walked him until he peed. A boy and girl with matching burgundy hair that stood straight up on their heads like flames smiled at them.

"Mohawk dog," the boy said. "You're twins." Dirk and Kaboodle smiled back.

They got in the car and drove by Oki Dogs on Santa Monica Boulevard. Punks, kids with long greasy hair and junky-bulky veins in shriveled arms, tall men with big cars and sharp teeth, sat on the scarred benches under fluorescent lights that buzzed like flies or fat cooking. Dirk stopped the Pontiac and got out. The man at the counter shouted at him, "Okay okay," so he just said, "Oki Dog and a Coke." The Oki Dog was a giant hot dog smothered with cheese and beans and pastrami slices and wrapped in a tortilla. Dirk ate a few bites. It tasted salty greasy rich dark danger like the night. He was so hungry.

Then he saw a shrink-wrap swastika earring. It was dangling from the ear of a girl with spikey hair. The girl was drinking a Coke and giggling with her friends. She could have been Tracey or Nancy with a punk haircut.

"Do you know what that earring means?" Dirk said. He had never spoken out like this but suddenly his nerves felt huge, fluorescent, explosive. Maybe from the music still in his head. Maybe from the symbol.

The girl giggled. "It's a punk thing."

"Do you know who Hitler was?" Dirk asked.

"Yeah sure."

"Really? You know about the concentration camps?"

"Kind of. I guess. Why?"

"Hitler massacred innocent people. I'm sure you heard about it sometime. That was his symbol. The swastika."

"I got it at Poseur. It's cool."

"It is so uncool. You can't even believe how uncool it is," Dirk said.

The girl lowered her eyes. She looked to her friends and back to Dirk.

Dirk left Oki Dogs and got in his car. Kaboodle kissed his face and Dirk gave him the rest of the Oki Dog. As they drove away Dirk saw the girl pull the earring out of her ear and look at it.

So maybe it wasn't what he thought, this scene. But it was a wild enough animal safari that his own beastliness might go unnoticed.

He drove over the city's shoulders tattooed with wandering, hungry children and used car lots, drove past hanging traffic light earrings into beery breath mist, up and up above the city, trying to shed it like a skin. On the city's shaved head was the crown of the Griffith Observatory. The viewing balcony was closed, but the star Dirk had come to see was the bronze bust of James Dean on its pedestal. He gazed into its light and would have exchanged his soul for that boy's if he could.

Because he couldn't give his soul to James Dean, Dirk kept going out. Just keep going out, he told himself.

The Vex was a club in an old ballroom. Dirk drove into the parking lot under a freeway, concrete shaking like an earthquake. Inside there was a long curved bar and columns and balconies and chandeliers but everything looked ready to crumble from age and the freeway vibrations. Dirk watched a boy and girl slamming. The boy threw the girl down on the ground. She was wearing a lot of metal that shocked against the wood of the floor. He started hitting her in the face. Finally some guys broke it up but to Dirk it seemed like it went on forever. There was blood the color of her lipstick on the girl's face.

Dirk felt the piece of pizza he had eaten for dinner hot in his throat and ran into the bathroom. When he looked up under the greenish-white chill of the lights, his head felt as if he had slammed it against porcelain.

After that, Dirk drove along Sunset to the Carney's hot dog train.

"Do you have a dollar?" The boy sitting in front of Carney's looked like Sid Vicious. "I'm Sinbad," he said.

He was really skinny so Dirk motioned for him to follow him in. But when they were sitting on the bench outside, Sinbad said he didn't want the hot dog Dirk had bought.

"I'm a vampire," he said.

"A what?"

"A vampire."

He bared his teeth. He had fangs.

"They're bonded on," he said. "They really work. Want to see?"

"No," Dirk said.

"Don't you want to exchange blood with me?" He leaned closer on the bench.

"Get away from me," said Dirk.

"You don't know what might happen," said Sinbad.

Two boys walked by, leaning against each other, sharing a frozen yogurt.

"If you ask me all those fags are going to die out," said Sinbad.

As he got in his car, wishing he had brought Kaboodle for a kiss and a wink, Dirk thought of Sinbad's eyes. They were familiar. Where had he seen them? Then Dirk knew

416

he had seen those eyes in the mirror when he scrutinized his face for blemishes and imperfections, when he imagined that no one would ever love him.

Fifi was volunteering at a local hospital the next night. Dirk was home listening to his Adolescents album.

"I hate them all—creatures."

The angry voice made Fifi's collection of plaster Jesus statues shake as if there were an earthquake, or as if they were about to start slamming, Dirk thought. He imagined a pit full of slamming plaster Jesuses. He didn't like the thought.

Suddenly Fifi's music box with the ballerina on top began to play, the ballerina going around and around on one toe. The china cabinet doors flew open and Fifi's coaster collection spun out like tiny Frisbees. Dirk covered his head to protect himself. The clown paintings on the walls swung back and forth, and Dirk thought he heard them laughing evil clown laughter. Dirk had never liked the clowns. He turned away from their leering mouths and saw the plaster Jesus statues slamming. Dirk stared into the eyes of one of them. The eyes were glowing. The statue fell from the shelf and its head broke off but the eyes kept sizzling like fried eggs. Finally the Adolescents' song was over and the house was quiet. Dirk heard an owl hooting in a branch outside the window and some cats screaming. He could have screamed like that. He plucked his wet T-shirt away from his sweating body and collapsed on the bed.

417

Fear, the band, was playing out in the valley. Dirk armed himself in chains and the leather motorcycle jacket. He rode the 101. The freeway made him think of loss instead of hope, stretching out under a hovering orangish buzz of night air, not seeming to lead anywhere. At night the valley felt deserted. Dirk drove down barren streets under tall streetlamps. The little houses looked blank, as if they wanted to deny that anything unpleasant happened in or around them, but the way they were nestling under the crackling telephone wires, Dirk knew they were afraid.

Dirk got to the place where Fear was. Punks were hanging out in the parking lot drinking beers, smoking, grimacing—everything out of the sides of their mouths. White-bleached hair bright under the blue lights, black-dyed hair stiff with hair spray, ears and noses pierced with metal, backs covered with leather. Some boys were giving each other tattoos with ink and needles. One boy was burning his arm with a cigarette butt while a girl shrieked at him. Dirk couldn't tell if she was laughing or crying.

He went inside. The lead singer's square white head and hate-filled mouth seemed blown up, larger than life. As the music speeded, Dirk climbed out of the pit, up onstage and flung himself into the slamming mash of bodies. As he fell into the sweating arms he felt desire inside and around him but it was a brutal thing, feverish and dangerous. He looked into the eyes of one boy and saw that the desire was mixed with a hate so deep it had the same shape as the swastika tattoo on the side of the boy's vein-corded neck. Dirk knew there was nothing he could say to the boy that would change what he thought about the thing inked so deep into his flesh, inked so deep into him. It wasn't like shrink wrap. But he said it anyway.

"Fuck fascist skinhead shit."

Swastika and two other boys with the same tattoo followed Dirk outside when the show was over.

"Where you going, faggot?" the first boy said.

Dirk felt they had looked inside of him to his most terrible secret and it shocked him so much that he lost all the quiet strength he had been trying to build for as long as he could remember.

"Fuck you," he whispered.

The skinheads were on him all at once. Dirk saw their eyes glittering like mica chips with the reflection of his own self-loathing. He wondered if he deserved this because he wanted to touch and kiss a boy. The sound of everything was so loud and he kept seeing the skinhead skulls with the stubble, the bunches of flesh at the back of the neck like a bulldog's. His own head felt like a shell. A thin one you could crush on the beach. He had never realized how delicate his head was. This pain was hardly different from what he had always felt inside—torn, jarred, pummeled. In a way it was a relief—a confirmation of that other pain. But he wanted to escape it all finally.

He wanted to die.

When the blood had stopped pouring enough for him

to see, Dirk drove home. He never knew, later, how he made it. He had to stop every so often to lean his head against the wheel. Blood was all over the car upholstery.

Once when he looked up from the steering wheel he saw a house crossing the road. It was a cheerful-looking yellow house moving on wheels through the valley night. Dirk thought at first he must be hallucinating. Then he thought, my father. He didn't know why but that was what he thought. He leaned his head back down and when he looked up the house was gone.

When he got home finally he managed somehow to get the lamp Fifi had given him off the front of the car and carry it inside. He staggered to the bathroom and washed the gashes on his face while Kaboodle whimpered at his feet and gently pawed his leg. His reflection pitched and blurred in the mirror. Blood was caking now, turning darker and thicker.

Dirk steadied himself by leaning against the wall until he got to his bed. He fell down there and closed his eyes.

Dirk dreamed of the train. It was moving through the hills, through the forests like a thought through his mind, like blood through a vein in him. There were the fathers taking their showers. They were naked and close together under the water. But something was different. Thin fathers. Emaciated bodies. Shaved scalps. Something was happening. What was happening? Not water. Gas. Coming through the pipes. Gas to make their lungs explode. Dying fathers as the train kept going kept going kept going. To hell.

PART II

Gazelle's Story

Kit was lying over Dirk's heart staring at him, her usually aloe-vera-green eyes now black with pupil. Even Kit could not take away the pain flashing and shrieking through Dirk's body like an ambulance. His blood shivered.

Help me; tell me a story, Dirk thought, knowing that somewhere in the room the lamp was waiting. Tell me a story that will make me want to live, because right now I don't want to live. Help me.

He shut his eyes.

The wind was tapping the peach tree's long thin leaf fingers against the window. The moon cast shadows of the branches across the floor. Dirk sat up in bed and Kit jumped off of him, yowling. It felt as if Dirk's heart leaped out of his body with her. In the corner of the room beside the golden lamp the figure of a woman was seated on a chair. She was wearing a long dress of creamy satin covered with satin roses and beads that shone like crystals under rushing water, raindrops in the moonlight. There was a veil over her face but Dirk could see her pallor, the sadness in her eyes. Eyes like his own. He clutched his wild-duck-printed flannel pajama shirt closer around his chest impulsively but he was no longer cold. And the pain was far away now—a fading red light, a retreating siren.

Am I alive? Dirk wondered.

He wished that the woman would go away. But she looked so sad; she looked as though she needed to talk to him.

"Who are you?" Dirk said softly into the darkness.

"My name is Gazelle Sunday. You want me to go."

"No I don't."

Was she about to cry? Dirk didn't want her to. He tried to think of something.

"Do you have a story?" Dirk asked.

"A story?"

"Yeah. I don't have one."

"I can't remember," she said.

"I bet you can. I bet you are full of stories. I can see in your eyes."

"No, no, not really."

"Try to think." He really wanted her to tell him something now. "Maybe something about that dress. Where did you get that dress?"

The woman reached her almost-transparent hand out to him.

"Please," he said.

"If you will dance with me."

"Okay," said Dirk, and then wondered if that was such a good idea. She looked like death. He wondered if she would dance away with him. Dance him to his grave. Maybe that was the best thing. Maybe that was what he wanted. Or it had happened already. And besides he had promised, and she, this white ghost lady, had begun to tell.

"I never knew my mother but I knew she had given me my name and I loved her for that. I imagined that my mother and father were from France, very young, very in love. In my mind they looked like children in the book of fairy tales—the only thing besides my name that my mother had left me. The book was big and full of intricate, jewel-colored pictures of castles with turrets, enchanted mossy forests, goblins, banshees, trolls, brownies, pixies, fairies with huge butterfly wings and djinns on magic carpets. I pretended that the two children in one story were my parents. I saw them walking into the woods, their faces as pale as the snow they trudged through, their eyes big dark mirrors like the frozen lakes they had to cross, their mouths like petals ripped from the red roses that they waited for all winter but never saw again, dying in each other's arms when I was born. At least that is the story I told myself, walking in circles, twisting my hair around one finger, sucking my lower lip, holding the book open in my arms.

"I lived with my aunt in a dark and musty building. The kitchen smelled of boiled cabbage and potatoes; the claw-foot bathtub behind the screen in the kitchen corner smelled of mildew no matter how hard I scrubbed it clean. I was always leaning my head out the window to smell the bay, the baking bread, to hear the trolley car ringing its bell as it crested the steep hill. In the parlor was a dressmaker's mannequin. I was afraid that if I misbehaved the mannequin would attack me with the needles and scissors my aunt used to make dresses.

"My aunt was a cold woman with raw hands and a mouth that looked as if it was always full of pins. She hated me. I knew that the only reason she let me live with her at all was because I helped her sew. I became a better and better seamstress. I could do the most elaborate embroidery and beadwork with my tiny fingers. I could make roses out of silk; they looked so real you hallucinated their fragrance. Women came from all over the city for my dresses. My aunt never let me wear what I made. I had one black frock and a brown one for Sunday church—the only day she let me out of the house. I didn't mind the hard work, really, or the plain clothes or even the fact that I couldn't leave and had no friends. But I wanted to dance. I needed it. Dancing was the only thing I wanted. I would do it in secret. With a child's wisdom I knew never to let my aunt see. She thought it was a sin."

That's like me, Dirk thought. Like me loving boys, not wanting anyone to know.

"When she went out I pulled back the carpets. It was very strange. Whenever she went out some beautiful music

426

would start to play in the apartment next door. I learned later that it was Chopin. It was like a magical being from my fairy book had entered my body when I heard the music. I felt the strong center of who I was pulsing with the sound of those fingers on the piano keys; it radiated out through my limbs until I became like a giant butterfly or a silk rose, a waterfall, fire. I never saw anyone come out of the next-door apartment but it didn't matter—the gift of their music made me feel I had finally found a friend. I danced wildly the story of my parents, of my birth, my life with my aunt. I saw worlds beyond the parlor as if I were soaring through the air on a magic carpet, cities twinkling like fairies or the crowns of giants, and forests green and singing with elves."

In just the way that Gazelle had seen those cities and forests, Dirk saw, there before him, a Victorian parlor and a slim girl dancing among coffinlike furniture draped in dark shawls. She had a child's body in old-fashioned white underwear but her eyes and mouth were a woman's. She was spinning as if she wanted to make herself dizzy, falling to the floor where she twisted and turned and tangled in her pale hair, each motion full of longing. Dirk heard, too, the faint strains of piano music ghosting the air.

"I danced till I was nauseous and sweating through my underthings," Gazelle went on. "I had to change before my aunt came home. I knew she was coming because the music always stopped in time for me to change and get back to work. But one day even when the music stopped I kept dancing. I couldn't stop. I heard the music inside of me still. So that when my aunt came into the room I didn't even look up. I was kneeling on the floor, running my hands all over my body. Then I opened my eyes and I realized there hadn't been music for quite a while. My aunt was looking at me with scissors in her eyes.

"She grabbed my arm and pulled me to my feet.

" 'What were you doing?' she said as if she were snipping pieces out of the air.

"I told her I was dancing.

" 'Do you know what happens to girls like you?' my aunt said.

"I saw the mannequin in the corner. The cloth I had covered it with had slipped off. I imagined that the mannequin had needles sticking out of her body and was ready to shoot them across the room at me.

" 'Girls who touch themselves grow up ugly,' my aunt said, like a curse. 'No one will ever marry you. No one will want you because you will be a little monster. You are the devil's bride. He plays music in your head.'

"And it was worse than being whipped. It was as if she had broken my legs with that. I never heard the music again. I never danced. I never told my story.

"When I bled for the first time a few months later my aunt saw the stains on my underthings and said, 'You see. You see what happens to girls who touch themselves. They bleed like little monsters. But they don't die. You will wish you died, I think, because you will always be alone.' "

"Oh my God," Dirk said. "How could she do that to you? She was sick."

Gazelle wrung her hands. She was trembling.

"Are you cold?" Dirk asked her. He took a blanket off the bed and held it out.

"Oh, no thank you. How kind you are. Kind, like him."

"Who?" Dirk asked.

Gazelle's eyes filled with tears. "He saved me, finally. I thought I was a monster. I huddled and hunched in my black dress. My fingers cramped like an old woman's. My face grew twisted with pain. There were always bruise-blue circles under my eyes from holding my tears back. Without my dancing I was like the mannequin in the corner, no arms or legs, swaddled and bound. I never left the apartment.

"But he came to me finally. It was my sixteenth birthday, and my aunt was out. It was a windy evening full of spirits. I almost thought I heard my piano player through the walls but it was only the wind. There was a knock on the door."

As she spoke, Dirk saw the parlor again, the image quivering as if behind smoke or water. The girl was older this time, and her body looked as if it had never danced and never would. Dirk gasped to see how different she was, almost as ravaged as the woman in white. He wished he could have waltzed her out of that place.

She hobbled over to a door and opened it. There stood a small man with dark skin and blue eyes. His head was

429

shaved so that his sharp cheekbones seemed to stick out even more.

"I shivered with awe when I saw him. I felt my whole life lived in that moment—blooming from a seed in my mother's belly, swimming like a tiny slippery fish, growing a birdlike skeleton, clawing forth—a baby lynx, dancing as a girl, becoming a woman with a child inside of me, lying in a satin-lined coffin beneath the earth while a young woman danced the story of her life above me.

"'I need you to make a dress for my beloved,' said the man in a voice like a purr.

"'Come in,' I said.

"He sat on the brown sofa. I noticed a red jewel embedded in his nose. It caught the light like a tiny fire.

"'I want you to make me the most beautiful dress,' he went on. He reached into the sack he was carrying— he must have had a sack of some kind although I don't really remember it now. But how else could he have brought the fabric in? I remember the fabric. It was a bolt of thick cream Florentine satin. And he also gave me the most fragile lace—all chrysanthemums and peonies and lilies and baby's breath—and a golden box full of tiny crystal beads.

"He put all these things in front of me.

"'I'll need to see the woman in order to make it,' I said. I imagined a fairy woman with dark skin and pale eyes like his, jewels in her ears and nose and on her fingers, chunks of rubies, emeralds and sapphires like her eyes. I would have been afraid to touch a woman like that—to have her there at my fingertips, just on the other side of the satin, vulnerable to my pins and needles. But I wanted to see her, too.

" 'I want the dress to be a surprise for her' was all he would say.

" 'Do you have her dress size and measurements?' I asked. I was very shy. I kept my head down the whole time I spoke to him. But I had to look up to see his answer because he was silent, just shaking his head and looking at me.

" 'Well, how will I know what size to make it?'

"His eyes on me were like the softest touch, a touch I had not known since the last time I let my own hands caress my now monstrous, bleeding body, since the last time I danced. They were the color of blue ball-gown taffeta.

'Looking at you . . . I think she is just your size,' he said.

"I blushed so much that I thought I was the color of the ruby in his nose. How could he know about my body beneath the black shawl I wore bundled around me? But I agreed to make the dress.

"Then he left. I almost danced again. I did dance in a way—my fingers danced over the satin. I sat at the black-and-gold sphinx sewing machine and made a ballet of a

431

dress—the most beautiful dress. When I was finished he came back. My aunt was away. He asked me to put the dress on.

"I went into the back bedroom, so dim and draped in dark fabrics to keep out the light, and I put on the dress. The satin against my skin made me want to weep. The dress felt cool and warm, light and soft, supple and strong the way I imagined a lover would feel. I looked at myself in the stained mirror and hardly recognized the gleaming woman, skin as pure and pale as the satin, eyes lit with the candleshine of the dress, lips moist with the pleasure of the dress, who stared back at me.

"I came out into the parlor and showed the stranger. He sat forward on the sofa and looked at me with a hypnotic blue gaze.

" 'Thank you,' he said. I started to leave the room to change but he called me back. He put a large stack of bills on the table and rose to leave.

" 'Wait,' I said. 'Don't you want it? Isn't it right?'

" 'It is perfect.'

My eyes were full of questions.

" 'The dress is for you, Gazelle. And there is something else I want to give you.' "

Dirk watched Gazelle take the golden lamp to her breast as if it were a nursing child. "I asked him what it was," she said.

"What did he say?" Dirk whispered.

432

"That it was the place to keep my secrets, the story of my love. But I told him I have no story."

Like me and Fifi, Dirk thought.

"He said, 'Yes you do. We all do. Someday you will know it.' He started to leave then, and I brushed my fingers against his shoulder. His eyes looked into mine—big pale sky crystals full of sorrow and wisdom. Lakes full of first stars that I wanted to leap into, wishing.

" 'Please,' I said.

"He took my hands in his. His hands weren't much bigger than mine but they were powerful and hot, the color of the cocoa velvet I used to sew winter hats. He put his lips to mine. I felt the room fill up with satiny light and a sweet powdery fragrance.

" 'You must not be afraid' were the last words he said to me.

"The next month I didn't bleed. At first I thought that my aunt's curse was over—I wasn't a monster anymore, I had been good. But when my belly got bigger and bigger I thought that her curse had become even more powerful.

" 'Oh, I knew you were evil,' she said. 'It must be the devil's child. Who else could have touched you? Who else would have touched you?'

"I thought about the stranger. Could he have been the devil? If he was the devil I would have gone with him anyway. I wished he would come back."

"How could she say those things to you?" Dirk asked.

"What happened? Did you have your baby?"

"Yes. She told me we would put it up for adoption when it was born. And she locked me in my room so the women who came over for fittings wouldn't see me. She only opened the door to give me food and the material to sew. I wanted to die. I might have killed myself with the sewing shears except for three things—the baby inside of me, the magical dress hidden in mothballs and tissue in my closet and the words I heard purring through my head. 'You must not be afraid.'

"Then just before my baby was born my aunt fell ill. She let me out of my room, and I sat at her bedside pressing damp lavender-soaked rags to her forehead and feeding her soft food."

"You should have strangled her," Dirk said. "Sorry. But I think she deserved it."

"She was a damaged woman. I would have been too if the stranger hadn't come. Someone had seen her touch herself, maybe even seen her dance, and told her those horrible lies."

Dirk said, "You're kinder than I am," and she answered, "No, not really. I was just trying to protect my baby, you know. I remembered all the fairy tales about the evil witch cursing the child. She'd almost destroyed me, and I wasn't going to let her hurt the baby."

"Did she?"

"No. She died rather peacefully with my hands on her

temples. Poor thing, I think I might have been the first one to touch her in all those years."

"Then what happened?"

"I gave birth to the most beautiful little girl! The most perfect little girl. She had tiny naturally turned-out feet and fluttering pink hands like wings and she danced everywhere. From the moment she came out of me she was dancing."

Dirk saw the phantom parlor again, although this time the walls were freshly painted white; the floral friezes along the ceiling were pale pink and blue. Lace curtains like bridal veils hung at the open windows. He thought he heard the piano music again.

"I painted the inside of the house and kept the windows open all day," Gazelle said. "I sewed large floral tapestry cloth pillows, pink, blue and gold, and stuffed them with dried lavender and rose petals. I re-covered the brown sofa in jade-green velvet. I made a chiffon canopy over the bed and lit long tapers so that through the draperies the house looked full of stars. I built fires in the fireplace that my aunt never used, and the house smelled of cedar smoke. I read poetry aloud—Shelley and Keats. 'The silver lamp—the ravishment—the wonder. The darkness—loneliness—the fearful thunder,' only it was a golden lamp and there was no more darkness.

"My daughter, who loved to draw, made a picture of a lovely face and put it on the mannequin under a big hat

435

covered with birds' nests full of pale blue eggs.

" 'Now you won't be afraid of her anymore,' she said, child-wise.

"No longer prisoners, we went out into the city that had been forbidden to me for so long. We walked up and down the hills until our legs ached, then rode the trolley car to feel rushes of salty, misty air. We had picnics and fed the swans on the lake under the flowering terra-cotta arches, drank tea and ate pastries in rooms with cupids and rosebuds painted on the walls, strolled through the park, green-dazzled, fragrance-drunk, gasped at treasures gleaming gold in the half-lit glass cases of the museum. Then we'd return with spices, fruits and vegetables from Chinatown, seafood and baguettes from the wharf.

"The piano music began again—coming through the walls every evening—and I watched my child dance. It was almost as if I were dancing myself. She danced among the spools of thread, the ribbons and laces, the silk flowers.

"After a while I took her for ballet lessons from Madame Joy. I brought her to the studio four times a week. She was the littlest in class but the very best; everyone thought so. I made her a garland of silk blossoms and some tiny pink net wings. She always played sprites or pixies in the dance recitals. I sat and watched her with such pride.

"Sometimes, though, she wouldn't stick to the choreography. She couldn't help it, she'd just start doing her own dances. Madame Joy hated that.

" 'What are you doing, idiot-child!' she screamed.

"She took her cane and hooked it around my baby's waist; she hit it against her backside. I was mortified when I found bruises on her.

" 'I don't want you going back there,' I said. 'You can dance at home.'

"But I knew she missed performing. I sat and watched her for hours, shining a light on her, but it wasn't the same.

"One day when we were walking down the street she started to jump up and down, tugging my fingers and pointing. Two little boys in spangled blue costumes were taking turns balancing on each other's shoulders in front of a crowd. She let go of my hand and before I could stop her she had jumped into the act, climbing up the tree of the boys to pose on top like a Christmas angel. They made her spin like a music box ballerina. The crowd cheered. I was so proud. After that Fifi joined the act."

"Fifi!" Dirk said.

"Yes. Your grandmother."

"I didn't know all this about her childhood," Dirk said. "Or about you." He was embarrassed that he hadn't even heard Gazelle's name before.

"That's because you never asked."

Dirk knew that was true. He had just assumed that Fifi was always a spun-sugar-haired grandmother living in the cottage, alone.

"And she never asked about my life," Gazelle said. "And I never asked about my aunt's. That's the way children are sometimes. Until it's too late. If I had asked my aunt about herself it might have helped her. It's important to tell your story. It's important to listen."

"Tell me more," Dirk said.

"The years went by. Fifi danced with Martin and Merlin, first on the street and then in cafés. Everyone thought that either Martin or Merlin was her beau so Fifi never had any gentleman callers. Sometimes I would find her crying into the tulle and silk of her dancing costume.

" 'What's wrong?' I would ask her. 'Your dress will be so heavy with tears the boys won't be able to lift you.'

" 'No man will like me,' she said. 'I'm such a cricket, an insect.'

" 'Don't say those things,' I scolded. I was afraid that somehow I had passed on to her the self-hatred my aunt had given me, although I was always telling her what a great beauty she was and that her size only added to it. Still, she did her stretches diligently, hoping they would make her taller. She wore the highest heels she could find, although I warned her about her feet, and did exercises to increase her bustline.

"I told her that I thought people believed she was engaged to Martin or Merlin, that she might not encourage that so much, but she wouldn't hear of it. She always held their arms when they walked down the street and let them introduce her as their fiancée sometimes. It was her way of protecting them, you see. In those days their feelings for each other weren't something people talked about. Of course, it was quite obvious to me. When they performed they would hand her back and forth between them like a love letter."

"Like a love letter," Dirk said.

"Yes. They loved each other."

"I know," said Dirk. "What do you think about that?"

"Any love that is love is right," Gazelle said. "It's the same as me touching myself when I was a child. Do you understand?"

"Yes," Dirk said. "I understand." Something in his body opened like a love letter. He wondered if Fifi would understand about him. . . . Maybe she had all along.

Gazelle went on.

"Fifi always played along with being engaged to Martin or Merlin, depending on whose relatives were at the show. But it enforced the feeling that no man would love her the way she dreamed of being loved. She became more shy, staying home all day drawing and painting in the parlor. Sometimes we went to the countryside where she set up an easel and painted the fields full of cows, the wildflowers and redwoods. She loved color. She used to say how she would paint everything if she could, eat orange or green porridge, cover the ceiling with flowers, make her hair pink or purple."

"Fifi the original punk," Dirk said. "She just needed a man as wild as she was."

"Well, she found him. One night she was performing at a supper club. As she left the theater in her gold brocade coat, peach roses in her hair, she was stopped by a tall,

439

dark, sad-eyed man. He tipped his hat to her and a hundred fireflies came swarming out, surrounding her and lighting her up as if she were still on stage."

" 'How did you learn that?' she gasped.

" 'I'm an entomologist,' he said. "But magic like this only happens when you meet your true love. My name is Derwood McDonald.' "

"McDonald," Dirk said. "My grandfather. He was a bug guy?"

"That's right," said Gazelle. "I wouldn't call him a bug guy. He was a magician really."

"That's what the bug ambulances are about, I guess," Dirk said. "When Grandma Fifi finds an insect in the house she gets an old yogurt container or something and makes this siren noise. She puts the bug into it and takes it outside. She calls it a bug ambulance."

"That's my daughter," Gazelle said. "Anyway, just then her partners appeared and took her arms.

"Derwood McDonald introduced himself to them and added, 'I was going to ask you to dinner, Fifi, but you look as if you already have plans.'

"She told him she didn't have plans, that she saw Martin and Merlin every day and every night.

" 'It's true,' they agreed, nodding in unison. From all their performances they had become accustomed to moving as one.

" 'Fifi might enjoy some new company.' They bowed and walked off, side by side.

"By the time Fifi and Derwood got to the restaurant there were so many ladybugs on Derwood's jacket collar that they looked like red polka dots.

" 'You must have very good luck,' she said.

" 'I am having it now,' he answered.

"They ate pasta and drank red wine. She told him about her dancing, how she loved to draw and had started to take art classes.

" 'I won't always be able to do those adagio tricks,' she said. 'I'm trying to plan for my future.'

"He told her, 'You will probably dance when you are ninety years old. You remind me of the fairies I saw in the countryside when I was a boy. My father—he was a naturalist too—pointed them out to me as if they were just another form of insect so I never understood why people thought they were made up. They had wings like large honeysuckle blossoms and were finger-size, but otherwise you look just like one. After I grew up I thought I'd never see another fairy,' he said. 'Until I laid eyes on you. Are you a fairy, Fifi?'

"Fifi giggled. Derwood laughed too but his fairy-filled eyes remained sad.

"He walked her home. She came into the house flushed and happier than I had ever seen her. I thought of the night the stranger had come to my door.

" 'What is it, Fifi?' I asked.

"She knew even then that she loved him, that she wanted to marry him."

"On Sundays Derwood took Fifi to the countryside. They caught butterflies in a net, studied the beautiful paintings of their wings and set them free. When Derwood found dead butterflies he would take them home and make collages that he framed behind glass. He and Fifi looked for fairies too, but never found any."

" 'It doesn't matter,' Derwood said as she came back with dirt on her hands and leaves in her hair from searching through grottos and barrows. 'You are my fairy.'

"In the evenings Derwood came calling with honey from his bees. It tasted like nothing less than nectar made for the love of a golden queen by a hundred droning drones. We slathered it on homemade bread, drizzled it over rice pudding, let big shining drops fall into our teacups and blended it into sauces for the salmon we ate on Fridays. I played the phonograph and Fifi danced. Sometimes Martin and Merlin came over too and they all performed for us. Derwood sat on the jade-green sofa among the rose- and lavender-stuffed pillows wringing his hands during the most precarious balances, clapping and stomping when a trick had been executed."

"But as much as Fifi loved Derwood I could tell something was wrong.

"Finally, after Fifi had known him for a few months and he still hadn't kissed her, she asked him what it was.

" 'I have a heart condition,' he told her. 'The doctors tell me I only have a few more years to live.'

"Fifi wanted to run away from him.

"Derwood said, 'I will understand if you don't want to see me anymore.'

"Fifi broke into tears but her sobs sounded like the flicker of crickets. Hundreds of ladybugs flew and landed on her hat. Cocoons opened and butterflies were released in a storm. She held on to Derwood in the forest of wings, and a golden powder covered their faces. Fifi was afraid they would be suffocated, but the butterflies only seemed to be kissing their cheeks.

" 'I want to be with you, Derwood McDonald,' Fifi said. 'No matter what.'

"A golden ring slid down out of the air and moved across the picnic cloth toward Fifi. She gasped when she saw the two tiny ring bearers.

" 'These are my pet spiders, Charlotte and Webster,' Derwood said. 'They want to know if you will marry me.'

"Not wanting to waste a moment, Fifi and Derwood were married the next day. Fifi wore the dress I had made for the stranger. Hundreds of pink doves flew alongside Derwood's car on the way home.

"Derwood and Fifi lived in a gingerbread house a few blocks away from me. It had two tall columns in front and cherubs bearing garlands over the windows. It was painted lavender but it was like a greenhouse full of flowering plants, butterflies, crickets, doves. Thin sheets of tin, pressed with the patterns of ribboned urns full of cascading leaves, covered the walls. Derwood studied his insects by the light of the Tiffany lamp. Fifi, who was still taking

443

art classes, drew the insects Derwood loved, and made them dance—balletic butterflies, tangoing tarantulas, waltzing caterpillars and tap-dancing bees.

"Fifi and Derwood hated to be separated, even for moments. Wherever they went they held hands. At night Fifi danced for him, swirling around in her glittery dresses, bringing tears of joy to Derwood's eyes.

" 'I knew you were a fairy,' he said.

"Fifi peeked at him from behind a lavender ostrich-feather fan.

" 'Then I can make all your dreams come true.'

"He took her in his arms and kissed her as the pink doves watched from the rafters and ladybugs and spiders and butterflies sang silently along with the radio. Fifi knew, though, that she and Derwood had only one dream and that she could not make it come true. It would take a much more powerful fairy than Fifi to cure what was wrong with Derwood's heart.

"At night she put her head on his lean chest and heard it ticking like an explosive. Fifi did make many of her dear Derwood's dreams come true before he died.

" 'You make my dreams come true every night,' he whispered into her wispy hair as they fell asleep, fearless from the wine of love.

"And one night, Fifi knew that she was pregnant.

" 'I'm pregnant,' she almost shouted.

" 'You mean just this second?'

" 'Yes.'

" 'How do you know?'

" 'I know. I'm a dancer. I've always known things about my body.'

"Derwood put his hand on her flat stomach. Her narrow waist and hips didn't look big enough to hold a baby. Fifi listened for Derwood's tears in the darkness. Instead she heard the soft, damp crackle of his smile.

"So she had made another of his dreams come true. His son, Dirby McDonald, your father.

"Dirby was born a very serious little boy. His father was afraid to get too close to him because he knew their time together would be so short. Fifi was so busy worrying about Derwood that she didn't give the child the attention he needed. I tried to care for him but he was always far away in his own world. He was a mystery to me.

"Finally one day, while Fifi and Derwood were out on one of their excursions to the countryside, Derwood sat down by the bank of a shallow, shimmering creek. A giant white butterfly flew past, and Fifi ran after it. She wanted to show it to Derwood. Maybe, she thought, the butterfly is really the fairy we have been looking for. But she couldn't catch it. When she got back to the creek Derwood was lying on his back. His face was covered with butterflies. They seemed to be trying to get inside of him or maybe they were coming out of him. But Derwood did not struggle. By the time Fifi had run to his side the butterflies were scattered and Derwood was dead. Fifi drove Derwood's car back to the house and collapsed on the front step before I had time to open the door with Dirby in my arms. There was Fifi lying in a heap. For a moment I didn't recognize her. Her hair was completely white. Dirby didn't cry. He just stared like an old man who has seen many deaths, his face tight and drawn. I put his white-haired mother to bed. She wouldn't eat for days. She seemed to be shrinking.

" 'I never really believed he would die. I don't want to live without him,' she said.

" 'You have to live, for Dirby and me,' I said, holding up her son for her to see. Oh, your father looked like you, young Dirk. He looked like his own father too.

"It made Fifi weep to see Derwood's eyes in that young face but she reached out for him, and when she did the doves in the rafters sang again, and the peonies in the arboretum unfolded layers and layers like Renaissance ruffs.

" 'You see,' I said, 'you must hold on.'

"Her art school teacher sent her work to an animation department in Hollywood. They wanted to hire her.

" 'I don't want to leave you, Mama,' she said. 'I stayed alive so I could be with you and Dirby.'

"I told her she had to go. 'There are groves of orange trees—you can pick your breakfast every morning—fountains in the hillsides, starlets in silk stockings driving colorful jalopies with leopards in the passenger seats, sunshine all the time. The sun will be good for Dirby. He's as pale as his old grandmother.'

" 'You should come with us,' Fifi said, but I couldn't. I

was afraid to travel and besides, what if my stranger returned and I was gone?

"So they prepared to leave, Fifi and Dirby with Martin and Merlin in a big old automobile with the glitter-and-paint dance backdrops of swans and heavens and circuses and fairylands fastened to the top.

"I gave Fifi the stranger's lamp as a good-bye gift. I still didn't believe I had a story to tell. A self-imposed shroud of silence had covered me long before the real shroud of death made it impossible for me to speak. But my daughter would have a story, I thought; Fifi would fill the lamp.

"She didn't want to take it from me but I made her promise. Just before she was to leave, the story that I still did not believe was mine came to an end.

"And now it's time for you to dance with me," Gazelle said softly.

Dirk stood up slowly, aware of how light he felt, and held out his arms. She was like Fifi's feather boa—not only that weightless but she brushed his skin with ticklish flicks of softness. She smelled like his grandma too—cookies baking, roses, almonds. Gently, gently Dirk and his Great-Grandmother Gazelle danced around the room while the peach tree tapped at the window and the moon made a shadow forest on the floor. Dirk saw the story of her life repeated now with the sway of the white dress, the pleatings and swishings of satin.

"Thank you, Dirk," Gazelle said, when the dance was over. "Bless you. You listened. You listened."

447

Death came for me, Dirk thought. She was fading away as she had come and he thought he would dissolve with her, molecules shifting without substance into veil of spirit.

Be-Bop Bo-Peep

And that was when the guitar in the corner began to play by itself.

Dirk opened his eyes. The guitar seemed to be floating on its side, strings trembling with music. Strands of smoke were flying out of the golden lamp and whirling around the guitar.

"Daddy," Dirk said out loud, remembering something he had lost a long time ago.

And Dirk's daddy Dirby McDonald's face appeared out of the smoke just above the guitar, as handsome as James Dean, not much older than Dirk, eyes soft with love like a lullaby behind his black-framed glasses. Lullaby eyes.

"Dirk," his father said, "hang on now."

Dirk nodded. He could taste blood in his mouth like he'd been sucking on a dirty metal harmonica.

"You came back," Dirk said.

"You want a story. A wake-up story. A come-back story."

"Yes. Please," Dirk said. "Please tell me who you are. I've always wanted to know. I feel like I don't exist. I feel

449

like I'm spinning through space losing atoms, becoming invisible, disintegrating. I . . ."

"Shhh, now," Dirk's father said. His voice was gentle. It was like his guitar. Like his eyes. Dirk thought, His eyes are guitars.

"What do you want to know?"

"What you felt. Who you were. Why you died."

"I always felt lonely," Dirby said. "It was just who I was born to be. I felt more like a part of nature than like a boy. Do you know what I mean?"

Dirk wasn't sure.

"I'd look at the stars in the sky or at trees and I'd want to be that. I worried Fifi. She was always trying to get me to be normal—play with the other kids, laugh more. She took me to her bungalow on the studio lot and showed me how she made the limbs of creatures move by drawing them again and again on clear sheets with light shining through. One of her projects was a story about herself and my father. The fireflies had devilish grins, the ladybugs had long eyelashes, the honeybees sang like Cab Calloway and the spiders danced like Fred and Ginger. She tried to get me to laugh, but I just asked questions about how butter-flies hatched from cocoons and how spiders made their webs. I wanted to walk in the hills at night and get as close to the moon and stars as I could. I wanted to lie in the dark grasses of the canyon and listen to the wind play them like the strings of a guitar. I wrote poetry from the time I could write. That was the only way I could begin to express who

I was but the poems didn't make sense to my teachers. They didn't rhyme. They were about the wind sounds, the planets' motion, never about who I was or how I felt. I didn't think I felt anything. I was this mind more than a body or a heart. My mind photographing the stars, hearing the wind. My forehead was lined before I was sixteen and I was always thin no matter how much Fifi tried to feed me."

Dirk looked at his father's body in the black turtleneck and jeans. Dirby's frame was just like Dirk's with the broad shoulders, narrow hips and long legs, but Dirk weighed at least fifteen pounds more and was lean himself.

"When my father died and I saw my mother's hair turn suddenly white I decided I was going to be like the clouds passing over the moon or the waves sliding up and back or the birds putting sounds together. That was the only way I could go on, accepting the way life was, being in the world.

"Then one night when I was sixteen I hitchhiked down into Topanga Canyon. I loved it there—the wild of it so near the sea, the thickness of trees and the smell of salt water all sharp and clean. I had to get away from the sugar smell in Fifi's kitchen and the roses; as much as I loved her I felt like I couldn't breathe—like it wasn't my world in any way.

"I walked inside this canyon bar and for the first time in my life I felt at home with walls around me. There was a cat onstage playing saxophone and chicks in black stockings sitting around watching him. There was beer and smoke—not just cigarettes, the kind of smoke that helps ease you into trees and wind. I knew I'd be coming back here.

"I came back all the time—every chance I could get away. All I needed was my thumb and my poetry journal. I also got a black turtleneck from my father's closet and a black beret from a thrift store so I'd look like the other cats hanging there in the mystic smoke and swinging sax night.

"One night a skinny old guy wearing shades asked me what I was writing in that journal all the time and I told him poetry.

" 'You're a baby. What do you know about poetry?' he said, all languid-like.

" 'I know enough,' I said.

" 'Yeah. I bet you know some nursery rhymes. Little Bo-Peep come blow your horn the cat's in the meadow the chick's in the corn. That's poetry, right?'

"I tried to walk away from him but he called after me, 'That's poetry, right, Bo-Peep?' "

"After that everyone called me Bo-Peep. Until the night I got up on that stage, sat down on a stool in the moon of light and read what I'd been writing all those nights.

"Everyone got still, especially that old man. They leaned in close to dig the words. But it was more than words. Something was happening. There was this bottle of red wine and four glasses on the table next to me and they started dancing, I mean really dancing, doing some kind of tango-fandango number. Then the shades on the face of the old man jumped right off and started floating in the air, moving just out of his reach when he grabbed for them. I saw his eyes with the pinpoint pupils and red whites and knew why he wore those shades but there was nothing I could do about what was going on. I just kept reading. They were all digging it more and more, even the old guy. More stuff kept going on. My beret flew off my head and went slinging across the room onto the head of this beautiful chick. She had short hair like a boy's, almond-shaped eyes and breasts that were the shape of one of those stiff padded bras but I could tell, even from the stage, that she wasn't wearing one. She was wearing a black dress and black fishnet stockings on the longest legs I'd ever seen. She laughed and put her hands to her head where my beret had landed. Her girlfriend handed her a joint but it didn't stay between her long fingers. It flew right out of those fingers and across the room, landing in my hand. I swear this is all true, buddy. Not that it sounds like the truth but it was."

Dirk was less stunned by the thought of his father's words making wineglasses dance than by what he saw hovering behind Dirby. When he saw her he remembered the way her long eyelashes had felt, ticklish as butterflies against his skin, he remembered the smoke of her voice and the patchouli smell in her hair, her long glamorous legs in black stockings. She was more beautiful than any girl in a magazine, she the boyish goddess. She was Edie Sedgwick and Twiggy and Bowie and like his father she was James Dean too. Just Silver. Mother. While Dirby kept talking she did a slow rhythmic dance, hands over her head, torso moving with sinuous snakey charm.

"Mom," Dirk said.

"After, I stopped reading my poetry, things settled down," Dirby went on. "I mean no more dancing wineglasses or flying joints, but everyone went wild.

"The old guy came up onstage—he had his shades again—and said, 'This, my friends, is Be-Bop Bo-Peep, beat guru.'

"I wanted to get out of there fast but the beautiful chick reached for my arm when I passed her table and put the beret back on my head. She smelled like incense and patchouli and orange blossoms. The light caught the big silver hoops she wore in her ears.

" 'I dug that, Be-Bop,' she said.

"I just nodded the way I'd seen the hipsters do when someone dug them.

" 'My name is Just Silver,' she said. 'Just Silver with a capital J capital S. The Just is because I renounced my father's name.'

" 'Are you a model?' I asked.

"She was. An actress too. She had done little theater and had a tiny part in a Fellini film once.

" 'You are very, very beautiful,' I told her. I knew I sounded more like Bo-Peep than Be-Bop talking like that but I felt she had dug right into my heart.

"She asked if I'd read *Siddhartha*. It was my favorite book. She told me I reminded her of him.

" 'Come home with me,' she said.

"She drove me in her black convertible VW Bug to her apartment above the Sunset Strip. There was no furniture in the apartment—just rugs. Just Silver's family had traveled all over India and the Mideast purchasing rugs when she was a child. She lit some Nag Champa incense—flowers turned to powdery stick stems, turned to clouds of smoke petals—put on some Ravi Shankar and made her head move from side to side on her neck like an Indian goddess. Then she cooked vegetable curry with rare saffron that was the color of poppy pollen.

" 'Do you know what this is?' she asked, showing me a dancing metal goddess holding a severed head and wearing a necklace made of skulls.

" 'I might think twice about getting into her car if I was hitching,' I said.

" 'Would you really? I don't believe you.'

" 'You're right. I'd get right in. She is beautiful.'

" 'She's Kali, the blessing, dancing goddess. She's also death. In the East those things can go together.'

"I knew what she meant. She danced for me for a while and then we lay on her mattress and made love all night.

"After that I didn't feel any less lonely, only that Just Silver had joined me in the wild blue windscape of my loneliness.

" 'I'm pregnant,' she said one night as I felt her draw me inside of her like a mouth on a pipe full of a burning dream-plant.

" 'What? Just this second?'

" 'Yes.'

" 'How do you know?'

" 'I am very in touch with my body.'

" 'I can tell.'

" 'What are we going to do?' She said we, knowing somehow that I wasn't going to leave even though I reminded her of Siddhartha.

" 'I never had a dad,' I said.

" 'I'm sorry. What happened?'

" 'Well I had him for a while but he died when I was five. He knew he was going to die so even when he was alive he kind of ignored me.'

"Just Silver kissed the angles of my face. Her hair smelled like Nag Champa and marijuana. Her eyelashes were so long they looked like they hurt her. Her legs were as long as mine when we lay hip to hip and measured. Steep thighs.

" 'So you don't want a baby,' Just Silver said. 'I mean, because of your dad.'

" 'No. I want a baby because of my dad. I want a baby so I can be a dad for him.'

" 'Or her,' Just Silver said.

" 'I think we will have a boy.'

" 'Why?'

" 'I'm very in touch with our bodies.'

" 'I can tell.'

"So we decided to have you, buddy. We almost named you Siddhartha but Fifi convinced us it was not going to be fun for a little boy to grow up with a name like Siddhartha, and Sid didn't have the right feeling. Fifi liked the name Dirk because of the sound of Derwood and Dirby and so we agreed, although your mother didn't see much difference between Dirk and Sid.

"Fifi loved your mom as if she were her very own daughter. She was so happy to see me with a friend. I had really never had any friends. Now Just Silver and I went everywhere together. I would recite my poetry and she would do her interpretive dancing on the stage. The wineglasses danced with her. I had expected things to stop moving around when I fell in love but I was just as telekinetic as ever. Maybe more so. Instead of grounding me, my love sent me spinning even deeper into the center of loneliness that was the stars and the night and the wind. I didn't feel that my love was anything to do with the planet I had been born on. I wanted to fly away with Just Silver.

"Then you were born. You presented me with this problem. How was I supposed to keep living this abstract way, trying to be like music from a horn, like sweat, like the dark skin of night peeling back at dawn? Although I'd wanted a baby so I could love it the way my father hadn't

457

been able to love me, when I saw you with your eyelashes and toes and everything, I realized what a big responsibility you really were. I had to care in a way I had never had to care before. I read you poetry and played my guitar. I made your toys fly around the room like planets in space. But I was drawn more and more to the waves and the wind. You made my heart hurt too much. It ached so much I thought it would stop pumping like my father's had.

"Your mother and I would leave you with your grandmother and go driving for hours. We liked to take Sunset all the way to the sea. We kissed in the furious Santa Anas that felt like jewel dust whirling around us as the sun went down.

"The night we gave up on life, I can't say it was a conscious decision. But we didn't struggle against it either. That was the year Martin Luther King and Robert Kennedy were killed. In a way I think it was all too much for us—this world."

Dirk thought of his parents on the precipice, wanting to sink into the cavern of night and wild coyote hills, away from the hammering headlines and screaming TVs and the death of fathers.

"That's why I want you to be different, Dirk," said Dirby. "I want you to fight. I love you, buddy. I want you not to be afraid."

"But I'm gay," Dirk said. "Dad, I'm gay."

"I know you are, buddy," Dirby said. And his lullaby eyes sang with love. "Do you know about the Greek gods, probably Walt Whitman—first beat father, Oscar Wilde, Ginsberg, even, maybe, your number one hero? You can't be afraid."

"Maybe it's too late," Dirk said. "Dad, am I alive now?"

"Yes. Still. Fight, Dirk."

"Mom?"

And then his mother, still dancing behind Dirby, all eyelashes and legs, spoke with that dream-plant smoke voice, "Tell us your story, Baby Be-Bop."

Genie

"One night when he was little Dirk McDonald woke to the sound of the telephone and his Grandma Fifi's voice," Dirk began.

"He had never heard a voice sound like that. Dirk looked up at the glow-in-the-dark stars Grandma Fifi had pasted on the ceiling for Dirk's father when he was a little boy. She had told Dirk they would keep nightmares away. But that night Dirk thought nothing would ever keep him safe from nightmares.

"Grandma Fifi ran into the bedroom and took Dirk in her arms. Her bones felt as light as the birdcage that hung in her kitchen. She wrapped Dirk in a coat that smelled sour from mothballs and lilac-sweet from her perfume.

"Dirk sat huddled next to his grandmother in her red-and-white 1955 Pontiac convertible and felt as if the night was going to eat him alive; he wished it would. Fifi hadn't taken time to put the top back on. She ran through red lights. Dirk had never seen her do that before.

"When they got to the hospital a doctor met them in

460

the hallway and led them back into the waiting room. Fifi took Dirk on her lap. Dirk could never remember, later, if the doctor had ever said the words, but he knew then that his parents were gone. He pressed his face into the velvet collar of Fifi's coat and their tears mingled together until they were drenched with salt water.

"Dirk listened for his parents' voices in the wind sometimes. But soon he forgot what they had sounded like. All he could hear was his Grandma Fifi whistling with her canaries in the kitchen or calling to him to come out and play in the yard or asking the pastry dough what shape it intended on taking this afternoon or singing him lullabies."

Dirk went on to tell the story of life in Fifi's cottage, the fathers in the shower, the story of Pup Lambert and the magic lamp. He told the story of Gazelle and the stranger, Fifi and Derwood, Dirby and Just Silver. All his ancestors' stories were also his own.

Each of us has a family tree full of stories inside of us, Dirk thought. Each of us has a story blossoming out of us.

"Dad?" he asked the darkness. "Mom?" but Dirby and Just Silver were gone.

He picked up the golden lamp. It was heavy with stories of love. It was light with stories of love. It could sink to the bottom of the sea, touch the core of the earth with the weight of love. It could soar into the clouds like a creature with wings.

Just then he saw that the lamp had begun to smoke— vapors writhing out from it like snakes. And Dirk saw

461

emerging from that mist the face and then the whole body of a man. There was a piece of sapphire silk with golden elephants on it wrapped turban-style around his head. Dirk knew that beneath the turban, the man's scalp was shaved; he was the stranger who had come to Gazelle's door with the very lamp out of which he was now materializing.

"Come with me," the man said.

"Where?"

"You'll see."

The braid rug on the floor of Dirk's room began to quiver. Then the corners furled off the wooden floor and the rug lifted from the ground, bringing with it Dirk in his bed. Dirk closed his eyes the way you do on a roller coaster, wind and gravity forcing lids down, forcing him to grip the brass posts as the bed levitated. Eyes still closed but he knew he was outside now careening through star-flecked space on warm wind, part of him wanting to scream, wake from the dream, part of him letting this be, this journey to wherever, this journey on the voice of the man.

Beneath him the city the way it looked from inside the Japanese restaurant on the hill where waitresses in flowered silk kimonos brought starbursts and blossoms of sushi maki and champagne in silver ice buckets. A platter of gleaming wineglasses and luminous liqueurs, main courses served on polished plates, towering flaming desserts, candlelit birthday cakes. And on to the edges where it was darker and on to the sea that broke against the shore in seaweed black against iced jade pale. Dark waves becoming pale foam like the banks of wild dill and evening primrose growing along the highway. Ancient stone creatures emerging from the sea. Fields full of cattle. Some were there to die. He saw a bull mount a cow like a wave of life in the midst of static death. Fields full of farm-workers, sweat stories hidden behind the clustering clean sea green, sea purple of the grapes they picked. Redwood groves purple shadows light fallen like pollen through high leaves. Sea going so far it looks like sky. Just blues for-ever. Sky like a field of lupine and white wildflower fluffs. Sheer rivulets of water a skin of light over the sand. On and on. Where was he going?

In a field at the edge of the sea was a white house with crystals and lace in the window. Trumpet vines grew over the trellis and picket fence in front. A hammock in the garden. On the porch were surfboards, sandals, sleeping golden retrievers.

Duck Drake and his family lived in the house that smelled of beeswax and lavender and home-baked bread. Duck's mother Darlene had wide-apart green eyes, frothy yellow hair and petite tan legs. She liked to stand on the porch having long conversations with the mockingbird who lived in the garden. She was always asking Duck questions about what his favorite flower was and why and what was his favorite color and time of day and animal and what dreams did he have last night? Duck's brothers and sisters, Peace, Granola, Crystal, Chi, Aura, Tahini and the twins Yin and Yang, were always careening through the house like a litter of blond puppies yelping, "I'm not delirious, I'm in love."

Duck was the only one who never talked about his crushes since his crushes were on boys and Duck knew Darlene wouldn't understand at all. He thought it was strange because of how free she was about other things. Once she tried some pot brownies that Peace made but she said they just made her depressed and unable to stop giggling. She let Crystal's boyfriend sleep over and she had told all the girls that when they were ready to have sex she would take them for birth control. But when it came to Duck's secret he knew she wouldn't accept it. He had heard her talking to her best friend Honey-Marie about Honey-Marie's son Harley. Harley was a few years older than Duck, and Duck had always admired him from afar. He looked like he was born to play Prince Charming with his fistfuls of curly dark hair, flashing dark eyes and ballet dancer's body. He spoke in a soft rich voice and wore baggy cotton trousers with Birkenstocks and colorful socks. Harley was a waiter at a café in Santa Cruz but he really wanted to go to San Francisco and perform Shakespeare. Finally, just before he left, he told Honey-Marie that he was gay. She was devastated. Duck heard her tell his mother, "My heart is broken."

Then he heard his mother say, "It could be worse. He could have something really wrong with him."

He breathed a sigh of relief on the other side of the kitchen door.

"Something *is* wrong with him," Honey-Marie said.

Then Duck's mother said, "I guess you're right. I'd probably feel the same way if it was my own son."

After that Duck tried. He took Cherish Marine to the prom and bought her a huge corsage of pink lilies. He even rented a tux (although he would not put his feet in weasel shoes and wore his Vans instead). Cherish Marine was a bathing suit model and all the boys wanted to be her date but she liked Duck with his lilting surfer slur and teenage-Kewpie beauty. They danced all the slow dances and Duck felt Cherish Marine's bathing-suit-model-breasts pressing through her peach satin prom dress. They went to the pier with a group of other kids and shared a bottle of champagne which Cherish Marine liked to drink with a straw. They sat next to each other on the roller coaster, Cherish Marine's slender thigh pressing against Duck's leg, her hands grabbing his knee as their light bodies were thrown from side to side of the car, bruising, the metal bar hardly enough to keep them from being flung into space. But when the evening was over Duck walked Cherish to her door and kissed her good night on her smooth peachy cheek. She looked into his eyes waiting for something more but he only said, "You are a total babe. Thank you for being my date," and left.

Cherish Marine was stunned.

Duck went surfing because it was the only thing that

comforted him. When he surfed he felt as aqua-blue and full and high as the waves but he also felt lost, a small human who could as easily be washed away as his father Eddie had been. Even the other surfers were separate from each other in their own tubes of water. Once in a while he'd see a guy holding his girlfriend and once he had seen a guy surfing with a pig on a leash. Duck wanted a boyfriend he could surf with, someone he could tell his secret to, someone who had the same secret inside. He wanted to reach inside his lover and touch that lonely secret with his own.

Duck decided to leave Santa Cruz. He drove his light-blue VW Bug along Highway 5 listening to the B-52s. He opened the windows and let the wind run its fingers through his shoulder-length hair that was bleached white from years of surfing in sun and salt water.

I am finally free, Duck thought, and then he thought about his brothers and sister and his mother telling them not to get sand all over everything and please be quiet so I can do my yoga, Duck could you please pick up some tofu patties for dinner, you look just like your daddy I miss him so much he would have been so proud of you the way you rode that wave.

The soaring free feeling was mixed with a sadness as Duck realized how alone he really was now. It was kind of like surfing—but then, Duck thought—everything was kind of like surfing.

Duck got to Zeroes at night and built a fire at the

campground. He heated up a can of beans and watched the waves, nodding with encouragement at the good ones like a proud father, watching the sun drop into the sea. He thought of how his father had died in the ocean and how instead of hating the water or being afraid of it he loved it even more. He didn't understand why that had happened to his dad but now he knew that his dad's spirit was there in the waves protecting him. He wondered if his father would understand about how he loved boys. Somehow he thought that if his dad were alive his mom wouldn't have agreed with Honey-Marie. She would have been too happy basking in her love for Eddie Drake. Around Eddie Drake everyone just basked—they felt safe, they didn't judge. Duck had never heard his dad say a negative thing about anyone's personal choice—just about things like the Vietnam War and the assassination of Martin Luther King and what was happening to the oceans. Even now after his death, he was like the sun—falling into the waves, rising again every morning—still with Duck like a god in an ancient myth.

Duck slept on top of a picnic table that night with his arm around his surfboard. He looked up at the stars and wondered if the future love of his life was looking up at them too. He couldn't have known about the glow-in-the-dark stars on the ceiling of a room where a boy lay wishing for Duck.

Duck waxed his board and surfed-in the dawn; he felt as if he was pulling the sun up behind him as he rode the waves. Then he rinsed at the outdoor showers. He wanted to stay out by the water forever but he knew that if he was going to live in Los Angeles he would have to try to get work.

He applied at a surf shop in Santa Monica. He had worked at one in Santa Cruz and he knew a lot about boards. Plus there was something about Duck that made people like him right away—his grin and the innocent openness in his blue bay-window eyes. The owner of the shop told him he could start the next day.

When evening came Duck drove into town—to Santa Monica Boulevard. He had never seen so many gay men all at once. He felt the buzz of desire making them all beautiful. Everything was sexy here—hamburgers and ice cream and books and boots and even supermarkets became sexy. There was even a billboard advertising gay cruises. The men on the billboards were all tan and muscular and the men on the streets looked like they had stepped off the billboards. Music thumped out of bars, and through the doors Duck saw strobe lights pulsing. He wanted to dance. He had never danced with another man. Some men came out of a club with their hands in each other's back pockets. Sweat was pouring down their necks and arms. Someone whistled at Duck. He was afraid to look at who it was.

"Do you have some money for food?" a boy asked him. The boy had huge brown eyes. Duck gave him a couple of dollars even though he hadn't had dinner himself.

"Thanks, man," the boy said. He was different from

some of the other guys around there—really young with a sweet mouth. When he smiled Duck saw that he had a gap between his front teeth. On the sidewalk in front of him was a huge chalk drawing of a beautiful blue angel.

"You new around here?" he asked.

Duck shrugged, not wanting to admit that this was his first time. His mouth felt dry and his heart was like the music coming out of the bars. "That's a good drawing," he said to change the subject.

"Thanks. Want to go to Rage?"

"Sure," Duck said.

The boy stood up and wiped his chalky hands on his jeans. Duck followed him into the bar that was crowded with men. A lot of the men knew the boy.

"Hey, Bam-Bam!"

"Is that you?" Duck asked.

The boy cocked his head. "Bam-Bam, yeah. Why?"

Duck started laughing. "My name is Duck," he said.

"Well at least it's not Pebbles."

Bam-Bam was a wild dancer, flinging his arms around and around over his head, gyrating his torso and hips. Duck found out later that sometimes he worked as a go-go boy when he could get a gig. Unfortunately it didn't pay much and most of the time Bam-Bam was out on the streets spare-changing or doing whatever else street kids did for some quick burger bucks.

"Where are you from?" Bam-Bam asked Duck over some beers that a guy in leather chaps had bought for them.

469

"Santa Cruz."

"And this is your first time out."

"What do you mean?"

"Out. Coming out."

"Oh. Yeah," said Duck. "I mean no."

"It's cool," Bam-Bam said. "Everyone has to have a first time."

"What about you?"

"I'm from all over. I was in Frisco last. I just keep moving. I'm a mover. I'm not from anywhere."

Duck nodded. He figured that wherever Bam-Bam was from—everyone had to come from somewhere, right?—it wasn't a two-story white wood frame house full of crystals and waffles and laughing golden children. Maybe Bam-Bam really did come from nowhere. Duck had noticed some cigarette burn marks on Bam-Bam's bare, thin arms. Parents that did stuff like that to you had to become nothing nowhere in your head if you were going to make it out alive.

Duck and Bam-Bam went to the beach and slept on the picnic tables. In the morning Duck surfed while Bam-Bam sat on the sand and sketched him. Duck made them coffee, boiling water over the campfire.

"Do you like L.A.?" Duck asked.

"It's okay I guess. It'll be better when I get my shit together. I design furniture."

"Like what?"

"Well for now it's just drawings." Bam-Bam opened his

sketch pad. He showed Duck pictures of tables made from surfboards and other ones covered with a mosaic of bottle caps and broken glass and china. There was some neo-Flintstone-style furniture made from broken slabs of stone and boulders, and some shaped like dinosaurs.

"You fully rip," Duck said.

Bam-Bam smiled so the gap between his teeth showed.

"So where do you live?" Duck finally asked.

"Sometimes I can find a squat. Sometimes I go to the shelter. When I have money I get a motel with some other kids. Why, you looking for a place?"

"Today I'm going to go look for an apartment," Duck said. "If you want you can stay with me for a while."

"How much?"

"It wouldn't cost you anything. And you could get off the streets."

Bam-Bam looked suspicious. Duck hoped he hadn't hurt his feelings. "I just don't know anybody out here," he added. "You could kind of show me around. You could design me a table. Just don't use my surfboard for a table!"

Duck and Bam-Bam found a one-bedroom apartment on Venice Beach. Duck surfed every morning and worked at the shop all day. At night he took an acting workshop but he was always too shy to present anything. After a while the teacher, Preston Delbert, just gave up and ignored Duck. But Duck kept going, sitting in the back, wondering if he would ever find a voice inside of him or something to say with it.

Bam-Bam stayed home painting murals of the ocean on the walls, designing furniture and making omelettes or peanut butter sandwiches for him and Duck to eat. He cut Duck's hair short so that it looked like the petals of a sunflower. Duck suggested that maybe Bam-Bam should take a class in furniture design at a city college or go to beauty school but Bam-Bam said he wasn't ready. He stopped going out altogether. He said he was afraid that he'd get caught back up in street life. At night, Duck and Bam-Bam slept in the same bed holding each other but they didn't make love. Bam-Bam said he didn't feel like it and Duck was too shy and inexperienced to push him. Duck wondered if he would ever know what it was like to make love to a boy he loved. Sometimes he wanted to go back to Rage or do something wild in a men's room or cruise in a park but he was afraid. He felt that he had to be responsible too, and set a good example for Bam-Bam.

One day Duck came back from work and saw that Bam-Bam's things were gone. There was a picture of an angel, like the chalk one on the sidewalk, painted above Duck's bed. Under it was written, "I love you, Duck. You will find your true angel. I am a dangerous one. Bam-Bam."

Duck sat on the bed and cried. He wasn't sure why he was crying so hard. I didn't know him that well, Duck told himself. He was a street kid. He couldn't stay inside with me forever. He wasn't my boyfriend, he didn't even want to make love with me. But still Duck cried. He was crying for the first person who knew his secret and for the painter of

472

angels and for the warmth of those thin, cigarette-burned arms and maybe for something else—a premonition of what would happen later.

After Bam-Bam left, Duck went out every night, prowling the streets, maneuvering through them as if he was surfing perilous waves. He never talked to the men he touched in bathrooms and parks and cars. Is this what it means to be gay? Duck wondered. He missed the clean, quiet beaches of Santa Cruz, the softer sun and the sparkling, swirling colors of the waves and sky, the cathedral forests of redwood trees and the way he saw rabbits or long-legged baby deer who hopped like rabbits and heard the soft motorcycle hum of quail in the woods near his house. He missed being cleansed by the ocean he had practically grown up in, hiking home with his smiling sunlit dogs, sitting in the reeds by the pond listening to the frogs as evening slowly settled. He even missed the skinned-looking yellow slime banana slugs on the forest paths. Mostly, though, Duck missed his mother and his little brothers and sisters. He thought he could hear them squeal, "I'm not delirious, I'm in love!"—the words Duck felt he could never say. I guess I deserve this, Duck thought, holding a man in a cold-tiled, sour-smelling men's room. In the dark he could not even see the man's face and he was glad because he knew the man couldn't see him either.

Where are you? he called silently to his soul mate, the love of his life whose name he did not yet know. By the time I find you I may be so old and messed up you won't even recognize me. Maybe this is what I deserve for wanting to find a man. Looking for you always, never finding you, poisoning myself.

Then the lights from a passing car revealed the eyes of the man whose hands were on Duck. The eyes were like tile. Duck shivered.

"Faggot," the man said. "How much do you hate yourself, faggot? Enough to come to piss stalls in the night? Enough to die?"

Duck tried to wrench away but the man had fingers in his arm like needles. He tried to scream but no sound came out of his throat to echo against the walls of the empty men's room.

"It is only a whisper now," the man hissed. "But it is coming. It is in your closest friend. Maybe it is in you, too."

That was when a light filled the doorway. In that radiance Duck was surprised to recognize something of himself. In that moment pulsing with a diffused rainbow mist of tenderness whispering, whispering, "Love comes, love comes," Duck was able to pull away and into the night. He felt as if he was surfing on a magic carpet and he thought he heard a voice calling to him, "Do you have a story to tell?"

When he got home Duck looked at his face in the mirror and saw that the bay windows in his eyes had clouded over and there was a roughness about his chin now. What story do I have to tell? Duck wondered.

The next night in his acting class Duck asked Preston Delbert if he could perform a monologue. Preston Delbert looked suspicious.

"I'd forgotten all about you, Duck," he said. "I don't think invisibility and muteness are very good traits for an actor."

"I know," said Duck. "But I have something to say now."

Duck got up in front of the class. His hands felt like they were covered with ice cream. He started to sit back down. Then he heard the voice asking if he had a story to tell. So Duck told the class the story of his mother and father and brothers and sisters. He told the story of Harley and Cherish Marine. And then Duck told the story of Bam-Bam. The class was silent. Some people had tears in their eyes. Duck felt as if his heart was an angel. Bam-Bam's sidewalk angel—that light, that full of light.

Soon Duck will meet his love. When Duck sees his love he will know that the rest of his story has begun. It will not be too late for either of them. The sweetness and openness they were born with will come back when they see each other in the swimming, surfing lights.

And we are still young, Duck will think. I wish I had met you when I was born, but we are still young pups.

They will still be young enough to do everything either of them has ever dreamed of doing, to feel everything they have always wanted to feel.

When they first kiss, there on the beach, they will kneel at the edge of the Pacific and say a prayer of thanks, sending all the stories of love inside them out in a fleet of bottles all across the oceans of the world.

And the story was over. Dirk felt he had lived it. Was it a story told to him by the man in the turban who now sat watching him from the foot of the bed? Had he dreamed it? Told it to himself? Whatever it was, it was already fading away leaving its warmth and tingle like the sun's rays after a day of surfing, still in the cells when evening comes.

"Who are you?" Dirk asked the man, his voice surfing over the waves of tears in his throat. "Who is Duck?"

"You know who I am, I think. You can call me by a lot of names. Stranger. Devil. Angel. Spirit. Guardian. You can call me Dirk. Genius if I do say so myself. Genie.

"Duck—you'll find out who he is someday."

"Why are you here?"

"Think about the word destroy," the man said. "Do you know what it is? De-story. Destroy. Destory. You see. And restore. That's re-story. Do you know that only two things have been proven to help survivors of the Holocaust? Massage is one. Telling their story is another. Being touched and touching. Telling your story is touching. It sets you free.

"You set some spirits free, Dirk," he went on. "You gave your story. And you have received the story that hasn't happened yet."

Dirk knew he had been given more than that. He was

alive. He didn't hate himself now. There was love waiting; love would come.

He was aware, suddenly, of being in a dark tunnel, as if his body was the train full of fathers speeding through space toward a strange and glowing luminescence. He wanted that light more than he had wanted anything in his life. It was like Dirby, brilliant and bracing; it was a poem animating objects, animating his heart, pulling him toward it; it was a huge dazzling theater of love. On the stage that was that light he saw Gazelle in white crystal satin and lace chrysanthemums dancing with the genie, spinning round and round like folds of saltwater taffy. Dirk also saw the slim treelike form of a man in top hat and tails, surrounded with butterflies. When he looked more closely Dirk saw that they were not regular butterflies at all but butterfly wings attached to tiny naked girls who resembled young Fifis. Grandfather Derwood, Dirk thought. And Dirk saw Dirby too, Be-Bop Bo-Peep, tossing into the air wineglasses that became stars while Just Silver, balanced on the skull of death, held up her long ring-flashing hands and moved her head back and forth on her neck. He wanted to go to them. But there was one thing they were all saying to him over and over again.

"Not yet, not your time."

Dirk McDonald saw his Grandma Fifi sitting beside him, her hair cotton-candy pink as the morning sun streamed in on it.

477

"Grandma," Dirk whispered. He looked around. White walls. The smell of disinfectant. Liquids dripping in tubes, into him.

"Where are we?"

"The hospital," Fifi said. "How do you feel?"

"Better."

"The doctor says you're going to be just fine."

"How long have you been here?"

"Oh, quite some time now. We've been telling each other stories, you and I, Baby Be-Bop. Past present future. Body mind soul," and Grandma Fifi squeezed Dirk's hand, knowing everything, loving him anyway.

Dirk closed his eyes. There was no tunnel but there was light—a sunflower-haired boy riding on waves the ever-changing colors of his irises.

Stories are like genies, Dirk thought. They can carry us into and through our sorrows. Sometimes they burn, sometimes they dance, sometimes they weep, sometimes they sing. Like genies, everyone has one. Like genies, sometimes we forget that we do.

Our stories can set us free, Dirk thought. When we set them free.

More titles by Francesca Lia Block!

Francesca Lia Block is a master at the art of lyrical storytelling. Written in spare, poetic prose, Block's characters explore both the magic and the hard realities of her vividly depicted urban landscapes. She has described her work as "contemporary fairy tales with an edge," where the real world finds solace for its troubles through "hope and magic."